COMPLETE. [PRICE ONE SHILLING.

NED NIMBLE
AMONGST THE INDIANS

EDWIN J. BRETT, "BOYS OF ENGLAND" OFFICE,
173, FLEET STREET, AND ALL BOOKSELLERS.

NIMBLE SERIES. VOL. 2

"HARRY, PLACING THE SQUIRT TO 'DOLF'S NECK, SENT A STREAM OF WATER DOWN HIS BACK."

NO. 1.   {No. 2 Presented GRATIS
With This Number. }   PRICE ONE HALFPENNY
[PUBLISHED EVERY MONDAY.]

With this Number is Presented Gratis a Splendid Coloured Picture.

NED NIMBLE AMONGST THE INDIANS;

OR,

THE SECRET OF THE PHANTOM CAVE.

CHAPTER I.

IN WHICH NED SETS FORTH FROM HOME, AND MEETS WITH A STRANGE CHARACTER.

"HERE'S success to Ned Nimble, God bless him and all his friends! You'll drink that toast, Nanetta, I am sure as willingly as you drank it when we decided to send him to school."

"As willingly, ay, even more so, were it possible, brother. With all my heart, with all my soul, I echo your words—success to Ned Nimble and all his friends!"

And Nanetta and Mr. Nimble drained their glasses to the health of the brave Ned and his noble-hearted friends.

Mr. Nicholas Nimble and Nanetta sat alone after dinner in the dining-room of the pretty house he had taken near Muswell Hill, the windows of which looked on to Alexandra Palace, the glass of which reflected in the light of a full moon.

It was a week after the destruction of his mansion by fire at Wood Green, and though Nanetta had recovered from the terrible shock of that night, Mr. Nimble had ever since been a sufferer from his old complaint the gout, which confined him to his chair.

The kind-hearted old gentleman, loth though he was to lose his nephew, yet consented to his following on the track of Minnie Sash and her abductors.

Like Ned, he believed that the torn letter had given the clue to the direction the two villains had taken with their victim.

Many a blessing did Nanetta and her brother heap on Ned's head for saving her from becoming the wife of a man who was himself already married.

To what a fate would she have been consigned but for her mischievous nephew and Doctor Whacker.

The thought made her tremble and turn pale.

And Ned had saved her.

How then could she refuse her permission to the noble-hearted boy to follow the villains who had stolen from him the girl he loved, and who had sought to destroy her and her brother out of revenge at the defeat of a worthless scoundrel?

Since that terrible night they had even learned more of the real character of Mr. Phinicky Phopps.

The publication of his name in connection with the fire had caused several of his actions to be looked into, and it was discovered that he had for some time past been committing forgery.

His friend, Squire Bombast, had been one of the victims, and to a very large amount, and he had also obtained large sums from usurers at great interest on the assertion that he was about to wed Miss Nimble, and would pay them out of her fortune.

He had also forged Nanetta's signature to letters promising to give the whole of her large fortune into his hands on the day of her marriage.

No wonder then that Nanetta and her brother had learned to hate and detest so desperate a villain, and prayed that Ned might succeed in hunting him down and bringing him to justice.

Harry Honour had obtained the permission of his father to accompany Ned, and 'Dolf had transferred his services from the uncle to the nephew.

As they were to leave England on the following day, Ned, Harry, and 'Dolf were upon this, their last evening at home, engaged in making their final preparations for their voyage to South America.

Hence it was that Mr. Nimble and his sister sat alone in the dining-room talking of their departure and wishing them success in their enterprise.

"I shall sadly miss 'Dolf," said Mr. Nimble, after a long pause. "He has been with us so long, and has got so used to our ways, and yet I am glad he is going with Ned."

"He has a great affection for our nephew," rejoined Nanetta, "and wild as Ned is, 'Dolf will be sure to have some slight control over him ; besides, he would never desert him in the greatest of danger."

"Of that I am convinced," said Mr. Nimble, "and if ever they come back safe to us I'll pension him for life to show my gratitude for his love for Ned."

"And Harry is a noble-hearted youth," said Nanetta ; "but for him we might now mourn for Ned."

"And you might have fallen into the trap laid for your fortune," added Mr. Nimble.

Nanetta shuddered.

"Brother, brother, don't speak on that subject," said Nanetta. "Never will I entertain the thoughts of marriage again."

Mr. Nimble was about to reply, when the door opened and Ned and Harry entered.

"We couldn't get back to dinner, uncle," said Ned ; "we were detained at the docks longer than we expected to be, so had a snack at a restaurant."

"And how do you like the look of the ship, Ned ?" asked Mr. Nimble.

"She's evidently a beautiful steamer is the 'Dancing Dolphin,' and splendidly fitted up. Her state rooms are equal to any gentleman's drawing-room, and her berths are first rate."

"Have you secured good ones ?" asked Nanetta.

"Capital, all close together," replied Ned, "and we've got all our traps aboard."

Nanetta sighed, and the tears came into her eyes.

"Have you seen her captain ?" asked Mr. Nimble, addressing Harry.

"Yes, sir and he is certainly a gentleman in every sense of the word."

"I am glad of that. I do not like your rough, bulldog of a commander. He may be all very well in a merchantman, but he is out of place in a passenger ship."

"He is all that your most fastidious lady could wish," said Ned.

"I hope you will not play him any pranks, Ned," said Nanetta.

"I should not like to," replied Ned. "But what do you think, aunt, of that 'Dolf ?"

"What, has he declined to go at last ?" asked Mr. Nimble.

"Oh, no, not he, but he will persist in wearing a livery. I can't persuade him out of it, although I have offered to supply him with any description of garments he would like."

"Why is that ?" asked Nanetta.

"He says he is my servant as he was yours, and that he is not going to presume to be my equal, and so he goes in livery or he don't go at all."

Mr. Nimble laughed.

"He will look all right on board," he said, "but how when you get to South America ?"

"Oh, perhaps by that time we shall be able to laugh him out of it. I do not look upon him as my servant but my friend."

"Well, let him have his way for the present," said Nanetta. "He is a good, faithful fellow."

"You may well say that, aunt," replied Ned.

"Could you learn anything at the docks or the shipping-office that might give you a clue by what vessels these villains may have sailed ?" asked Mr. Nimble.

"Nothing definite, sir," replied Ned. "But three persons shipped on board the ' Kicking Kangaroo ' on the morning after the fire who bear some slight resemblance to those we are going in search of."

"What sort of ship was it, Ned. Did you learn ?"

"Yes ; she's one of the fastest steamers afloat they say, and being bound direct for the island of Trinidad, there is no chance of coming up with her ere she can reach her destination."

"After all, they may not be on board this vessel," said Mr. Nimble.

"That's true, sir," said Ned; "there's no certainty that those who shipped in her when she was on the point of sailing are those we seek. But it is enough for me that Minnie is being carried to South America, and thither we go in search of her. And though to seek her in so vast a place is like searching for the finest needle in the largest haystack, yet I believe we shall find her, and I for one do not despair."

"Nor I," said Harry.

"May Heaven guide you to her," said Nanetta, "and permit you to bring her back unarmed to those who will ever love her."

"I say Amen to that," said Mr. Nimble, "and may Heaven have you also in its keeping, my dear boys."

And the old gentleman held forth both his hands.

Ned took one and Harry grasped the other.

"Thank you, uncle," said Ned; "and now, since we may not meet again for a long time, I ask your pardon for the many annoyances I have caused you."

"Not only my pardon, Ned, shall you have, but my blessing. God bless and prosper you, and send you back safe to me and your aunt."

"I feel that I shall return safe and bring Minnie with me," returned Ned. "I have hope, and he who has hope seldom fails."

His uncle wrung his hand, and looked affectionately into Ned's face.

"Hope on, Ned, hope ever," he said, "and you will succeed. To despair is to fail, but he who has hope and faith is sure in the end to conquer."

"And we will conquer, uncle, won't we, Harry?" said Ned.

"If we fail it shall not be for the want of trying to succeed," replied Harry. "But we shall not fail, for like you, Ned, I have hope in our success and faith in Providence."

"Bravo, bravo!" cried Mr. Nimble. "In spite of your youth I fear not to see you go forth on your venture. You have stout hearts and determined wills, and know not the meaning of the word fail."

"And now, dear uncle and aunt—more than father and mother to me—

since every arrangement has been made and we must be on board early to-morrow morning, let us bid you farewell."

"Does the vessel sail so early then?" asked Nanetta, in a voice choked with emotion.

"She will endeavour to get out of dock at ten in the morning, or she will have to wait another tide. Her officers and crew are on board, and all is in readiness to put to sea."

"So soon, so soon!" moaned Nanetta, flinging her arms round Ned's neck.

"Don't cry, aunt, don't make me regret the step I take," said Ned, kissing her.

"No, no, dear boy," she said, dashing away her tears. "I will be brave for your sake. God bless you, Ned, God bless you."

She turned and left the room hurriedly to hide the tears she could not control, shaking Harry's hand and kissing him as she went.

As she passed out 'Dolf entered the apartment.

"I've come to say good-bye, sir," he said.

"Good-bye, 'Dolf," said Mr. Nimble, shaking his hand. "Take care of my boy and bring him safe back to me."

"I will, sir, or I will never look on your face again," replied 'Dolf, retiring.

"And now, Ned, once more good-bye, and Heaven have you in its keeping."

Harry and Ned once more shook hands with Mr. Nimble and then left the room, unwilling to render their farewell more painful to him.

"Before I go to bed," said Ned, "I'll bid Dorothy and Betsy good-bye. You go and turn in, old man, for we must be off early."

The friends shook hands, and Harry went to his room, while Ned sought the kitchen.

But on the threshold Ned stopped in amazement.

In the centre of the apartment stood 'Dolf, and hanging round his neck, sobbing, were both Dorothy and Betsy.

'Dolf was evidently using all his powers to compose the two frantic females, but evidently in vain.

Ned felt he must come to 'Dolf's aid, so he coughed loudly.

With a little shriek both women let go their hold and sank into their chairs, and put their aprons to their faces.

'Dolf turned and looked terribly sheepish at Ned, then bolted out of the kitchen.

"I've come to bid you good-bye," said Ned.

"Good—good-bye," sobbed Dorothy, holding out her hand.

"Good-bye," replied Ned, taking her hand, and pulling her apron from her face kissed her.

Then turning to Betsy he served her the same, much to her surprise.

Before she recovered from it Ned was gone.

Five minutes later he was in bed, and in five minutes more fast asleep.

At six o'clock a tap at his door aroused him, and, dressing, he descended, to find breakfast ready, and Harry and 'Dolf awaiting him.

The meal was soon disposed of, and the carriage waiting at the door to take them to the docks.

"Are you ready?" asked Ned.

"Yes," replied Harry and 'Dolf.

"There is nothing more you think we may want?"

"Nothing," replied Harry.

"Then lets begone, for I fear I cannot bear another farewell with my aunt."

They started for the hall.

But on the threshold of the breakfast-room they met Miss Nimble.

Ned started back.

"Dear aunt," he gasped, "why—why have you risen so early?"

"Oh my dear boy, I could not let you go without an embrace and a God bless you."

And her arms went round his neck, and her lips pressed his own.

"Good-bye, aunt, good-bye, and Heaven guard you till I come back."

He pressed her to his heart, and glued his lips to hers for a moment, then releasing her, sprang along the hall, out of the doorway, and into the carriage.

Harry followed him.

'Dolf mounted beside the coachman, and the carriage was driven rapidly away.

Ned could not trust himself to look back, least the face of his weeping aunt should unman him and cause him to regret the expedition he had undertaken.

Harry read his thoughts and tried to cheer him.

And in this he succeeded, for by the time they had reached the gates of the docks in which the "Dancing Dolphin" lay, he was laughing as heartily as ever he had laughed in his life.

They bade farewell to Dan Driver and dismissed the carriage and entered the docks.

Early as it still was in the morning, there were many persons about; several had come to see their friends off, others because they had nothing else to do or out of idle curiosity.

They stood mostly in groups, but there was one solitary individual seated on a cask, alone, who was looking with a hungry look at the ship, on which some sailors were busily engaged.

He was evidently a man of extraordinary stature, for his feet touched the ground as he sat, and his thin body rose up high above the barrel.

His arms were immensely long, his body and legs were thin, and his face the colour of old parchment.

His eyes were deep sunken, and his mouth and nose very large, while the hair that peeped from under his well worn silk hat was of a dirty tow colour.

His face was smooth shaven, his cheeks sunken and his cheek-bones immensely high.

He looked like a man, or rather a giant attenuated by starvation.

Ned's sympathies were aroused in a moment, and taking a shilling from his purse, he approached him.

"I beg pardon," he said; "but you look ill and in want. Will you accept this shilling to purchase you some food.

The man looked at him for a moment, then dropped off the barrel, and stood before him, nearly seven feet in height.

"Noble youth," he said; "your offer shows the tenderness of your heart, but think you that he who can eat shavings and from between his lips extract deal boards, yea, he who could feed upon fire wants the wherewithal to support the inner man? No, were I hungered I would swallow the barrel on which I sat."

"I beg your pardon, I did not intend to offend you," said Ned, turning away.

"Stay," said the man; "'tis you who are offended, not the fire-king, Hanky-panky Jack."

"Mad," thought Ned.

"Ah, I read your thoughts," said the man. "You think I'm mad, but I am only mad to think that I can't go off in that vessel, for if I could I'd make a fortune among the savages of South America."

"Indeed," said Ned; "may I ask how?"

"By hanky-panky, hey presto, fly, begone and that sort of fun. It don't pay here now. Them ere music hall duffers spoils the buskin business. The time was when I could get a couple of shillings chucked into the ring for swallowing a lighted torch, but those days are gone for ever."

"You are a conjurer?" said Ned.

"I am; and I only wish as I could conjure some fellow to pay my passage in that ship, and then farewell to the ungrateful British for ever."

"Suppose I was to pay it for you?" said Ned.

"If you would, I'd be your slave for ever. I swear it on the honour of Hanky-panky Jack, the immortal fire-king."

CHAPTER II.

IN WHICH HANKY-PANKY JACK SHOWS HIS GRATITUDE AND HIS STRENGTH, AND IN WHICH NED AND HIS FELLOW PASSENGERS BID FAREWELL.

As the man gave utterance to the words, he slipped his long thin right hand into that of Ned's, and seizing his left foot with his left hand, held it above his head.

"You'll do it," he cried, as he balanced himself on one leg, "say you'll do it, and I'll be a father and a mother to you, nay, a brother and sister, an uncle and aunt, all rolled into one."

"You are a strange fellow," said Ned; "but I think you are an honest one, and so if you are really anxious to go, I'll pay your passage for the steerage."

"Hurrah! hurrah!" cried the fellow, dropping hand and leg, and throwing a somersault. "My fortune's made. I must get my props though, for what's a hanky-panky without his props?"

"Props!" said Ned, in surprise.

"Yes; don't you know my properties that I do the hanky-panky with? I only live a little way off. They're all in one box. I can get them in five minutes. Now you ain't larking, are you?"

"No," replied Ned. "What I have promised I will do, and while you go home for your props I'll step on board and speak to the captain, for there's no time to go to the office."

"May the blessings of Hanky-panky Jack fall on your head with the force of my fifty-six pound cannon ball!" cried the man. "My props weigh at least three hundred weight, but what of that? My heart is light, my arm is strong, and blow me tight, I won't be long."

And thus saying, the tall man dashed out of the dock gate like a rocket.

"Well, Harry, what do you think of him?" asked Ned.

"He's a character," replied Harry; "and I believe he is really grateful for your offer."

"So do I," said Ned; "and who knows but we may find him serviceable when we get to South America?"

"I fancy we may," said Harry.

"Then come along. I must see the captain if he is on board."

'Dolf had already gone on board to put things right in their bunks.

The lads went aboard and inquired for the captain.

Captain Cruiser was on board, and Ned was shown to his cabin.

Ned inquired if there was a vacant berth in the steerage, and if he paid for the passage, a person he wished to take with him could be allowed to go.

The captain having replied in the affirmative, and Ned having paid the passage-money and received a receipt and ticket, went on deck.

Scarce had he reached it, than he saw the tall man staggering along the dock with an enormous chest on his back and carrying his hat in his mouth.

"Here, here!" cried Ned, "mind how you come, or you'll be off the gangway into the water."

The fellow staggered along the planks on to the deck of the vessel, and two sailors sprang forward to lift the box off his shoulders.

This, by the aid of the man, they did.

"Is it all right?" he asked, turning to Ned.

"It is, and here is your ticket," replied Ned, "with the number of your berth on it."

The man took it and drew his sleeve across his eyes.

"God bless you!" he said. "I've conjured a penny out of many a fellow's pocket, but you've conjured that out of me that no man ever did before."

"And what's that?" asked Ned.

"A tear—a tear of gratitude," was the reply. "I don't know who you are yet, but if you were the devil himself, I'd be your slave for ever."

And the fervour with which he wrung Ned's hand was proof sufficient that our hero had found another friend who would stand by him to the death.

"Say no more about it," said Ned, "I am only too happy if I have been able to serve you."

"Now then, out of the way here, and let's get this box off the deck," said one of the sailors.

And two brawny, bearded fellows essayed to lift the trunk and carry it away.

They let go and looked at each other in amazement.

They could not move it, so great was its weight.

"Look here, my infants," said the tall man, "you must eat more pudding before you can lift Jack Jones's box; just show me where to stow it."

And stooping, Jack Jones lifted the box on to his shoulder.

"By gosh, you're a strong un," said one of the sailors.

"And a long un," replied Jack; "heave ahead, my hearties, and point out the particular position for the resting-place of these props."

The men obeyed, still gazing at him in wonder.

"What do you think of that, Harry?" asked Ned.

"That if that fellow does not desert us when we reach our journey's end we shall have a most valuable ally."

"He'll stick to us, I'm sure he will," said Ned.

"Through thick and thin, if he don't may Hanky-panky Jack never taste fire again," said the man, coming up behind them.

"I believe you," said Ned, "and one day I'll tell you what takes me and my friends to South America."

"And one day I hope to be able to show you that I am not all words," said Jack.

At this moment came the loud ringing of a bell.

And then the sailors cried out—

"All ashore! all ashore!"

The captain came on deck.

"All who are not passengers by this vessel on shore, please," he said; "we are about to cast off."

There were hurried embraces on all sides, and sounds of sobs, as friend took leave of friend whom they never might see more.

Again the voice of the captain rang out clear from the bridge—

"All ashore there, please, or you will be left aboard!"

"All ashore!" echoed the sailors.

And still the bell kept up its mournful tones.

Slowly, oh, how slowly, those who have come to see their friends off make for the gangway, holding on to their friend's hand and turning every moment to take one more embrace, to whisper one more word of farewell!

At last all who are not passengers have crossed the gangway, but they gather on the quay with streaming eyes, and impede the duties of those who stand at the mooring-ropes.

At the side of the vessel crowd the passengers, to be pushed aside by the sailors as they find themselves hampered in their work, only to crowd forward again and wave hat or handkerchief to those but a few yards distant.

The captain whistles down the tube to the engineer.

There is the stroke of the engine and the paddles revolve slowly.

The water washes up in foam about the bows of the vessel.

"Bear on the stern hawser!" cried the captain.

"Ay, ay, sir," return the sailors.

"Cast off the bow hawser!"

"It's off!" cry the men ashore, as from the huge pin they throw the stout hempen noose.

But the tones of the men and the orders of the captain are scarcely heard, so many voices are speaking on ship and shore.

Dangerously near to the edge of the quay crowd the friends.

Dangerously high over the rails hang the passengers as the ship slowly draws away from the shore.

The throb of the engines becomes stronger.

The water, lashed to foam, rises higher and higher about the vessel's hull.

The voices of the passengers and those on shore become more and more husky.

And further and further out drifts the gallant ship.

High above mothers' heads children are raised who may never see their fathers more.

Wives with eyes blinded with tears gaze longingly, lovingly on the faces of their husbands as they recede further and further from their sides.

Lovers shriek their farewells in husky tones.

Wildly and more wildly hats and handkerchiefs are waved, while women weep and men press firmly their lips together to choke back their emotions.

And so the ship drifts out of dock.

Will she ever return?—who can tell?

Ned laid his hand on Harry's shoulder; there was a big lump in his throat and his voice was husky as he said—

"Let's go below, old man. I can stand a lot, but I confess I feel that a fellow's heart must be as cold as stone who is not moved by such a sight, and whose soul does not sink at those solemn words—'Farewell, farewell!'"

CHAPTER III.

IN WHICH 'DOLF AND BIRCHER FIND THERE IS NOT MUCH PLEASURE IN A LIFE ON THE OCEAN WAVE.

The engines of the "Dancing Dolphin" were stopped at Gravesend to allow two persons to come on board.

Ned and Harry were below, so that they did not see them.

If they had they would have certainly been surprised, for in the slight-built, spectacled gentleman, and in the prim, rosy-faced lady they would have recognised their old acquaintances, Mr. Benjamin Bircher and Mary, now Mrs. Bircher.

Mr. Bircher looked more nervous than ever, and Mary certainly showed some trepidation as she looked along the deck of the vessel on which she stood.

They however soon disappeared from the deck, for the steward advanced and led them to their berth, which they did not leave till the following day.

The morning was bright and beautiful when Ned and Harry came on deck.

They looked round.

Not a sight of land.

Above the sky was blue and calm.

Below the waves rolled, chasing each other or broke in foam against the steamer's bows.

There was an unsteady motion too which rendered standing still perfectly impossible.

"Adieu, my native land, adieu," said Harry, looking towards the stern.

"Oh, blow it, don't get poetical, old man!" said Ned. "Just look at that big wave; there's a lot of reality in it, I can tell you."

"And a lot of fishes perhaps," said Harry. "Wonder if we shall get a bloater for breakfast?"

"Get out. Do you think they catch them ready dried?" said Ned.

"Ain't quite such a fool, dear boy," said Harry; "but I feel awful peckish."

"So do I," said Ned. "I feel as if I could eat a shark."

"More likely a shark eat you," said Harry.

"But I say, old fellow, where are all the passengers got to? There was plenty of them yesterday, and I don't see any now."

"The lazy beggars won't get up I suppose," said Ned. "Oh, blow these waves; they almost knock a fellow off his pins."

"Good morning, Master Ned; good morning, Master Harry," said 'Dolf, coming up, clutching every moment at the rail to steady himself.

"Halloa, 'Dolf, is that you?" cried

Ned. "Ain't this jolly? It's as good as a penny swing at a fair."

"Do you think so, sir?" said 'Dolf, clutching wildly at the rail as the vessel gave a lurch.

"Don't call me 'sir' or 'Master Nimble' now, 'Dolf, call me Ned. But I say, old fellow, ain't you white about the gills!"

"It's the soap, sir. I think I noticed how different it was to what we were in the habit of using."

"Soap be blowed," said Ned "Never mind, 'Dolf, breakfast will soon be ready, and that will put some colour into you."

"I—I ain't at all hungry," said 'Dolf. "I don't think I want any breakfast this morning."

"Oh, nonsense! I ain't going to let you starve yourself. I don't want to take a skeleton ashore with me. Halloa! what's that bell mean?"

"Breakfast, sir," said a midshipman, who passed at that moment.

"Is it?" said Ned. "All right. I'm on."

"So am I," said Harry. "Come on, 'Dolf."

"No, sir. I don't breakfast at the captain's table," said 'Dolf, looking at his livery.

"That's your fault; you should have had other things, as I wanted you to," said Ned.

"Sir, I know my place," said 'Dolf.

"That's more than many do," said Ned. "However, I'm going to breakfast, for I could eat a donkey."

And Ned and Harry went below.

There were but few of the passengers assembled at breakfast, and the captain, evidently observing Ned's surprised looks at the empty seats, said—

"We shall not have much company at meals to-day, young sir. They will be only too glad to keep their berths."

"On account of sickness, I suppose, sir," remarked Harry.

"Yes. But they'll be ready to do justice to the food before long, never fear. You may consider yourselves fortunate."

"In what, sir?" asked Ned, looking up from his plate.

"In not being sea-sick yourselves," was the reply. "But I suppose you have sniffed the salt water before."

"Very little of it, sir," said Ned. "Only at Brighton and Hastings."

"And I have never been near the sea before," said Harry.

"Well, you will be lucky if it don't lay hold of you yet," said the captain. "Make a good breakfast. It's the best preventative."

"No fear of my doing so," said Ned. "I can't remember ever having felt so hungry before."

One or two of the passengers suddenly grew pale, rose from the table, and left the apartment.

Nor did they return.

Having made a good meal, the boys rose and went on deck.

There were several of the passengers sitting about and leaning over the rail.

Ned cast a glance round, paused suddenly, and caught Harry by the sleeve.

"What is it, old man? are you going to be sick?" asked Harry.

"Look—look!" said Ned, pointing.

"Where?"

"There, don't you see?"

Harry followed the direction of Ned's finger, and gave a long, low whistle. Then he burst forth—

"Bircher, by Jupiter!"

"His very self," said Ned. "Who'd have thought he'd be here?"

"And there's Mary, Mrs. Bircher, with her arm round his waist."

"Yes, and don't he look awful bad, I wish he didn't for I should like to have a lark with him."

"Oh, let the poor beggar get well first said Harry. "Where's 'Dolf."

The lads looked round, and at last caught sight of the livery 'Dolf wore.

"There he is leaning over the side looking at the water," cried Ned.

"Looks in a reverie," said Harry. "Dreaming of home."

"And Dorothy," said Ned. "Let's wake the beggar up."

"So we will."

Ned stooped and picked up a long stiff straw which had been a portion of the packing of some article, for the decks were not yet wholly ship-shape.

"What do you want with that?" asked Harry.

"I'll tickle 'Dolf's ear with this," said Ned. "That will rouse him."

"I've got something better than that in my pocket," said H

And he winked at Ned.

"What?" asked Ned.

"A squirt, if I can only find some water," said Harry.

"There's plenty without looking far for it," said Ned pointing over the side.

"Can't reach it, dear boy," said Harry, "Oh, here's a bucket full. Stunning!"

"What could be nicer?" said Ned, with a grin.

And extracting a large squirt from his jacket pocket Harry thrust it into the bucket and filled it with water.

"There," cried Harry, "if there ain't nearly half-a-pint in it I'll eat it."

"Let's creep gently up behind him," said Ned; "you let him have it down his back while I draw his attention off by tickling his ear."

"I'll let him have it never fear," said Harry, with a laugh.

Softly the two boys stole up to where 'Dolf stood holding his hat in his hand, and his head low over the bulwarks.

"Why, if the beggar ain't sea-sick, I'm blowed," whispered Ned.

"This will cure him," said Harry.

"Oh! ugh! oh!" came from 'Dolf, as he thrust his head further over the side.

"Oh, I—I shall die—ugh!"

As his head came up Ned thrust the end of the straw into his ear, and then sank down laughing uproariously as 'Dolf turned a white and miserable face towards him.

Harry sprang upon a seat, and placing the squirt to 'Dolf's neck, sent a stream of water down his back, then jumped back to see Bircher with his hand over his mouth and supported on the arm of his wife.

"Ugh!" gasped 'Dolf, as his head again went over the side.

"Ugh!" gulped Bircher. "Oh Mary! I shall—ugh!"

And then down he went flop on the deck, pulling Mary with him.

"I—ugh!—wish I was back at Pickleton," gasped Bircher. "Oh, I'm going to die! I know I'm going to die!"

"No, you won't, old boy, for I'll keep you alive," said Ned.

Bircher looked up, his eyes started out of his head, and his face turned green.

"It's a ghost—a warning!" he cried. "Mary, kiss me; I'm going to die!"

CHAPTER IV.

IN WHICH SOME OF OUR CHARACTERS ENJOY ANYTHING BUT PLEASURABLE SENSATIONS.

NED and Harry fairly shrieked with laughter as Bircher turned his ghastly green face up to his wife in order that she might give him the salute he begged for.

But Mary did not comply with the request of her husband.

She herself began to experience the inconvenient motion of the steamer, and clasped her handkerchief over her mouth as her bosom gave a convulsive heave, and even her very hands went deadly white.

"Why don't you kiss the poor fellow?" said Ned; "you used to before you were married, for I've seen you do it."

Bircher gave an awful groan.

"Is it a spirit?—or is it—oh!"

Bircher could get no further.

He turned his face to the deck and allowed his wife's head to drop on to the collar of his coat.

"Poor devils," said Harry, "they are bad; come away, Ned, and let's send the steward to them."

"All right, old man. It would be too bad to make fun of them now," said Ned.

And taking hold of Harry's arm he went towards the cabin.

In vain they called for the steward and stewardess.

Those persons were too much engaged with the first-class passengers to care to look after the second.

"It's a beastly shame," said Ned; "let's go back, old man, and see what we can do for them; old Bircher's a cad, but with all his faults I love him still."

"I'll go and get some brandy and water," said Harry. "Perhaps that will do them good."

"Run on then, dear boy."

Harry went to the steward's room for the brandy and Ned went on deck.

Two more pitiable objects than Mr. and Mrs. Bircher he had never gazed upon.

There they lay where he had left them, Bircher on his face and his wife's head lying on his shoulder.

Ned looked round.

'Dolf still hung with his head over the side, but he had sunk down on to the seat before it as if unable longer to stand.

His hat had fallen from his powerless hand and lay at his feet, or rather with one of his feet thrust into it, and pinning it to the deck.

Harry came up with the brandy.

"Here, let me help you up, Mary—Mrs. Bircher, I mean," said Ned, sinking on his knee and lifting Mary from off her husband's shoulder.

It was an awful moan that the poor woman gave utterance to as Ned turned her white face upwards.

"Oh, let me die—let me die!" she gasped.

"Not if I know it," said Ned; "here, drink some of this."

And taking the glass from Harry's hand he held it to her lips and forced her to swallow a small portion of its contents.

"There! you'll soon be better," he said, tenderly. "Take hold of the glass, Harry; now let me lift you into that chair."

And Ned tenderly lifted her up and sat her in a folding-chair, gently drawing her head back till it rested on the cane work.

"Now let's get Bircher up," he said to Harry. "Put the glass down, old man, and bear a hand."

Harry placed the glass on the deck, and together with Ned caught hold of Bircher.

"Now then," cried Ned, pull yourself together, Mr. Bircher! up you come."

And up he did come on to his feet, but they slipped away from under him and down he went into a sitting posture on the deck, bringing Ned and Harry down with him.

"Well you are a fellow," said Ned; "you might have sat down somewhere else instead of in that precious mess."

"Oh—ugh—oh!" gasped Bircher; "it's all over with me."

"It's all over you and no mistake," said Ned; "get up and we'll help you to the side."

"Mary," moaned Bircher; "Mary, I'm going home; my last hour has come, and Bircher's occupation has gone."

"Open your eyes and don't be a fool," said Ned.

"Eh, ay," said Bircher, opening his eyes; "you here, You?—Hence—avaunt—horrible——"

"Shut up," said Ned, "and take a pull at some Brandy. Harry give him a drink."

Harry seized the glass and placed it to Mr. Bircher's lips.

"Poi—no, brandy," he gasped and took a gulp.

"That's enough," said Ned, pushing the glass away, "you shall have some more presently. Didn't expect to meet friends here, did you, Mr. Bircher.

Bircher looked wildly from the face of Ned to that of Harry and then back again.

"Friends," he muttered; "friends or fiends, which?"

"A little bit of both, sir." said Ned; "we did not expect to meet you, nor you to meet us, but we're very glad to see you, and now let's help you to the side."

"My wife, my wife!" cried Bircher, staggering to his feet.

"Oh, she's all right," said Ned; "I've made her comfortable in that chair."

Bircher stretched out his arms and took a step towards her, but the sickness again seized him and down he sank on his knees.

"Well he's a treat," said Ned, who still held the tutor by the arm.

"Glad you think so, old man," replied Harry; "I'm blest if I don't think he'll make me as bad as himself."

"Confound him, what a dead weight he is!" said Ned; "I wish we could get the obstinate beggar to endeavour to walk to the side of the vessel."

"I'll carry him, sir."

Ned looked up and saw Hanky-panky Jack standing before him.

"Oh do, please," said Ned.

"Friend of yours, sir?" said Jack, as he put his arms round Bircher.

"Particular friend," replied Ned.

"Then I'll see to him, sir, for your sake," said Jack, "trust me."

And with the greatest ease he swung Bircher off his feet, carried him to the side, and sat him down beside 'Dolf.

Then hanging Bircher's arms up over the rails, he gently lowered the tutor's head over the side of the ship.

"There," he said, gazing upon his work, "you'll be better in an hour ; then take my advice and have a basin of gruel and to-morrow you'll be as right as a trivet."

The only reply Bircher gave was a low moan.

"Hold on to the rail and keep your face turned from the wind," said Jack, "and then hey presto, fly, begone ! "

And the tall fellow turned to look for his new-found friends.

But he turned the wrong way.

Ned and Harry had approached 'Dolf.

"Well, 'Dolf, how are you getting on ? " asked Ned.

"Don't you feel thirsty, old man ? " asked Harry.

And he offered 'Dolf the brandy.

But 'Dolf, raising his head slowly, pushed the glass away.

"Oh, Master Ned," he gasped, " why didn't you go to South America by road ? If the horses had galloped ever so hard they wouldn't have made me so ill as this blessed steamboat ! "

"Well, you see, 'Dolf, I never thought of that," said Ned.

"I wish you had, Master Ned," moaned 'Dolf.

Ned burst out laughing.

"You silly beggar ! how could we cross the ocean in a carriage ? " asked Ned.

"We could have gone round it, sir, you know," said 'Dolf.

"No, I don't know," said Ned. "I never heard of such a thing being done nor you either."

"Well, sir, I thought you could," said 'Dolf, "and if you can't, all I know is I wish you could, for there'll only be half of me left before we get to our journey's end."

And 'Dolf again thrust his head over the side.

"Pick up his hat, Harry," said Ned. "Don't let the beggar set a new fashion by wearing it on his feet instead of his head."

Harry essayed to lift 'Dolf's hat from the deck, but his head grew dizzy, and he staggered back, and set the glass hurriedly down by 'Dolf's side.

"Halloa! old man, what's the matter ? " asked Ned.

"Blest if I know," said Harry, his face growing paler and paler, and his limbs trembling; "unless it's these beggars have turned me up."

"By your leave, sir," said an under steward, as he came along with a basin of soup.

Harry looked at the soup, gave a gulp, and rushing to the side thrust his head over the rail.

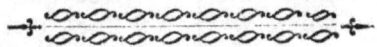

CHAPTER V.

IN WHICH NED AND HIS FRIENDS RESOLVE TO AMUSE THE ENLIGHTENED BRITISH PUBLIC.

THERE were few passengers on board the "Dancing Dolphin" who did not suffer from that painful malady, sea-sickness.

Amongst those who fortunately escaped was Ned Nimble.

The motion of the vessel had no more effect upon him than the jolting of his uncle's carriage would have had over the stones of London.

But Harry was not so fortunate, and though not near so bad as Bircher or 'Dolf, he yet suffered considerably.

But all things have an end, and among them *mal de mer*.

In a week all had thoroughly recovered, and began to enjoy the invigorating breezes of the ocean.

Cheeks wore a rosy tint, features a smile, and limbs felt strong and active.

Instead of moanings, laughter was heard on all sides.

When not at meals, and when the weather was fine, the passengers crowded the deck.

Still, a sea voyage becomes monotonous without some amusement, at least, so felt Ned and Harry, and many were the practical jokes they played 'Dolf and Bircher, who took them in good part.

Ned had told Bircher and Hanky-panky Jack the cause of him and his friends going to South America, and Bircher, in turn, had told Ned that it was to Venezuela he was bound, to become assistant-master in a large school.

"And so I thought I'd get married before I went," said the tutor, looking up lovingly at his wife, "especially as Mary was willing to go abroad."

"The best thing you could do, sir," said Ned, "for you'll have somebody to keep you in order."

At which Mary smiled and said she thought she'd be able to do that.

Hanky-panky Jack, who had found conjuring in the streets of London but a poor game, had imagined that if he could get amongst the Indians, that he might persuade them he was a great medicine man, and by taking advantage of their ignorance, build up for himself a fortune ; now that he had learned the object of his friend's visit to America, he had decided to join him in his search for Minnie.

This was an offer which Ned only too gladly availed himself of, especially as Jack possessed the strength of three ordinary men.

"Look here, old fellow," said Ned to Jack one bright morning when they had been about nine days at sea, "can't you break some of the monotony of this confounded voyage by giving us a specimen of your conjuring ?"

"I did not like to offer, sir," replied Jack ; "but if you would like to see a little hanky-panky I should be only too glad to show you."

"Do then, old fellow," said Ned.

"And I'll go round with the hat," said Harry.

"Keep your eye on him if he does," said Ned, with a grin.

"No need of that, Mr. Nimble," said Jack. "There's a nice clear space forward, so I'll get some of my props out."

"But can you get at your box ?" asked Harry.

"Oh yes," replied Jack ; "I had it put where I could get at it."

"Go on then," said Harry.

Hanky-panky Jack departed in search of his box.

"I say, Harry," cried Ned, "do you happen to have such a thing about you as a small tooth-comb."

"A small tooth-comb ?" cried Harry in surprise. "What should I want with such a thing ?"

"I don't know what you might want with such a thing, dear boy. I only know that I want one and haven't got one."

"Good Heavens, Ned, you don't mean to say——"

"I mean to say that I have got a use for one," said Ned, "if I can get it."

"You do, Ned ?" said Harry, "and no joking ?"

"Honour," said Ned, looking very serious.

Then seeing the look of pain and surprise on Harry's face, Ned burst out laughing.

"Don't be alarmed, dear boy," said Ned, "I only want it for music."

"Music," repeated Harry. "I don't understand you."

"We ought to have music for the performance you know."

"Well ?"

"So in the absense of fiddles, flutes, etc., we could make shift with small tooth-combs," said Ned.

"How ?"

"By wrapping a piece of paper over it and blowing through the teeth. It's fine music I can tell you."

"Get out," said Harry.

"Fact, dear boy. Didn't you never see the fellows do it at school ?" asked Ned.

"Never saw such a thing at school," said Harry. "But of course I've seen plenty of the ordinary combs. Why won't one of them do ?"

"Don't play so well," said Ned. "And we ought to have music to make the entertainment go."

Harry slapped his hand on his thigh.

"I know something better than that, Ned," he cried.

"What is it ?"

"Cymbals."

"But where can we get them ?"

"I know," replied Harry, "I'll get them. They'll make more row than your combs."

And away dashed Harry.

"I wish I'd got a big drum or even a

pair of clappers to wake the beggars up," muttered Ned. "The passengers all seem half asleep."

And he looked round upon the persons seated about the deck reading and dozing for the day was very warm.

"Wonder where 'Dolf is?" he muttered. "He can whistle stunning, and can make up the orchestra."

As if in answer to his thoughts 'Dolf came on deck.

"Here, 'Dolf, I want you," cried Ned.

"Yes, sir," said 'Dolf, moving forward.

"Do call me Ned, there's a good fellow. You can whistle 'Dolf?"

"Yes, Ned."

"That's right," replied Ned. "We are going to have an entertainment and I want you to be one of the musicians."

"But I can't play any instrument."

"You can whistle, that's enough. Do it as loud as you can. Give them regular ear piercers. You know. 'The ducks' march over a field of wheat,' 'The turkeys' gallop,' anything that's lively."

"I don't know those tunes, sir," said 'Dolf.

"Then 'Yankee Doodle,' 'Jack Robinson,' 'Slap bang, here we are again,' or if they are dull give the 'Burial of Sir John Moore,' d'ye hear?"

"I'll do the best I can," said 'Dolf. "But I whistle 'Mary Blane' best."

"Oh blow 'Mary Blane'" said Ned. "That's too lively. Chuck out 'Biddy the Basket-woman' for a beginning."

"Am I to begin now?"

"No, wait till we are ready. I'll tell you when."

Harry came up carrying in his hand a tin fish kettle and two iron saucepan lids.

"Here, old man," said Harry, "I've bounced these out of the cook. You take the drum I'll take the cymbals."

"Stunning," cried Ned. "Harry you're a brick."

"Rather a soft one, old man," returned Harry. "That marline-spike there will make a first-rate drumstick."

"Good," said Ned, seizing the small iron bar that lay on the capstan.

"We only want a flute or a fife now, and we should have a first-rate band," said Harry.

"'Dolf's going to whistle, that will do," replied Ned.

"First rate. Shall we strike up, Ned?"

"Wait till the great star is ready to come on," said Ned.

"Here he comes," said Harry.

"Bravo!"

Hanky-panky Jack came along the deck carrying a bag in his hand.

"Come on, forward, sir, we shall have more room there," said Jack, as he passed the lads.

The boys and 'Dolf followed him.

Selecting a clear spot Jack pitched his bag on the deck and from the noise it made the things within were of no light nature.

"Shall I summon the audience?" asked Ned.

"I'm ready, sir, when you are," replied Jack, turning back his shirt sleeves.

"Now, 'Dolf and Harry, strike up," said Ned, "and let the enlightend British public know that the performance is about to begin."

CHAPTER VI.

IN WHICH NED TAKES A LESSON IN JUGGLING, AND BIRCHER AND 'DOLF DO A LITTLE TUMBLING.

As Ned finished speaking he brought down the marline-spike with all the force of his good right arm on the bottom of the fish kettle.

Harry at the same time clashed the saucepan lids together and Dolf whistled.

But though 'Dolf's whistle was a failure as he had to stop for laughing,

the iron and tin instruments were very effective, for the drowsy passengers sprang to their feet and came hurrying forward to see the cause of the din.

Ned and Harry continued to make all the row they could till they had drawn around them the whole of the wondering passengers; then, while Jack was selecting his juggling tools from the heap he had poured out of the bag, Ned said—

"Walk up, ladies and gentlemen, walk up; we are just going to begin."

He paused and rattled the spike on the kettle, and then continued—

"Ladies and gentlemen, you see before you the world-renowned magician, Senor Hanky-panky Jacobi Jonesi, who, to put you in a good humour and break the monotony of your lives, has kindly consented to give his wonderful entertainment, never before performed on the bosom of the ocean. Strike the cymbals, Harry, to give effect to my words."

Clang, clang, went the saucepan lids together.

"That will do; you are a little out of tune, but let that pass," cried Ned.

"Yes, ladies and gentlemen, we have decided to give this entertainment for the benefit of the remorseless sharks in order to provide them with spectacles, so that if any of you should fall overboard, they may fancy you are too large to swallow; but lest you should forget after the entertainment and go away without paying, my friend will go round with his hat before the performance begins. 'Dolf, yours is the largest; make the circuit of the company."

Jack had fixed a wooden cup to his forehead by means of a strap which passed round his head, and was standing with several gilt balls in either hand, and Ned and Harry had again begun making a most horrible din, when Captain Cruiser strolled up to the spot.

"What is this?" he asked of Ned.

"That, sir," said Ned, pointing to 'Dolf's hat.

"And pray, sir, what is that?"

"Those," said Ned, pointing to the balls in Jack's hand.

The captain laughed and Ned again beat away at the kettle.

"Young sir," said the captain, "I'm afraid that kettle will be of little use to the cook."

"Never mind, sir. If the kettle won't cook for the cook, then I'll cook it, that's only fair."

"Sir," said Jack, stepping forward, "for the amusement of my friends and the passengers generally, I am going to do a little bit of juggling, if you have no objection."

"Not the least," said the captain; "but have you not a somewhat noisy band?"

"That's because you have not got a good ear for music, sir," said Ned; "it might be improved if you would lend us your large tabby cat and let 'Dolf tread on its tail."

The captain turned away with a smile.

"Don't go, sir," said Ned; "you forget that music hath charms to soothe the savage breast. Blow the cymbals, Harry, and strike the whistle, 'Dolf; now, senor, are you ready?"

"Quite," said Jack.

"Then go ahead."

Up went a ball high in the air, to be caught in the cup on the man's forehead.

And then, while a murmur of admiration rang through the crowd, several gilt balls went spinning round the man's head one after the other with the greatest velocity.

"Bravo, Jack," cried Ned; "keep the pot a-boiling, while Harry winds the cymbals and I blow the drum."

"Why don't you scrape that whistle of yours, 'Dolf?" said Harry; "don't let us be short in the orchestra."

In vain 'Dolf tried to whistle, he could only grin.

Jack jerked the ball out of the cup, caught another in it, jerked it out, and so went on, the boys keeping up a most infernal din the while.

"Blow the drum, I think it's cracked," cried Ned, as he gave the kettle a blow and drove the end of the marline-spike clean through the bottom.

"Now you've done it," said Bircher.

"Beg pardon, sir," said Ned, "it wasn't me, it was this beastly piece of iron. It's no good now, for that hole will let all the wind out."

And Ned threw the kettle and spike from him.

Harry was laughing so immoderately that he gave his knuckles a sharp blow with the edge of one of the saucepan lids, and handing them to 'Dolf he remarked—

"I fancy the senor can go through his business best without music."

Jack had caught the last ball in the cup, and paused in his work, and the passengers, highly gratified, bestowed on him a round of applause.

Jack took off the cup, bowed, and turned to place the balls on the deck.

NED NIMBLE AMONGST THE INDIANS; OR, THE SECRET OF THE PHANTOM CAVE.

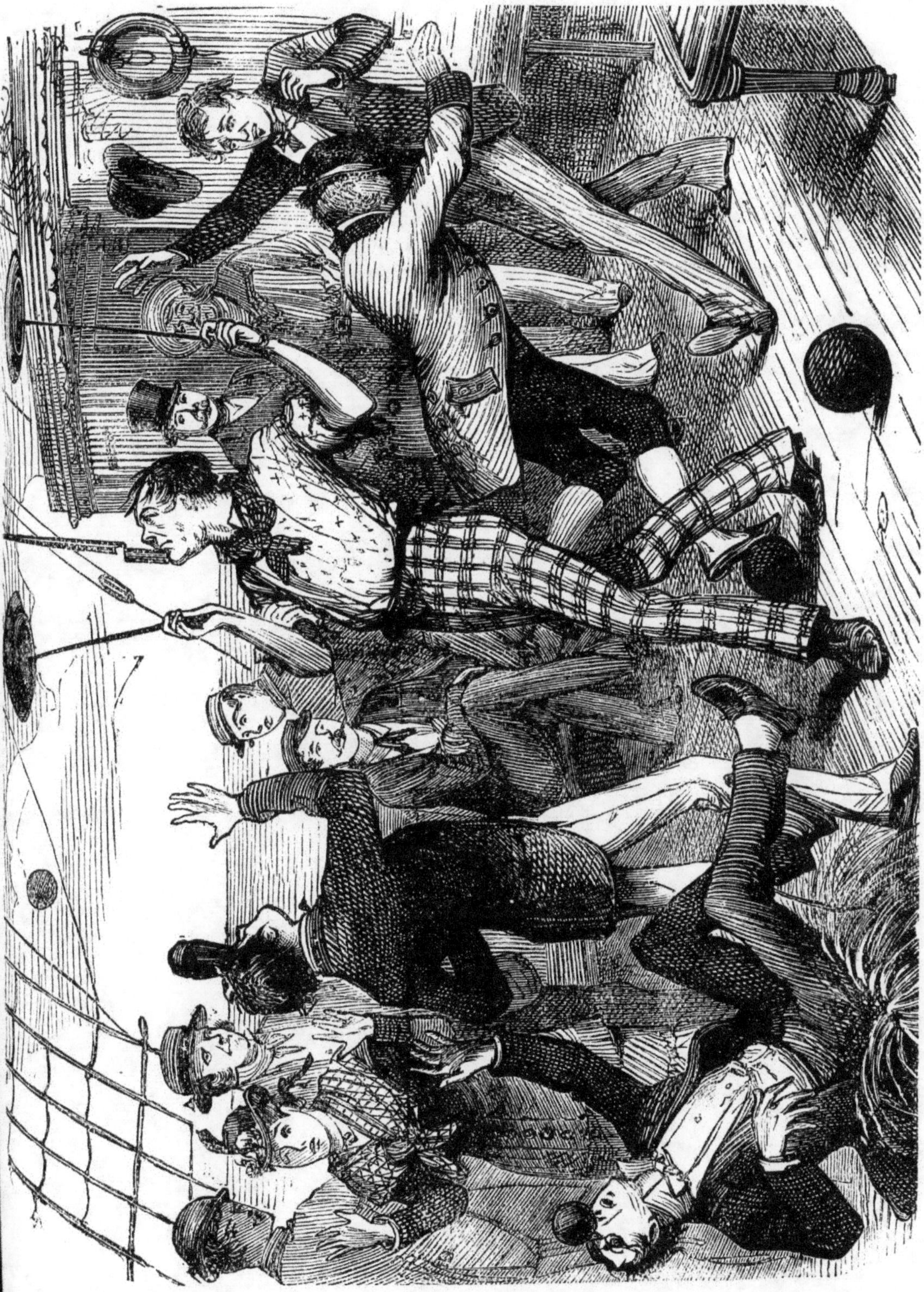

"UTTERING A LOUD YELL, BIRCHER FELL BACKWARD INTO A BUCKET OF WATER."

Gratis with No. 1.

"I say, senor," cried Ned, "you ain't done yet, have you?"

"No, sir, I have several other tricks to perform. You have only seen the easiest."

"Easy as it is, wouldn't you like to be able to do it, Nimble?" asked Bircher.

"I was just thinking I'd have a try," replied Ned.

"Go on, old man," said Harry; "two performers will be more interesting than one."

"I'm on," said Ned. "Senor, lend me that cup and those balls, and while you do your next trick I'll astound the natives with mine."

Jack handed the cup to Ned, who instantly placed the strap round his head.

"Keep the cup fair between the eyes, sir," whispered Jack, "and you'll catch them all right."

"Never fear," said Ned.

And he gathered up the balls, or as many as he could hold in his hands conveniently.

"We'll both operate together," said Ned; "then if I make a mess of it I shan't look so foolish."

"Mind your nose, old man," whispered Harry.

"I knows," returned Ned.

Jack now balanced a bayonet on his chin, and on the point of it he lifted a large cannon ball.

Steadying it, he stooped and picked up a couple of thin sticks about a foot and a half long, and a couple of plates.

With these in his hands he rose to an upright position.

And then flinging the plates up he dexterously caught one on the end of each stick and set them spinning.

And there he stood with the bayonet balanced on his chin and holding the spinning plates in either hand.

"Now," said Ned, "here goes."

And he flung one of the gilt balls in the air and his head back to catch it in the cup.

The onlookers drew back lest the falling ball should strike them, all except Mr. Bircher, who stood just behind Ned watching the ball in the air.

"Told you I could do it," said Ned, as the ball came with a thud into the cup.

Ned threw up another ball as high as he could, and in doing so dropped one out of his hand, which went rolling on the deck.

Down came the ball through the air, and striking the ball which Ned had forgot to jerk out of the cup, bounded over his head, and hitting Mr. Bircher a violent blow on the nose, caused that gentleman to utter a loud yell and spring back with such velocity that he lost his balance and fell backwards fair into a bucket of water which one of the sailors had just hauled over the side.

At the same moment 'Dolf started forward, and treading on the ball on the deck, pitched head first into Harry's stomach, against which he doubled up his hat like an accordion.

CHAPTER VII.

IN WHICH HANKY-PANKY JACK PROVES TO NED THAT ACCIDENTS SOMETIMES PROVE VERY BENEFICIAL.

THE laughter which greeted the mishaps of Bircher and 'Dolf was certainly not joined in by Mary.

As she saw her husband fall flop into the bucket she gave a loud scream and sprang forward with upraised hands.

Her cry of terror caused Jack to start, and the bayonet being thrown out of its balance, down came the cannon ball with a crash to the deck.

"Look out!" cried Jack, catching the plates in his hand.

But Ned instead of looking out was looking up.

A lurch of the boat sent the cannon ball rolling over his feet and against his ancles.

"Oh!" cried Ned, leaping up, to come down with both feet on the cannon ball, which, shooting from under him sent his legs up in the air and caused him to turn fairly head over heels on the deck.

Fortunately the strap was loose, or the cup might have caused him some injury.

As it was it fell from his forehead as he pitched forward.

Recovering himself in a moment, Ned sprang to his feet, and making a low bow, said, as if his fall was intentional—

"Ladies and gentlemen, the performance is ended, and we hope that we have afforded you both satisfaction and amusement."

"Well, if that ain't cool," said Jack, as he stooped and slipped the cannon ball into the bag to hide his laughter.

"Halloa, what's the matter with Bircher?" said Ned, looking at the tutor being lifted from the bucket by Mary and one of the passengers.

"You hit him on the nose with a ball," said Harry, holding his hands across his waist and standing half doubled up, "and knocked him into that bucket of water."

"I?" said Ned. "What do you mean?"

"What I say, old man. The second ball you threw bounced off the cup and hit him on the nose, and flop he went into the bucket."

Ned roared with laughter.

"Upon my soul, old man, I didn't mean it," he said.

"I know that," replied Harry. "And I know that you didn't mean to dash 'Dolf's head into my victualling department, but you did."

And Harry doubled himself up again.

"Here, cut it," said Ned; "blest if I know what you are talking about."

"Look at 'Dolf's hat."

And Harry pointed to where 'Dolf stood trying to force his hat out of its accordion shape, and looking dolefully at his damaged *chapeau*.

"I don't tumble to it at all," said Ned, "blest if I do."

"I wish 'Dolf hadn't, for he has knocked all the wind out of me," said Harry.

"And taken the bark off his own nose as well, seemingly," said Ned.

"I wonder he has got any nose at all the force he came," said Harry. "Look here, dear boy, when you try conjuring again you had better engage a ten acre field all to yourself to do it in."

And Harry went and sat down.

"My luck," said Ned; "I'm always in for it. I'm sure to bring somebody to grief whether I mean to do it or not. Just my luck!"

"Well, young gentleman, are you satisfied with your freak?" asked Captain Cruiser, strolling up to Ned.

"Perfectly, sir," replied Ned, "and hope that everybody else is."

"I should scarcely think that gentleman there was," said the captain, pointing to Bircher, "or that the cook will be either when he sees the state of his kettle."

"As to the kettle I understand that," said Ned, "but I cannot understand what brought Mr. Bircher to grief."

"Your failure to jerk the first ball out of the cup," said the captain; the second bounded off it and struck that gentleman on the nose causing him to fall backwards into a bucket of water."

"Oh, was that it?" said Ned. "It was very careless of me, I admit, and I regret the accident. I shall be able to make my peace with Mr. Bircher, for he and I are old friends and understand each other."

"I hope you may, sir," said the captain, drily. "But no more borrowing kettles of the cook or juggling on board this ship mind."

"Your commands, sir, are law," said Ned, "and I shall not presume to break them."

And bowing, Ned crossed over to Bircher who was standing in a most uncomfortable position holding a handkerchief to his bleeding nose.

"Mr. Bircher," said Ned, "I regret that my want of thought should have caused you this pain and annoyance. Believe me it was unintentional."

"I believe it was an accident this time, Nimble," gasped Bircher. "But you know what you are."

"And so do you, sir," said Ned.

"Yes, to my sorrow. Here I am bleeding in front, and dripping behind, and I don't believe I've got any nose left," cried Bircher, jerking out his words between each dab of the handkerchief.

"Oh yes, you have, sir," said Ned; "quite as much as ever you require, I assure you. It ain't a bit smaller than it was—if anything it's larger."

"It's large enough for—"

"A prize porker at a cattle show," interrupted Ned.

"Nimble, dare you compare me to a pig?" shrieked Bircher.

And he made a furious rush at Ned dragging Mary along with him.

Ned sprang back, laughing.

"Come to your berth, dear," said Mary, "or you'll catch your death of cold."

And she strove to force Bircher away.

"Go to my death, you mean," cried Bircher. "I wish I'd never been born."

"Oh, then what should I have done?" said Mary, tears starting to her eyes.

Bircher saw that he had wounded her, and he replied quickly—

"Found a better husband than I am."

"Bravo, Mr. Bircher!" said Ned. "That's the best thing you ever said in your life."

"Nimble, I do not require your remarks," said Bircher.

And taking his wife's arm he went below.

"Well, he's good cause to be wild. I know I should be if anyone gave me a crack like that," muttered Ned, turning to Jack, who had finished packing his props into the bag.

"Accidents will occur in the best regulated families, you know, sir," said Jack. "Lor', sir, that's nothing to what happened to me once."

"What was that, Jack?" asked Ned.

"Well, you see, I'd pitched in a square where there was no horses allowed to come, and had got a goodish crowd round me and was manipulating the balls when one hit the edge of the cup and flew off just like yours did."

"Well?" said Ned.

"Well, sir, I'd got a lot of balls up in the air, and an old lady stood with her mouth wide open a-watching them and never saw the ball that had hit the cup a-coming, and I'm blessed if it didn't fly smack into her mouth."

"Indeed," said Ned; "that's strange."

"Not at all, sir; you see the old lady had no teeth to stop it, and it went right in. Well, though it went right in it wouldn't come out. She tried, and I tried, and then the doctor tried, but there it stuck, and out it wouldn't come."

"It killed her then?" said Ned.

"Not a bit of it, sir. As it wouldn't come out in front they determined to take it out behind. So they opened her skull and took it out at the back of her head."

"With what result?" asked Ned, with difficulty suppressing a smile.

"With this, sir," replied Jack; "that old lady, who had been a martyr to headache ever since her childhood, never suffered with it afterwards. The doctor not only extracted the ball but also the pain at the same time. And out of gratitude she has promised to leave me something in her will when she dies."

CHAPTER VIII.

IN WHICH THE "DANCING DOLPHIN" COMES INTO HARBOUR, AND IN WHICH NED GAINS SOME INFORMATION.

IT must not be thought that Ned had forgotten or even partially ignored the desperate errand on which he was bound because he had given full play to his mischievous nature.

Ned was one of those who did not believe in sitting down and brooding over misfortune or sorrow.

He was anxious to reach South America, anxious to come up with the villains who had carried off Minnie and fired his uncle's house; but he knew that fretting and fuming would not bring him one hour nearer his wishes, and so made the best of circumstances.

"It's no good, old man, being downhearted," he said to Harry, when that youth murmured at the slowness of the vessel; "it's best to take things comfortable, grumbling only makes them worse."

"Which is the philosophical way of putting it," remarked Jack; "you have only got to be patient, sir, and things come all right at last."

"You're a patient fellow, ain't you?" said Harry.

"Which I am, sir," replied Jack; "it's only patient men as can learn to do the hanky-panky, I can tell you, which if you don't believe, just you try to balance that fifty-six pound cannon ball on the point of the bayonet."

"No thank you," said Harry; "it might drop on my nose."

"Bless your soul, sir, if it did it wouldn't hurt the ball," said Jack.

"But it might hurt me," said Harry, "so I'd rather not try."

"It's a beastly shame that Captain Cruiser has put his veto against our having a lark," said Ned, "or we might do something to cheer ourselves up."

"There's a place for everything, sir, as the old woman said when she swallowed a cup of tea," remarked Jack.

"Well, we are getting near the end of our voyage," said Ned, "and that's something; by the way, I haven't seen Bircher these two days."

"He's hard at studying Spanish in his berth," said Harry.

"What's he want Spanish for?" asked Ned.

"It's spoken a good deal in South America, and he is eager to learn it, and we ought to try to do so as well," said Harry.

"Look here, dear boy," said Ned; "you learn it and then you can act as interpreter for me."

"Thank you, but suppose you learn it?"

"I ain't got time," said Ned.

"Nor patience," said Harry.

"A little bit of both perhaps," remarked Ned.

"Still it wouldn't be a bad thing to try and lay hold of a little of it," said Harry; "it might be handy where we are going."

"Right you are," said Ned; "let's see if old Bircher will learn us while he is learning himself."

"Agreed," cried Harry.

Mr. Bircher had forgiven Ned for the blow he had received from the ball, and thanks to the captain's orders, that gentleman met with no more annoyance from Ned's freaks.

He willingly undertook to allow Ned and Harry to study with him.

And so the days passed till land was sighted, and the "Dancing Dolphin" bore up for the island of Trinidad.

Lessons and study were now thrown aside.

All was excitement as the good ship drew nearer and nearer to the island

Ned could scarcely control his feelings, for now he felt he would gain some information of Minnie and her abductors.

Already he felt himself within reach of Boaster and Phopps.

And he clenched his hands and set his teeth together, and there was a look on his face which, had Boaster seen it, he would indeed have had cause to tremble.

Bircher came and stood by Ned's side.

"We shall soon say good-bye to each other now, Nimble," he said, "so I hope we shall part friends."

"I hope so, sir," said Ned.

"You have caused me much pain and annoyance, Nimble, but I bear no animosity, for I believe your high spirits are more to be blamed than the badness of your heart."

"Mr. Bircher," said Ned, "I know I am a beast, but I can't help it; I ain't so bad as some people think me; I must have a lark if I can, but I never sought to injure another by word or deed."

"I believe you, Nimble," said the tutor; "but as we shall so soon separate, let me ask you to put a curb on your spirits, and be a little more thoughtful and considerate."

"I'll try, sir," said Ned. "Indeed, I feel that there is too much stern reality before me now to permit me to think of play; and yet," he added, with a smile, "all work and no play makes Jack a dull boy, and I'm sure even you would not like me to grow dull."

"No, no," cried Bircher; "I only enjoin moderation in all your pursuits."

"I'm afraid, sir, it will always be the whole hog with me," said Ned. "However, thank you for your advice, Mr. Bircher, and I wish you all the success you deserve."

"Thank you, Nimble, thank you. Now I must go and look after my luggage, for the captain expects to anchor at sunset."

"And I must get 'Dolf to look after ours, for we've got a cartload at least."

And Ned went in search of 'Dolf.

The sun was setting as the "Dancing Dolphin" steamed into the harbour of Port Spain.

Little notice did Ned take of the place, he gave but a glance at the large forests and magnificent scenery.

The fortifications had no charm for him.

He had but one thought now, one desire.

That was to discover Minnie, to track down Boaster and his companion, to learn if they had been seen, and if so, in what direction they had gone.

"It was too late when the vessel came to an anchor for the passengers to land that night.

Ned paced the deck excitedly.

At last he paused, and leaning over the rail, gazed down into the water of the harbour.

"What a fool I am," he muttered, " to vex myself about things that can't be helped. Ned, Ned, where's your philosophy ? "

"Halloa, Ned, got the blues ? " cried Harry.

"It's the blacks, I think," said Ned. ' Glad you come, Harry. I was getting melancholy."

"Take a pill, old fellow. For you to be melancholy is a sure sign that you are out of health."

"I feel wild we can't land to-night," said Ned.

"If we could we should have to wait till to-morrow for our luggage."

"I'd forgotten that."

"The town looks pretty from here with its lights and background of forest about it."

Ned looked up.

"It does," he said. " I wonder if those we seek are hiding there ? "

"I don't expect so," said Harry. "I asked that big-bearded fellow that came on board if he had seen any persons like those we are in search of on board the Kicking Kangaroo.' "

"You did ? " cried Ned. " What did he say ? "

"At first he said he did not. But after awhile he remembered seeing two of the passengers answering the description of Phopps and Boaster."

"And Minnie ? " cried Ned, eagerly.

"There was a female with them, but whether young or old he couldn't say."

"Why not ? "

" It seems she was heavily veiled and evidently very ill or prostrated, for she was lowered over the side into the boat in a chair and carried ashore in the same."

"If they have harmed her," cried Ned, clenching his fist, "I'll kill them both."

"Don't get excited, Ned. It may not be them, you know," said Harry.

"But it is; I feel sure it is ! " cried Ned. "Minnie ill !—prostrate !—unable to walk ! Oh, if they have caused this !—if they have harmed but a single hair of her head, they shall answer to me for it. I'd kill them, Harry; kill them, even if I bring about my own doom ! "

"Be calm, old man," said Harry. "As I said before, it may not be them after all. Indeed, Ned, we are not positive that they were really passengers by the 'Kicking Kangaroo.' "

"Harry, dear boy, I have no doubt of it myself. Some inward voice tells me they were, and that Minnie is suffering at their hands. Where is this man ? He may know more than he cares to say. Gold may open his mouth. I will try him."

"He went forward in company of the first mate," said Harry. "Oh, see here he is, standing by himself.'

"I will speak to him," said Ned. "He may place me on their track."

He sprang away from Harry's side and approached the bearded man, who, by the light of a ship's lantern, was making entries in a pocket-book.

As he closed the book and put it in his pocket, Ned touched his arm, and in a husky and tremulous voice implored him to give what information he could respecting the persons of whom he had spoken to Harry.

At first he hesitated, but the promise of ten pounds opened his mouth, and Ned learned that they had crossed the straits to the mainland, purchased a small boat, manned it with two whites and six Indians, and set sail for the Orinoko, but their actual destination he could not tell.

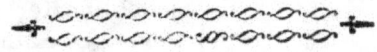

CHAPTER IX.

IN WHICH NED'S DOUBTS ARE SET AT REST, AND THE ADVENTURERS SET SAIL FOR THE ORINOKO.

NED was forced to remain content for the present with the information the man could give him.

There was no doubt in his own mind as to their being the parties of whom he was in search.

On receiving the ten pounds, however, the bearded fellow said—

"I shall go ashore early and I'll speak to them as is likely to know where the boat is bound for, and when you land I'll let you know the result."

Ned thanked him and turned away to tell Harry what he had heard.

"And if it should turn out to be them, what will you do ?" asked his friend.

"I have letters of credit from my uncle and shall be able to obtain money to any amount," replied Ned, "so I'll buy or hire a boat and well go in pursuit of them."

He also made 'Dolf and Jack acquainted with what he had learned.

That night Ned found it difficult to sleep, and the sun had scarcely risen when he was again on deck.

He inquired for the bearded man, but he had gone ashore.

It was still early when passengers began to assemble on the deck and the sailors to bring up their luggage.

Suddenly a boat put off for the ship and a man came on board with letters.

One of these was for Mr. Bircher, and Ned noticed as he read it that his face turned pale and that the sheet dropped from his hand to his feet as he turned to speak to Mary.

Mary clasped her hands together and seemed to become as much agitated as her husband.

"No bad news, sir, I hope ?" said Ned.

"I'm ruined, Nimble; I'm ruined !" moaned Bircher.

"I hope not, sir."

"Only to think, Nimble, of crossing the ocean to be disappointed."

"How, sir, may I ask ?"

"He's dead, Nimble ; dead !"

"Who is dead ?"

"My employer. The gentleman whose assistant I was to become has died of yellow fever, and the school is broken up."

"That's unfortunate," said Ned.

"It's ruin, Nimble ; ruin ! I've spent all my money for my passage, and I'm in a foreign land a beggar."

"Not so bad as that, sir ; I have plenty of money," said Ned, "and another engagement may be found in time."

"That's what it says in the letter," moaned Bircher, "but where am I to find it."

"That I can't say. But don't distress yourself, you shan't want."

"Thank you. And then the insult ?"

"What insult, sir ?"

"The writer says he can take my wife into his service till I find employment."

"I do not call that an insult, sir, as it provides for Mrs. Bircher, and leaves you free to look about you."

"Well, so it does," said Bircher.

"Of course, and if I may advise, I certainly should accept his offer."

"Well, I don't know but what it would be the best thing to do under the circumstances."

"Of course it would, and I daresay Mrs. Bircher would not object."

"Oh no," said Mary ; "for I should not then be a drag upon him in his search for employment."

"Then accept it," said Ned. "Mr. Bircher will know you are safe and comfortable, and that will take a great deal of anxiety off his mind."

"But schools I expect are few and far between in these parts," said Bircher.

"Doubtless they are," replied Ned; "but if you fail in finding employment in one you can turn your hand to something else you know."

"How can I ? What's the good of a schoolmaster at anything else. I shall never get an engagement outside a school-house."

"Oh yes you will," said Ned, "for I'll engage you if all else fails."

"What to do, Nimble?"

"To be my travelling companion and secretary. Wages to commence with one hundred and fifty pounds a year. What do you say to that?"

"It's too good to be true."

"No it ain't for I mean it."

"You do?" cried Bircher.

"On my honour I do."

"Then Mary could stay with me."

"No, for this reason," said Ned. "We may be called upon to travel hundreds of miles, and meet with many hardships and perhaps dangers, and she would be safer and far more comfortable in the house of the gentleman who has offered to take her. However talk it over between yourselves, and give me your answer in an hour."

And Ned turned away.

But in five minutes Bircher approached him.

"Nimble," he said, "I know you to be a lad of your word. I and Mary have talked it over. She will go into service in Venezuela, and I will follow you and your fortunes."

"Bravo, Bircher!" said Ned, grasping his hand. "I'm glad you have decided thus, for I want friends badly enough now."

Preparations were now being made for landing the passengers and luggage.

And one of the first to touch the shore was Ned.

To 'Dolf and Jack he had left the work of looking after the luggage, for he was far too intent upon meeting the man with the large beard.

The fellow, true to his word, met our hero as he sprang ashore.

"Well?" asked Ned, eagerly.

"I have learned that the boat would go up the Orinoco, but how far, is doubtful from the conversation of the white men. However it appears that they intend joining one of the wandering tribes of Carribs that infest the forests, caves, and shores of that river and its tributaries."

"And the girl?" cried Ned.

"None saw her face; so whether girl or woman is uncertain, but I think I can show you something that may give you an idea whether you are on the right track or not."

"Ah," cried Ned; "what is it?"

"Only this handkerchief left behind by one of the party where they stopped while the boat was being got ready."

Ned took the handkerchief and examined its corners eagerly.

"'Tis she, 'tis she!" he cried, pointing to one of the corners where marked in red silk were the initials M. S. "There is no mistake, we are on the right track and I'll rescue her from their hands or die."

And he thrust the handkerchief into his bosom.

"If he joins the Carribs you'll have all your work to do," said the man; "they're a desperate lot, I can tell you."

"Were they fiends from Hades, I'd care not," said Ned. "Now will you earn another ten pounds by obtaining for me a boat and a crew who know this river and its banks?"

"I will but you will have to buy the boat, and it will cost you a heap of money."

"No matter the price. How soon could it be done?"

"To-day."

"Then get me a serviceable boat and crew. My own party will consist of five, and I have a great deal of luggage. You are a sailor and will know better than I the sort of craft I require."

"And I'll get you one," said the man, "I know just where to pick it up, but your crew will have to be Indians if you want them to know where the others are likely to be hiding."

"Be it so," said Ned; "but stay, how shall we understand each other?"

"They speak Spanish or something like it."

"That will do. Do not delay an instant, so eager am I to be on my way. What start have they?"

"Eight days."

"Would it were but eight minutes," said Ned. "But I'll run them down, and when I do, may Heaven have mercy on them!"

"Amen to that."

Ned swung round to see Harry at his elbow.

"There is no longer any doubt, dear boy," said Ned, showing the handkerchief to Harry. "Here are her initials. Oh, Heaven! what may she not have been made to suffer?"

"Bill will not dare harm her," said Harry; "coward as he is, he will not dare do her any injury."

Ned shook his head, and together they walked away from the shore.

There was a boat ready to start for the mainland, and the captain having offered to see Mary safe into the hands of the gentleman who had offered her a home, she bade farewell to our hero and his friends, and accompanied her husband on board.

Here Bircher took an affectionate leave of his wife, made cheerful by the good account the captain gave of Senor Velasquez, who, he asserted, would prove not only a good master to Mary but a true friend.

Bircher then returned to Ned, and the whole party had a long and serious talk about their plans for the future.

Ned and Harry had provided themselves with serviceable suits, but neither 'Dolf, nor Bircher, nor Jack would agree to dress as hunters.

Arms and ammunition they had in plenty, and by the time the boat and crew were ready, provisions for a long journey had been procured.

Early next morning the party went on board, and set sail for the Orinoco.

CHAPTER X.

IN WHICH THERE IS A GREAT NOISE AND A LITTLE FIGHTING.

Now that Ned felt sure he was on the right track, and that every hour brought him nearer and nearer to Minnie, his spirits revived.

Jack kept them amused with his sleight-of-hand tricks, and astounded the Indians who worked the boat.

'Dolf they could not understand.

They had never before seen a man dressed as he was, and they paid such deference to his laced hat and plush breeches that the footman felt as though he were a king.

There was nothing to call for any attention, or any event worthy of notice on the part of the voyagers till some time after they had entered the Orinoco.

Then the wild and varied scenery on its banks engaged their attention.

Hitherto they had not left the boat, but tempted by the beauty of the scene they resolved to land and partake of a meal.

The Indians, however, were ordered to remain in charge of the vessel.

The forest came down to within twenty or thirty feet of the bank on which they landed, but the flowering vines that encircled the trunks of the trees and spread along the ground, made the spot odourous and beautiful.

"Is this not lovely, Harry?" said Ned.

"It is a pretty scene, indeed," replied his friend: "but amid so much beauty may lurk the poisoned snake and the deadly panther."

"Satan in Paradise," said Jack.

"Halloa! what's the matter with you?" said Ned. "Now if Bircher had said that I shouldn't have been surprised."

"Why, what's Bircher up to, Ned?" asked Harry.

"He's afraid of spoiling his complexion, I suppose," replied Ned.

Mr. Bircher had brought with him a huge green umbrella, which he had opened and held above his head.

"Nimble," he said, "you shouldn't expose yourself to the vertical rays of the sun in this climate."

"And why not, sir?" asked Ned.

"You might get sunstroke, you know."

"I'll chance that."

"I would advise you to place a silk handkerchief inside your hat, or a cabbage leaf."

"Can you tell me where I can find a cabbage leaf?" asked Ned.

"Well—er, you might get such a thing, I think."

"In Covent Garden Market," said Harry. "'Dolf, just run and fetch one."

"Afraid it's almost too far, sir, and I might find all the dinner eaten before I got back," said 'Dolf, as he raked some sticks together to kindle a fire on which to cook some bacon they had brought ashore with them.

"I'll go and get my fifty-six pound cannon-ball," said Jack. "If you put that in your hat there'll be no fear of the sun getting at your head."

"Thank you," said Ned; "but you may save yourself the trouble."

"Besides, it might melt," said 'Dolf, with a wink at Jack.

"You look alive with that fire, 'Dolf," else I'll melt you," said Ned.

"Welt him, you meant, Ned," said Harry.

"Which wouldn't be the sort of thing to do this hot day," said 'Dolf, as he set light to the sticks and filled his eyes with smoke.

"Blest if he ain't crying!" said Harry.

"Let the poor beggar be; he's thinking of Betsy Baker."

"Betsy be blowed!" said 'Dolf. "Lor', Master Ned, I wonder how that new footman likes her jaw?"

"Perhaps he likes Dorothy's lips better," said Ned.

"He'd better hang off there," said 'Dolf, "or he'll get some of the buttons knocked off his coat when I get back."

"Oh, they'll be married long before that, 'Dolf," said Ned.

"What? when she swore to wait——"

"Oh, oh, so the cat's out of the bag, is it?" cried Ned.

"I didn't mean to say that," stammered 'Dolf.

"Now, then, don't burn the bottom out of that frying-pan; we can't get it mended out here, you know," cried Ned.

"Well, you do talk so, Master Ned; I'd quite forgot I hadn't put the rashers in it."

And 'Dolf proceeded to lay some rashers of bacon in the pan.

"We ought to have brought some rifles on shore," said Ned; "then we might have had a shot or two while dinner is getting ready."

"So we might," said Harry; "but it's hardly worth while fetching them now."

"No. The dinner sniffs nice, don't it? And I'm awfully peckish."

"Ditto," said Harry. "Halloa! Jack, what are you up to?"

"Getting up an appetite," replied Jack, as he caught hold of a branch of a tree, drew himself up, and sat astride of it.

"You have practiced gymnastics, I see," said Bircher, looking from under his umbrella.

"Yes, I used to do a little on the trapeze one time," said Jack.

"Dinner's ready," cried 'Dolf.

"I'm on," said Ned. "Come along, you fellows, and grease your windpipes."

In a minute the party were seated in a circle, engaged in cutting up slices of bacon.

"I forgot the table-cloth," said 'Dolf, "and if you want finger-napkins you'll have to use the legs of your trousers."

"Not I," said Ned, "I shall wipe my fingers in your hair.'

"Don't do that, sir; Mr. Bircher's umbrella is more convenient."

The meal went on amid jests and laughter, when suddenly a blood-curdling yell from the forest brought the whole party to their feet.

"Wha—what's that?" gasped Bircher, dropping his food and shutting up his umbrella.

"Indians," said Ned.

Bircher grew paler and turned to run for the boat.

But the vessel had drifted some two hundred yards higher up the river.

"Look out," cried Ned; "here they come."

As he spoke some half-dozen naked savages burst into view.

"Stand firm," said Ned. "I fear they mean mischief, and we are unarmed."

Another yell from the savages as they sprang forward, brandishing their knives.

"Yes, yes, yes! stand firm; oh do stand firm!" gasped Bircher.

And he made a bolt for the nearest tree.

He caught the lowermost branch and swung himself up on to it, and then with his umbrella still in his grasp, drew himself higher.

"Show a bold front, lads," cried Ned. "If they mean mischief, let them have it hot."

"And strong," said Harry.

"Here they come," cried 'Dolf, seizing the frying-pan in which some more of the bacon was cooking.

"And there they'll go," said Jack, pointing to the earth, and then spitting on his hands.

With a whoop one savage flung himself upon Harry to find the grip of that youth's hands like a vice on his throat.

"Oh that's your game is it?" cried Harry, giving the savage a swing round and planting his foot in his back.

"Let them have it, Harry," cried Ned.

"Wire in, boys, and show them what Britishers can do. Don't be frightened of their knives."

Ned struck out straight from the shoulder, planting a blow on the nose of a savage that sent him toppling backwards as if shot.

Jack had watched his opportunity, and as two of the savages dashed upon him he put out his long arms and caught each by the back of the neck.

"You murdering sons of Satan!" yelled Jack; you'll use your knives on peaceable travellers, will you?"

"Ugh, ugh!" growled the savages, struggling to drive their weapons into his chest.

"I'll give you 'ugh' and me too, you greasey-hided varmints," cried Jack. "Dance, you black beggars, and I'll sing 'Every morning as true as the clock somebody hears the postmans knock.' Never heard it, did you? Then blest it you shan't feel it."

For a moment he held them at arms' length, then putting out all his enormous strength he brought their heads together with a crash that completely stunned and rendered them insensible.

Meantime one of the savages had sprung to the tree in which the tutor had taken refuge, and clutching at the lowermost branch was drawing himself up when Bircher, terrified half out of his wits and rendered desperate by fear, prodded him fiercely in the eye with his umbrella.

"Go away, black man, don't you come a-nigh me," yelled Bircher, prodding the face of the savage.

"Ugh, kill," yelled the savage, striking desperately with his knife.

"No, don't," cried Bircher; I ain't fit to kill. You couldn't even make a stew of me, I'm so tough. Go away, go away."

And Bircher began to tremble, and he could hardly hold the umbrella, while the branch across which he lay began to sway in such a manner as to render him fearful of being precipitated on to the knife of the savage.

Frantically he prodded at the black, upturned face, yelling as he did so for help.

'Dolf, perceiving the state of affairs in Bircher's direction, sprang to his aid, frying-pan in hand.

"One for his nob!" yelled 'Dolf, bringing the hot pan down on the Indian's back, and flinging bacon and fat around him.

"Hit him again—hit him again, 'Dolf," cried Bircher.

"You let him have it at top, and I'll let him have it bottom, sir," cried 'Dolf.

And 'Dolf smashed away at the savage with the hot pan, while Bircher, gaining courage now that he had got assistance, jobbed furiously at the face of his black opponent.

Maddened with pain and rage, the Indian still struggled to get at Bircher, but 'Dolf, seizing him by one leg, wired into him so desperately with the frying-pan, that the savage was fain to let go and howl for mercy.

A howl which was echoed by the opponents of Ned and Harry as they went floundering to the earth, sent them senseless and bleeding by the heavy and well aimed blows of the two brave British boys.

CHAPTER XI.

IN WHICH BIRCHER TAKES A BATH AND THE INDIANS TAKE AN AIM.

HARRY had succeeded in saving himself from being gashed by the knife of the savage and giving the Indian such a neat back fall as to shake half the life out of his body.

Jack holding the two stunned savages for a moment let them drop limp and powerless at his feet.

"Now that's what I call the double knock," he said; "and if their skulls ain't as solid as my fifty-six pound cannon ball they'll fancy their heads are full of parched peas for a month."

"And if this fellow is able to sit down for double that time I'd eat him," said 'Dolf.

And he dragged the now howling savage away from the tree.

"Hold your hullabaloo, you son of a black kangaroo," cried 'Dolf, giving him a blow on the top of his head with the flat of the frying-pan.

"Come down, Bircher," said Ned. "I don't think there's any more of them."

"I think I'll stop where I am," said Bircher. "I can use my weapon better here. See how I've paid that wretch out."

"Come down and don't be a fool," said Ned, angrily.

Very fearfully Bircher descended to the ground.

"Just keep your eyes on those fellows while I question this one," said Ned. "Or, rather, Bircher, you repeat my questions to him in Spanish. I daresay he speaks that lingo. And you, 'Dolf, hail the boat back."

'Dolf went to the edge of the bank and hailed the boat.

"Why did you attack us?" asked Ned of the Indian.

"See smoke, smell meat," was the reply.

"Who told you to do so?"

The Indian pointed to the savage Ned had struck to the earth.

"Where are the two white men and the white girl?" asked Ned.

The Indian's look of surprise convinced Ned that the savage knew nothing of Boaster and his companions.

He had hoped to learn from him the whereabouts of those he sought.

He was disappointed.

"When did a boat with white men and a white woman go up the river?" asked Ned.

The Indian shook his head.

"Tell me or I'll kill you," cried Ned.

But evidently the savage had not seen the boat.

"Those fellows will soon recover," said Ned, addressing Jack. "What shall we do with them?"

"The safest way to prevent them doing us or others harm would be to kill them," replied Jack. "But I don't like the idea of that."

"No, no," said Ned. "I am ready to defend my own life, and if in so doing I shed blood I cannot help it. But I cannot commit murder."

"I've gathered up all their knives," said Harry, "and they do not seem to have any other weapons."

"We'll keep them," said Ned. "Here's the boat. Perhaps we'd better let them be; they have been punished enough for attacking us."

"I don't think they will try it on again, at least, not these two in a hurry," said Jack, pointing to the men at his feet.

"There! start that fellow, 'Dolf, and we'll get aboard," said Ned.

"Now, then, you copper-skinned varmint, off you go," cried 'Dolf, giving the Indian a sound thwack with the frying-pan.

"Distance lends enchantment to the view of all such greasy-hided things as you," said Bircher, giving the savage a prod in the ribs with the ferule of his umbrella.

The Indian gave Bircher a fearful look, and then bounded away into the forest.

The savage who had been Ned's opponent, and also the Indian who had been Harry's, showed signs of recovery.

But the two whose heads Jack had brought together lay as though utterly bereft of life.

"Gather up the things, 'Dolf," said Ned, "and let's get aboard before that fellow can bring any of his tribe down upon us."

"We ought not to have let him go," said Jack; "we should have secured him to a tree to prevent him giving an alarm."

"We should, but I didn't think of that," said Ned.

"That was because you allowed yourself to get excited, Nimble," said Bircher. "Calmness in danger is the proper thing, you know."

"Oh, that accounts for your hurried flight up into the tree, I suppose?" said Ned.

"I gazed calmly around me, Nimble, and I saw that that tree was a post of vantage; I calculated how much more powerful would be the downward stroke of the umbrella than——"

"Look out, Bircher, here's a lot more coming," interrupted Ned.

"The devil!" yelled Bircher, making a rush for the boat, into which he attempted to scramble.

But in his eagerness to get in he pushed it away from the shore, and down he went between the boat and the bank, head first into the water.

One of the Indian crew made a grab at him as he sank, but he only saved the umbrella.

Ned and the others sprang to the bank.

Up came Bircher, and the moment his head rose above the surface, he yelled lustily for help.

Jack thrust out his long arms, and seized him by the hair of his head, while Harry secured his hat as it floated by.

"Oh, save me, save me!" yelled Bircher, waving his arms frantically.

"Don't get excited," said Ned. "Remember your calmness, you'll want it now, for there's an awful big crocodile a-coming."

"Oh, help me out, help me out, or I shall be killed!"

"Put your finger in the reptile's eye, Bircher, and he won't hurt you," said Ned.

Bircher clutched fiercely at the arm of Jack and dragged himself out of the water and up the bank.

"Saved, saved! oh, thank Heaven!" gasped the tutor.

"Yes, from the crocodile, but how about the Indians?" asked Ned.

"Oh, let me get into the boat, let me get into the boat!" groaned Bircher, terrified half out of his life.

The Indians had now brought the boat close to the shore again.

"In you go, then," said Jack.

And lifting Bircher off his feet he pitched him into the boat, where he sank down, utterly exhausted by fear.

"Don't think much of his calmness," said Jack.

"Nor his courage either," said Ned.

"Now then, calves, pitch those things aboard," said Jack.

"None of your impudence, if you please," said 'Dolf."

"Oh," said Jack, "I'm sorry I spoke."

"And so am I," said 'Dolf, "for I object to impertinent 'sinuations."

Ned and Harry laughed.

"Don't be riled, 'Dolf," said the former; "you must expect to get chaffed out here if you will persist in wearing those togs."

"Sir, I know my place, and besides, I feel it an honour to wear the livery of the Nimbles," said 'Dolf.

"All right, 'Dolf, but if you get among the snakes you'll wish you had something thicker on your legs than silk stockings."

"I've got my drab gaiters, sir," said 'Dolf, "and as they are part of the livery of course I'll wear them."

And with this 'Dolf handed the frying-pan and other utensils into the boat and followed himself.

In a few moments Jack, Ned, and Harry were aboard, and the Indians set to work.

Suddenly a loud whoop rang in their ears.

"By Jingo!" cried Ned; "that fellow has given the alarm and we shall have the whole tribe down upon us."

"Pull out into the stream," said Harry; "pull for your lives!"

The Indians bent to their oars, and the boat shot away towards the middle of the river.

But ere the boat had got a hundred yards from the shore a crowd of Indians, yelling and whooping, came tearing down to the bank.

Another moment and a flight of arrows came hurling and whizzing through the air.

CHAPTER XII.

IN WHICH JACK STOPS A MUTINY AND HARRY STOPS A TOOTH.

BIRCHER had sprung to his feet on hearing the savage yell, but when he saw the arrows coming he flung himself down again, striking his nose a severe blow on the toe of Jack's boot.

"Oh, Lor', oh, Lor'! we shall all be killed!" moaned Bircher.

"Hold your row," cried Ned. "Jack, hand me that rifle."

Jack did as requested.

The arrows had fallen short of the boat and plunged into the water with a hiss.

Leaning the rifle barrel on the side of the boat, Ned knelt and took a sight along it.

"I don't like to kill any of the beggars," he said; "but we must prevent them if possible following us."

And he pulled the trigger.

The shot was a true one.

One of the savages on the shore threw up his arms and then pitched head first off the bank into the river.

A fearful yell arose from his companions.

Again they sent a shower of arrows towards the boat, and then turning plunged into the forest, evidently to escape another shot from Ned's rifle.

Of course not an arrow reached those in the boat.

But Bircher, fearful that they might, had seized the umbrella and opened it before him.

"What do you want with that gingham up for?" asked Harry.

"It's my shield, Honour, my warlike shield, which I throw before me," replied Bircher.

"Put it down, you fool," said Ned.

"Nimble, you forget yourself," said Bircher.

"Shut up," said Ned. "A lot of good that thing would be if we were within range of their arrows, wouldn't it?"

"That shot seems to have frightened them," said Harry; "but I should keep well out in the stream lest the niggers are following us under the shelter of the trees."

"I thought of that, Harry," said Ned "Jack, load that barrel, we must be ready for any emergency."

"Right you are," said Jack; "nothing like being always ready."

"And now, since it is evident we may come upon foes at any moment," said Ned, "I think we had better put a revolver each in our belts."

"But where are they to come from?" asked Jack.

"Oh, I've got a perfect arsenal," said Ned.

And he went into the cabin of the boat.

When he came back he carried with him five revolvers and as many pouches of ammunition.

These he distributed among his friends, much to the surprise of Bircher and Jack.

"Now look here, Bircher," said Ned, "don't go and shoot yourself in a fright."

"Nimble, I am never frightened, I'm only cautious," said Bircher.

"Then when you get filled with an extra amount of caution don't forget to turn the muzzle away from your own body, that's all."

"And mine too," said Jack.

"Don't have any anxiety about me," said Bircher. "But I say, Nimble, is this weapon loaded?"

"Every chamber," replied Ned.

"Don't you think it had better be unloaded till it's wanted?—it might go off you know by itself."

"Look here, Bircher, if you are afraid of it you'd better give it me back," said Ned.

"Afraid! I'm not afraid, Nimble, I'm only cautious."

"Then don't put the trigger up until you want to use it and it can't go off."

And Ned turned away.

Bircher, half fearfully, placed the weapon in his breast-pocket.

Jack, looking up suddenly, caught the eyes of one of the Indians looking greedily at the weapon he was examining.

He touched Ned's foot with his own,

and signed for him to look at the savage.

Ned turned a meaning gaze on the conjurer.

"If that fellow meditates treachery," whispered Jack, "we had better frighten it out of him."

"How?" asked Ned.

"Watch me," replied Jack.

He took a small glass marble from his pocket, and holding it between his finger and thumb, said—

"Woe to him who would not serve faithfully the great white medicine man or his friends, he would be shattered even as this ball."

Then he whispered to Bircher to translate his words to the Indians.

Bircher did so, and then Jack, flinging the marble into the air, raised his revolver and fired.

The next moment a shower of small pieces of glass descended on the heads and hands of the rowers.

So surprised were the Indians at this feat that they ceased rowing, and leaning on their oars gazed with awe and admiration at Hanky-panky Jack.

"That's stopped their little game," said Jack; "if they could turn upon us after that they wouldn't look so white about the gills."

"Great medicine," muttered one Indian.

"Yes," laughed Jack, "and that's some of my physic."

"Now then, pull away," cried Ned.

The men again bent to their oars.

It was evident from their looks and gestures that if they had meditated turning upon the whites, that trick of Jack's had frightened them out of such an act, and that they believed it was better to be their friends than their foes.

On went the boat.

The travellers seemed to have the mighty river all to themselves.

Not another vessel was in view.

Now and then they caught sight of a crocodile basking on the bank, and then their gaze wandered away to the forest beyond.

And so the shades of night fell over the scene.

The silence that during the heat of the day had been oppressive was now broken.

The beasts of the forest now gave voice, and Ned shuddered as he thought to what danger Minnie might be exposed, not only from those who had abducted her, but from the wild denizens of the primeval forests.

The musquitoes, too, caused them great annoyance.

In their small cabin they could find no means of avoiding the stings of these pestiferous insects.

Bircher in vain tried to sleep.

As he dozed off he felt a sting on his nose, and putting up his hand gave his injured proboscis a blow that caused him to jump up with a howl of pain and sit down again immediately, from having knocked his head against the low roof of the cabin.

"Blow the blow!" he growled.

"Blow you!" said Harry. "Why don't you let a fellow go to sleep?"

"It ain't me, it's the musquitoes," said Bircher. "They sting worse than a wasp. This is a beastly country."

"And no wonder, when such a beast as you are in it," said Harry. "Take that, you beggar!"

And he aimed a blow at a buzzing musquito that he heard near his ear.

Unfortunately he forgot that Bircher was lying, or rather sitting up, close by his side.

Harry missed the troublesome insect, but not Mr. Bircher.

His open hand came across Mr. Bircher's lips, and Mr. Bircher's body went down flop.

"What the devil do you mean by that, Honour?" he cried. "How dare you strike me?"

"I beg your pardon," said Harry. "I forgot you were so close. I hit at a musquito."

"You hit me, sir."

"I did; but I certainly had no intention of doing so," said Harry.

"I believe it was done on purpose," said Bircher; "and you have loosened my tooth."

"Never mind, sir; pull it out and say no more about it," said Harry.

"But I will say something about it. I will not submit to have my teeth loosened in that way."

"Don't be angry, sir. I assure you it was unintentional," said Harry.

"'YER BERRY HUMBLE SARBENT, GEN'LEM'S,' SAID THE NEGRO."

PRICE ONE HALFPENNY
[PUBLISHED EVERY MONDAY.]

"The musquito made me mad," Harry added, "and I hit out without thinking."

"Then don't do it again," said Bircher, covering up his head.

"All right," said Harry, "I won't if I can help it."

And following Bircher's example, he tried to go to sleep.

But the insects, buzzing and biting, kept him awake a long time, and when he arose to give place to Ned, he felt anything but refreshed.

CHAPTER XIII.

IN WHICH NED HAS AN INTERVIEW WITH FRIENDLY INDIANS AND AN UNFRIENDLY JAGUAR.

NED and his party ascended the river for many miles before they discovered any evidence of human life on its banks.

At last they caught sight of an Indian village, and on questioning the rowers, they learned that the savages were friendly and well disposed to the whites.

On hearing this Ned resolved to land and make inquiries about those whom he was in pursuit of.

He had procured at Trinidad several pieces of coloured cloth, beads, and small ornaments, and providing himself with some of these, he went on shore.

The village was inhabited by a tribe of Taumans.

The Indians were tattooed with a red pigment on face and body.

This gave them a fierce look, but their looks belied their nature, and they received the whites kindly.

Having made several of them presents of beads and pieces of cloth, Ned began to question one who appeared to be the head man of the village.

Bircher translated what Ned said, and as the savage knew some little of Spanish, he was able to make his replies understood.

From this savage they learned that some days before a boat containing four white men and a white woman had passed up the river.

Believing that the savage could give more information if he liked, Ned made him further presents, and then learned that some of his people had come in who said that at the mouth of the Meta, a tributary of the Orinoco, the boat had been surrounded by the canoes of Tiger Claws, a chief of a powerful tribe of Orinoco Indians.

Ned felt his heart sink within him.

Had Minnie then fallen into the hands of savages?

A few questions, however, and Ned learned that the white men had made friends with Tiger Claws, and that they had all gone on together.

"To where?" asked Ned.

The Indian shook his head.

The tribe had no settled abode.

They might encamp for a time near the falls, or take up their residence in the caves, or they might land on one of the islands; beyond this he could not tell.

"Anyhow," said Ned, "we are on their track, and sooner or later will come up with them."

"And when we do," said Harry, "I fear we shall only have begun our work if they have pulled in with a band of savages. We are only five, and they may now number five score."

Ned breathed a deep sigh.

"Don't be down on your luck if there should be five hundred of them," said Jack; "they are sure to be a superstitious set of beggars, and my hanky-panky will count for something."

"Come what will, I will never go back without Minnie," said Ned.

"Nor I," cried Harry.

"Then let us on," said Ned.

And he went to the boat.

The others followed him.

As soon as all were on board Bircher opened his umbrella and held it low down over his body.

"There's no trusting savages," he said, "and they may send a shower of arrows after us."

"If they do I hope one will give you a clip of the ear," said Harry; "you are a cowardly beggar."

" My shield will save my ear," replied Bircher. " Prudence, you know, Honour, is the better part of valour."

" Then you've got more of the first than the last part," said Harry. " But don't you think, Mr. Bircher, that in your case prudence is only an excuse for cowardice ? "

" Certainly not," said Bircher. " And to prove that such a feeling cannot find a resting-place in my breast, I'll put down my umbrella."

Bircher peeped from under it though before he lowered it to make sure that the boat was far beyond arrow-shot of the shore.

Ned questioned his rowers and learned that Tiger Claws was one of the most desperate chiefs of the Orinoco Indians, and that his band were the most merciless of any that roamed the shores of that mighty river and infested the forests and mountains beyond.

Still Ned did not lose heart.

Indeed, the greater appeared the danger the greater his resolve to meet it.

He felt that he could not hope to come up with the fugitives for some days at least.

The start Boaster and Phopps had got was indeed a long one.

However, he thought he must make the best of it, and trust to Providence to aid him in his difficult and dangerous enterprise.

On the following day he resolved to go ashore, for the boat was small and the travellers had become cramped and stiff in sitting and lying in such a narrow compass.

Besides, provisions were falling short and he wanted to shoot something for their larder.

So at midday the boat was paddled up to the bank, the travellers landed, taking with them not only their rifles and pistols but everything necessary for their use.

The Indians fastened the boat under the overhanging branches of a huge tree and laid down in its shade to sleep or smoke as they felt disposed.

On either side of the spot chosen for the bivouac the forest ran down almost to the water's edge.

Flowers sprang up beneath their feet, the most gorgeous bells and clusters of red and yellow dropped from the branches of the trees, and the hum of insect life was heard on all sides.

Here and there mighty palms raised their giant heads high above the surrounding vegetation.

And insects of beautiful hues flitted from flower to flower.

The party were charmed at the glorious sight.

'Dolf and Jack made preparations for a meal, while Bircher looked on, with his umbrella shielding his body from the sun.

Ned threw his rifle on to his shoulder and bidding Harry accompany him strode into the forest.

" I daresay we can pot a bird or two, Harry," said Ned.

" Mind how you hold that rifle, old man," said Harry. " If you catch the trigger in one of these boughs perhaps you'll pot yourself or me."

" All right, Harry, I'll look out."

Suddenly they heard a rustling in the undergrowth, and as they pressed towards the spot whence the sound had come Harry sprang back and brought his rifle rapidly to bear in the direction.

" Look, Ned ! " cried Harry. " Don't you see its eyes ? "

Before Ned could reply there came a low growl, the bushes were parted, and the head and shoulders of a jaguar presented themselves to their gaze.

" Don't stir, Harry," cried Ned.

As he spoke Ned brought his rifle to his shoulder.

The beast crouched for the spring, its eyes blazing, its lips drawn back from before its gleaming teeth.

" Fire ! " hissed Ned. " Fire, ere he springs ! "

The boys fired together as the animal bounded upwards.

Both balls took effect in its shoulders, and the brute fell with a heavy thud, breaking down in its fall the bushes from which it had emerged.

In his excitement Harry sprang forward.

" Back," cried Ned, " the beast is only wounded. Let's give him another dose before we approach him."

Harry again brought up his gun, and both lads fired, this time at the animal's head.

Both had aimed well, and the brute gave a convulsive shudder and then lay motionless amid the prickly shrubs.

CHAPTER XIV.

IN WHICH OUR FRIENDS MAKE THE ACQUAINTANCE OF TWO STRANGE CHARACTERS.

THE sound of their rifles brought Jack and 'Dolf to the spot, and warmly did those two worthies congratulate our heroes upon their escape from the claws of the terrible beast.

"Let him lay there," said Ned, "and after dinner, if you like, you may take off his skin."

"All right, sir," said 'Dolf. "Dinner is quite ready, if you are."

"I am," said Harry; "so let's go and have a tuck in, Ned."

The four went back to where Bircher stood, white and trembling.

He recovered his composure, however, on seeing Ned and Harry safe and sound, and on hearing that they had shot a jaguar he fell on Ned's neck and blessed him.

"If you hadn't shot him he might have bolted us," cried Bircher.

"Bosh," said Ned. "Here, let us bolt some dinner."

They seated themselves around the food which 'Dolf and Jack had spread for them, and fell to.

"Whew!" said Harry, flinging his wide-awake over his shoulder and wiping his face with his handkerchief. "Pity jaguar ain't fit to eat. Don't know what's the use of such things at all."

"There's lots of things besides jaguars that don't to us appear of any use; but I suppose there's a use for everything in this world," said Ned.

"That's just the observation I often make to my respected and highly respectable friend, Jumbo Jingle. A very sensible observation—very, and I am proud to make your acquaintance."

And as Ned and his companions started in surprise at this observation, a young man strode into the circle in which they were sitting.

He was a white man of about twenty years of age, slightly above the middle height, and rather thin.

His expression was that of mingled impudence and cunning.

He was attired in a dirty shirt and trousers, with large holes at the elbows and the knees, through which his flesh could be seen.

On his head he wore a brimless silk hat, almost devoid of nap, and very battered and greasy.

One foot possessed a shoe and the other a top boot.

The former fastened with a piece of string.

A more dirty or impudent-looking rascal it would have been impossible to imagine.

"Gentlemen," he went on, "allow me to present my most honoured of honourable companion, the prince of niggers, and honestest of fellows in creation. Jumbo, step this way, and make your bow to our noble friends."

"Yer bery humble sarbent, gen'lems. Bery happy to allow you to make de acquaintance of dis mos' 'oner'ble cullered gen'lman."

And the negro, who had slipped round from behind Harry and Ned, stood beside his friend, bending before them.

If the first comer did not show a prepossessing appearance the second was certainly not a patch upon him.

He was a negro of about thirty years of age.

His face was black as ebony, his nose flat, and his lips protruding.

His expression was even more cunning than that of his white companion.

He was attired in an old blue sparrow-tailed coat, minus one of its tails, and possessing only two brass buttons on its breast.

On his legs he wore a pair of dirty linen drawers, one leg of which reached just below the knee; but a large hole left the black knee open to view.

The other leg had been torn off midway between the thigh and knee, leaving the rest of the leg bare.

He had neither shirt nor boots, but round his head he wore the brim of his companion's hat.

As he stood before Ned and Harry, this brim he raised with one hand, while with the other he was endeavouring to conceal beneath the single tail of his coat Harry's hat, which he had snatched from the ground.

In this piece of rascality he was not successful, for 'Dolf having observed the movement, crept up behind him, and raising the tail of his coat exposed the hat to view.

Jack no sooner saw this than he raised his foot to inflict vengeance on the would-be thief.

While this bit of play was going on with the black, Bircher had risen, and was moving out of reach of the negro's companion.

"Don't make way for me, my boy," said the fellow. "Bless your soul, though you may not consider yourself worthy to breathe the same air as I do, I'm not a bit proud, oh dear no, not a bit of it."

And he chucked Bircher under the chin.

"Sir, this insolence is unpardonable," said Bircher, starting back and waving him off. "You are a low, dirty, and extremely impudent fellow."

"And you are a thundering black thief," cried 'Dolf, snatching Harry's hat from the negro's hand.

"You don't come here thieving," cried Jack. "If you want something I'll make you a present of that."

And he dealt Jumbo such a kick on his coat-tail that the negro went floundering into the arms of his companion.

"Gor-a'mighty! what's dat broke?" cried the nigger, clutching at his coat-tail.

"Not your head, you scoundrel!" cried Jack. "But I'll break that for you if you try to collar anything belonging to us."

"He had got your hat hidden under his coat-tail, Harry," said 'Dolf. "I lifted up the tail and twigged it there."

"What do you mean by trying to steal my hat?" cried Harry.

"'Dere now," said the negro, addressing his companion; "just hear dat, as if Jumbo Jingle, de honestest nigger on dis here blessed globe, would steal dat gen'leman's hat."

"How came it under your coat then?" said Ned.

"Oh, sar, dat's jest it; it's de force ob 'traction; dis yar cullered gen'leman hab got such a lot ob 'traction in his body

dat things is drawn towards it and stick dere."

"You'd better take yourself and your attraction off," said Jack, "or I shall feel called upon to knock that same attraction out of you if you try to attract anything else belonging to us," and Jack doubled his fists and took a step towards the negro.

Ned motioned to Jack not to molest the negro, and then asked—

"Who are you both?"

"I'm myself and dis fellow is hisself," replied the black.

"You are a pretty pair, whoever you are."

"By golly, you are right dere; we's bofe so 'ansome an' so bery respec'able dat to prevent being run away wid by all de white gals, we had to run away from dem."

"Your beauty is on a par with your respectability, certainly," said Ned; "what brought you here?"

"Our legs," said the white man.

"And you had to use them pretty sharp, I expect," said Ned, "to save your bodies; but now you are here, what do you want?"

"I'll take a slice of that meat, I tink," said the negro.

"And I'll take two slices," said the other.

"Well, you've got plenty of cheek," said Harry.

"Tries to come it comic, too," said Ned.

"Ob course he does," replied the negro; "dat's why he's named Comic Charley."

"Oh, Comic Charley is his name, is it?" said Ned.

"I was christened Charles," said the man, "but my surname being Comic, my friends thought it sounded better to call me Comic Charley."

"And they had good reason for doing so, no doubt."

"The innocent expression of my features, and my retiring and modest disposition, brought it about, I expect."

"You look modest and retiring," said Jack, "don't you?"

"Appearances are very deceptive," said Charley.

"I don't think I should be deceived in either you or your friend," said Jack.

"Wonderful opinion of your own powers of discernment," said the fellow.

"I think I can tell a jail-bird when I see him," said Jack.

"Of course you could, having been so long amongst them."

Jack clenched his fist.

Both Ned and Harry burst out laughing.

"That's one to him, Jack," said Ned.

"He's a cheeky beggar," growled Jack.

"Bless your soul, it's his natur'," said Jumbo; "he could no more help it dan dis yer child can help being black."

"Or so respectably attired," said Jack.

"Sar,' said Jumbo, drawing himself up, "I don't wear my Sunday clothes ebery day."

"If they are like those you wear now, they must be very light and airy," said Ned; "I should like to see them."

"Den, sar, while you get de dinner ready for us I'll show you dem."

"Give the beggars some grub, Harry," said Ned, in a whisper.

"They are a pair of characters, and no mistake."

"I'll give you some food if you want it," said Ned; "though you don't deserve it for trying to rob us."

"Dere you go again," said Jumbo. "Didn't I tell you dat it was de force ob 'traction dat did it?"

"Well, don't do it again, that's all," said Ned.

"Look here," said Charley, "I'll take a good lump of fat with mine."

"Perhaps you'd like to take it all?" said 'Dolf."

"Yes, I'll take it all, I'm not particular. Oh, I say, old man, I see you have broken that hat of yours, it would just fit me."

And Charley took 'Dolf's hat off his head and raised it to his own.

"Here, drop it," said 'Dolf, "don't put that on your head."

"Why not?" cried Charley; "I don't mind you putting mine on yours; there! it fits you stunning."

And before 'Dolf could prevent him he whipped his brimless hat off his own head, and thrusting it on 'Dolf's forced it down with a blow on the top fairly on to 'Dolf's nose.

Then putting on 'Dolf's hat he stood with his arms akimbo.

"How's that, old nigger?" he said. "Spiffin', ain't it?"

The fellow's cool impudence quite prevented Jack or Ned resenting the liberty.

But 'Dolf, forcing the hat off, flung it in the fellow's face, and tore his own away from him.

"Here, let's see how I look in dat," said Jumbo, advancing.

"Keep back," cried 'Dolf, "or I'll smash you."

The negro recoiled.

He did not relish 'Dolf's look.

"Now that's what I call a dirty trick," said Charley, picking up his hat and wiping it round with his arm; "here's a new hat positively spoilt, and I hold that it's only fair that having destroyed my hat you should give me yours."

"I'll give you my fist on your nose," cried 'Dolf, "if you put your dirty paws on it again."

"You?" said Charley.

"Yes, I," cried 'Dolf, his face red as the comb of a turkey-cock; "touch it again and I'll make your head too big for the biggest hat ever made."

Charley had put on a swaggering air, but he drew back as 'Dolf held his clenched fist under his nose.

But if his courage failed him his impudence did not.

"Bah!" he said, "how your hands smell of onions, and I never could a-bear the smell—never."

"Never mind my hands," said 'Dolf; "don't you touch my hat again, that's all."

"Look here, flunkey, don't stand jawing there," said Charley, "but just bring our dinners, will you?"

"You certainly are the most insolent fellow I ever met," said Bircher.

"Halloa, four eyes, what's the matter with you?" said Charley.

"I am grieved and disgusted——"

"Are you now? Well, take my advice, don't be."

"I wonder that Nimble tolerates——"

"Who?" interrupted Charley.

"You and your dirty comrade here," said Bircher.

"Don't insult a man's colour," said Charley; "he can't wash himself white, can he?"

"Course not," chimed in Jumbo; "dat's de misfortune of de poor nigger. When him a piccaninny his mother feed him on pitch instead of milk, and so de pitch get into the skin and dere it stick, and you can't wash it out."

"Here pitch into this," said Ned, handing a plate of meat and bread; "share it between you."

The nigger made a dart at the food, and seizing the plate flopped himself down on the ground.

Charley flung himself down beside him.

"Here, I'll share it," he said.

"Get out, I'll share it," cried Jumbo.

"No, you won't. I always do the sharing, you know."

"Ob course you does, and you always gets de lot."

"Now how can you say so; look at that coat; ain't that a proof that you have the best of it?"

"No, 'tain't, you got de trousers and de shirt."

"And you've got the coat and drawers, ain't that fair?" said Charley.

"No, 'tain't, 'cos you got de boots and de hat, and you wears dem all de days but Sunday."

"What's it one suit between the two?" asked Ned.

"That's it," said Charley; "I wear these togs all the week and Jumbo has them on Sundays, when I wear his, and now the beggar's grumbling."

"I should think so," said Ned, turning away with a laugh.

"Come, hand over that plate," said Charley; "fair's fair, you know, and right's right."

"So it am," said Jumbo, as he resigned the plate; "but it's little fair and little right dat dis chile gets."

"Not fair," said Charley; "now look here, that's one piece for you, and one piece two for me, that's fair, ain't it?"

The negro scratched his head.

"Dat's one piece you gib me," he said, "but dat's two pieces you gib yourself."

"Well, ain't that right? one for you, two for me," cried Charley. "Look alive and eat yours, or I shall have to help you when I am done."

And Charley set to on the food as if he had not tasted any for a week.

The negro looked at his share and shook his head.

"Brest if dis chile can make it out," he said; "one for you and two for me; no, dat ain't it, two for me and one for you—no, dat's not right. What de debbil am it?"

"Beef," said Charley, with his mouth full.

"Beef be——"

"Look alive, Jumbo. I've nearly got through mine," said Charley; "first done help the other, you know; that's fair."

"Gor'-a'mighty, am it? Den look out, for I'll hab yours," cried Jumbo.

And he thrust a large piece of beef into his mouth, and the next moment he was spluttering, coughing, and choking fearfully.

Charley shrugged his shoulders and kept on eating.

"That fellow's choking; pat his back, Jack," said Ned.

Jack stepped up behind the negro and with his open hand he struck him a blow between the shoulders, with a force that not only put a stop to his coughing but sent him floundering across the plate and legs of Charley.

"Gor'-a'mighty, was dat a elephant fell atop of me?" gasped Jumbo, as he scrambled up.

"Where's my meat?" asked Charley, looking on the ground on discovering that his plate was empty.

"I seed a big lump jump out dere," said Jumbo, pointing.

Charley rose and proceeded in the direction indicated.

Jumbo did a broad grin and slyly slipped his hand into the pocket of his coat tail.

"Dat's one for him and two for me dis time." he muttered. "Golly, tink I know how to divide it fair, yah, yah!"

When Charley returned to his side, Jumbo was sitting quietly tearing a piece of meat apart with his teeth.

"I can't find it," he said.

"Can't you?" replied Jumbo.

"No, so I'll have to help you with yours."

"Not for dis chile," said Jumbo; "you divided it bery fair; you eat one piece and I'm eating one piece two."

"Here, I shall have that," cried Charley, making a grab at the meat.

"Guess you won't neither," said Jumbo, as he made a snap at Charley's fingers and caught them firmly between his teeth.

CHAPTER XV.

IN WHICH NED MAKES AN OFFER AND CHARLEY AND JUMBO JUMP AT IT.

THE yell which Charley gave utterance to was only equalled by the shriek of laughter that burst from Ned and his companions as they heard the cry and saw the expression of comical pain on the features of the white youth.

The only composed person was Jumbo himself.

His thick lips drawn back showed his gleaming white teeth, and his eyes glared with the fire of mischief and satisfaction.

"Let go, you black hound!" cried Charley, raising his hand to deal the negro a blow.

But ere he could do so, Jumbo drew up his leg and planting his foot in the pit of Charley's stomach caused that young man to flop down into a sitting position before him.

"Caught in a trap," said Ned.

"Yes, a tater-trap," laughed 'Dolf.

"A meat-trap, rather," said Harry. "Should like to find potatoes out here."

"There, young man," said Bircher, addressing the discomfited Charley; "you have the illustration of the truth that honesty is the best policy."

"Go it, Bircher, read him a lecture," said Ned. "He can't run away from it while the nigger holds him."

"Young man," began Bircher, "let this be a lesson to you never again to——"

"Shut up, four eyes," cried Charley. "Let go, you black thief, or I'll smash you."

The negro opened his teeth and his friend sprang to his feet.

"Bress my soul!" said Jumbo, "what you put your finger in dis chile's mouf for?"

"Don't do that again," cried Charley, as he thrust his hand under his arm, "or you and I will dissolve partnership."

"Golly! what's that?" asked the black. "Am it good to eat? 'Cos if it am, I'm brest if you won't want double share. Dar, go along. Dat's one for you, and dat's two for me—yah! yah!"

"Here," said Ned, "don't quarrel. I can spare you a bit more, though our larder is getting empty."

And he gave Charley another piece of meat and a biscuit.

"Golly! now just you share dat fair dis time," cried Jumbo.

"So I will," said Charley. "I'll stick to the lot."

And he moved away, as if he was afraid the negro would make a grab at his food.

But Jumbo never moved.

He sat and ate the food he had kept in his hand, chuckling every now and then to himself, and muttering—

"Dat's one to him and two to me. Yah! yah!"

"What do you think of these fellows?" asked Ned of Jack, as he led him out of earshot of the negro and Charley.

"I think they are a pair of rascals," replied Jack.

"That's my opinion," said Ned; "but I fancy if I made it worth their while we might ensure their services."

"How do you mean?" asked Jack.

"Well, we know that Boaster has more aid to depend on than I have, and that if I hope to rescue Minnie from his grasp that I can't have too many to help me, so I thought that if I could enlist these fellows in my service I might find them useful."

"If you could depend upon them not to desert you at the very moment you most needed them," said Jack.

"Or rob me, and be off some fine morning," said Ned.

"I shouldn't like to trust them far out of my sight," said Jack. "They're a pair of awfully cunning birds."

"Yes; but their cunning may also teach them that it may be more to their interest to serve me faithfully than play me any scurvy tricks."

"Well, that's true," said Jack, stroking his chin; "if they are cunning they are evidently not fools."

"Besides, we can keep a sharp eye on them."

"And if I found them up to any nonsense I could soon take their cheek out of them," said Jack.

"I think I'll have a talk with them," said Ned. "I can't stand too particular out here. Better a weak friend than a strong enemy."

And so saying, Ned joined Bircher and Harry, and called Charley and Jumbo to him.

"Sar," said Jumbo, "dis chile will divide what you are going to gib us now."

"No, you won't," said Charley. "I always do the division of what we get."

"Stop!" said Ned. "You'll get nothing more out of me unless you earn it, and that you earn it honestly."

"Bress my soul! hear dat now, as if we was not de honestest gen'lems in dis here world."

"We have seen a specimen of your honesty," said Ned, "and appreciate it at its full value."

"Dar now, dat's a compliment to dis nigger; but dis chile'll share it fair whateber you gibs de two honestest gen'lemens in dis here company."

"Just shut that big mouth of yours," said Charley.

"Sartingly, if you'll put your fingers in it," said the negro, with a grin.

"Listen to me," said Ned, "and hold your jaw."

Jumbo clasped his jaw in one hand, and bent forward his ear with the other.

"Most happy to oblige you with our attentions," said Charley, sitting down familiarly beside Ned.

"I may as well be candid," said Ned, "and tell you that I look upon you both as a pair of most consummate scoundrels; but bad as I believe you to be, I am willing to make it worth your while to serve me faithfully and honourably."

"Wat's dat?" cried Jumbo.

"It's the way of the world to judge uncharitably of the poor," said Charley, turning up the whites of his eyes. "I pity your ignorance of human nature. Is it because a man wears a ragged garment that his heart is cold and his mind diseased?"

"Look here," said Ned, "I'm not to be fooled by that look. I can read you like a book. How long have you been out of jail?"

"Never was in one," said Charley, dropping his canting tone and injured look when he found it did not deceive Ned.

"Then you ought to have been," said Jack, "and would have been if you hadn't given the officers leg-bail."

"Oh, you seem to know all about it," said Charley.

"Perhaps I know a lot more than you think," said Jack.

"Well, we won't bandy words," said Ned. "What I want to know is if you are willing to act fairly and honestly by me if I pay you for doing so? If not you can take yourselves off, and the sooner the better."

"Now I like a fellow to speak out plain and fair," said Charley.

"And so does dis child," said Jumbo. "Dis nigger's so berry fair himself that he likes to be treated fair."

"So you always are," said Charley.

"Dat's a big lie," cried Jumbo. "Is one for me and two for you fair? Eh, golly! don't I know you?"

"No quarrelling," said Ned, "but answer my question."

"What do you want us to do?" said Charley.

"Enter my service, act faithfully to me and my friends, assist us in any danger we may encounter, and do as you are bid without question or hesitation, for which I'll pay you well."

"I hope the business is strictly honest," said Charley.

"If it were not I should not be engaged in it," said Ned.

"And I should decline to join you," said Charley. "Wouldn't we, Jumbo?"

"Shua as dis child's a nigger," said Jumbo, with a grin.

"Do you think it would be safe to trust two such persons as these, Nimble?" asked Bircher.

"Lor bless you," said Charley, "if we don't dress in black coats and wear white chokers and spectacles we're more to be trusted than plenty who do."

"Your remarks are quite uncalled for, young man," said Bircher.

"Were they?" retorted Charley; "that's because you know them to be true. If a fellow looks a ruffian he puts people on their guard against him. It's sanctimonious-looking rascals that's more to be feared after all."

"Well, well," said Ned, "perhaps you are right, but certainly not as regards my friend here. As you bear the impress of rascal on your face I'm on my guard against you."

"You flatter me," said Charley.

"And I should flatten you if you come any of your dodges with me," said Jack; "so remember that."

"To the point," said Ned. "Is it worth the while of yourself and companion to serve me honestly and well. I may not require your services long or I may want them for some time. Decide quickly for I've no time to lose."

"Do you find our livery?" asked Charley, looking at 'Dolf.

"No," cried Ned; "for were I to supply you with the clothes you would take yourselves off."

"And so should I, Master Ned, for I could not stand the livery of the Nimbles being degraded."

"No fear of that, 'Dolf," said Ned. "Look here, you fellows, I promise you this—food and a pound a week each, and if you serve us faithfully and aid us to succeed in the mission on which we are here, the present of a suit of clothes and a hundred pounds each when I no longer require your services."

"Do you mean it?" cried Charley, springing to his feet.

"Golly!" cried Jumbo, "is dat true?"

"I mean what I say, and will faithfully perform what I promise if Heaven spares me," said Ned. "But I tell you the errand I am on is one full of danger, and we may have to fight for our lives."

"Will you tell us what the enterprise is and where it may lead you?" asked Charley.

"Yes," replied Ned. "I think that only right before I ask you to decide."

And he explained sufficient to show them what danger they might have to encounter and the object of his coming from England.

"And now that I have taken you thus far into my confidence," said Ned, "just give me a plain yes or no."

"I say yes, I'll go with you," said Charley.

"And dis child say so too," added Jumbo.

"And you mean to conduct yourselves honestly and truly towards myself and my friends?" asked Ned.

"It's worth my while," said Charley.

"And you?" asked Ned, turning to Jumbo.

"Gorra, massa, dis child couldn't be bad if he wanted to," replied the negro. "He serb you right and fair, by golly he will!"

"It is agreed then that you enter my service and remain with me so long as I need your aid?"

"Count on me," said Charley, "and I'll be answerable for my friend Jumbo here."

"I suppose you have no friends you wish to take leave of?" said Ned.

"Oh, lots," said Charley. "But I shan't go and see them, they might prevent my going at all."

And he winked at Jumbo.

"You mean the officers of justice, do you not, young man?" asked Bircher.

"Something of that sort," replied Charley. "In fact they have been so anxious about our healths lately that we found it convenient to get beyond the radius of their solicitude."

"I thought you were a bad lot," said Jack.

"Thought!" said Charley. "Why I thought you knew it?"

"Don't come any games with us," said Ned. "On your good conduct rests your ultimate reward remember."

"No fear," said Charley. "Only make it pay and we'll stick to you like wax."

"Enough," said Ned. "Now, Jack, if you want the skin of the jaguar take these fellows with you and get it, and let's be off to the boat."

Jack and his two new companions soon took the skin off the jaguar, and then the whole party went into the boat, which again started on its voyage.

CHAPTER XVI.

IN WHICH OUR FRIENDS VISIT AN ISLAND, AND MEET THERE WITH WHAT THEY DID NOT EXPECT TO FIND.

NED soon found that the boat was far too small for the party now that it had been increased, and he resolved to try and obtain either a larger vessel or another one at the earliest opportunity.

But no chance presented itself that day or the next, but on the following they came upon an Indian village, and succeeded in purchasing of the natives a large canoe.

In so doing they were greatly assisted by Charley and Jumbo, who were able to converse with the savages.

They had now more room, and started on again, more comfortable than they had been for some time.

Charley and Jumbo made no secret of what they had been, and Ned had drawn from them an account of their lives, which had been one of mingled misery and villainy for some time past.

Charley had been thrown a waif on one of the American cities at an early age, and like many another without friends or home had drifted into crime.

Jumbo had been a slave on a cotton plantation, but the war had robbed him of a master and the means of a livelihood, though it gave him his liberty.

Had he remained a slave, probably he had still been an honest man, but he was free, and his freedom had led him into the company of Charley and others as bad, and like his friend, he had found it necessary to fly from justice.

But bad as they both had been, they served Ned faithfully, and our hero hoped that when he should no longer need them his generosity would enable them to retrieve the character they had lost.

Their acquaintance with the Indian dialect proved of great service to Ned, and when they came to a village, he sent them on shore to obtain information and provisions.

For some time they could learn nothing regarding Boaster or the band of Tiger Claw, but at length they fell in with a canoe, in which were two Indians,

and from these they learned that Tiger Claw and his followers were encamped on a small island some thirty miles further up the river.

Ned rewarded his informants for the information, and urged the rowers and paddlers to the greatest exertion.

Was there then only thirty miles between him and Minnie?

How his face flushed and his heart beat.

What cared he for numbers?

Were all the world arrayed against him he would defy all the world for her sake.

Thirty miles, and if all worked well the boats might reach the island by daylight.

"Heaven grant we can land," he said to Harry, "and rescue Minnie before our foes know of our presence."

"Don't get excited, dear boy," said Harry.

"I can't help it," replied Ned. "Only think; not more than a few hours' distance between us at last."

"I hope so," replied Harry; "but don't be disappointed if when we reach the island we should find them gone."

"Oh, don't say that, old man," cried Ned.

"Well, let's hope they will be there," said Harry. "If the beggars pull hard we shall reach the island by daylight."

Throughout the night the men paddled incessantly, and at daylight the boats reached the island.

At the first streak of day they partook of food and then landed on the island.

Determined upon no delay, Ned placed himself at the head of the party and proceeded into the interior.

Forcing their way through the shrubs and undergrowth they had gone about a quarter of a mile when a voice reached their ears.

The whole party came to a stop on the instant.

"Get out, you varmint, take that, s'cat," cried the voice in a shrill tone;

"Oh Lor', oh dear, the beasts will tear me all up into little bits—s'cat, s'cat."

Everybody looked towards the spot from whence the sound came.

"Why, it's somebody up in that tree yonder," cried Ned; "and what's that leaping among the branches? see, there's another and another!"

"It's wild cats," cried Charley; "blowed if the beasts haven't treed somebody. They're awful things is wild cats."

Again the voice rang out loud and shrill.

"Get out, you murdering varmints, get out! S'cat, s'cat."

"Whoever it is will be torn to pieces," said Charley.

"Not if I can help it," cried Ned.

And raising his rifle he fired into the tree.

There was a scream and down crashing through the branches to the earth fell a wild cat.

Harry fired at another with the same result.

"Blest if I don't pop that one off," said Charley. "There, how you like that, massa scratcher?—yah, yah?"

Down came a third cat to the earth.

"Hurrah," cried the shrill voice, "that's give the varmints pepper. If there's anything I abhor it's cats, it is."

And down the trunk of the tree slid a human form, which no sooner reached the ground than looking half-fearfully around it bounded to where the party stood.

It was a woman attired as an Indian squaw, and great indeed was the surprise of all when they saw that she was a white woman, though her face was tattooed on one cheek by a crocodile, and on the other with a serpent.

These tattoo marks gave her otherwise comely face a hideous appearance as she turned it towards them.

Her red hair streamed over her shoulders, and her rough head was surmounted by a bunch of feathers.

"If there's anything I abhor it's cats," she cried; then fixing her gaze on Jack, she shrieked—"Is it? yes—no—can it be Jack? It is, it is, my long lost Johnny—my Jack, my Jack, my jolly, jolly Jack."

And the woman opening her arms, flung herself heavily on Jack's bosom, and clutched him fiercely round the neck.

"What the dev——!" yelled Jack, as he retreated a step, flinging out his arms in surprise.

"Oh," yelled 'Dolf as he went tottering backwards from an unintentional blow from one of Jack's hands as he flung them out.

"Murder," cried Bircher, who, stooping down at that moment, found 'Dolf sitting on the top of his head, and sank under his weight.

"Gor-a'mighty! what's dat?" yelled Jumbo, as Charley started back on receiving a blow, which sent his hat flying from his head, from the other extended hand of Jack's and dropped the butt of his rifle fair on to the uncovered toes of the negro.

"Jack, Jack!" cried the woman, clinging round the neck of the conjurer.

"Get away, you ugly painted squaw," cried Jack. "Take your hands off I say."

"My love—my life!" shrieked the woman.

"Get out, you confounded wild cat! Let go I say," cried Jack.

"Never will we be parted again—never—never!" cried the squaw, as she clung round Jack's neck and leaned her head on the bosom of his shirt.

"Hang it all! somebody take this she-devil away will you?" cried Jack, "or else she'll throttle me."

Ned and Harry could not resist their laughter.

The painted face of the woman, the fierceness with which she clung to Jack, and the misfortunes of which she had been the cause to 'Dolf, Bircher, and Jumbo, rendered them forgetful of any danger that might be near them, and they shrieked aloud.

"Never shall they take me away!" shrieked the woman; "Never more shall they part us—mine now, and mine for ever."

"If you don't let go I'll pitch you into the river," cried Jack. "What do you mean? Who are you, you painted she-viper?"

"Viper!" shrieked the woman, as she let go her hold and gazed at Jack. "And has it come to this after all these years. Oh Jack, Jack, you've broken the heart of Sally Scrubbins all into little bits."

"Sally Scrubbins!" cried Jack; "you—you Sally Scrubbins?"

"Your Sally Scrubbins; yours, Jack, yours!"

And down went the head of Sally into his bosom again, and her arms clung round his neck with a closeness that threatened to choke him.

CHAPTER XVII.

IN WHICH SALLY SCRUBBINS GIVES AN EXPLANATION.

EITHER Sally Scrubbins's weight was too great, or Jack's surprise deprived him of strength, for he suddenly sank under one or the other and came down flop into a sitting posture on the earth.

As Sally made no attempt to hold him up or to unfold her arms from around his neck, down she went with him, giving utterance to mingled sobs and laughter.

"Sally Scrubbins! Sally Scrubbins!" was all Jack said, and this he uttered in the tone a man might use who did not know whether he stood on his head or his heels.

"Yes, Jack, your own faithful Sally," gasped the woman; "the Sally of your boyhood's love; the Sally you used to walk out with on a Sunday evening when her missus let her out to church; the Sally you used to sneak down the area steps to see. Yes, Jack, it's your Sally, who's always been true to you, though you was jealous of the Bobby on our beat.

Still Jack could only murmur—

"Sally Scrubbins!"

"Golly! dat dar gal'll gnaw a big hole in his cheek afore long," said Jumbo; "brest if she won't."

"Shut up, you fool; don't you see it's how she shows her love," said Charley.

"Jus you keep dat gun away from my toes," cried Jumbo. "I don't like that sort ob love as you gib me just now wid it."

"You should have kept your toes out of the way then," said Charley. "What did you want to put your toes under my gun for? You're always up to something, you are."

And Charley turned his attention again to Jack and his companion.

Jack slowly rose to his feet.

Catching Sally's hands in his he held her at full length and gazed into her tattooed face for some moments, and then he cried—

"So it is—I'm blowed if it ain't."

"And I'm blowed if I'll stand it any longer," cried Bircher, striding up to Ned. "If you don't compel this flunkey of yours to behave himself properly and treat me with due respect, Nimble, I'll resign my position and leave you all to your fate."

"Who are you calling a flunkey?" cried 'Dolf.

"You, sir, you," returned Bircher, hotly.

"Don't call me names," cried 'Dolf.

"But I shall, sir, I shall," cried Bircher. "I say you are a low, insolent fellow. How dare you play your pranks upon me? How dare you sit upon my head?"

"How could I help it?" cried 'Dolf. "I was knocked on to it, and you'd no right to put your head where it was."

"Come, come, what are you quarrelling about?" cried Ned. "Has everybody gone mad, or am I dreaming?"

"Mad, who wouldn't be mad to have eleven stone of flesh balancing itself on the top of his head, I'd like to know?"

"Or to have the big end of um gun come flop down on um toe?" said Jumbo, as he held his foot in his hand and hopped about on one leg to prevent himself falling.

"Both were accidents," said Harry. "I saw how it all happened. For Heaven's sake do not let us quarrel. Remember we may be surrounded by enemies."

"Anyone would think we were either in a playhouse or a madhouse," said Ned. "Blest if I can make it all out, can you, Harry?"

"I can pretty well guess," said Harry, "but Jack will tell us all about it."

Jack now approached them with one arm round Sally's waist and one hand holding hers.

"Ladies and gentlemen," said Jack; "beg pardon, I mean gentlemen only; here's a rum go."

"Whar?" said Jumbo.

"Shut your tater-trap, you black snob," said Jack. "Blest if I know how to explain this here strange business. I'm knocked all of a heap."

"Not so much of a heap, sir, as I have been knocked," said Bircher; "indeed, I have my doubts whether my neck is not broken and my spine seriously affected."

"Pity it ain't," said 'Dolf.

"Be quiet 'Dolf," said Ned; "and allow us to hear what Jack wishes to say."

"Well, blow me if I know how to say it, it's such a jolly strange affair "

"Never mind, Jack, out with it," said Harry.

"Well, my friends," began Jack, "you see this lady, she's——"

"Sally Scrubbins," interrupted the woman, "and I won't own no other name."

"Yes, she's Sally Scrubbins," said Jack, "and we used to keep company a many years ago in London."

"And though they did try to make an Indian of me, I ain't," said Sally; "I'm as white as you are, excepting where I'm tattooed. You know, Jack, I wasn't tattooed when you used to come a courting me."

"No, you was a nice looking gal then," said Jack, "a regular beauty. But look here, Sally, you just tell 'em how it all happened, for I can't you know."

"Well, you see, Jack, this was how it was; when you got jealous of the police-man, and I declared I never gave him nothing but a cup of coffee one night when it was very cold, and said as how you wouldn't have no more to do with me, it broke my heart and I gave notice."

"Yes," said Jack, "I know I was a fool."

"Dat's trufe," said Jumbo.
But he darted back as he spoke lest Jack should resent the insult."

"Well, I was mad with you, Jack, because I didn't deserve your suspicions, and I came to America, but I didn't like t and I made up my mind to go back

to England and see you and make it up."

"And why didn't you?" asked Jack.

"Because I couldn't; I was in service at a farm up the country, and the night afore I meant to leave the Indians came down upon us; the farmer and his family were killed, and I was carried away captive."

"And became a squaw," said Bircher.

"Yes, but against my will. Red Feather, the chief of the tribe, gave me my choice either to be burnt or become his squaw, and as I didn't care about being frizzled all up, I consented to be his wife to save my life."

"And did he tattoo you like this?" asked Jack.

"It was done by his orders," replied Sally.

"If ever I catch sight of him I'll tattoo him," hissed Jack.

"You won't get a chance," said Sally.

"Is he dead then?"

"Yes, he was killed by a great chief named Tiger Claws; the two tribes quarrelled and fought; Red Feather and his people were destroyed, and I alone lived, a captive of Tiger Claws."

"And he—he is here on this island," cried Ned, grasping her arm.

"No he ain't," said Sally; "he was here two days ago. He gave me the chance to save my life as Red Feather did, and pretending that I was willing I managed to escape from him and hid in a tree. He thought I had fled from the island, and so he set out with four white men and a white woman after searching in vain for me."

"Gone," said Ned; "whither?"

"I don't know, but I think it's likely he's gone to the phantom cave near the great falls."

"And you," said Jack, "have been alone on this island since."

"Not I. I've had company worse than Indians," replied Sally. "The wild cats found me out if Tiger Claws didn't and if it hadn't been for you shooting them, I should have been soon torn to pieces. Oh, if there's anything I abhor worse nor Indians it's cats."

"The phantom cave," cried Ned, "do you know where it is situated? You can lead us to it? You will aid us to save one whom I dearly love?"

"If you want to go to it I can show

you where it is," replied Sally. "But you don't catch me going into it—not I. If there's anything I mortally abhor besides Indians and cats it's ghostesses."

"Ghosts!" said Bircher. "Poor ignorant creature, do you not know that there is no such things as ghosts?"

"I know there is, 'cos I've seen 'em," cried Sally; "and look here whoever you are, don't call me a poor ignorant creature or I'll get my Jack to thrash you."

"Poor benighted heathen," said Bircher.

"I ain't a heathen," screamed Sally. "I'm a real born true English girl, and my name's Sally Scrubbins; and if you give me any of your imperence I'll show you that I wasn't brought up in Drury Lane for nothing."

"That shows your respectability," said Bircher.

"Shut up," said Ned.

"Or you'll go down if you don't, Mr. Bircher," said Jack. "I look upon this here young woman as my property, so just you mind what you are after."

"That's my dear Jack," cried Sally, flinging her arms round his neck. "Only to think as how we should meet again like this. I left you once, Jack, but I'll stick to you now. If I don't my name ain't Sally Scrubbins."

CHAPTER XVIII.

IN WHICH SALLY AND JUMBO GO ON A VOYAGE OF DISCOVERY AND FIND NOTHING.

As it was evident that Sally had made up her mind that she would not be parted from her former lover, and as Ned did not feel disposed to part with Jack, he had no alternative but to decide that she must become one of their party and share their fortune.

He was more willing to allow this since she might act as guide, her wanderings with the tribe of Red Feather having made her acquainted with the towns and villages in the vicinity of the Orinoco.

In order to have some command over her however he induced her to accept a wage for her services, which she consented to do, intimating to Jack that it would form her dowry when they got married.

All arrangements being made the boats again set sail, but this time under the direction of Sally, who advised that certain places should be visited on their way to the falls, as the Indians with whom Boaster and Phopps had joined were likely to make a stop on their way to the Phantom Cave, for the purpose of hunting or obtaining provisions.

Sally, though a little rough in her manner and plain-spoken, proved herself to be far from hard-hearted, and soon became a favourite with all but Bircher, whom she teased and chaffed unmercifully."

Throughout the day the boats were kept moving, and towards sundown they approached an Indian village.

"The village lays back from the shore," said Sally, "and is partially hidden by the trees. We must be cautious, for though the inhabitants are friendly, if Tiger Claws is amongst them he may induce them to become enemies."

"Then it will be as well to look out for squalls," said Jack.

"We will land under the cover of the darkness," said Ned, "and Heaven grant we may surprise Boaster in or near the village and be able to rescue Minnie.

"But he may be too sharp for us, dear boy, even if he is there," said Harry.

"Tiger Claws is not likely to have proceeded farther by this time," said Sally. "His band would require food and must have it."

"Then ere long I and he whom I hate may stand face to face," said Ned, "for Boaster don't know we are on his track so will have no reason to try to avoid us."

"But the movements of the savages with whom he has leagued himself may have compelled him to leave the place," said Harry.

"Yes, yes; you are right," said Ned; "but he cannot be far off."

"'KEEP BACK—KEEP BACK,' CRIED SALLY."

"We must soon come up with them," added Ned.

"I hope so," replied Harry; "but I would not be too sanguine, Ned, because the higher we raise our hopes the deeper we may get plunged into despair."

"Don't be so gloomy, dear boy. It's hope that keeps me up, and I feel that I could do battle with a hundred foes if necessary."

"I hope it won't be, Ned; but rest assured of this, that come on them when we may we shall have to fight. Boaster is too wary a card to give anyone an opportunity of rescuing Minnie without a struggle."

"Would he faced me now!" cried Ned. "Oh, how I'd make him regret his villainy."

And Ned hurried into the cabin to see that every rifle was loaded, every weapon ready for a struggle if it were needed.

As the shades of evening became deeper they came in sight of the village.

"Harry," said Ned, "are all the men armed?"

"Yes," replied his friend, "and I believe if it comes to a struggle that our new friends will not be the most backward."

"I'm glad of that. Do you think we can depend upon the Indians?"

"To look after the boats, yes; but to fight, no," replied Harry.

"Do you fear treachery?"

"No," replied Harry; "but I do not think they can be depended on to fight for us."

"Then we must fight all the harder for ourselves," said Ned.

Gradually the moon rose, and the shore and village beyond stood out clear in the moonlight.

Nothing gave the least notice that a single human being was stirring.

All but the rowers stood rifle in hand ready to spring on shore the moment the boat touched a spot that would admit of their landing.

They reached the shore, but the bank was high and they had to still paddle on in search of a spot where they could land.

The silence was alone broken by the soft dip of oar and paddle.

At length they reached a spot where the bank sloped down into the water, and the trunks of the trees were washed by the stream.

Here Ned signalled for the boats to be brought to, and this being done he sprang ashore.

He was instantly followed by Harry, Jack, 'Dolf, Bircher, Charley, Sally, and Jumbo.

Each was armed with rifle, revolver, and knife.

"See that the boats are secured, Jack," whispered Ned; "we must not let those Indians drift off lest we have to seek them in a hurry. Let them be secured to these trees; we can easily cut the ropes if need be."

"I'll see to that,' said Jack; "never fear."

"Jumbo, you get up into one of the trees and see if you can see any fire or anything that points out where savages are encamped," said Ned.

"And mind you don't tear your clothes," said Charley.

"Don't care if I do," said Jumbo; "Sunday soon come, den I wear yours."

"Silence," said Ned.

Jumbo climbed into a tree, and after about five minutes returned to the ground.

"Not a bressed light nor nuffin," he said.

"We will get further on," said Ned.

"Stop, sir," said Jack; "had you not better send Jumbo and Sally out on the scout? They are better hands at that work than white men, and await their return."

"If you think so," said Ned.

"I do not see how anything else can be done till daylight," said Jack.

Sally and Sambo consented to scout round the village, and both armed with a knife and revolver they set out.

An hour passed and then they joined Ned.

"Well?" asked Ned.

"The village is deserted," said Sally, "but there are signs of Indians about. I think they are on a hunting expedition, but the huts are deserted even by the squaws."

"Foiled again," said Ned, bitterly.

"Perhaps not," said Sally. "You don't know them as I do. At daylight they may return to the village laden with spoils of the chase."

"Better perhaps wait till daylight," said Harry.

"Your advice is good," said Bircher.

"Be it so, then," said Ned. "Let's return to the boat and wait till it is light enough to see better. But saw you not any signs of the white men or white woman?"

"None," replied Sally. "But don't give up. To-morrow may prove whether she is in these parts or not."

"Then till to-morrow I must rest satisfied," said Ned. "To the boats, and let's rest till daylight."

CHAPTER XIX.

IN WHICH JACK AND JUMBO PERFORM FEATS THAT SURPRISE THE INDIANS.

As soon as it was daylight Ned was eager to land.

"Get your breakfast," he said, "and then let's get on shore. I feel that every moment's delay may put space between me and the villains I have come so far to seek."

"Mr. Ned," said Jack, "I and Sally have been having a sort of a palaver."

"Well?" said Ned.

"And I've told her she'd better speak out plain like to you."

"I do not understand you," said Ned; "has she any cause of complaint?"

"Not against you," said Jack; "but I think you'd better hear what she's got to say."

"What is it, Sally?" asked Ned. "Speak plain and do not hesitate."

"Well, then it's just this. If you go tearing off to that there village after the girl, as you want to do, you're a fool, and that's plain, ain't it?"

"It's certainly plain," said Ned, "but I do not think it is polite."

"Perhaps you don't; but it's true, I can tell you. It's no use going like a bull at a gate, is it, Jack?"

"So you say, and of course you ought to know," replied Jack.

"What I does, to my sorrow," said Sally. "Now look here, Mr. Nimble, I'm only a woman, but I know what's what, and you don't."

"I do not understand what you are driving at," said Ned.

"Well, it's just this; that no matter how plucky a fellow might be, he can't expect he's a match for twenty."

"I should say not," replied Ned.

"And yet you seem to fancy you are," said Sally.

"I do not think so," said Ned.

"Oh, yes, you do, or you wouldn't be so eager to run agin Tiger Claws and his band."

"But I must; I will rescue Minnie or perish," said Ned.

"No one wants to stop you," said Sally; "but what I want to do is to show you how you may stand a chance of getting at the poor girl without running yourself into danger."

"I wish you could," said Ned.

"I'll try," said Sally. "I know something about Indians."

"Pray go on," said Ned; "what do you propose?"

"Well I and Jack have talked it over, and Jack sees the sense of it, and it's just this."

"What?"

"That if you attempt to get hold of the girl by tearing her from those who have got her you'll find you must use stratagem; that's what they call it, ain't it, when they want to fool anybody?"

"Yes, I believe so."

"All right, then. Now as you half dozen fellows would stand no chance against four whites and a hundred reds, it stands to reason it's no use fighting them if you can help it."

"But how are we to help it? I have no desire to injure a single Indian. All I want is to rescue Minnie from her two abductors and punish the two villains who have so deeply wronged me and mine."

"That's all right enough; but if they have got a lot of Indians at their back you must fail. Now I and Jack have hit on a plan."

"What is it?"

"The Indians have a great reverence and superstition for what they call medicine men, but what you'd call conjurors, and we call hanky-panky dodgers, eh, Jack?"

"Right you are, Sally," said Jack.

"So we've agreed that Jack should dress up as the fire king—he's got the props you know—and that he should land with me and Jumbo and Charley, and go through an entertainment."

"What good would that do?" asked Ned.

"Don't you be too impatient," said Sally. "Wouldn't the Indians get excited and come to see the hanky-panky, and then while we kept them surprised and amused mightn't you and the others find out where the girl was hidden and carry her off to the boats—that is if she was there."

"A capital idea," said Harry. "While they rivet the attention of the Indians we might escape their notice and succeed in finding Minnie."

"It would be much better than fighting, Nimble," said Bircher. "Violence you know should never be resorted to if it could be avoided."

"Thought you were getting funky, old man," said Charley, giving Bircher a dig in the ribs.

"Keep your hands and your observations to yourself, if you please, you ragamuffin," said Bircher.

"Looks white about the gills, don't he, Jumbo?" said Charley.

"He jus do dat," replied the negro; "bress me! jus' you look at dat now. Don't you see him heart go flop, flop? Golly! won't him run when he see Indian knife. Yah, yah."

"Hadn't you better make your will and leave us your togs?" said Charley.

"Better him gib'em to us now," said Jumbo, "before dey gets cut by de knives of de Indians."

Mr. Bircher turned very green about the eyes, and strode away to another part of the boat, while Charley and Jumbo winked at each other.

"I think, Ned," said Jack, "that Sally's proposition is a good one, and that if we can keep the attention of the Indians fixed on us, you may be enabled to discover whether the girl is in the village or not, and if she is carry her to the boats."

"It is indeed a capital idea," said

Ned! "but you have forgotten one thing."

"What is that?" asked Jack.

"That Sally is in danger of falling into the hands of those from whom she has escaped, should Tiger Claws or any of his band be there."

"Not so," replied Jack; "no Indian would dare molest her if under the protection of a medicine man; the savages have a greater respect for the medicine men than for their chiefs."

"Then be it as you wish."

"If I did not know that I could serve you better by my hanky-panky than my fists, I would keep by your side, Ned," said Jack; "but if you are cool and cautious you will not need my aid."

"Well, what is to be the programme," said Harry.

"As our boats may have been seen, the savages would know that there must be a party on board, so it would be necessary to prevent suspicion that others beside Sally accompanied me on shore."

"That's true," said Ned.

"Then what Sally proposes is this: that I go ashore as a great medicine man, accompanied by my attendants, and that you keep out of sight and land further up the river, and steal down upon the village from the opposite side to where we are, and taking advantage of our entertainment try to discover if Minnie is there, and if so carry her back to the boats."

"But who shall accompany you?" asked Ned.

"Those that you can least depend upon," said Jack, in a whisper; "Bircher, Charley, and Jumbo, and of course Sally, whom I learned a few tricks years ago."

"Harry and 'Dolf then will be with me?"

"Yes, they are cool bold fellows, and as it is not so much strength but coolness you will require I think you will find them best to join you."

"And should I succeed in recovering Minnie?" said Ned.

"Make for the boats and wait our coming," said Jack.

"Be it as you wish," said Ned.

"All right then, I'll get my togs on. Just tell that fellow Bircher he must obey me in all I command, for I don't want him to spoil our game."

Ned promised and spoke to the tutor, who finding that there was no chance of his being engaged in a fight, willingly consented to follow Jack's orders.

Jack proceeded to the cabin, and attired himself in a long red robe which he tied round his waist, and then taking from the box a large tin crown placed it on his head.

Beneath his robe he concealed a revolver and a knife.

Then he took from his box a powder, a rope torch, and a long fork.

He dissolved some of the powder in water and rinsed his mouth with it, smeared it over his lips and face and then his hands.

This done he took from his box a long rope with a ball of rag covered with wash-leather attached to each end.

"You know how to use this, Sally?" he said.

"Rather," she replied; "what a pity we ain't got a drum! It would put me in mind of the time when I used to go buskin about with father, afore he died and I went into service."

"Here's a tin whistle," said Jack, taking one from the box, "wonder who can play it?"

"I can play a tune on a whistle," said Bircher.

"Then you shall be head man of the orchestra," said Jack.

"What am dis chile to play?" asked Jumbo.

"And here, what am I to do?" said Charley; "go round for the ha'pence, if so Bircher will have to change hats."

"I'll tell you what you can have," said Harry; "take a couple of saucepan lids ashore, they make first-rate cymbals, don't they, Ned?"

"Yes, but they must not have one of our saucepans for a drum, we can't afford that."

"Gorra, is dis chile, to go without anything," said Jumbo.

"Here, niggers always play a banjo," said Harry; "make one out of that; you can't hurt it, for I see 'Dolf's burnt a hole in the bottom."

And he thrust the frying-pan into the negro's hand.

"Yah, yah, dat just do," said Jumbo, holding it across his breast as he would a banjo, and beating at the bottom of the pan with his knuckles.

"First-rate," said Harry, "but you must look the character. Ned, get us a yard of that calico you bought, to make the nigger a tie and collar."

Ned brought the calico, and Harry soon formed it into a tie and collar for Jumbo's neck.

"Golly, dis chile am a swell," cried the negro. "Brest if um share dese close. Yah, yah!"

"Now are you all ready?" said Jack, for I can see smoke rising above the trees yonder, a sure sign that some of the Indians have come back to the village.

All professed to be ready.

"Are you all armed?" asked Ned.

All were though they kept their weapons out of sight.

"Then you lay down and don't be seen," said Jack; "and when we have landed pull up the river at least a mile before you land yourselves. Should you need help fire a rifle and we will rush to your aid."

Ned promised to do this and orders were given to pull close to the shore.

Reaching this Jack, crown on head and torch in hand, landed, followed by Sally, Charley, Jumbo, and Bircher.

Then the boats were pulled away and headed up river.

"We'll make for the smoke yonder," said Charley, "and as soon as we get sight of the Indians make as much row on your instruments as you can, and do all that is possible to keep the savages' attention fixed on ourselves."

A quarter of an hour brought the party in full view of the Indian village, and also into view of a number of savages gathered in front of the huts partaking of their morning meal.

The moment they caught sight of Jack and his party they sprang to their feet and came towards them.

"Make all the row you can," cried Jack. "Now, Bircher, put all your wind into that whistle."

The band struck up. Bircher blew the whistle, Charlie clashed the saucepan lids, and Jumbo beat on the frying-pan, holding it on his chest with the handle pointing over his shoulder.

As the Indians approached Jack asked—

"Is that chief Tiger Claws?"

"No," replied Sally, "none of these

are his band; that I know by the tattoo."

Jack called a halt, and when the Indians came up he told Sally to explain that he was a great white medicine, that he loved the Indians, and had come to bring strength to their warriors and fruitfulness to their fields by his incantations.

Sally explained this to the wondering savages, and then asked if they had any guests or friends whom they would like to see the power of the great white chief.

The chief whom she now particularly addressed replied—

"My friends hunt in the forest, and will not return till the sun sinks into the waters. There is a stranger in my lodge but she is the captive of Tiger Claws, therefore she comes not forth to see the works of the great white chief."

"Will you not let your squaws and papooses see the wonders the white chief will perform?"

"The squaws hoe the corn and the papooses have no sense," was the reply; "so let the great medicine begin."

And they pressed forward.

"Stand back," said Jack. "Keep them back, Sally,"

Then he set fire to his torch.

When it was well ablaze he took a portion of the flaming rope on the end of his fork, and shouting out—

"Behold the power of the white medicine!" thrust the fire into his mouth.

The chief darted forward in his uncontrollable excitement.

"Keep back, keep back!" cried Sally.

And twirling the long rope with both hands the savages recoiled before the balls that flew first in one direction and then the other.

Meantime Jack had taken another forkfull of fire to convey to his mouth, and the band set to work, making a most fearful din.

"Great medicine," cried the chief. "Eat fire—no burn—no kill—ugh!"

The last expression died in a gulp, for coming within reach of the rope Sally was twirling, one of the balls caught him a blow on the eye and sent him floundering against Jumbo.

"Hold on dar!" yelled the negro, colliding against Charlie, and driving the end of the handle of the frying-pan against that youth's nose.

"Oh — murder — fire — oh!" yelled Bircher, as the other ball caught him a blow in the stomach and doubling him up he thrust his head against the torch, singeing his forehead.

"Fire and fury!" cried Jack, starting on one side. "What the devil——"

A yell from Jumbo drowned the rest of the sentence.

In his pain and rage Charley had flung the negro against the Indian chief, who instantly pitched him off.

Jumbo came with a crash up against Jack, shaking the flaming pitch off the point of the fork on his black chest and legs.

"Gorra, gorra, dis chile's burnt to def!" yelled Jumbo, capering wildly about. "Put um out—put um out! Dat's all fru you, you cuss Injun—take dat!"

And without thinking of the consequences of the act, the negro struck the chief on the head with the frying-pan, knocking out the bottom and leaving the rim firmly fixed round the Indian's neck.

CHAPTER XX.

IN WHICH NED FINDS MINNIE AND LOSES HIS LIBERTY.

AFTER about a quarter of an hour's rowing and paddling Ned gave orders for the boat and the canoe to be again headed for the shore, and directing both vessels to be drawn into the shadow of some overhanging branches, he armed himself with revolver and rifle and sprang on to the bank.

Harry and 'Dolf, armed like himself, followed him.

"By this time," said Ned, " I expect Jack will have commenced business, and it may therefore be safe for us to advance towards the village, or rather the cluster of wigwams they call a village."

"But we must keep a sharp look-out," said Harry, " or we may find ourselves surrounded or led into an ambush."

"I have little fear of encountering any obstruction before we reach the village," replied Ned ; " but, as Bircher says, prudence is the better part of valour, so we will not neglect it."

They moved on through a forest of trees in the direction of the village, every moment finding the undergrowth more and more dense.

"Wonder how far this forest reaches ? " said Harry.

" Not far in the direction we are going as we know," said Ned ; " but in the other it is impossible to say."

" Or inland either, remarked Harry , " but we must make sure we are going in the right direction, for we have to twist about so through this confounded underbrush that if we are not careful we shall be going from instead of to the village."

"That's true, dear boy ; I just thought of that. Let's get on for a time and then I'll climb one of the highest trees and take an observation."

"Look out for wild cats when you do," said 'Dolf.

" And snakes too," said Harry.

"Ah, that reminds me," said Ned ; " you should have put on your gaiters, Dolf."

" I shall soon have to wear them for stockings," said 'Dolf, " for I've worn all mine into holes."

"Oh, I've got plenty of hose," said Ned. " I laid in a good stock. Let's halt here and I'll take a survey from the top of this tree."

Giving 'Dolf his rifle to hold, Ned clambered into the branches of a large tree.

Up he went till he could see above the surrounding vegetation.

Then he took a good look about him.

Before him lay the Indian village.

On his right the waters of the Orinoco glided on to the sea.

Keeping his face turned in the direction of the village he descended to his friends.

"We are right as yet," he said ; " this forest does not seem to break till we reach the village."

"Could you see anything of our friends ? " asked Harry.

"Nothing from where I was. Indeed, but that we know there is sure to be a clear space about the Indian village, I should have imagined there was no break in the trees at all."

" If we keep the sun on our right we shall not go astray then," said Harry.

"No," replied Ned, as he took his rifle from 'Dolf and again led the way.

Thicker and thicker became the undergrowth as they advanced, and many a scratch did the unprotected legs of 'Dolf get from the prickly branches through which they had to force their way.

Here and there, too, the sun was almost hidden from their sight, so dense was the foliage overhead, for the tops of the trees were laced together with vines, whose leaves and flowers made a dark canopy above them.

Birds of most gorgeous plumage flew from bough to bough, and round the heads of the young adventurers fluttered butterflies of the most beautiful colours.

Beetles, shining like burnished gold, crawled about the stems at their feet, and insects of every shape and hue met their gaze at every step.

It was a scene of wild beauty through which they travelled, but it was also one of danger, for they knew not from whence the poisoned snake might dart its venomed fangs, from out of what bush the jaguar might spring.

Bravely but cautiously they proceeded till a sound met their ears that caused them to pause.

"What is that?" asked Ned.

Harry listened for a moment and then burst out laughing.

"That?" he said. "Why, Ned, don't you remember hearing that music on board the 'Dancing Dolphin?'"

Ned's face wreathed in smiles.

"To be sure I do, dear boy, and it was you who discoursed it. It's the clash of the cymbals—beg pardon—the clash of the saucepan lids. The beggars are at it."

"And we are close to the village," said Harry.

"Yes, we must be doubly cautious now," said Ned. "Look to your weapons in case we want to use them."

And he loosened the knife in its sheath at his waist.

"Don't you think it would be better to take another squint around before we go any further?" said Harry; "there's a good tall tree."

"Right, dear boy," said Ned, holding his rifle for 'Dolf to mind.

"I'll go up, Ned," said Harry.

Ned consented, and taking Harry's rifle that youth began to climb the tree.

On getting up a good height he saw the Indian village just beneath him, and over the tops of the wigwams he could distinguish Jack and his companions and a crowd of Indians surrounding them.

One look only Harry cast around him.

Away to the left and further from the river he saw the country for some distance was open and then it was closed in again by forests.

Beneath him he gazed upon a lovely sight, the crowns of the trees around him were one gorgeous mass of flowers lit up by the sunlight.

These were the flowers of the vines, which creeping up the limbs of the forest giants spread themselves over the tops, and covered them with the most gorgeous bells of every colour and size.

Harry could have gazed upon this scene for an hour, but he knew time was precious and he began to descend.

On reaching the ground he told Ned what he had seen.

Grasping their rifles they made their way along till they could see the habitations of the Indians ranged before them, and stretching away for some little distance to the right and the left.

Beyond the wigwams they knew the Indians were looking on at the performance of Jack the conjuror.

On the edge of the timber they paused.

"Now to find whether my hopes are to be realised or not," said Ned; "these huts or whatever they are called are not built like London houses or country cottages, and as their entrances seem to be on the opposite side, we must make openings for ourselves."

"Not much trouble in that, I expect. They are built of reeds and skins, it seems, so it won't take so very much to make a hole in them."

"Let's set to work at once," said Ned.

They stole noiselessly from the shelter of the forest and approached the huts.

They were nearly all of a size, but one in the centre of the row was of more conical shape and somewhat higher than the rest.

"That must be the habitation of the chief," said Ned, "and if Minnie is here she would be taken doubtless."

"Well, you see if you can get a squint inside of it," said Harry, "and leave me and 'Dolf to scrutinise some of the others; but I say, old man?"

"What?" asked Ned.

"Mind you are not seen as you pass the openings between the wigwams."

"I'll be careful," said Ned, as he moved away towards the highest habitation.

Harry and 'Dolf found little difficulty in obtaining a view of the interior of the wigwams.

"Look here, 'Dolf, this is how to do it," said Harry; "put the blade of your knife between the reeds and then give it a turn and you force them wide enough apart to take a squint."

In this manner they managed to obtain a view of the interior of the dwellings.

A couch of reeds and skins and a few vessels of Indian culinary was all that they saw.

Not one was occupied.

The women and old men had gone to the corn-fields and taken the children with them.

Ned gained the building where he hoped to see Minnie, and perhaps Boaster or Phopps.

It was built of tougher material than its fellows, the reeds being stronger and stouter and more closely secured together, and these were plastered over with clay and moss.

Ned laid his ear against the wall and listened.

Not a sound.

He looked about for an opening.

There was none on the side he stood.

He peered along either side of the building.

But nothing like an opening could he see.

To go round to the front he dared not, lest he should be discovered by the savages at that side assembled.

Suddenly a thought struck him.

The roof was conical. If he could get on to it from where he stood he might still be beyond the range of the vision of the Indians on the opposite side.

He drew back several paces and took a view of the roof.

There was an opening in it, probably to allow of the smoke escaping.

It was not more than eight feet to the lowest part of the roof, and through the opening therein he could learn whether Minnie was confined in the hut or not.

"I've done harder things than that," muttered Ned, "so here goes."

He lodged his rifle against the wall of the hut, walked backwards a few steps, then running forward, made a spring and drew himself up on to the sloping roof.

Although the roof looked strong it was far from it.

Scarcely had Ned's full weight come down upon it, than, with a crackling sound, it sank beneath him.

Ned, finding himself sinking, clutched tightly at the bark and reeds of which it was formed, but in vain.

The reeds parted, and he fell through the opening flat on to the earthern floor below.

Half stunned he sprang to his feet.

A scream rang in his ears, and as he swung round to learn its cause a terrific yell from the Indians beyond pealed through the place.

Before Ned could recover from the effects of his fall and the noise that had assailed his ears, he saw what he imagined to be a bear or some other wild animal move at his feet.

Instinctively he sprang back and clutched the butt of his revolver.

Then he stood as if rooted to the spot.

"Ned, Ned! Oh, Heaven, at last, at last!"

And the heap of skins were thrown aside, and from amidst them sat up the form of Minnie Sash.

Ned's hand dropped from the butt of his revolver, and with a cry he sank down on his knees and enfolded the sitting form of Minnie in his arms.

"Thank Heaven, I have found you, Minnie!" he cried. "Oh, speak to me —speak; say it is not all a dream."

"Ned, Ned!" was all she could utter as she clung to him.

Ned folded her to his heart.

He forgot everything but that she was leaning on his bosom, forgot the yell of the Indians he had heard, forgot where he was, the danger he was running of being discovered, forgot all but that he had found her, the girl he had crossed the seas to save or die for.

"At last, at last!" he cried. "Saved, saved!"

"Lost, fool, lost!" shouted a voice behind him, as a crushing blow descended upon his head.

"Ah, 'tis he, Boaster—villain!" cried Ned, as he staggered up to receive again a cruel blow on his forehead that sent him to the earth as if shot.

"Yes, fool, Boaster," cried his assailant.

"You come to save her, but you come to your death. Ned Nimble, I swore I'd kill you, and thus I keep my oath."

With the blood streaming over his eyes, Ned essayed to draw his revolver from its case, but a blow from Boaster's weapon struck down his arm

Again the villain raised his hand to strike, but with a shriek, Minnie threw herself across Ned, and spread forth her arms appealingly.

"Mercy, mercy!" she cried. "Oh monster, spare him! in mercy spare him!"

As her words rang out in agonised accents the curtain of the wigwam was thrust aside, and with loud yells several of the Indians bounded into the hut

CHAPTER XXI.

IN WHICH NED'S FRIENDS PUT THEIR HEADS TOGETHER ON NED'S BEHALF.

THE indignity offered to the savage chief by Jumbo nearly cost the negro his life, for with a yell of rage the Indian drew his tomahawk and aimed a blow at the man who had struck him with a frying-pan, and who grinning in his face still held that article by the handle.

The blow was cleverly turned aside by one of the saucepan lids which Charley thrust forward to intercept it.

"Hold!" cried Jack; "strike another blow and I will rain down fire upon your heads. Back. Jumbo, back all."

And he waved Jumbo one way, and the Indians who were advancing upon them another.

"Back, or I spit fire upon and destroy you," cried Jack.

And then as they hesitated he thrust his hand to his mouth and the next moment he blew from between his lips a shower of sparks.

Seeing this the Indians together with their chief, turned and fled panic-stricken and yelling to their huts.

"Quick," cried Jack, "if we would escape let's away, for in a few moments they will recover from their terror and be down upon us with tomahawk and arrow; while they are terror-stricken it is best to vanish."

"But the girl?" said Charley, "she is here."

"We must wait till night; to attempt her rescue now is to court death, come!"

As he spoke he darted across the open towards the forest.

Bircher trembling in every limb, followed him, clinging to his robe.

"Don't leave me behind, don't, don't!" he gasped.

"Coward," hissed Sally, "save your breath, you may want it."

So terrified were the savages by what they had seen that it was their belief that Jack could annihilate them with a breath.

They never turned to see whence he and his companions fled.

They were too eager to seek the shelter of their huts.

By taking advantage of their terror Jack and his party gained the other side of the village, but scarcely had they done so than they were confronted by Harry and 'Dolf.

"To the forest; to the woods," cried Jack, seizing Harry by the arm.

"But Ned, Ned," cried Harry; "where is he?"

Jack paused.

"Where?" he said.

"Yes, he was here just now; has any harm befallen him?"

"I know not; we are in a deuce of a mess through the stupidity of this nigger and must make ourselves scarce while we can."

"But Ned, I wont go without Ned," cried Harry, wrenching himself free.

"Nor I," cried 'Dolf, "where can he be?"

"Whither did he go?" asked Jack.

"To yonder hut; if danger has befallen him I share it!"

"And I," said 'Dolf.

"Then you don't have it all to yourself," said Jack; "if we could hide to-night all the better, but if Nimble's in danger hang me if I desert him."

And he followed Harry and 'Dolf, who now rushed towards the hut with the conical roof.

At the back of this they paused for loud voices broke upon their ears as they clearly penetrated the shattered roof.

"I tell you, Swift Arrow, that you are a fool. They were but jugglers and you flee from them like children; away with all such rot; attend to me or fear the anger of Tiger Claws."

"What would my white brother."

"That he should listen and obey," replied the voice that seemed to hold Harry spellbound; "this youth is my foe and the foe of Tiger Claw; he must not escape or woe to you and your people."

Harry placed his hand to his forehead and staggered back.

"It is he—Boaster," he gasped; "and Ned, poor Ned, is a captive."

"Let my white brother command," said Swift Arrow; "and the friend of Tiger Claw will obey."

"Bind him, that when he recovers his senses he may not escape, and keep your braves posted round the hut; when Tiger Claw returns with his white friend the boy shall die."

"And the pale faced maiden?"

"I will look to her. See that he cannot leave here. He has friends at hand therefore keep sentry on all sides; Tiger Claw will soon return, and then your braves shall dance round the fire that burns the body of my foe."

"It is my brother's will and he shall be obeyed. Let the captive be bound hand and foot, and sentinels guard the village that none may steal upon us. 'Tis well, Swift Arrow has spoken."

The words reached the ears of those without.

Jack seized the arm of Harry and whispered—

"We cannot aid him now, to attempt it were madness."

"I'll save him or die with him," said Harry.

"Be warned," said Jack; "as you may destroy him as well as yourself. Let's get into the forest and hold a council; I fear no man living, but I am not fool enough to throw my life away when I may keep it to serve my friends! be advised, come."

"His words are good," whispered Sally. "It is our only chance to save your friend."

And she took Harry's arm.

Harry saw the wisdom of the advice and suffered Jack and Sally to lead him away.

'Dolf fain would have lingered behind, but Charley whispered in his ear—

"Flunkey it's no go now. Trust me we'll save him yet."

And he followed after the others.

'Dolf gave a sigh and a look round.

His eye lighted on Ned's rifle, and he seized it, then hurried after the others.

"I'll never go back if I can't take him with me," he muttered. "I shouldn't dare show my face to Dorothy if I did."

The next minute he had plunged into the forest and joined his companions.

"Now what's to be did?" asked Charley when by mutual consent they came to a pause in the thick of the wood.

"Bress if this chile knows," said Jumbo. "If dat curse Injun hadn't hit dis nigger, dis nigger hadn't bit him and caused all the hullabaloo dey kicked up."

"Never mind the Indians," said Jack. "Our friend is a prisoner, and in the hands of one evidently more cruel than any savage; the thing to consider is how to rescue him."

"And that is a most difficult problem to solve," said Bircher.

"Perhaps it is; but we mean to solve it," said Jack; "'Dolf and Harry are for going bull rush at them and chancing it, but that won't do; we should have to fight fifty of them. We must think how we may circumvent the beggars."

"Besides," said Sally, "if they saw a chance of a rescue they would kill him before our eyes. I know Indians, and they are almost as savage as wild cats."

"Poor Ned," said Harry, "he must have discovered Minnie was there, and in his eagerness to save her, fallen into a trap."

"That's about it," said Jack, "and now we've got to hit upon some plan to get him out of the trap."

"And if we delay, Tiger Claw and his band will be against us as well as those now in the village," said Harry.

"I overheard as much," said Jack.

"Then why not throw all upon the chance of a rescue now?" said Harry.

"Because everybody don't want to get killed if you do," said Sally. "There, I don't want to hurt your feelings, young man, but you don't know Indians like I do. You may fool a hundred but you can't fight twenty. They're just like wild cats; you may bamboozle 'em, but try to fight them and see who'll get the best of it. Lor'! don't I know— rather!"

"In course you do," said Charley, "for you are half an Indian yourself."

"Look here, Mr. Imperance," said

Sally, "you be careful, or I'll be Indian enough to go for your scalp."

"Don't," said Charley. "If you want anybody's wool take his."

And he pushed Jumbo towards her.

"Stop that fooling," said Jack, angrily.

And as he swung round on his heel with his fists clenched, Charley and Jumbo retreated a few paces and looked as grave as mutes.

"Now look here," said Jack, "the business we have now got on hand is too serious for nonsense. The white fellow, whoever he may be, who is in that Indian camp will take good care to point out to the savages that my hanky-panky tricks are not to be feared, so I can't hope to fool them any longer in that way; so we must hit upon something by which we may get Nimble out of the scrape he's got into."

"I'm afraid it's no use," said Bircher.

"You are afraid of everything," said Sally. "I don't know what good you are at all."

Bircher shut up.

"I don't expect it's any use to try any dodge till night comes," said Jack.

"But then it may be too late," said Harry.

"No it won't," said Sally. "If they mean to kill the lad they won't attempt it till Tiger Claw returns to the village."

"And then," said 'Dolf, "there'll be more enemies to encounter."

"That's true," said Sally; "but I know Indians as well as wild cats, and I tell you they'll have a long palaver before they do anything, and it's while they are doing that we shall have the best chance."

"You think so," said Harry.

"I know so, don't I?" said Sally. "Ain't I been an Indian squaw, though it was against my will?"

"Of course you are better acquainted with their ways than we can be."

"To be sure I am. So you just follow my advice."

"What then do you propose?" asked Harry, eagerly.

"That we wait patiently the arrival of Tiger Claw and his braves. Then a council will be held, and while the Indians are engaged in it we steal upon the hut and rescue the prisoner, if possible."

"But suppose he is not left there? Suppose they keep him in their midst?"

"That they won't do, though he is sure to be well guarded. Anyhow, nothing can be attempted till dark, and then we must act according to circumstances."

"And in the meantime?" asked Harry.

"One of us will go and bring the boats back to the spot where Jack and I landed, to be handy. Sentinels must be stationed in the tree-tops to watch the village, and all get ready to act when the moment arrives, that action may be successful, or at least, present hopes of success."

"You cannot do better than follow her advice," said Jack; "and now who will go and recall the boats?"

"I think, perhaps, I had better do so," said Bircher.

"All right," said Jack.

"You'll have to keep a sharp look-out for snakes and wild beasts," said 'Dolf.

"I—I forgot," stammered Bircher; "I don't know where the boats are to be found. Perhaps somebody else had better go."

"Not a bit of it," said Charley. "You're the ugliest, and if a jaguar met you he'd be so frightened at the sight that he'd be safe to bolt."

"Gorra, dat's truf," said Jumbo; "he bolt Massa Bircher, spec'lls and all."

"Don't, don't," said Bircher. "I—I don't like jesting on such a subject."

"It's trufe—solemn trufe," said Jumbo; "dat ain't no jes'. De animal open his jaws and down you go."

Bircher looked awfully white.

"I don't think he's any good," said Jack. "Look here, Charley, you shall go."

"Right you are, I'm on," said Charley. "Just what I wanted, for I'm feeling peckish and there's plenty of grub on board."

"Harry will give you a hint about where you will find the boats, and having found them, bring them as near where we landed as possible, but have them kept out of sight of the savages."

"I tink dis chile will go too," said Jumbo.

"No, you can keep a look-out from one of the trees," said Jack.

"Den look here, Charley, jus' you bring a lot of grub when you comes back, 'cos de wearing ob dis yere collar makes me hungry."

"All right," said Charley, "I will if I don't eat it all."

"Don't you go for to do that, or gorra! I'll eat you," said the negro. "We go shares you know."

"One of you fellows must let me have your rifle," said Charley. "I may need it on the journey."

"Here take Ned's," said Harry.

"And bring a gun for each ashore with you," said Jack, "for we may need them. But be careful not to expose yourself to our foes. We will keep a look-out for you. Now start."

"Like a bird," said Charley.

And shouldering Ned's rifle he darted off in the direction which Harry pointed out to him.

CHAPTER XXII.

IN WHICH BOASTER PLAYS A GAME AND WINS IT.

NEITHER Boaster nor Phopps had imagined that Ned or his uncle would suffer them to escape without some attempt to bring them to justice and punish them for the crimes they had committed.

But when they set sail for South America they believed they had succeeded in escaping pursuit.

But as they proceeded on their voyage the fear stole upon them that they would be tracked, and this feeling grew in intensity till at length it became almost certainty.

Hence it was that they had purchased a boat and engaged two white ruffians to manage it, and resolved to hide somewhere in Peru or one of the Republican states.

Revenge on Ned and his friends was, however, their first thought, and through Minnie they resolved to obtain it.

Bad as they were, neither of them could take the life of the innocent girl, and next to slaying her Boaster knew he could not take a greater revenge on Ned than by forcing her to become his wife.

To effect this he must bear her to a spot where there was no possibility of her obtaining a friend or assistant, and thus it was that instead of making their way to a civilised part they had entered into a compact with the savage chief Tiger Claw.

It was on their way to the camping-ground of that Indian's followers that in order to hunt Tiger Claw had landed and made friends with Swift Arrow, over whose hunting-grounds he desired to wander in search of provisions.

The red chief had professed the greatest kindness for his new companions and had promised to befriend them, but he had resolved to possess for himself the captive girl as soon as he should return to the hunting-grounds of his tribe.

But the wily chief so comported himself that neither Boaster nor Phopps dreamed for one moment of treachery, and the former was looking anxiously forward to the moment when Minnie, perceiving all hope of escape impossible would consent to be his bride, when the arrival at the Indian village of Jack and his companions told him how premature his hopes and speculations were.

Great indeed was his surprise and consternation when on looking forth from the hut of Swift Arrow his eye rested on the well-known form of Mr. Bircher.

Shabby as that unusually prim gentleman was, he recognised him in a moment and then like a flash it came to him the certainty that he had been tracked down.

Bircher had always been his friend shielded him from punishment, almost defended him in his villainy in days gone by?"

But he dared not hope that he was other than his enemy now.

What could have brought him there? —what but to aid Ned Nimble in rescuing Minnie and punishing him for his villany?

Eagerly he scanned the faces of the others, expecting to find Ned in disguise but he was soon convinced Ned was not one of the party.

But he felt equally convinced Ned was

not far off, and he drew back into the hut resolved to wait and watch, and if need be kill Minnie ere she should be taken from him.

Ill in health, worn out by despair, Minnie lay slumbering beneath the skins that covered the bed of rushes where usually the form of the Indian chief, Swift Arrow, reposed.

Assuring himself that she slept, Boaster examined his revolver and loosened the knife he wore in a sheath at his belt.

"Danger is nearer than I dreamed," he muttered. "I see it all. Ned is on my track, and those fools whom the Indians are looking upon with such awe are but aiding him to defeat me and run me down. Ned is good at stratagems, but I may foil him, clever as he is."

He lifted the skin before the opening and peeped out.

"He is not far off, I'll swear," he muttered, as he suffered the skin to fall again into its place. "I wish Tiger Claw were here. Those fellows may frighten Swift Arrow into betraying me. But I'll kill her before he shall take her from me."

He stood over the sleeping girl and levelled his weapon at her head.

"Fool," he muttered, as he turned away. "Time enough for that when all else fails. Let me think."

Suddenly he started.

"Yes, Ned may seek to capture her while those fools of Indians are wonder-stricken at the scene got up to attract their attention. I must be ready, for the blow may fall at any moment.

He stooped and raised from the floor a thick knotted bludgeon, and looking at it, said—

"A blow with this would fell an ox. It may be handy."

He flung the skins off a couch on the opposite side of the place to where Minnie lay, and then sinking down upon it, drew the heavy coverings over him.

These he adjusted in such a manner that though they completely hid him from view, he could yet see the whole of the interior of the dwelling.

Under the coverlet he kept firm hold of the knotted stick.

"The moment he shows his face I strike," he muttered. "I may fall, but I will not fall unavenged."

The shouts which the Indians in their terror had given utterance to drowned the noise which Ned had made in clambering on to the roof of the hut.

While wondering what could have caused the commotion among the savages the roof gave way, and the body of Ned shot down to the floor.

So suddenly and so unexpectedly was Ned's appearance in the Indian hut that Bill was for the moment rendered powerless by surprise.

Nor did he recover himself till he saw Minnie in the arms of her lover.

He saw not the face of Ned, for his back was turned towards him, but he heard his tones and recognised them in a moment.

Then rage, jealousy, hatred, revenge leaped to his heart, and he flung aside the skins and sprang from the couch.

With a bound he crossed the earthern floor unseen, raised the bludgeon high in the air, then brought it down upon the head of Ned.

Then as the youth sank under the effects of the blow Boaster found voice and gave utterance to the threats he had spoken.

Again the weapon was raised and again it descended ere Ned, stunned and bewildered, could attempt to defend himself from the murderous attack of his cruel and revengeful foe.

As Ned sank under the second blow the eyes of Boaster flamed with fury, and he would have finished the work of murder there and then but for Minnie, who flung herself over her lover, and the sudden appearance of Swift Arrow and his terrified braves.

Then his upraised hand fell.

His look of fury gave place to one of cold-blooded pleasure, and he resolved that Ned should live to be tortured as only Indians can torture; that he should suffer the agonies of a thousand deaths to satisfy his great revenge.

Stooping he dragged Minnie from her lover, and flinging her brutally back on to the couch he cried—

"Spare him? Ay, I'll spare him for a death a hundred thousand times worse than I could inflict. I'll spare him to encounter a doom that demons would shrink from in horror. Ay, fear not that

I will kill him now. To do so would be to rob myself of half my revenge."

And then he gave orders for the securing of Ned from all chance of escape, and set about ridiculing the fears of the Indians, in which he succeeded even better than he had hoped.

CHAPTER XXIII.

IN WHICH SALLY SCRUBBINS THROWS A LINE AND HOOKS HER FISH.

CHARLEY having started on his journey through the forest in search of the boats, Jack said—

"A sharp look-out must be kept both on the village and its approaches, and that of course can best be done from the top of one of the highest trees."

"I will climb into one," said Harry.

"I was going to suggest that the nigger should do that," replied Jack.

"Why he ?" asked Harry.

"His black face is not so likely to be seen among the foliage as your white one."

"Dar's de beauty in being brack," said Jumbo. "Guess you white folks envy dis gemmen now."

"You'll have to take off that sheet you've got round your neck though," said Jack.

And he caught hold of the piece of calico which formed collar and tie and gave it a pull.

"Gor'-a-'mighty ! What for you choke dis chile ?" yelled the negro, as the calico instead of coming away in Jack's hand tightened round Jumbo's throat.

"Hold your row, you son of Satan !" cried Jack. "Do you want to bring the whole village down on us ?"

"No, nor I don't want you to choke me," replied Jumbo. "Brest if him didn't tink him head come off."

"Off with it and get up into that tree and keep a good look-out," said Jack.

"It am all bery well to say off wid it, but you pushed dis here garment right inside dis nigger's neck, and it won't come out again."

And the negro tugged away at the piece of calico with all his might, but instead of unfastening it he drew it tighter and tighter.

"Look here, you fool," said 'Dolf, "that's not the way. Let me."

And 'Dolf took hold of the necktie.

"No you don't," said Jumbo. "Jus' you keep your distance."

And he planted his foot in Dolf's stomach, causing that gentleman to double up so quickly that before Jumbo could draw back the top of 'Dolf's hat caught him a sharp blow across the nose that instantly filled his eyes with water.

"What you do dat for ?" gasped Jumbo.

"What did you do that for ?" retorted 'Dolf.

And the two men doubled their fists menacingly.

"Stop," said Harry; "for Heaven's sake don't quarrel now."

"Well, what did he kick me for when I only wanted to help him ?" growled 'Dolf.

"And what for you hit me ?" said Jumbo.

"It was your own fault," said 'Dolf.

"No it wasn't; it was yours," returned Jumbo.

"Look here," said Jack, "I'll maul you both if you don't shut up."

And he thrust them apart.

"'Dolf," said Harry, "if you love Ned you will not forget that any private quarrel now may be the cause of misery to him."

"I am sure, Master Harry, I should be the last to be the cause of any harm befalling Ned. I was a fool to lose my temper with that black fellow."

"And dis brack fellow was a fool to lose him temper wid you," said Jumbo. "So dere's my paw; chuck out yours."

And Jumbo held out his hand.

"Take it," said Harry.

'Dolf did so, and they shook hands.

"We are a pair of fools," said 'Dolf.

"Dat's trufe," replied Jumbo. "I was a fool and you was a fool, too."

"Here, let me untie that thing," said 'Dolf; "you've got it in a knot."

NED NIMBLE AMONGST THE INDIANS; OR, THE SECRET OF THE PHANTOM CAVE

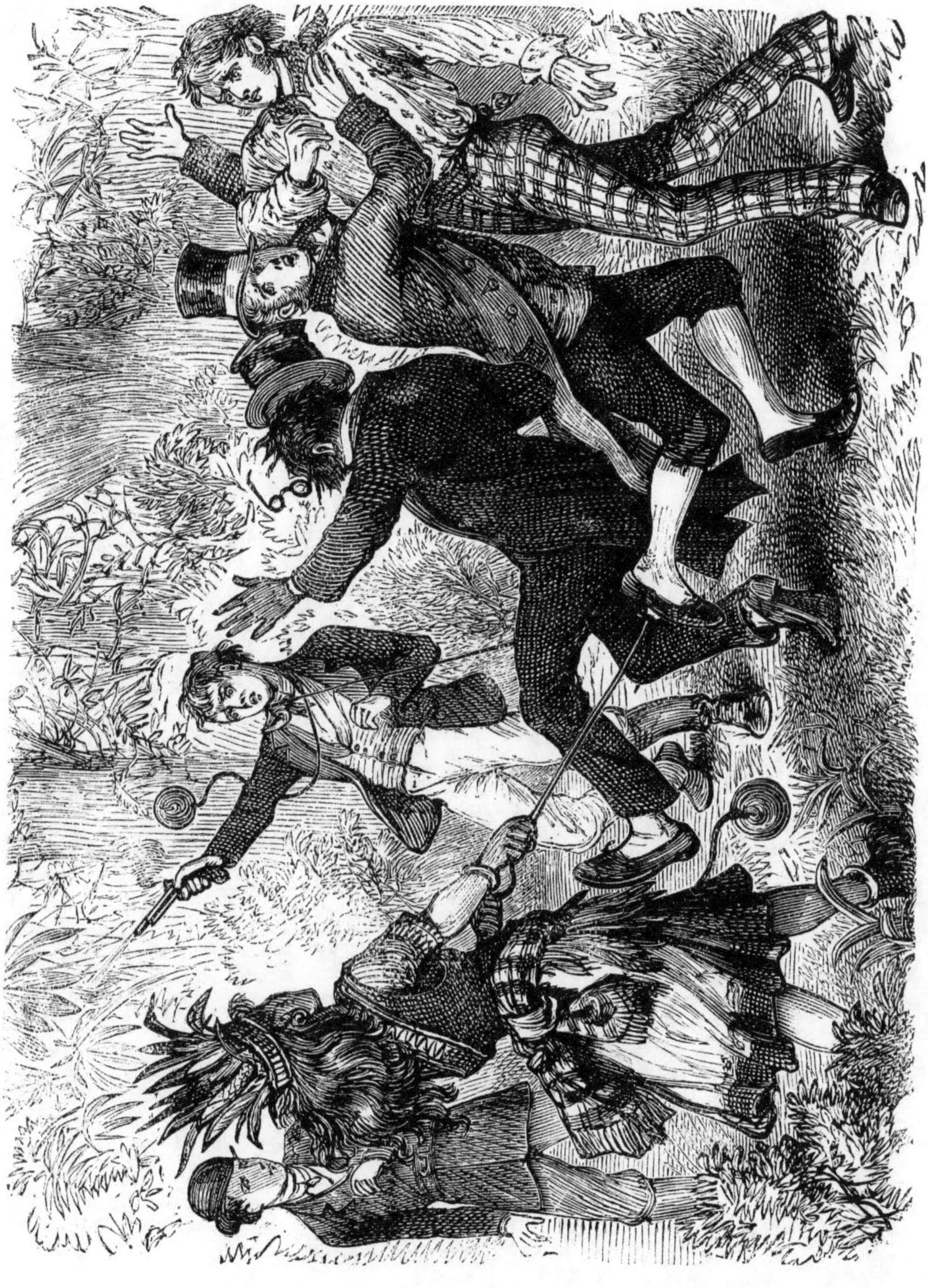

"THE ROPE CAUGHT BIRCHER'S LEGS AND PITCHED HIM BACKWARDS."

No. 5.

PRICE ONE HALFPENNY

[Published Every Monday.]

" It's very evident you ain't used to a cravat," Dolf added.

" Brest if I tink I ever will get used to it," said Jumbo. " Now mind, no choking ; dat's it."

Off came the calico.

" It's big enough for a shirt," said 'Dolf.

" Den I'll wear it next time for a shirt," said Jumbo, rolling it up and thrusting it into the pocket of his coat. " Now den, am dat dar de tree from which dis yar nigger am to take a sight ? "

" That one there ; it is higher than the others," said Harry, pointing to a tall tree. " Keep well hid in the branches, and if you see anything particular going on come down directly."

" Guess dis chile will," said Jumbo.

And he began to climb the tree, being assisted to mount by 'Dolf.

Up he went, till the foliage almost hid him from their view.

" I wish I'd gone for the boats myself," said Jack.

" Why ? " asked Sally.

" Then I would have left these togs aboard. This robe is in my way, and if it comes to a fight will be precious awkward."

" Can't you take it off and hide it somewhere ? " asked Harry.

" Yes, but if we should find it necessary to get out of here in a hurry I should have to leave it behind, and it may be of service to us yet, you know."

" It's a pity you didn't give it to Charley to take with him," said 'Dolf.

" Didn't think of it. Well, off it goes, lose or no lose it."

And Jack took off the long red coat and tinsel crown and placed them in some bushes that grew near.

" Now I feel ready for anything," he said. " Hush ! "

He held up his finger.

All listened.

There was a sound as of the crushing of twigs.

" Per—perhaps it's a wild beast," whispered Bircher, creeping close to Jack's side.

" Hush ! " hissed Jack.

The sound came nearer.

Jack grasped his pistol.

Harry and 'Dolf did the same.

There was a moment of suspense, and then the form of a man came crouching through the underbush, paused a moment, gave utterance to a cry of alarm, and turned to flee.

" It's Boaster ! " exclaimed Harry and Bircher in a breath.

Jack and Harry sprang forward to seize him.

But Jack caught his foot in a low branch and came tumbling to the earth, and Harry stumbled over him.

Boaster had turned again on hearing his name pronounced, and in his hand he held his revolver.

" Ha ! " he muttered, " he too here."

As he spoke he pointed his weapon at Harry as the youth rose to his feet.

His finger was on the trigger, but ere he could pull it a ball shot through the air and a rope coiled round Boaster's neck.

The next moment he was jerked aside and throwing up his arms the weapon was fired in the air.

Even as the report came Bircher was hurled to the earth.

Sally had thrown the rope, using it as a lasso, and caught the bully cleverly round the neck.

As she drew the rope tight it caught Bircher's legs and lifting him from off his feet pitched him backwards over the line.

'Dolf, who had also sprang forward on seeing Boaster raise his pistol, found himself hurled violently aside for Bircher's head and shoulders came with a thud against his back as the tutor performed his unintentional somersault over the rope.

Like a shot from a catapult—away went 'Dolf flying into the broad chest of Jack the Conjuror.

Before Boaster could realise how it happened, Harry had flung himself upon the baffled villain.

Pinning Boaster to the earth with one hand, he tore the revolver from his grasp with the other.

" Wretch ! " he cried ; " again we are face to face."

Boaster turned his eyes upwards full of baffled rage.

Harry laid the barrel of the revolver against his forehead.

" Villain, why should I hesitate to kill you ? " he said.

" Let me get up," cried Boaster, in a

hissing voice; "fool, 'tis you are in danger, not I."

Jack, thrusting 'Dolf aside, grasped Boaster by the neck, and waving Harry off him, dragged the bully to his feet and held him as in a vice."

"Is this the villain?" he said.

"That is the wretch, Boaster; the abductor of Minnie Sash," said Harry; "and the villain who is the cause of our friend's captivity now."

"Boaster, poor misguided youth," said Bircher, coming forward now that he knew the bully was powerless to do harm; "how could you so far disgrace yourself——"

"Bah!" interrupted Boaster; "keep your canting to yourself. Even you it seems have turned against me."

"What shall I do with him?" said Jack.

"Blow his brains out," said 'Dolf.

"I am your captive," said Boaster, "but if you would save Ned Nimble you will spare me."

"Did you spare him?" asked Harry, fiercely. "Why then should we spare you?"

"To save your friend," said Boaster, who had recovered his coolness.

"How?" asked Harry.

"By an exchange of prisoners," replied Boaster; "give me my liberty and I swear to release Ned."

"You have lied to me before to serve your purpose, and would do so again," returned Harry. "I dare not trust you; even now you said 'twas I who was in danger, not you."

"I did not mean that, I ——"

"De Injuns, de Injuns!" yelled Jumbo, as he came crashing down out of the branches in such a hurry that he lost his hold and fell all of a heap at the foot of the tree; "dat dar shot bring dem; dey run like mad dis way."

Harry and Jack both noticed the smile that came into Boaster's eyes.

He struggled desperately to escape.

"Fools," he cried, "if you would escape fly."

The yells of the savages now broke upon their ears.

"Kill him," cried 'Dolf; "quick, kill him and fly."

"This to avenge Ned," cried Harry, levelling the revolver at Boaster's head.

The villain blanched to a deadly white.

"No, no," cried Jack, thrusting the weapon aside; "dead he's but carrion, alive he may save Ned. We'll keep him hostage for Ned's safety; while Ned lives his life is safe, if Ned dies he dies, by Heaven I swear it. Now follow me; quick, this way!"

And Jack, still grasping Boaster by the throat, dashed among the trees.

CHAPTER XXIV.

IN WHICH A PALAVER IS INTERRUPTED BY A SURPRISE.

WHEN Ned awoke to consciousness he found himself bound hand and foot lying on the earthern floor of the Indian's wigwam.

Seated beside him was the Indian chief Swift Arrow, and standing in the opening beside the curtain stood a tall savage leaning on his long spear.

For some moments Ned could not realise where he was or what had happened to him.

But gradually recollection came back, and he realised his position and his danger.

His arm was stiff and painful, and his hair was matted and plastered to his forehead by the blood which had flowed from his wound.

Instinctively he turned his gaze towards the couch from which Minnie had risen to greet him.

It was empty.

His gaze wandered round the wigwam in search of her and Boaster.

But in vain.

He was alone with his Indian jailor.

A sigh he could not stifle burst from his lips, and at its utterance the Indian cheif grasped the long spear that laid on the floor at his side and rose to his feet.

"Where is she? Where are you Minnie?" cried Ned.

"What says the pale-face?" asked the savage chief. "Does he ask for the white maiden whom he sought to steal away from the white brother of Swift Arrow?"

"The white maiden was a captive; she was stolen from me by a villain. Where is she?" cried Ned.

"In the keeping of my white brother by whose will you are a captive in the wigwam of Swift Arrow."

"Are you he?"

"I am."

"You are a chief?"

"The pale-face speaks truly."

"What harm have I done you or your people that you should bind me thus and keep me prisoner?" asked Ned.

"You stole into my wigwam and would have carried away the captive of the white man who is my friend."

"Your friend?"

"The friend of my friend Tiger Claw," replied the chief.

"I came but for my own. If a villain tore from you one you loved would you not seek her?"

"Is the Indian a squaw that you ask him that?" said Swift Arrow.

"No, he is a man—a warrior, and he would die for the woman he loved."

"There the pale-faced spake with a tongue that is not crooked."

"Then why should the warrior be my foe, when I have but tried to do what he would have done."

"If the warrior failed he would die by the hand of him he sought to slay, and his tongue would not have asked mercy, his eye would not have dulled with fear, his limbs would scorn to tremble. He would have died laughing at the tortures and sung his song of defiance amid the flames to which his enemy consigned him."

"I do not fear for myself," said Ned.

"Then let the pale-face keep silent or speak to defy his foe. 'Tis the coward only who murmurs at his fate. If my white brother had fallen by your hand would you have suffered him to go free?"

"But I fell not fairly. The villain struck me from behind," said Ned. "He gave me no chance to defend myself, but like a coward fell upon me unawares."

"Does the panther wait till the hunter raises his rifle," said Swift Arrow; "or the snake hide its sting till the enemy is prepared."

"No, but man does not crawl like the snake in the grass, or spring without warning on his foes. He faces him boldly and gives him a chance to defend himself," said Ned.

The Indian shook his head.

"The pale-face is a squaw," he said, contemptuously, "and he will die howling like a dog."

Ned felt his blood fairly boil at this remark.

His brain throbbed.

He felt faint and weak, almost powerless, yet he made an effort to burst his bonds.

"You call me coward," he cried. "Release me from these bonds and I'll prove that you lie."

"Does the hunter take his hand from the panther's throat till he has slain the brute? Does the Indian let the wild cat out of the trap till he has killed it? Again I say the pale-face is a fool."

"It is Swift Arrow who fears now," said Ned, "but his fears are foolish. I have no wish to harm him; I would assail only the wretch he calls his white brother. The villain who has robbed me of mine and holds captive against her will the pale-faced maiden."

"The Indian betrays not his friend," replied Swift Arrow.

"You refuse then to release me?"

"I do."

"Then beware, for if you lend aid to a villain you become the accomplice of his crime, and will be called on to suffer for it."

"The threats of the pale-face fall like rain from the bird's wing," said Swift Arrow.

Ned saw it was no use to appeal to or threaten the Indian chief.

"At least tell me where is the maiden?" he asked.

"She is in another wigwam guarded by my white brother."

"What do you mean to do with me?" asked Ned, after a pause.

"That which is the will of my white brother and his friend Tiger Claw."

"Where is Tiger Claw?"

"Gone to the hunt. When he returns the council will be held and the doom of the pale-face spoken."

Ned was silent for some moments.

Then he said—

"I cannot escape ; I can see that I am too well guarded for that ; why then should Swift Arrow refuse to loosen my bonds that I may stretch my limbs and sit up?"

The Indian smiled and shook his head.

"I swear that I will not attempt to assail him or his people," said Ned ; "it would be madness to do so, for I could not hope, weak as I am, to harm them or escape."

"Swift Arrow fears you not but he breaks not his word with his white brother, therefore let the pale-face speak no more."

Ned saw it was no good trying to induce the Indian to remove his bonds.

His only chance now of escape was by the aid of his friends.

But could they aid him.

Could Jack's conjuring be of service to him now.

"Does not Swift Arrow fear the vengeance of the great white medicine?" he asked after a pause.

"No," replied Swift Arrow ; "my white brother, who is wise, tells me his power is not derived from the spirits but a trick of his own which can do no harm."

"And you believe him?"

"I do."

"Then you know not his power. Woe to you and your tribe if harm befall me. He will burn you with fire, change you to dogs, or blight your corn, so that you starve to death."

"My white brother says the white medicine lies."

"'Tis the white man who lies," cried Ned, seeing a look of doubt on the Indian's face ; "he is more powerful than all your medicine men put together. He will spit fire from his mouth that will burn you up, your squaws, your wigwams, and your fields if harm befall me."

"Is he the friend and brother of the pale-face captive?"

"He is," cried Ned.

"And he would save him?"

"Yes, a hundred times," replied Ned.

"Then if he be a powerful medicine, why did he not give the victory to his friend instead of his friend's enemy?"

Ned was silent.

This was a question he could not answer.

A low chuckle escaped the Indian's lips.

"The tongue of my white brother is straight," he said, "and that of the pale-face at my feet is crooked."

"We shall see," said Ned ; "even now he is making the punishment that shall fall heavily on you and those you aid to harm me and mine."

"The tongue of the pale-face is crooked and his heart is white. He shall die like a dog, and Swift Arrow will laugh at his fears, and drown his death cries with his laughter. Ugh, pale-face, you shall die!"

"You lie, cowardly savage," cried Ned, "I shall live to be revenged on you and yours for these taunts and insults."

The Indian was about to make some reply when the sound of a pistol shot awoke the echoes around.

The chief started, sprang to the opening and looked forth.

Then motioning to the sentinel to enter the hut he darted away.

The next minute loud voices broke upon Ned's ears.

Then past the opening to the wigwam hurried several Indians brandishing their spears.

What did it all mean?

Did it augur good or ill for Ned Nimble?

CHAPTER XXV.

IN WHICH BOASTER FINDS HIMSELF IN THE COILS.

"THERE, I think we are all right for the present," cried Jack, as after a run of some minutes he flung Boaster panting and breathless to the ground; "we've thrown them off the scent a bit I think."

"Blow the scent," moaned 'Dolf, rubbing his calves. "It's feeling I've got. There's a couple of hundred thorns sticking into my legs."

Mr. Bircher very white and very exhausted held his hands to his sides and panted for breath.

"Yes," said Harry, "I think we've given the beasts the slip for a while, but in so doing we shall miss Charley."

"We'll make for the river," said Jack, "and follow its bank till we reach the spot where the boats will be brought to. We must not let this fellow be rescued; he will be more secure on the boat."

"So that's the varmint is it that run away with Ned's girl?" said Sally, stooping over Boaster.

"That's the wretch," replied Harry.

"Well, he's a beauty to think any girl would care for him, ain't he now?" said Sally; "what do you think of yourself, eh?"

"What's that to you?" growled Boaster.

"Oh, you cut up surly do you," said Sally; "look here, young man, when I asks a question I expect a civil answer."

"Do you?"

"Yes, I do, and when I don't get it do you know what I do?"

"No, nor don't care," growled the bully.

"I just put my tattoo on their mugs, that's what I does," said Sally; "so none of your imperence to me."

"Just hand over that rope, Sally," said Jack; "I've got a use for it."

"Are you going to give him a good larruping with it?" said Sally; "'cos if you are double it a good many times."

"I'm going to bind his arms with it," replied Jack.

"You don't bind me," said Boaster.

"Don't you tell lies, young man," said Jack, "because I am."

"You dare not."

"What?" cried Jack; "you'll soon see whether I dare or no."

And he caught Boaster round the waist and flung him down as easily as though he had been an infant, and despite his struggles he tied the rope round him and had his arms pinioned to his side in a minute.

"There you are," said Jack; "that's cut your capers. Now then, on to your feet. Up you get!"

And Jack lifted the bully to his feet.

"Now friends, for the river," said Jack; "lets get this fellow aboard, and then we'll return and try to rescue Ned."

"You'll never do that," said Boaster.

"Oh yes we will," said Jack! "or it will be the worse for you."

"Gorra, dat it jus' will," said Jumbo. "Guess if dat poor chap suffer dere'll be a row, and dis chile'll hab a hand in it."

"Boaster may rest assured that it will be to his interest to prevent any harm befalling Ned," said Harry.

"Then let me go," said Boaster. "How can I prevent harm coming to him if you keep me away from the village. I can help him there, but not if I am absent."

"We cannot trust you," said Harry; "and never could."

"Then if ill befall him the fault is yours, not mine."

"You and your villainous companion Phopps are hand and glove with the savages, and through Phopps you can ensure Ned's liberty."

"How?"

"You shall write a letter to Phopps, when we get into the boat, telling him that if Nimble is not set at liberty at once and allowed to come to us your own life will be taken. Phopps is your friend, and of course will see that no harm befall Ned."

"A good idea," said Jack. "His life for Ned's; so bring him along, 'Dolf."

'Dolf caught hold of the end of the rope.

"I'll not go," said Boaster.

"Won't you ?" said 'Dolf.

"No."

"Jus' twist dat end round him neck," said Jumbo, "and I'll help you get him on."

'Dolf threw one of the ends of the rope round the neck of Boaster.

The ball attached to the end of it caught Jumbo a blow on the nose, and the negro uttering a yell leaped back on to Bircher's toes.

"Mur—oh !" cried Bircher, lifting up his foot, and hopping from side to side. "You black fool, I'm half a mind to smash you !"

And in his rage he aimed a blow at Jumbo.

"Gorra, tink dis chile stan' dat ?" cried the negro. "Brest if um do ! Jus' you take dat, an' dat, an' dat !"

And seizing the rope he beat Bircher about the head and shoulders, the padded ball falling with a loud thud at each blow.

'Dolf, hanging on to the other end of the rope shrieked with laughter.

If the antics of the negro amused him they certainly did not gratify Boaster, who expected his neck would be dislocated every moment.

Jack lost all patience, and giving Bircher a thrust and Jumbo a kick, promised to soundly thrash them both if they quarrelled again.

"Now let's get on," he said. Then addressing Boaster, he added—"Now young man, stir your stumps, or it will be the worse for you."

"Boaster," said Bircher, "prudence is the better part of valour. Come along quietly."

"Go to the devil !" cried Boaster.

"He'll go there fast enough," said Sally. "Now are you going to move ?"

"No I am not," said Boaster.

He hoped that delay might bring the savages to his aid.

"Then if you won't walk I'll carry you," said Jack.

"Don't you do anything of the kind," said Sally. "He'll walk, and sharp too, or I'll serve him worse nor wild cats would."

And Sally made pretence of clawing at Boaster's face.

"We can't stop here any longer," said Harry, "and if you refuse to walk, by Heaven, these men shall drag you at the end of the rope."

"Pull away," cried Jumbo, giving the rope a jerk, that caused Boaster to wince with pain.

"You black hound !" he hissed, "my turn will come yet."

"Yes, and it will come sooner than you expect if you are not careful," said Jack. "Don't try it on too far or I'll hang you from one of these trees."

"Boaster, be careful," said Bircher.

"Shut up, you double-dealing cad !" cried the bully. "Be what I am, I ain't one to pal in with a fellow at one time and then go against him another. Don't talk to me."

"And don't you talk to him," said Jumbo, "but sabe your breath for yourself and come along."

Boaster looked at the speaker as if he would annihilate him, and then gave a loud " halloa " in hopes that the savages would hear it.

"Clap a stopper on your tater-trap !" cried 'Dolf, as he placed his hand across Boaster's mouth.

"He but wastes time in hopes that the Indians will reach us," said Harry. "By Heaven, if he utters another cry like that I'll blow his brains out."

"Keep him covered with your pistol, Harry," said Jack, "and let the next cry he gives be his last. Now on, and if he won't march drag him; and if he speaks, kill him."

Jack hissed out these words, and Boaster saw that further resistance was useless, and suffered himself to be led along by 'Dolf and Jumbo.

Bircher and Sally preceded him, and Jack and Harry pistol in hand, brought up the rear.

They straggled through the forest in the direction of the river.

Boaster glanced nervously and eagerly round at every step in hopes of seeing the savages whom he knew his pistol-shot had brought into the forest.

But not a savage met his sight.

The fiends had eluded their pursuit entirely.

Still there was the hope that they would follow up the trail and reach them ere they could get to the boat.

Once on board he felt all hope of escape was gone.

Jumbo observed the eagerness with which Boaster looked around him.

"It no good you look," he said. "If de red men's come dey no get you—suah ob dat."

And he gave the rope a fierce tug.

"Dont like dat, do you?" said the negro. "Golly, dat nuffin to what I gib you if savage show his nose. Den I pull your head off suah, brest if I don't."

"If I am your prisoner you have no need to torture me," said Boaster.

"You would not torture poor Ned, would you?" said Harry. "The less you say about mercy to a captive the better. I heard your orders to the Indians in the hut, you cold blooded cad I did."

Boaster bit his lips.

How could he plead for mercy when he had shown none.

He felt it would be useless, and so in sullen silence he suffered himself to be led onwards, till through a break in the trees he saw the waters of the Orinoco.

CHAPTER XXVI.

IN WHICH NED FOOLS HIS INDIAN GUARD AND MAKES HIMSELF SCARCE.

THE sentinel who had stood guard at the door of the hut in which Ned was a prisoner was a young man of not very prepossessing appearance.

He stood gazing down at Ned for some moments in silence, leaning on his long spear as he took his survey of our hero.

At last, as if satisfied with his scrutiny, he uttered a guttural exclamation, but whether of admiration or contempt Ned did not know.

His forbidding features, made even more than naturally so by the red pigment with which they were smeared, led Ned to believe that any attempt on his part to induce the warrior to befriend him would be in vain, so he closed his eyes and pretended to sink into slumber.

After a few minutes he opened them again, and found the young savage seated by his side, his long spear resting across his knees and his eyes fixed intently on the ground.

"I wonder if it would be any use to appeal to him to release my arms?" thought Ned.

But another look at the forbidding features convinced him that it would be useless.

"I'm in for it now," thought Ned, "unless Harry and the others can hit upon some way of getting me out of this mess. Good Heaven's!" he added, "perhaps they too are in the power of these fiends."

As this thought flashed through his brain, Ned felt he could keep silent no longer.

"What captives has Swift Arrow in the village?" he asked suddenly of his guard.

"Ugh!" grunted the savage; "Swift Arrow has buried the hatchet and all the tribe are at peace."

"I do not mean prisoners of his own race, but mine," said Ned; "how many has he made captive?"

"None," was the reply.

"What! am I not a captive?" asked Ned.

"You are white man's prisoner," replied the savage.

"Then why does the red man guard me?" asked Ned.

"Because Swift Arrow is the friend of the pale-face brave, and the pale-face is the brother of the great chief Tiger Claw," was the reply.

"Does the red man then assist his brother to do wrong?"

"Ugh!" grunted the savage.

"If by that you mean yes," said Ned, "then is the red man worse than the pale-face. You saw the great white medicine?"

"I did."

"He is my friend. Do you not fear him, or have you not seen his power?"

"I saw him eat fire and blow it from his mouth," was the reply.

"Can your medicine men do that?" asked Ned.

The savage shook his head.

"No," said Ned, "he cannot, for he is not so great as the pale-face medicine, to anger whom is to die."

The young savage looked hard at Ned as he spoke in solemn tones.

"The white chief told the Indian it was lies—all lies."

"It is the white chief who lies, as the Indians will find if harm comes to the friend of the great medicine. The ears of Swift Arrow are closed to my warnings; the false tongue of his white friend has stopped them, and he will die."

"Swift Arrow?" asked the young savage.

"Your chief, yes," returned Ned; "he will not see his danger. He will suffer because he listens to the words of the white friend of Tiger Claw and he will bring ruin on himself and his people."

The young savage listened intently.

"You have seen some of the wonders of the great white medicine," said Ned, after a pause, during which he was intently scanning the Indian's features."

"I have."

"They were as nothing to those he has the power to perform. Poor deluded red man, would you and your brothers help Swift Arrow to bring destruction on your tribe."

The Indian only shook his head.

"You love your chief?"

"Ugh!"

"Then save him and yourselves from destruction," said Ned.

"What means the pale-face?" asked the Indian.

"That if harm befall me the great white medicine will smite the red man to the earth. Even now he weaves the spells that shall crush him. If you would escape his fury, do so before it is too late. Save yourself, your squaw, your wigwams, from the blight he will blow upon you with his breath. You have seen him blow fire from his mouth. Oh, beware, beware of his power or perish!"

The features of the savage grew gloomy and thoughtful.

"Did the pale-face friend of Tiger Claw lie?" he asked.

"His tongue is crooked," replied Ned, "and when he said that the white medicine could not destroy you with even a breath he lied."

The Indian shook his head doubtingly.

"You believe I speak with a crooked tongue. Where is Swift Arrow?"

"He has gone to the forest with his braves," was the reply.

"Yes," said Ned, "gone with his braves to his death unless I am permitted to return to my friends."

"What does the pale-face mean?" asked the young savage.

"That the shot we heard fired was to lure him into the power of the white medicine."

The savage sprang to his feet.

"Ugh!" he grunted, "I must warn him."

"Too late," cried Ned; "if you follow him, you too are lost."

The Indian paused irresolutely on the threshold of the hut.

"Stay!" cried Ned, "stay, or you are lost. If you would save your chief and his braves release my arms and suffer me to seek the great medicine and implore his mercy."

The Indian neither moved nor spoke.

Ned saw that the savage was half convinced that Jack had the power to perform what he had said he would.

He resolved to work upon his fears still further, and endeavour to induce him to cut his bonds ere Swift Arrow returned.

As Ned lay, through the hole in the roof, he could see the sky above.

Floating along the blue expanse was a white cloud bearing somewhat the shape of a crocodile.

He knew the belief of savages in signs, and he called the Indian to his side.

"The red man doubts my words," he said; "but the pale-face will prove them true. Let my red brother go forth from the hut and gaze upon the sky, and there he shall read how truly I speak."

"The sky?" cried the savage.

"Yes. When the white medicine is angered he calls forth the spirits of the skies to destroy his enemies and they come in the shape of a huge white crocodile. In the wind that blows I can even now hear their angry moanings as they hurry to do the bidding of the great white medicine."

"I hear them not," said the savage.

"No, for the red man's ears are closed by the white medicine's power; but the ears of the pale-face are open; the Indian's eyes are not blinded, let him therefore look forth and say if the white captive lies."

Ned threw such solemnity into his tones, and gave the savage such a look of pity, that the Indian walked from the hut and gazed up at the sky.

Ned saw the start he gave as his gaze rested on the white cloud floating towards the forest.

Slowly he came back into the hut.

"Well," said Ned, "is the red man blind as well as deaf, are his eyes closed as well as his ears, and must the pale-face who would save the red man from the white medicine's anger lay powerless to aid them?"

"The spirits are there," said the savage, pointing upwards.

"Then Swift Arrow and his braves must perish unless I—oh, but I am bound and a prisoner; how can I fly to appease the wrath of the great white medicine?"

"Pale-face," said the savage, "will the white medicine listen to your words when he is angry?"

"He will."

"Will you save my people from his anger?"

"I am powerless," said Ned; "am I not bound and a captive?"

"But were you unbound and free?" asked the Indian, bending lower and lower as he spoke.

"I would, because I know the ears of Swift Arrow have been charmed by the lying words of his white friend."

"Then save then," cried the Indian, whose superstitious fears had overpowered his reason. "Fly, pale-face, save my brothers from the white man's anger."

And drawing his knife he severed the thongs that bound the arms and legs of Ned.

Ned felt his heart leap to his throat with joy, then sink again as he attempted to rise but fell back.

"Good Heavens!" he thought, "am I so powerless? the chance of escape before me and I cannot grasp it."

Again he essayed to rise, and this time succeeded; and the blood beginning to circulate through his benumbed limbs he moved towards the doorway.

Staggering out he looked up as if searching for the cloud.

"Behold it," he said, pointing, "'tis there—there. Do you not hear the voices of the spirits? Yonder are your people, and thither I go to save them."

He hastened away as he spoke, and the young Indian stood gazing at his retreating form till it was hidden in the forest.

CHAPTER XXVII.

IN WHICH THE FLIGHT OF SWIFT ARROW IS STOPPED BY A BULLET.

NED staggered on through the forest, every moment getting a better use of his limbs, as the blood, stopped by the thongs that had bound him, circulated more freely through his veins.

His temples throbbed painfully, and the exertions he made caused his wound to bleed afresh.

He was hatless, and he drew his handkerchief from his pocket and tied it round his head.

His knife and revolver were gone, and he was totally unarmed.

If he met with any of the savages he knew that he was powerless to resist them.

If attacked by any of the wild denizens of the forest he must speedily succumb.

"It will not do to follow the same course as that cloud," he muttered, "or as soon as that Indian or his fellows find

how I have fooled him through his fears that is the course they will take in pursuit of me."

So saying he struck out in the opposite direction.

"Where can Harry and the others be," he said; "they would not have deserted me if they could have seen any chance of a rescue; perhaps they are hiding near, and yet to give them any signal of my presence would perhaps be to bring Swift Arrow and his fellows down upon me."

He paused at the base of a tree and leaned against the trunk for a moment.

"I must climb it," he said, "and see if there is any sign of them, and yet my limbs are so stiff I hardly feel equal to the task."

He grasped the stem of a stout vine

that encircled the trunk and drew himself up.

Every movement was painful, but he persevered, and up he went and sat among the branches.

He could discover nothing of his friends.

His gaze rested on the Indian village.

"Poor Minnie," he sighed, "I will not desert you though I am powerless yet to aid you."

Then he looked away beyond the village and saw a number of black forms emerging from the distant forest into the open.

"That is doubtless the band of Tiger Claw returning from the hunt," he said. "Ah, would to Heaven I could rescue that poor girl before they reach the village."

But he knew that to be impossible now.

With a sigh he descended the tree.

Though he had failed to discover the whereabouts of his friends or Swift Arrow he doubted not they were still in the forest, and he resolved to search for the former and at the same time made his way towards the spot where he expected the boats to be in waiting.

"I can do nothing unarmed as I am," he thought. "Now I know that Minnie is here I must bide time and opportunity to effect her rescue."

He had reached the ground again, but so cramped were his limbs, and so sick did he feel from the pains in his head, that he staggered forward a few steps and sank to the earth.

"I must rest awhile," he said, "and yet to pause here is madness. The bushes yonder are dense and dark. I'll crawl into them and rest and hide till I feel stronger."

He parted the bushes and dragged himself into them.

"What's this?" he muttered. "Why it's Jack's coat and tinsel crown. How come they here? They must have gone this way, but whither?"

He sat down, and the bushes closing up around him he felt that he was safely concealed from view of any prowling savage.

His only danger there was from some wild beast or a poisonous snake.

"Oh, well," he muttered, "I must take my chance. I have seen Minnie, and I must think how to save her."

He leaned his head on his hands and fell into deep thought.

How long he remained in his reverie he knew not, but suddenly he looked up with a start.

"S'elp me never! this licks me, blest if it don't."

Such were the words that fell on his ears.

"I know I'm right; didn't I cut my coat of arms on some of the trees so that I shouldn't lose my way? In course I did, and they've namussed. Even that black cuss of a nigger ain't here. Well, this is a go."

Ned listened intently and waited, for at present he did not recognise the voice of the speaker.

"Here have I been sweating all my fat off to bring these shooters along and not a blessed cove here to handle them. Oh, blow it! I'll sit down and eat the grub I brought for Jumbo. 'Tain't no use carrying that any further. Eh, who's that? Stand, or I'll put half-a-dozen bullets into you in the twinkling of a fly's hind leg!"

"Charley!" said Ned.

"Who says Charley? If you're a pal of mine come on; if you ain't, just show your ugly mug and I'll make a hole in it before you can say Jack Robinson."

"Charley, it is I—Ned Nimble."

"What?" cried Charley.

"Ned."

"The devil!"

"No, myself," said Ned.

"Hold on, my pippin," cried Charley, "whoever you are don't try to come the blarney over me, or I'll riddle you like a cullender."

"It is indeed I," said Ned, parting the bushes.

Charley dropped the gun he had raised to his shoulder and levelled at the place from whence the voice had come, and exclaimed—

"It is, by Jupiter!"

"Yes," said Ned, "it is I; but I am so weak; lend me your hand to get out of here."

"All right, take my leg as well if you want it," said Charley, as he drew Ned out; "why what's the matter, and how did you come here?"

Then he added quickly, as he put down his gun beside the others that lay at his feet—

"Here, take a pull at this before you speak; you look as if you want it."

He thrust his hand into the bosom of his ragged shirt, drew forth a leather flask and extracted the cork.

Ned placed it to his lips.

"Thank Heaven for that," he cried, as he gave it back.

"I brought it for Jumbo, together with this grub; but where's the other fellows?"

"I do not know," said Ned. "I succeeded in escaping from the hut where I found Minnie, and know nothing of them."

"Well, that fool of a Jumbo spoilt the whole affair, and we had to hook it into the forest. The others said they'd stop here till dark and then try to rescue you, and they sent me to bring the boat and the canoe back to where we landed this morning and get them some rifles, and now I've done so they have namussed."

"Are you sure is was here they promised to stay?" asked Ned. "A forest is not like a town, you know."

"Of course it ain't; but I marked the trees so that I should be sure. Oh, I'm right, but I'm licked. What's to be done? Halloa! is that blood on your face?"

"Yes; my head has been cut open by the villain who carried Minnie away, and I have been insensible for some time and tied hand and foot."

"I heard him give the order, but I didn't know you was hurt like that. And you managed to escape?"

"Yes, but alone, and so we shall have to go over the work again. I wish I knew where Harry was."

"So do I, and the others too, for it ain't no fun carrying a perfect arsenal of guns like that. Hush!" hissed Charley.

And he seized Ned's arm.

"What is it?" whispered Ned.

"Savages," replied Charley, in a whisper; "quick, into the bushes."

He parted the bushes as he spoke and thrust Ned among them, then handed him the guns one after another.

Still holding the branches apart, he listened intently.

The voices of the Indians came nearer.

Charley sprang into the bushes and crouched down beside Ned.

Peering through the interstices, the two watchers perceived four savages coming towards them, their eyes fixed on the earth.

Suddenly one of them paused and looked up.

It was Swift Arrow.

Ned recognised him by his stature and his paint.

"See," he said, "the signs are all around. Here is where they struggled; the branches are broken and lay on the ground. Look into those bushes; the pale-face may be killed and hidden there."

He pointed to the bushes where Ned and Charley lay.

"We're gone coons if we don't let them have it straight," said Charley, whispering the words in Ned's ears. "The rifles are all loaded. They're after you; wish they may get you."

"They won't," said Ned, hissing the words between his teeth and cocking the trigger of one of the rifles.

Charley followed suit with the other.

With the weapons pointed in the direction of the savages they waited.

Two of the companions of Swift Arrow advanced to within a few feet of the bushes, and then paused and gave utterance to a gruff—

"Ugh!"

"Seen us, by Jingo!" hissed Charley. "Let them have it—sharp."

As he spoke he thrust his rifle through the branches.

Ned did the same with his.

Swift Arrow and his companion bounded forward to their companions' side, their hands grasping their tomahawks.

Ned and Charley pulled the triggers of their rifles.

The two reports sounded as one.

The two foremost Indians sprang into the air, and Swift Arrow and the fourth savage turned to fly as their companions with a cry fell dead to the earth.

Ned flung aside the rifle he had used, seized another, and sprang through the bushes into the open.

"Stay!" he cried.

Swift Arrow turned at the sound of his voice.

"Ha, the white captive," he cried poising his hatchet for the throw.

He had come in search of Boaster and great indeed was his surprise to behold the youth he had left captive in his hut.

Ned gave him no time to recover from

his surprise, or throw his weapon, but covering him with his rifle, cried—

"Dog of an Indian, it is you who are now at my mercy. Die!"

And he fired as the savage yelled out his war-cry.

Charley, fearful of shooting Ned, flung down his rifle and springing from among the branches, dashed the tomahawk from the hands of the other savage, and throwing his arm round the Indian's neck, dragged down his head, and began punching away at his face with all his might.

Flinging his hands above his head, Swift Arrow pitched forward on his face, and his death-cry was echoed by loud yells from a score of Indian throats.

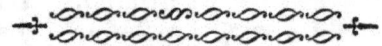

CHAPTER XXVIII.

IN WHICH SALLY PROVES HERSELF TOO MUCH FOR A COUPLE OF INDIANS.

As Boaster's gaze rested upon the flashing waters of the river he felt his heart sink within him.

All chance of rescue by the Indians he believed was now gone.

While they continued in the forest there was the probability of a surprise and recapture, but once on board the boat of his enemies, and a good start, the chances were few indeed of his Indian allies being able to wrest him from his captors.

Sally, turning suddenly noted the pallor of the bully's features and the quiver of his ashen lips.

"Don't like the look of things, do you Mr. Girl-stealer?" she sneered. "Begin to feel a little bit uncomfortable, don't you?"

"You will feel anything but comfortable soon, the whole lot of you," cried Bill, striving to put on a look of indifference, but making a very bad attempt indeed.

"Oh, shall we indeed," said Sally. "And pray, Mr. Boaster, how may that be?"

"You'll soon find out when Tiger Claw gets you in his talons," said Bill, "and that won't be long first."

"Won't it now," said Sally. "Think it will though. I'm just the girl that knows how to fool that red coon. Ha, ha!"

"You'll laugh the other side of your mouth before long," growled Bill.

"Jus' you be a little more perlite to dat young lady," said Jumbo, "or dis chile'll hab to make you. 'Spects I ain't going to 'low no one to cheek Sally, 'cos when Master Jack leabs her a young widder she's going to flop all her 'fections on dis nigger—yah, yah!"

"There wouldn't be another man left in the world then besides yourself," said 'Dolf.

"Dat observation just shows how jealous you are of dis chile's good looks," said Jumbo. "Why, bress your soul, I'se so hansum dat if I hadn't a-stepped it out of old Kentucky sharp dere'ud been a Solomon in 'Merica, for every bressed girl was a-wanting to marry me."

"Pity you came away then," said Sally.

"Dats trufe," said Jumbo.

"And what you've been telling us is lies," said Sally.

"Now jus' you hear dat," cried Jumbo; "as if dis chile could tell a lie. I couldn't do it, no not if I was to try eber so hard."

"Shut up," said Jack, "and keep a look-out for the boats."

"What de good ob looking for what you can't see?" said Jumbo. "Hold on, dar, or I'll pull your head slap off."

This was addressed to Bill, who suddenly made an attempt to jerk the rope from Jumbo's hand.

"Oh, you'll choke me!" gasped Bill, as the negro gave the rope such a fierce tug that it almost strangled the bully.

"Don't mind if I do," said Jumbo. "Don't you go for to try dat 'ere game on again, cos if you does off comes your head suah."

"It's no go," said Jack. "You'd better not try to escape or it will be the worse for you."

Boaster bit his lips and scowled.

"If I only had my hands free," he said.

"But then you ain't, you see," said Sally, "and what's more, you won't get them free either, leastways, not till you are safe in the boat."

"Do not bring pain and anguish upon yourself by useless resistance," said Bircher. "Always keep in mind the lesson I sought to instil into your bosom, that prudence is ever the better part of valour."

"Get out," said Sally, giving the tutor a push. "Wonder you wasn't prudent enough to keep away from these parts, for I don't know what good you are here."

"It was because I allowed my valour to——"

Sally and Jack shouted with laughter, and Mr. Bircher said no more.

"You have got about as much valour in your composition as a sick mouse," said Sally. "Lor' how I would like to see him and a wild cat have a spar."

"I guess den dat we'd better make a ring so as you and Massa Bircher can go at it at once," said Jumbo.

"What's that?" said Sally.

"Just what it am," said the negro.

"Do you mean to say as I'm a wild cat?" cried Sally.

"Guess this chile ain't going to tell a story and say you is a tame one," replied Jumbo.

"Jack," cried Sally, "will you stand by and hear me insulted like that? If you don't go for that nigger's scalp I will."

"Suah den if you gets it, it won't be much use to you," said Jumbo, grinning. "Why, bress de gal, dere ain't enough wool on dis here nigger's head to make a bustle for a young school miss let alone a great big——"

"Jack," cried Sally, "if you love me punch that nigger's head."

But the person addressed either did not or would not hear her request.

"What is that yonder?" said Jack, suddenly pointing up the stream. "There, just creeping round the island."

"That's," said Sally, shading her eyes with her hand, "that's the boats I take it."

"Come on then, sharp," said Jack. "Let's keep as close to the river as we can. Charley performed the journey safe then."

"Seems like it," said Harry, "and lost no time about it, or the boat would not be so far on its way back."

"Keep your eyes open as you go," said Sally. "The savages will naturally make for the river in pursuit of us, and may surprise us at any moment."

"It will be as well then if you do not talk," said Harry. "The sound of our voices may give note of our whereabouts."

They kept along the bank, following the direction the boats were taking.

But the black speck that had shot round the island grew smaller and smaller as the distance increased between them.

For every now and then they had to move away from the beach and go round clumps of trees and rocks that came right down to the water's edge.

In making one of these detours the party came upon an inlet or small bay running some three hundred yards into the forest, and which until our friends stood upon the very edge of its shore had been hidden from their gaze by the thick foliage that grew upon its bank.

This sight alone gratified Boaster.

"Hist!" cried Jack. "Back, back every one of you."

The others drew back.

"They are the canoes in which Tiger Claw and his braves left the island," said Sally. "A guard may be left over them. Keep concealed and I will go round and see."

She was about to move away, when turning to speak some order, she observed the expression on Bill's face that caused her hurriedly to say—

"Keep your revolver, Harry, pressed to that fellow's head. If he attempts to utter an alarm kill him. I don't like his looks."

"I will," said Harry, as he pressed his revolver against Bill's forehead.

A look of baffled fury came into the bully's eyes.

His object was defeated.

The hope that had sprung to his heart died within him.

Oh, how he cursed Sally in his heart, and vowed that if ever the tables should be turned that he would have a terrible vengeance alike on her and Harry Honour.

Sally Scrubbins, holding a revolver in her hand, started on her journey.

Jack made no attempt to follow her.

Her Indian life had given her a knowledge which he knew he could not possess, and rendered her the best fitted for the work she had in hand.

Stealthily as a panther she crept along behind the bushes that shaded the bay.

Not a twig snapped under her light footfall.

At length she threw herself flat on the earth, and gliding like a serpent along the ground, she parted the bushes and looked out upon the bay.

Her gaze wandered along the line of canoes.

They were empty.

Not one of them possessed an occupant.

But Sally was too well acquainted with savage customs to jump to the conclusion that the coast was clear for her and her friends to advance in safety.

Drawing back, she again crawled through the bushes for some distance, then once more made her way to the edge of the bay.

"I thought so," she muttered. "They are there."

Seated but a few yards from her, on the very edge of the bay, were two Indians.

They were smoking and bathing their feet in the water.

Sally suffered the branches to close before her and loosened the knife she wore at her belt.

"It's awful work," she muttered to herself; "but if I don't do it for them they'll do it for me, and perhaps be the destruction of all of us. If I were sure there were none others within call I'd go back without, but I ain't, and so there's no help for it."

Shifting her revolver to her left hand and her knife to her right, she crept towards the Indians till she lay within a foot of the nearest.

Then she rose to her feet.

Swiftly as had been her movements, the quick ears of the savages caught the sound, and they sprang to their feet with a gruff "ugh!" and parted the bushes.

To hesitate Sally knew was to be lost.

A moment and it would be too late.

The Indians had seen her.

Their hands flew to the handles of their tomahawks.

But swift as a flash Sally raised her knife.

It gleamed before the eyes of one of the savages, and then was buried up to its hilt in his bosom.

Ere she could withdraw it his companion seized her by the throat and whirled his hatchet over his head.

Sally gave a shriek.

She felt her last hour had come.

She closed her eyes and pressed the revolver against the Indian's bosom.

Her finger touched the trigger.

The grasp on her throat relaxed.

The tomahawk fell from the hand of the savage, grazing her shoulder in its fall.

Then the savage sank down in a heap at her feet, beside his comrade, and Sally, holding the smoking weapon in her hand, staggered backwards into the arms of Jack the conjuror, who, fearful for her safety, had followed her just in time to receive the half fainting form on his bosom.

CHAPTER XXIX.

IN WHICH NED GAINS THE BOAT AND MEETS WITH FRIENDS AND ENEMIES.

THE sound of the savage war-whoop told Ned and Charley how great was their danger, and how necessary it was that they should make themselves scarce.

So Charley flung his opponent heavily to the earth, and turned to seize the guns he had hidden in the bushes.

The savage, however, caught the ragged youth by the leg as he moved away, and Charley, losing his balance, came down with a crash by the Indian's side.

Quick as lightning the savage was over his prostrate body, and his knife raised just above Charley's heart.

Ned saw his friend's danger.

Uttering a cry he swung his rifle round, and striking the Indian with the butt of the weapon full on the temple, sent the knife flying from his grasp and his body lifeless across the plunging form of the white youth.

"'IS THAT THE DOG THE PALE-FACE MAIDEN WOULD HOE THE CORN FOR?' CRIED TIGER CLAW."

To fling the Indian off him was the work of a moment, and then Charley sprang to his feet.

"Collar the traps and scarper," he cried. "Hear the beggars, they'll have us if we don't mind; double, sharp."

Even as he spoke Charley gathered up the rifles and handed them to Ned.

Then seizing upon Jack's robe and tinsel crown, which he hurriedly placed on himself, Charley snatched a couple of guns from Ned and cried—

"Come on, quick! This way, this way!"

Ned was fain to leave the vicinity of the spot where he knew that Minnie was a captive, but to remain he felt sure was certain death now, so with a sigh he dashed after his companion.

They had not gone far when a loud wailing sound told them that the savages had discovered the dead bodies of their chief and his companions.

"Not a minute too soon," said Charley. "If we hadn't took our hook when we did they'd have copped us for certain. Guess they don't like the look of affairs by the row they are making."

Ned made no reply, his head pained him, and his thoughts were with poor Minnie.

"Scissors, talk about a dozen cats having a concert, if that yelling don't beat all the pussy music in creation I'm no judge of sweet sounds," cried Charley.

"They'll be yelling at our heels in a moment, I fear," said Ned.

"Very likely," said Charley, "but it can't be helped. Hang those twigs, they're always catching in my coat-tails."

And he gave the robe a pull from a branch to which it had clung, and split it from top to bottom.

"Throw it away," said Ned; "it only hampers your movements."

"What," cried Charley, "throw away a coat when I haven't had one for so long? Ask a starving man to fling away his dinner. Not I."

"Are we in the right route to meet our friends?" asked Ned.

"All right, trust to me," said Charley. "I know just where to spot the boats, never fear."

"I'm afraid we shall never reach them," said Ned, as a blood-curdling yell from a score of savage throats broke upon their ears and awoke the echoes of the woods.

"Jerusalem! they're after us now," said Charley. "It's a run for it and no mistake."

Together they started off at a run, crashing through the branches heedless of torn garments and scratched limbs.

But nearer and nearer came the cries of the pursuing savages, panting for the life blood of the lads who had slain their chief.

On, on, without a word now.

It was a race for life, and Ned forgot his wounds, forgot all but that death was pursuing them.

"Hurrah, hurrah!" yelled Charley, as breaking cover they came suddenly upon the bank of the river, and saw some few yards from the shore the boat and the canoe, the rowers resting upon their oars and their faces turned to learn the meaning of the shout they heard from the shore.

"Pull in, you beggars, pull in!" yelled Charley, motioning to those in the boats to come nearer and take them on board.

"Quick, quick," cried Ned, "we are pursued."

The crews bent to their oars and the boats neared the bank.

But again came the loud yell of the savages.

"Holy Moses, look alive," cried Charley, or we shall be gobbled up."

As the boats drifted in Ned flung his rifles on board.

Charley did the same.

"Jump, jump," cried one of the rowers, gesticulating wildly.

Ned turned his head.

There was a crushing of branches behind him and he saw the reason of the man's motion.

The Indians had broken cover.

Fearful was the yell that burst from their throats as they caught sight of Ned and Charley.

Not a dozen yards separated them.

They dashed forward to secure their prey, but both Ned and Charley had realised their danger, and without a moment's hesitation plunged into the stream

A yell of fury burst from the throats of the baffled savages as they saw half-a-dozen hands stretched forth to drag Ned and Charley into the boat.

They hurriedly fitted arrows to their bows.

"Quick, quick, give them a volley," gasped Ned as he was drawn over the side.

The rowers let go their oars and seized the guns.

The next moment they delivered a volley, and the savages turned and fled into the cover of the woods.

But from there they sent forth a shower of arrows, two of which struck the side of the boat.

"It's no use wasting powder," said Ned, as the rowers loaded again, "so long as we can't see where to fire, and they are sheltered by the trees. Wait till I give the order, and keep the boat meanwhile under the cover of that high ground."

He pointed to where the shore rose somewhat higher from the river.

Still the Arrows came hurtling through the air, but passed harmlessly over the boat.

"Have Jack, or Sally, or any of the others been seen?" asked Ned.

There was a general shake of the heads.

"I hope no danger has befallen them," said Ned. "If they are safe and expect to find the boats here we cannot leave this part, and to remain is danger if not death."

"Guess we're in a bit of a mess," said Charley. "If we stop here we may get chawed up ourselves, and if we take our hook we may leave the others to get chawed up instead. Well, there's only one thing that's cheering, and that is, if they have to knock under and we don't, I shall be heir to Jack's togs."

"Very gratifying that, certainly," said Ned.

"As you say, so it is," replied Charley. "Guess this red coat suits my complexion first rate. Halloa! what the devil's that?"

Away went the tinsel crown flying off Charley's head, shot away by an Indian arrow.

"Serves you right for coveting another man's property," said Ned, as he levelled his rifle in the direction the arrow had come from, but waited to pull the trigger till he could detect either the form of an Indian or a movement of the vegetation that should proclaim the spot where the savage was sheltered.

"Oh blow it!" said Charley; "if these togs are only fit for a target, off they go."

And Charley instantly flung off the red coat that made him so conspicuous an object in the boat.

"Would to Heaven they would come, or that I knew where they were!" said Ned, speaking rather to himself than to any one else.

"Who—the Indians?" said Charley.

"No, our friends."

"Oh," said Charley, "I thought you meant the reds, because there ain't much mistake about where they are, I reckon."

Keeping their gaze fixed in the direction from whence the last arrow had come, the party in the boat waited rifle in hand, wondering whether their foes meant to fire or break cover again or whether they had retreated.

"I expect they fancy it's no go," said Charley, "and have gone back to hold a palaver over their pals we wiped out so neatly."

But as if to contradict this a body of savages suddenly made their appearance, crawling over the high mound just under which the boat lay on its oars.

A cry from one of the Indians in the canoe gave timely warning of their presence, and before they could spring up and send a shower of arrows into the boat, half-a-dozen rifles belched forth and as many bullets ploughed through their recumbent forms.

With a yell the savages sprang to their feet and plunged down the bank.

But as they did so a volley was poured into their backs, and as they turned in consternation at finding a foe in their rear, those in the boats uttered a cry of surprise and joy.

Over the mound plunged Jack, Harry, and 'Dolf, giving utterance to a loud hurrah as they ran.

The next moment Jumbo dragged Boaster into view, and Ned uttered a cry of exultation when he saw that one of his enemies was at last in his power.

CHAPTER XXX.

IN WHICH THE RED CHIEF BECOMES RED-HANDED.

"WHY comes not my brother Swift Arrow to welcome Tiger Claw and his braves when they return to his wigwams loaded with trophies of the chase, to make a feast in which our tribes may join ere we seek our hunting-grounds by the great falls? Is my brother angry that he hides his head and speaks no word of welcome?"

Such were the words that a stalwart warrior addressed to the Indian whom Ned had induced to sever his bonds and allow him to escape from the hut in which he had been a prisoner.

"And where is the white man I left to guard the pale-faced girl when I went forth with my friend Tiger Claw?" asked a young man, fixing a glass in his eye and scrutinising the painted features of the Indians through it, to the mingled amusement and disgust of the savages congregated around the door of Swift Arrow's hut.

It was Mr. Phinicky Phopps, who even in these savage wilds was attired in a ridiculously loud London fashion, and used his eyeglass more from habit than necessity.

The Indian addressed bowed his head and replied—

"The Great Spirit has been angry with Swift Arrow and his braves, and the hand of the pale-face has turned red in their blood."

"What?" cried Phopps.

"Let my brother speak so that the ears of Tiger Claw may drink in his words!" cried the chief. "Let his talk be straight as the bound of the panther not crooked like the motion of the serpent."

The savage then told the chief all that had transpired since he had gone forth from the village with his braves.

Of the visit of the white conjuror to the village.

Of the attempt of Ned to rescue Minnie.

His escape; the absense of Boaster and the finding of the dead bodies of Swift Arrow and his braves in the forest, and

his suspicion that those who had slain the Indians had also killed their white friend.

On hearing this the chief's fingers closed tightly over his tomahawk, and a savage and revengeful look gleamed in his eyes.

Phopps however smiled and rubbed his hands together.

Boaster dead, he would possess Minnie and was for ever rid of the man who, once his tool, was now his master.

No better news could he have heard than that the man he had learned to both hate and fear was no more.

"Swift Arrow was my brother," said Tiger Claw, "and he who slays my brother or my friend must die. I have spoken."

Then turning to his followers he said—

"The feast must wait till the scalps of my brother's foes hang at our belts. Let my braves string their bows and point their arrows, and get ready to march on the trail of our common enemy."

"I don't think it's worth your while, Tiger Claw," said Phopps; "what are the lives of a few savages?—and as for the white man he was a rascal and deserved his fate."

Tiger Claw swung himself round on the speaker and fixed his gaze fiercely upon him.

"Are these the words of a pale-face," he said; "would he not avenge his white brother?"

"Well, yes, of course, if he was a proper sort of a fellow, you know; but the fact is, Tiger Claw, he was getting a little too fast, and if some one else hadn't put him out of the way I should have had to do it myself."

"Was he not your friend?" asked the chief.

"Yes, at one time, but I can't say he showed much friendship lately; you see I paid him to do a certain service for me, and when he'd done it he ought to have been satisfied with the pay, but he wasn't. He began to crow over me, and try to get the girl away from me, and indeed if he hadn't been taken off as he was I should have had to offer you something handsome to get rid of him for me, for I was getting tired of his impudence and bounce."

The chief never moved his eyes from the face of Phopps.

Savage though he was the words of the exquisite disgusted him.

He saw in a moment that Phopps expected to benefit by Boaster's absence or death.

In fact he could read plainly that having got the youth to aid him in his villainy he was now only too glad to get rid of him.

And for what?

That he might obtain Minnie.

All the savage chivalry of the chief rose against the white man.

He had resolved to wrest the poor girl from both Phopps and Boaster and force her to share his own wild life, but still he was disgusted with Phopps.

He put forth his arm and seized the startled swell by the shoulders.

"Dog," he hissed "Tiger Claw can see into your white heart and knows why you speak thus. He will not aid you to steal the pale-face maiden, for he has said she shall share his wigwam, and the coward who covets her must die."

"What," gasped Phopps, "would you rob me of my prize?"

"She is too good, too beautiful, for the bride of a white-hearted coward," he replied; "she is mine. I have spoken."

"Never," cried Phopps, foaming with rage, and in his anger becoming unguarded in his words. "I stole her from her home; I have paid for all the trouble she has cost me, and my revenge on those I hated and who loved her, and she shall be mine or I will stab her to the heart."

"Does the white dog threaten?" cried the chief.

"I do; she is mine, and woe to him who would take her from me. Who are you? If you are a chief you are but my servant, for I paid you for what you have done for me. Your bride! as though a white girl would ever look with aught but disgust and loathing on a red-skinned savage."

"Has the white dog spoken?" said Tiger Claw.

"He has; but this more he will say; I need your aid no longer and I will take the white girl away with me and my servants at once. Here is pay for your services and we are quits."

And as he spoke Phinicky Phopps took several gold pieces from his pocket and offered them to the chief.

Tiger Claw motioned to one of his followers to take them, wh h he did.

"Has the white dog no more to say?" he asked.

"Nothing."

"It is well," said Tiger Claw; "then can the red chief speak, and let the white man mark his words. The pale-face maiden goes with Tiger Claw to the camping-grounds of his tribe, and the body of the white dog who defies the red chief shall roast in the fire that my braves shall kindle. I have spoken."

"You dare not," yelled Phopps, "I am a white man."

"And a dog and a coward," cried the savage, "and you shall die."

And the chief drew his tomahawk.

Phopps saw his danger, and rendered desperate he drew a revolver and levelled it at the head of the chief.

But ere he could pull the trigger a couple of stalwart braves threw themselves upon him and pinioned his arms behind him.

One of the savages, taking off his head-dress of feathers, put on the hat of Phopps and then with a chuckle forced his own head covering over the brow of the swell.

"You greasy villains!" yelled Phopps.

Then he stopped short, for the savages brandished their tomahawks threateningly above his head.

At that moment a scream of terror caused the chief to turn, and he saw the trembling form and agonised face of Minnie Sash standing in the doorway of the nearest wigwam.

With a bound he sprang to her side, and seizing her arm he dragged her into the circle of Indians, and pointing with his tomahawk to Phopps, he cried—

"Is that the dog the pale-face maiden would hoe the corn for or weave the moccasin? Is that the coward on whose bosom she would rest and into whose ears she would sing the song when he returns from the fight or the chase? Is the Indian a fool that he should ask? No. The pale-face loves the brave red chief, and she shall be his squaw."

Minnie, speechless, terrified, half fainting, drew back in horror.

A chuckle broke from the lips of Tiger Claw, and holding the girl at arm's length he took a step forward and poised his weapon.

"Mercy! what would you do?" shrieked Minnie.

"Slay the dog with the white heart and the crooked tongue," he replied.

All the courage of Phopps vanished in a moment and sinking on his knees, he cried—"Mercy, mercy, I——"

But the prayer died on his lips as the tomahawk of the red chief crashed heavily into his brain.

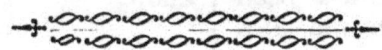

CHAPTER XXXI.

IN WHICH BOASTER FINDS HIMSELF IN A FIX.

THE surprise into which the Indians were thrown by the sudden appearance of Harry and his companions made them easy victims to the desperate onslaught of Jack and his companions, and the unerring rifles of Ned and Charley.

In less than a couple of minutes those who were not killed or severely wounded had fled into the forest.

While the fracas raged Boaster made desperate efforts to escape, but Jumbo held so tightly to the rope that if he had not desisted he would certainly have been strangled.

To pursue those who fled would have been madness, so the boats being brought close in shore, the party were taken on board.

"Thank Heaven for your timely arrival," said Ned, pressing the hand of Harry. "You saved us to a certainty."

"Glad to see you again, old man. But how did you escape?"

"I'll tell you another time, Harry," said Ned. "How did you get hold of Boaster?"

Harry told him.

Boaster had been placed in the stern of the boat, and Jumbo still held the rope that bound him.

"Get out into the stream," said Ned, "lest we have another visit, and then we will hold a council as to what can be done."

As he saw the rowers set to work to obey his order he walked over to where Boaster sat.

"Your triumph was but short-lived," said Ned, addressing him.

"Was it?" replied Boaster, sulkily.

"Yes, thank Heaven, it was," replied Ned. "Your villainy has been foiled."

"Perhaps," said Boaster. "Don't make too sure."

"You are in my power now," said Ned.

"I know that," replied the bully.

"And do you expect me to have any mercy on you?"

"If I did I might be disappointed," replied Boaster.

"Did you have any on me," asked Ned.

The bully did not reply.

"No," said Ned, "never; and why then should I have any on you?"

"I don't ask it," said Boaster.

"Because you know you don't deserve it," replied Ned. "Were I as revengeful and merciless as yourself I should kill you where you sit."

"Dat's just what I should do, sah," said Jumbo.

"It would only be a just punishment for all his crimes," said Ned.

"Dat's de trufe," said Jumbo. "Jus' you say de word, Massa Ned, and I'll drop him ober into de water and hold de rope till him kick de bucket."

"I cannot murder in cold blood," said Ned.

"Of course you are very tender-hearted," sneered Boaster.

"I thank Heaven I am not wholly heartless," replied Ned. "But of this rest assured. If any harm comes to poor Minnie I will kill you."

"I cannot help what harm may come to her," replied Boaster. "I could prevent it when I was near her, but now you hold me prisoner here if harm befall her it is you who will be to blame."

Ned turned away from him with disgust, and joined Harry and Jack.

Charley and 'Dolf came over to the side of Jumbo.

"Well, my charming nigger, it does my eyesight good to gaze once more on your ugly profile," said Charley. "I was afraid you was a gone coon and busted up."

"Dat's talk what's not perlite," replied Jumbo. "Dis yer chile's been doing his duty and making ob himself a hero."

"Shouldn't wonder but what they'll put you up a statue one of these days," said Charley.

"Guess dat's what dey will do," replied the nigger, grinning.

"Only they won't know where to fix it." said Charley.

"Why in de very centre of de biggest square, suah."

"Oh, that ain't likely."

"Why not?"

"'Cos the kids, you know, play in the squares," said Charley.

"What dat matter? All de better, 'cos dey can see it dere."

"But it wouldn't do to let them see it, you kuow."

"Why not?"

"They'd think it was the devil, and it would frighten them into fits," said Charley.

"Guess dat's one to you," said Jumbo. "Jus' you sit down here and collar hold ob dis rope so as dis cove can't slope, and I'll punch your head."

"Ain't got time," said Charley. "Besides, if the devil ain't quite got hold of him yet his brother has, and he can't be in better hands."

"Dat's two to you," said Jumbo; "but you look out. If dis child don't hab you den he don't, dat's all."

"Quite right," said 'Dolf. "If you don't you don't."

"Look heah, flunkey, dis chile don't want no more ob your say. Jus' you keep your place, and don't you presume to talk to gemmen like me."

"What?" cried 'Dolf.

"Gemmen."

"Oh," said 'Dolf, "a pretty specimen of a gentleman certainly. I could make a better one out of putty."

"Jus' you go and get dis chile some grub," said Jumbo. "If you don't I'll

hab to eat you, for I'm mortal hungry."

"I ain't," said Charley. "Do you know why, old man?"

"No, I don't."

"I'll tell you. 'Cos I eat yours as well as mine."

"Dat's true, I know, 'cos dat's what you always do."

"Yes," said Charley, "and I daresay I always shall. It's a way I've got, you know."

"Don't I just," said Jumbo. "Guess it's bery little anybody gets where you is. Wonder you ain't eat yourself afore now, and belieb you would, only you so tough and so nasty it 'ud make you sick."

This badinage was broken in upon by Ned coming aft, accompanied by Harry, Jack, and Bircher.

"Boaster," said Ned, "if you would save yourself from a terrible fate you will restore Minnie Sash to me uninjured."

"How can I?" said Boaster.

"You are in league with Phopps and the Indians, and as you must have considerable control over their actions, Harry has proposed that you should prevail upon them to give her up to my protection. If you succeed, base as your conduct has been, I promise to set you ashore."

"And if I failed?" said Boaster.

"Then we have decided to hang you from a branch of a tree, and leave your body to be pecked at by the birds of the air and your bones to whiten in the sun.

Boaster shuddered.

But he replied—

"How can I do anything, bound and captive as I am?"

"You can write."

"Well?"

"Indite a letter to Phopps. We will find some means of getting it conveyed to him. Tell him in it that if Minnie is restored to me you are at liberty to depart, but that if he refuses you die."

"And do you think he would give her up?" said Boaster.

"Ay, to save the life of his fellow-villain," replied Ned.

"Then you don't know him," said Boaster. "He'd be only too glad to keep her for himself. Give me my liberty and I swear to send her to you."

"I cannot do that."

"Why not—what's to prevent it?"

"I dare not trust you," said Ned. "A liar is never to be trusted."

"Then you'll never get her," said Boaster. "It's your only chance, and if you won't take advantage of it it's your fault not mine."

"Perhaps it would be best to let him go, and trust to his word," said Bircher. "You know, Nimble, that there is an old proverb that 'it is a long lane that has no turning,'" and Boaster, havivg seen the error of his ways, may repent in time and——'

"Shut up!" said Harry. "You forget that 'once a fool is to be always a fool,' or you wouldn't believe there was such a thing as repentance in Bill Boaster."

"I will neither believe in his honour nor his truth," said Ned; "but I believe in his fear of death, and by Heaven! if he finds not the means to place Minnie in my hands, he dies!"

"Then let me go and I'll do it," said Bill.

"No," replied Ned. "I keep you here till Minnie comes; then I promise you to let you go. But mark me—and you know I will keep my word—if she be not given into my hands in two days from this, I'll hang you as sure as the sun will rise to-morrow, though my own life pay the forfeit of the deed.

Bill read in Ned's look and his determined tones that he would keep his word, and his heart sank within his guilty bosom.

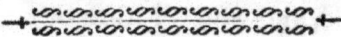

CHAPTER XXXII.

IN WHICH BIRCHER SHOWS HIS KINDNESS AND BOASTER SHOWS HIS CRUELTY.

NIGHT was stealing on apace, and Ned, now that the excitement had somewhat abated, began to experience considerable pain from his wound.

The rest of the party were tired and hungry, and all felt assured that there was little that could be done till daylight.

So Ned gave orders for Boaster to be taken to the cabin and the boat and the canoe to make for an island about two miles further down the river, where Sally said there was a small bay in which they could take shelter for the night.

While the boats made for this island the friends partook of refreshment, and Boaster's arms were unbound to allow him to eat.

But the meal ended, his arms were again secured and the rope that bound them made fast to a staple in the boats timbers, but in such a way as to allow him to take up any position he pleased.

But for the fact that the Indians would be on the alert, an attempt would have been made to rescue Minnie during the darkness; but as affairs had turned out it was thought better to lead the savages to imagine the white men had taken their departure from those parts, and ises perhaps throw them off their guard.

By the time the meal was ended and every preparation made to guard against surprise and be ready for any sudden emergency, the boats had entered the little bay in the island, the entrance to which was almost hidden, by the dense vegetation that grew on its banks and stretched out over the water.

The vessels being made fast, a guard was set and the tired travellers sought refreshment in sleep

Sally, who would insist in taking her turn with the others was on the watch together with Bircher, the former leaning on the bow of the boat while the tutor kept guard in the cabin where Ned slumbered and Boaster tossed uneasily on the floor.

The breathing of Ned proclaimed that he slept soundly, and Bill suddenly sitting up, motioned Bircher to draw near him.

The tutor bent his head to hear what he had to say.

"Mr. Bircher," whispered Bill; "I've done you many a good turn in England Will you not do me one now?"

"What do you wish me to do?" asked Bircher.

"Loosen my arms, the cords cut into my flesh, and I cannot sleep."

"I dare not," replied Bircher, "oh, how could you act as you have done, and thus bring disgrace upon my teaching! It pains me to see you thus, but your own wickedness has brought it all about."

"Don't preach," said Bill; "if you had not often shielded me in my wrong-doing, I might have acted differently. If at school you did not positively encourage me to assail Ned Nimble, you yet shielded me from punishment."

"I am sorry to say I did," returned the tutor.

"You know you hated him."

"I did."

"And you do now in your heart."

"No, I do not," said Bircher, "for I have learned that though one of the most mischievous, he is one of the noblest hearted lads in the world."

"Is he?" sneered Bill.

"Yes, and but for him I might now be starving on a foriegn shore, and when I think how unjustly I have acted to him in the past I feel ashamed of myself, and vow that I will atone by doing all that lays in my power to aid him now."

Boaster turned his face away to hide his passion-couvulsed features and the murderous expression that gleamed in his eyes.

Suppressing with difficulty his intense rage, Boaster said—

"Then you won't release my arms?— you'll let me lie here with the cords cutting into my flesh and causing me awful pain. Very well, only I did think that for the sake of old times you might try to render my captivity less painful and cruel than it is."

"I'll speak to Ned about it when he awakes," said Bircher.

"As well ask a tiger not to claw you," growled Bill; "never mind, I'm sorry I asked you; it's the way of the world, friends become foes when a fellow's down, and you are like all the rest."

"Now, Boaster, you know if I thought it safe to do so I would loosen your hands," said Bircher.

"Safe! what do you fear? tied up here as I am, and with enemies all around me; loosening the cords is not taking them off; I don't ask you to do that, because I know you won't, I only ask you to loosen them a little, to give room to my swelling flesh."

"If I thought that was all——"

"What more can it be," interrupted Bill; "but there, at school you liked to see a boy tortured, and it's not to be wondered at that you still feel a pleasure in seeing a fellow in pain."

"Now, Bill, don't say that, I'm sure I should be only too glad to prevent you suffering."

"Then loosen the cords an inch—only an inch will do; just see how my hands have swollen. I haven't any feeling left in my fingers; they are dead and numbed and I couldn't use them even if I had a chance."

Bircher's heart began to soften towards his old ally.

Not for the world would he have done anything to injure or annoy our hero, since his kindness to him.

But he was weak and easily persuaded and he bent down and placed his hand on the cords that bound the arms of Boaster.

"They are tight," he whispered "I'll wake Nimble and ask him to have them loosened."

"Yes, because you know he hates me, and instead of loosening them would have them drawn tighter if that were possible. There, I'm sorry I condescended to ask a favour of you, I might have known that you would not grant it."

"Boaster, I'm sure I——"

"There don't try to excuse your heartlessness," said Bill, "I know you of old and was a fool to speak to you."

And Boaster flung himself round as if disgusted in having asked the favour.

Bircher hesitated.

He felt pained that Bill should imagine he gloried in his suffering.

He felt annoyed too that he himself could imagine for a moment that by loosening the cords he would allow the prisoner to regain his liberty.

He felt that Bill must look upon him as a coward, who feared that by permitting a free circulation of the blood, he gave him a chance to assail him.

And so the tutor laid his revolver on the floor of the cabin and set about loosening the cords.

Bill pretended to be unaware of what he was doing, but with his face turned to the floor and his teeth set hard, he waited the slightest relaxation of the pressure of his bonds.

Well was it for him that Bircher saw not the expression of his face or the fiendish gleam in his eye.

Had he done so he would have quickly put another knot into the cord, seized his discarded revolver and held it pressed to the bully's head.

But Bircher saw not the look nor suspected the other's motive, and so he kept to his work, believing that he was only doing that which Ned would order to be done when he awoke.

But he was quickly undeceived.

As Boaster felt the cords loosen he put forth all his strength, and drawing the rope through the hands of the tutor freed his arms.

The next moment he had clutched Bircher's revolver, and springing to his feet levelled it at the tutor's head.

"A word, a breath, and you die!" he hissed.

Bircher recoiled, terrified and horror-stricken at the fiendish look and deter-termined mien of the desperate youth.

"Boaster," he gasped.

"This then to ensure your silence, fool."

As Boaster spoke he turned the weapon in his hand, and striking Bircher a crashing blow, bounded from the cabin.

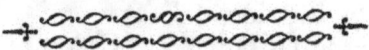

CHAPTER XXXIII.

IN WHICH BOASTER GOES FIRST AND JUMBO FOLLOWS AFTER.

"HALLOA, there! who are you? Why blest if it ain't—no you don't, my hearty."

And as Sally Scrubbins jerked out these words, she sprang upon Bill as he ran along the deck and seized him by the arm.

"Back, you she fiend, or I'll kill you!" hissed Bill, trying to shake off her hold.

"She what? What did you call me? I'll she fiend you!" cried Sally.

"If you're tired of life then, I'll end——" gasped Bill, as he jerked up the revolver and fired.

But Sally's grip on his arm sent the bullet far over her head.

"You murderous vampire!" cried Sally. "Help, Jack! help here! the rascal is trying to escape."

"And so he will," cried Bill, fiercely "Let go, you tiger cat there," and he tore himself free and again levelled the revolver.

Bang!

But Sally escaped again.

She saw her danger, and as Boaster raised his arm, flung herself to the deck.

The moment he had fired, Bill turned, dashed along the deck, and sprang upon the bulwarks, thinking he could jump from the boat to the shore, deceived in the distance by the vegetation which stretched out into the bay.

Well he knew the cries of Sally and the sound of the shots he had fired would arouse all on board.

He had not a moment to lose.

Once off the boat he might escape.

He gathered himself for the spring and bounded into the air.

But as he rose a hand gripped his ankle, and a voice cried, "No you don't, suah; you don't foole dis chile."

Down came Boaster, but not on to the deck.

He had sprung out too far for that, and down he shot into the waters of the bay.

Jumbo too, intent upon securing him, clung to his hold, and before he knew where he was, the black was dragged over the side of the boat.

Then the nigger let go his hold.

The cry he gave utterance to as he felt himself flying downwards, was stifled by the water that rushed into his mouth.

Up he rose, striking his head against the boat's side.

"Golly, take dat," yelled the negro, imagining that it was Bill who had hit him, and launching out his arm to retaliate. "Gor-a-mighty! oh, yah."

Jumbo had hit the boat's timbers, and they being too hard to make any impression on, he had only cut his knuckles and benumbed his hands and arms.

"Quick, a light here, a light!" cried a voice on deck.

It was Ned who spoke.

Aroused by the shouts and cries, he had sprung from his bed to find Bircher bleeding on the floor of the cabin and Boaster fled.

In a moment he had realised what had happened, and hurried on deck.

The noise in the water brought him to the vessel's side.

Even as he called for a light, Jack, Harry, Charley, and 'Dolf joined him.

"What's the matter, Ned?" cried Harry.

"What's up?" echoed Jack.

"A light! get a light!" cried Ned; "Boaster's escaped, but I can hear some one in the water."

"Den jus' chuck out dat ere paw ob yours, Massa Ned," cried Jumbo, " or brest if dis child'll eber lib to be hung."

"It's Jumbo," cried Charley.

"Yes," said Sally, coming to his side, "it's the nigger, but the other ain't far off. I tried to stop him but he fired at me, and jumped over the side."

"The rascal, and I thought I had him secure," said Ned. "Oh, here's a light."

'Dolf, who had turned away to obtain a light, now returned with a lamp from the cabin.

"Hold it over the side, 'Dolf."

'Dolf did as he was requested.

The rays of the lamp streamed down upon the upturned face of Jumbo as he clung with one hand to the boat's side, and upon the surrounding water.

But Boaster was nowhere to be seen.

"Bill has given us the go-by," said Harry.

"So it seems," said Ned, "but whether he is drowned or on the island is doubtful."

"If on the island we shall capture him again. He can't get away without a boat," said Jack.

"True," said Ned, "it is too far for him to swim to enable him to join his savage friends. But how came Jumbo in the water?"

"Better ask him," said Harry, "when he's aboard again."

Sally had taken the lamp, and 'Dolf was aiding Charley to assist the negro to the deck.

Charley, having made several attempts to reach the head or arm of the negro and failed, had clambered on to the side of the boat and lowered himself head downwards over it, trusting to 'Dolf to keep a firm hold of his legs to prevent him falling into the water.

"Hold tight, good luck to you!" cried Charley, as he made a grab at Jumbo's extended arm.

"Jus you hole tight," said the negro, "Catch hold, quick!"

But before Charley could catch hold, Jumbo was out of sight.

On letting go his grasp of the boat, he had sunk like a stone.

Missing his hand Charley made a grab for his head, but Jumbo's hair was too short to give his friend a hold.

"The poor devil will be drowned," said Ned, "if something ain't done. Stand aside, I'll fetch him out"

And Ned sprang on to the side of the boat.

"Hold on, Ned; here he is," said Harry, catching hold of Ned, as the head of the negro appeared again above the surface.

"Give us your hand," said Charley.

"Golly, make haste and take it," gasped Jumbo, "I've got such a lot of water in me dat it won't let this chile swim long, suah."

"That's it; I've got you; hold on, 'Dolf, good luck to you."

"All right, I'll stick to you," said 'Dolf.

"Haul up then."

"Here, Jack, lend a hand," said Sally.

"Like a bird," said Jack.

And seizing hold of Charley, he dragged him up on to the top of the side of the boat.

Charley stuck tight to his friend, and Jumbo's head came with a loud bang against the side of the vessel.

"Gor-a-mighty, what's dat noise," cried the negro.

'Dolf now seized the African, and in another moment he stood on the deck, the water running from him in streams.

Seeing Jumbo safe, Ned said—

"Come with me, Harry, and let's see to Bircher; Jack and 'Dolf will look after the nigger."

"But what about Bill?" said Harry.

"We can do nothing till it's light. Jumbo where's Boaster, do you know for certain?"

"Guess he's in de water," said Jumbo "dats where he was when I went arter him."

"Did he sink do you think?" asked Ned.

"Dis chile rather tink he did," replied Jumbo, "dis yer woolly nob ob mine jammed him down to de bottom, and I calkerlate dat it rammed him so tight into de mud dat he'll nebber get out ob it—yah, yah!"

"Get out," said Charley.

"But dis chile say he won't get out; golly, didn't I feel him go in about half-a-mile, suah!"

"If he rose again after he sank, he'd certainly strike out for the shore," said Harry.

"And that I expect he has done," said Ned; "however, we cannot pursue him till daylight; it is an unfortunate circumstance, but it can't be helped."

"How could he have got out of his bonds?" said Harry.

"I know not," replied Ned; "perhaps Bircher can enlighten us, but I am afraid not, for evidently the villain surprised him and laid him senseless before he was aware he was free of the ropes."

"Is Bircher hurt much then?" said Harry.

"Badly, I fear; but come on, dear boy, and let us see what's best to be done for him."

And Ned led the way to the cabin.

CHAPTER XXXIV.

IN WHICH JUMBO AND CHARLEY GO SHARES.

"WELL, you are all right now, old man," said Jack, addressing Jumbo, as Ned and Harry disappeared into the cabin.

"Don't you tell no lies," said Jumbo, "dis yar chile is all wrong."

"Why, what's the matter with you, you're safe on deck, ain't you?"

"Didn't say I wasn't," replied Jumbo.

"Get that coat off, and I'll ask Ned for a drop of brandy for you, and your ducking won't do you any harm."

"It will do him lots of good," said 'Dolf.

"Hows dat?" asked Jumbo.

"It will wash that elegant pair of drawers you wear."

"Don't you make remarks about 'nother gen'lman's clothes," said Jumbo, as he wrung the water out of the tail of his coat.

"Here, hold on mate," cried Charley, "don't twist that coat-tail like that; remember you've got my Sunday suit on, and I don't want it spoilt."

"Oh, your Sunday suit, am it?" said Jumbo, as he drew the soaking wet garments off him with some difficulty.

"Yes, it is."

"Den perhaps you'll jes take care ob it," said Jumbo.

And he flung the wet coat in Charley's face.

"Pah," cried Charley; "you ungrateful beggar, is that how you reward a fellow for getting you out of the bay."

Sally had gone into the cabin, and Jumbo took off the rest of his wet garments."

"You said the coat was yours, didn't you?" he cried, "and so I give it you, dese here drawers are yours as well. Dere dey are, take 'em. An' now perhaps you'll jes hand over de togs you got on. 'Cos according to 'greement when you claims de coat I claims de trousers. Fair's fair, you know, so jes hand over.

"Don't you wish you may get 'em," said Charley.

"Dat's right, ain't it?" asked Jumbo, turning to Jack and 'Dolf.

"Of course it is," said Jack.

"Rather," put in 'Dolf.

"Walker," said Charley, "I ain't such a fool as that."

"What dis chile to wear den?" asked Jumbo. "'Taint likely I can only wear dis skin suit when dere's a lady aboard."

"Get 'Dolf to lend you a suit of his clothes," said Charley.

"What!" cried Jumbo; "do you tink dis cullered gentleman would wear a flunkey's breeches? Well, you must tink I've come to suffin."

"I'll take good care you don't either," said 'Dolf.

"I'll lend you something to put on," said Jack; "there's my red robe, how will that do?"

"If it's perfectly clean I'll condescend to wear it," said Jumbo.

"Clean!" said Jack. "Why you don't think I am——"

"Don't you get in a passion, Massa Jack," interrupted the negro. "No, ob course I don't mean to defer anytink against you; but den, you see, dat Mr. Charley wored it for a little wbile, and he might have 'fected it, you know."

"All right," said Charley. "Want some brandy, don't you?"

"Dat I jes' do."

"I'll get Ned to give me some for you," said Jack.

"I'll fetch it," said Charley.

"All right," said Jack. "I'll get the coat meanwhile."

Charley went to the cabin, and Jack to overhaul his box, where he had placed the red robe Charley had found in the forest.

"Well, you'll be all right now," said 'Dolf; "so I'll go and finish my snooze."

And he moved away.

In a minute Charley came up with a glass of Brandy in his hand.

"Golly! dat's your sort," said Jumbo.

"It's good stuff, ain't it?" said Charley. "First-rate stuff to prevent a fellow catching cold."

"It jes' am."

"Capital," said Charley, carrying the glass to his lips.

"Here you jes' hold on dere."

"Eh?" said Charley.

"Dat for dis chile."

"What?"

"Why, dat ere brandy, to be suah," said the negro.

"Well, ain't what's yours mine, and what's mine's my own, eh?" asked Charley.

"What's dat?" asked Jumbo.

"What's mine is my own, ain't it?"

"Ob course it is," replied Jumbo. "Who said it wasn't Not dis chile."

"Just so. What's yours is mine, ain't it, according to agreement, you know."

"Don't understand dat no how," said the negro, reaching out his hand for the glass.

"Oh, don't you?"

"No."

"Not when we agreed to share and share alike? Now, do you want to cry off that?"

"Who's a-crying off?" said Jumbo. "I always agree to share fair, but you don't; you always collars de biggest share ob everyting."

"Now that's unkind of you," said Charley; "such a friend as I am too. Why, if you were ill, I'd even take your medicine for you, so that you shouldn't have the nasty taste in your mouth, and I'd even let you have the sugar to eat after it, I would."

"Guess you wouldn't," said Jumbo. "De only tings what's eber shared fair 'tween us is what dis chile shares out."

"Do you mean to say you always give me a fair half?"

"Always," said the negro; "and de biggest half too."

"And you always will?"

"Suah."

"That's a promise, mind."

"Course it is," replied the negro.

"Then, I'll trust you. There take the brandy; but halves, you know—share fair."

"What?" cried Jumbo. "Share dis?"

"Everything, you know; that's the agreement."

"Oh, wery well," said the negro. "You wants half of dis what I holds in my hand?"

"Yes, half, and a good half, mind."

"All right, you shall have half, and de biggest half too."

And Jumbo tossed down the brandy at a gulp, and handed Charley the glass.

"Do you call that sharing fair, you greedy hound, when you've drank the whole lot of it?" asked Charley.

"Ob course dis chile does," replied Jumbo. "I drink de brandy, dat my half; and I gib you de glass, and dat your half. And if dat ain't sharing fair den I neber shared fair in my life, neber."

"But I can't drink the glass," said Charley.

"Dis chile didn't say you could," replied Jumbo; "and dat's where you got the best ob it. You got your share to look at, and my share's gone."

"All right," said Charley, "I'll be even with you yet. I'll share the next lot myself."

"Dat's a good boy," said Jumbo.

"Halloa! what are you two growling about?" said Jack, as he strode to the spot. "Here's the coat; you can wear it till your own is dry."

"Guess I will," said Jumbo. "Golly! but dis gen'lemen'll look a swell, an' no mistake. Dar, what you think ob me now?"

And Jumbo having, with the assistance of Jack, got into the long red robe, turned himself round and round before Charley.

"Not much," replied Charley.

"Dat shows you no 'preciation. Guess dat licks you. Golly! what ud um gals down Broadway tink of dis chile? Guess dey'd take him for a prince or president —yah, yah!"

"Or a fool," said Charley.

"Dat's trufe," said Jumbo; "leastways, dey'd take him for a fool if they knowed he 'sociated with such poor vulgar fellows as you."

"You're a lot to be proud of, you are," said Charley.

"Dat's trufe again," replied Jumbo; "and so jes' go, and drink dis chile's healf out of dat are glass—yah, yah!"

And Jumbo strode away laughing loudly.

CHAPTER XXXV.

IN WHICH BOASTER RUNS AWAY IN THE DARK, AND SEES SOMETHING THAT SURPRISES HIM.

WHEN Boaster rose to the surface he struck out for the shore of the bay, and catching at the overhanging branches drew himself to land.

Scarcely had he done so, than he heard the voice of Ned calling for a light.

Fearing discovery, he went further inland, and creeping into the bushes he crouched down shivering with wet and fear.

He had lost the revolver in the bay, and even had he retained his hold of it, it would have been useless now.

Still he wished he had a knife or some weapon, for he knew that the Indian rowers were on shore.

So cramped were they for room in the boat, that they had been sent on shore to sleep.

He was fearful least one of these should detect him and either carry him back to the boat or give note of his whereabouts to those on board.

Suddenly he saw a light in the boat, and crouched lower among the bushes.

He could see those on board and hear most that was said, and when he heard Ned say that nothing could be done till day-light, he gave a sigh of relief.

Had he a pistol in his hand then he would have shot Ned as he leant over the side of the boat.

When all was again darkness he tried to hit upon some plan to get away.

If he remained on the island his chance of escaping Ned was very little, for the island was small, and his discovery would only be a matter of time.

But if he could get away he might return to the Indians, who he doubted not would befriend him.

Had he known the fate of his companion in crime how different would have been his thoughts.

"I cannot swim across," he muttered; "it is too far to the opposite shore. Ah," he added, suddenly, "the canoe! If I can unmoor that I might float out of the bay in the darkness and escape them yet."

This thought once formed, Bill crawled cautiously through the bushes in the direction where he knew the canoe was moored.

In the darkness it was some time ere he came upon it, and then another fear seized him.

Might not one or more of the Indian rowers be sleeping in it?

Drawn up as it was under the overhanging branches, he could not in the gloom in which the canoe was shrouded be certain whether or not it was tenanted.

He felt about for the rope which secured it to the trees on shore, and drew the vessel gently towards him till it struck the bank.

Intently he listened.

There was not a sound or movement within the vessel.

He let the rope slacken, and the canoe drifted to the length of the line, then he drew it in again more quickly than before.

Again its bows struck the bank, but still there was no sound to tell that any one had been disturbed.

Boaster now felt satisfied that none of

the Indians were on board the canoe, and feeling cautiously for the fastening of the rope, he untied the knot that secured it to the tree.

This done, he drew the canoe close up to him and got into it, and catching hold of the branches drew it along towards the opening to the bay.

Sheltered by the dense vegetation that formed a perfect bower over the light craft, he gradually urged it along past the boat and close to the narrow entrance of the cave.

His heart beat with apprehension lest the snapping of a twig should betray him either to those on the boat or those on shore.

At length the opening to the bay was reached, and giving the boat a lurch out from the shore, he sank down flat in the canoe.

His suspense now was fearful.

Would the canoe pass out into the river unseen ?

Or would it be detected, and those on board the boat, suspecting the truth, send a volley into it.

He held his very breath least it should betray him.

Slowly the canoe floated through the narrow entrance into the wide river beyond, and caught by the current swung round and swept up the stream.

Then Bill drew a deep sigh of relief and sat up.

They might search the island now, for the bird was flown.

He would have laughed aloud had he dared.

Carried by the tide the canoe swept on at a good rate

But Boaster wished to gain the opposite shore.

Were the paddles in the boat.

He searched about for them.

Yes, they were there.

He seized one, and soon brought the head of the canoe across the stream.

Then he set to work to cross the river.

"Ha, ha! Ned Nimble," he muttered, " I shall foil you yet. You will have had your long journey for nothing. Minnie shall yet be mine, and I shall glory in my revenge."

And for a moment he ceased to paddle that he might shake his fist at the bay in which Ned lay.

Having thus eased his heart, he sat to work again and sent the light craft dancing over the water.

But the stream was strong, and he was not good at paddling.

He paddled so that he made slow headway in the direction he wished to go.

But he was cheered by the reflection that every stroke took him further from Ned, and nearer to Minnie.

"Oh, that I could see his rage and disappointment when he learns that I have escaped him," muttered Boaster, " but that the canoe will be gone, he might fancy I had been drowned in the bay, but soon he will know I am alive, and eager to be avenged on him. Ah, ha—and I will—I will—bitterly, fearfully avenged."

He found his arms begin to tire, and he rested on his paddle.

"This won't do," he said, as he felt the light craft borne along by the current, " I must stick to my work, tired though I am, or I shall drift too far."

And he set to work again.

But it was weary work, and the day had broken when he was still far from the shore, and much further up the river he believed than he wanted to be to reach the Indian village where he had left Minnie.

The exertion and the excitement he had undergone began now to tell upon him.

Still he dared not rest.

He must keep on paddling.

His arms ached and his head throbbed.

He began to curse his weakness.

Slowly and more slowly he plied his paddle.

The light grew brighter and brighter, and then the sun rose and tinted the waters.

Still on, still the paddle rose and fell.

Gradually, but oh, so gradually, the shore drew nearer and nearer.

At length it was reached, and perspiring and faint, he sprang to land.

The forest came down to the water's edge, and he drew the canoe high on to the shore.

How far he was from the Indian village he knew not, but he felt, had it been close at hand, he could go no further then.

He flung himself down, and closing his eyes fell into a sound sleep, from which he was suddenly startled.

"SALLY UTTERED A SCREAM, AND BOUNDED CLEAN OVER DOLF'S BACK."

PRICE ONE HALFPENNY
[PUBLISHED EVERY MONDAY.]

It was the sound of voices that arou-ed Boaster, and, starting up, he saw a fleet of canoes gliding up the stream.

In one of these sat the chief, Tiger Claw, and by his side was Minnie Sash.

A horrible suspicion flashed across Boaster's mind, and he sank again to the earth.

CHAPTER XXXVI.

IN WHICH NED HEARS SOMETHING NOT TO HIS ADVANTAGE.

Mr. BIRCHER was soon brought out of the insensible state into which the blow of Boaster had sent him, and, his face and head bathed and bandaged, he had been placed on Ned's bed, where he soon sank into slumber.

Ned had forborne to ask him any questions.

He had taken it for granted that the bully had himself succeeded in getting free of his bonds, had thrown himself unawares upon Bircher, and inflicted the wound on the tutor's forehead ere he could give an alarm.

Ned and Harry watched Bircher till he fell asleep, and then the former said—

"This escape of Bill may prove unfortunate for poor Minnie, I fear."

"Yes, for if he succeeds in getting away from the island, he'll join Tiger Claw, and then our chances of rescuing the girl will be more remote than ever."

"But do you think he has got on to the island?" asked Ned. "You heard what the nigger said?"

"Yes," replied Harry; "but he said too much. If the black rascal had not asserted he had forced him into the mud at the bottom of the river, I might have fancied Bill had been drowned, but that assertion proved to me that Jumbo has no idea what became of him."

"And of course he was only too intent on escaping drowning himself," said Ned, "however, we'll search the island as soon as it is light."

"Then get some sleep, yourself, Ned. You know you are about as bad as Bircher."

"Oh, don't mind me, I am nearly all right again, and yet I can't help thinking that perhaps Bill is done for."

"How?" asked Harry.

"The Indians you know are aroused at the least sound, and if Bill had reached the shore, depend on it some of them would have detected him."

"Possibly, but Boaster's an artful card."

"True; well we can't do anything for the present, so you turn in, Harry. I don't think I could sleep again if I tried."

After some persuasion Harry flung himself down, and was soon fast asleep.

So also was Jack, Jumbo, and Sally.

Charley and Ned kept watch during the rest of the night.

At sunrise however all except Bircher were on deck.

"Just give the signal for those fellows to come on board and get their breakfast," said Ned; and then we shall learn if either of them have seen or heard anything of Bill on the island."

Jack placed his fingers to his mouth and gave a loud shrill whistle.

But scarcely had he done so than he swung quickly round on his heel, and confronted Ned.

Jack's face wore a look of surprise and consternation as he blurted out—

"Why where's the canoe? It ain't there!"

Ned and Harry sprang to the side.

The canoe that they had seen moored to the shore was gone, and the Indians coming down to the spot in answer to Jack's call, were gazing thunderstruck at the water.

"Gone!" said Ned.

"Yes, gone," replied Harry, "and Boaster in it."

"It must be so," said Ned. "Confound it! we are foiled again, even after all seemed to be working so well for us."

"Well, I'm licked," said Charley; "that coon's fooled us all and no mistake."

"All 'cept dis chile," put in Jumbo, "and dis chile fooled him."

"You have fooled us," said Jack; "didn't you swear you'd drowned the varmint in the bay?"

"Now look yer, Massa Jack," cried Jumbo, "dis yer chile's too much ob a genlemens to swear 'bout anyting."

"Oh, go to Jericho!" said Jack, turning away impatiently.

"Don't know the way, but perhaps you'll show me," said Jumbo.

"Shut up," said Charley; "you're always fooling somebody."

"Take a long while to fool you," said Jumbo, "and now jus' yo look here, don't you go for to speak 'spectfully to me now 'cos dere's a lot ob diff'rence in our position. Jus' you remember that you're only a ragged wagabone, while I am a 'spectably tired gentleman."

And Jumbo drew Jack's robe tightly round him, and turned loftily away.

In spite of his annoyance, Ned could not help smiling.

"A jackdaw in borrowed plume," said Sally.

"Thinks himself somebody now, don't he, Sally?" said Charley.

"We must take the boat in close to shore, so that those fellows can come on board," said Ned. "This is unfortunate, for not only have we lost Boaster, but we shall be terribly overcrowded."

"And besides, there's a lot of our things in the canoe," said Harry.

"That rascal's got the laugh of us after all," said Ned.

"Better have knocked him on the head in the forest," said 'Dolf.

"I wish I had," said Jack.

"Well it can't be helped now," said Ned; "get the boat nearer the shore, and let those fellows come on deck,"

The boat was soon brought near enough to the shore to allow the rowers to come on board.

Ned eagerly questioned them.

Not one had seen or heard anything of Boaster, or knew of the loss of the canoe till after they heard Jack's call.

"Well, get your breakfast," said Ned, and in the meantime we'll decide what's best to be done."

Rations were served out to the Indians and the others went to the cabin to snatch a hasty meal and hold a council as to their next proceeding.

Bircher still slumbered, and so that they should not awaken him, they spoke in a low tone.

It was decided to send two of the Indian rowers on shore to scout round the village and try to learn whether Boaster had returned, and the movements of Tiger Claw, and scarcely had they decided upon this than a confusion on deck caused the men to rush out of the cabin to learn its cause.

On reaching the deck, Ned saw a canoe entering the bay paddled by a white man.

His heavy moustache, long beard, dark hair and bronzed face, proclaimed him a Spaniard.

Intent upon paddling his canoe through the narrow entrance to the bay, he did not look up till he had forced the vessel through the bushes, which almost hid the opening, and then his features bore a look of surprise as he saw the boat moored in the bay.

With his paddle raised in the air he seemed to hesitate for a few moments whether to advance or retreat.

Evidently he decided upon the latter course, for he hurriedly dipped his paddle into the water and struck out for the opening.

Ned seized a rifle, and levelling it at him, cried—

"Hold, or you are a dead man!"

The fellow ceased paddling on the instant.

"Come on board and report yourself," cried Ned; "if you are a friend you have nothing to fear."

"Who are you?" cried the fellow, "who order men to come on board your boat?"

"Honest men," said Ned, "and we are determined to know whether you are the same or not, so paddle this way unless you want to get a bullet in your head."

The fellow seeing Jack and Harry also level a rifle at him, brought his canoe alongside the boat.

"Now what do you want with me?" asked the fellow, surlily.

"A truthful reply to a few plain questions," returned Ned, "which, if you give, you shall be rewarded with gold, but if you lie, you shall get lead instead."

"What do you want to know?" asked the man.

"First, have you seen a white man in a canoe on the river?"

"No."

"Where have you come from?"

"From an Indian village about five

miles down the river. I've had to fly for my life."

"The village of which Swift Arrow is the Chief?" asked Ned.

"Yes, the same. Since you know it, perhaps you are the whites that caused all the row over there."

"Perhaps we are," said Ned, "and if I mistake not, you are one of the white men engaged to manage the boat of a couple of rascals who had a young girl captive, are you not?"

"Myself and three companions were engaged by two white men to row them up the Orinoco," said the man.

"And fell in with the band of which Tiger Claw is the chief?"

"Yes, and accompanied him to the village of Swift Arrow?"

"Now, hark you," said Ned, "I am in pursuit of those white men who have carried off the girl. Answer me truly and I will reward you handsomely."

"What do you want to know," asked the fellow.

"Has the youngest of the white men passed you on the river on his return to the village?"

"I have not seen him," replied the man, "and if he returns to the village he won't find either his friend or the girl there."

"Why not?"

"Because the chief Tiger Claw, has taken the girl prisoner."

"Taken her prisoner! Why?" asked Ned.

"There was a dispute about her between him and Phopps, and the Englishman was slain with the Indian's hatchet."

"Phopps slain!" cried Ned.

"As dead as a herring," replied the man, "and such will be the fate of his companion, if Tiger Claw gets hold of him; my mates also fell by the hands of the Indians, and I should have done the same had I not escaped in one of their canoes."

"And Minnie the white girl?" said Ned, excitedly.

"Will become the squaw of Tiger Claw. He has carried her off; and it was to hide from him and his band as they paddle up the river towards their camping-grounds that I sought cover in this place."

Ned pressed his hand to his forehead, and staggered back like one shot through the heart.

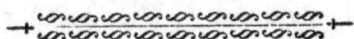

CHAPTER XXXVII.

IN WHICH SALLY GIVES HER HAND TO JUMBO AND CHARLEY RECEIVES JACK'S FOOT.

HARRY dropped over the side of the boat into the canoe, and taking the paddle from the man's hand, said—

"I will prove the truth or falsehood of your words."

And before the Spaniard could reply, Harry sent the light craft skimming towards the river.

A few strokes brought the canoe out of the bay, and looking in the direction the man pointed, Harry saw a fleet of canoes in the distance.

Laying the paddle across his knee he took a small but powerful glass from his pocket, and placed it to his eye.

A moment he held it, and then dropped it with a sigh.

"It is too true, only too true," he said. "Poor Minnie! poor girl!"

Then raising himself he said—

"Ned promised you some reward. Come and get it."

And he set the paddle to work, re-entered the bay, and brought the canoe to the side of the boat.

Leaping on board he grasped Ned's hand.

"Old man," he cried, "that fellow I am sorry to say spoke the truth. I've seen her."

"Who, Minnie?" cried Ned.

"Yes; she's in one of a large fleet of canoes now going up the river," he cried.

"Quick!" cried Ned, breaking away from his chum. "Cast off the ropes. Get out the oars. We must pursue them at once or they'll escape us!"

"Don't you be a fool!"

It was Sally who said this.

She had heard all that had transpired

and when Ned gave the order to unmoor the boat had given utterance to the words.

"What!" cried Ned, indignantly. "How dare you?"

"Hoity toity!" cried Sally. "So you're getting your back up, are you? And what for? Because I tell you not to be a fool, eh? Suppose you want us all to be made prisoners of, don't you, eh?"

"I must rescue Minnie!" cried Ned. "Cast loose those ropes."

"Look here, you fellows!" said Sally; "don't you do nothing of the kind, leastways not yet."

"I don't understand this," said Ned.

"Don't you? Well, I understand it if you don't, and you ain't a-going to commit suicide if I knows it."

"I shall go mad if I am not quickly obeyed!" replied Ned.

"And you'll go to your death sharp if you are!" said Sally.

Ned looked at her half surprised, half angrily.

"What do you mean?" he cried, impatiently.

"I'll tell you," replied Sally. "If you want the whole lot of us to be gobbled up in double quick time, or expect we ought to furnish a lot of amusement for the savages on the occasion of Tiger Claw's marriage with that white girl, you'll just give the Indians a chance by going after them now; but if on the other hand you wish to rescue the girl from their clutches, you will wait till you can get a chance of doing so with safety to her and yourself. Why there's a couple of hundred of them at least, and what chance would you have with them, tell me that?"

Ned clasped his hand to his forehead, and leaned against the side of the boat.

"If you save that girl, it won't be by attacking Tiger Claw surrounded by his braves," said Sally. "You'll have to come the artful over him, or you're a gone coon and no mistake."

"Sally, is quite correct, old man," said Harry. "Our only chance of rescuing Minnie will be by using stratagem."

"I am a fool?" said Ned.

"Open confession is good for the soul," said Sally. "And now, since you own you are a fool, perhaps you'll be ready to listen to reason."

"Of course Ned will," said Harry. "He thought only of poor Minnie and not of the danger he would himself run. It will require consideration before we act."

"And a lot of it, too," said Sally. "Nothing can be done just at present. In fact, to attempt it will only make it bad for ourselves and worse for the poor girl."

"I think you are right," said Ned. "Forgive me for speaking so harshly to you, Sally,"

"Lor, I ain't offended," said Sally, "not a bit of it. If you think I am, that'll show I ain't."

And Sally flung her arms round Ned's neck and kissed him.

"Halloa, there!" said Jack, "pretty goings on, ain't it?"

"Guess dere's no objection to serbing all alike," said Jumbo, putting his face forward.

"Not the least," said Sally. "There's your smack!"

And her hand came with a loud smack across the black face of the negro.

"Gor-a-mighty!" cried Jumbo, rubbing his cheek.

"Serve you right," said Charley, "it's only white men as gets her favours. Sweet Sally, permit me to take a salute from your fair lips."

"Hold off, there. I allow no poaching on my preserves!" said Jack, "or look out for spring guns."

And raising his foot, Jack gave Charley a kick which sent him flying into Jumbo's arms.

"Dat's fair," said Jumbo, "got your share, ain't you?—yah, yah!"

"Look here, Ned," said Harry, drawing him to the other side of the vessel, "how about that Spanish fellow there?"

"Oh, I had forgotten all about him," replied Ned; "I promised to give him something, didn't I?"

"You did if he spoke truly, and he did so. Do you think he could be of any use to us?"

"No," replied Ned, "we dare not trust him."

"I fear not. He must have known that Minnie was a captive of the fellows who employed him."

"Of course he did. He's a bad one, depend upon it, but I'll keep word with him."

So saying Ned walked over to the opposite side and addressed the Spaniard.

"Here," he said, "are a couple of pounds for you for the information you gave me. Take them, and try if you can't earn money honestly in the future."

"I earned this honestly, didn't I?" asked the man.

"Yes, but you knew while with Boaster and Phopps that you were aiding them in a piece of villainous rascality."

"Men can't be too particular sometimes," said the fellow.

"They can always be honest and just if they will," said Ned.

"I'm quite willing if it pays," said the man, "so if you want a hand I'm ready to engage with you."

"No doubt," said Ned, "but I'd rather have your room than your company."

And he turned away.

The Spaniard muttered an oath between his set teeth and pocketed the coins.

Paddling out a few yards from the boat he called to Ned.

"What do you want?" asked Ned.

"Will you give me some provisions? I have a long journey to go and no firearms with which to hunt for food."

"Yes," said Ned, "though I don't think you deserve any pity from me, seeing that you have aided my foes."

"I didn't know that," was the reply.

"Give that man some food to help him on his way," said Ned, addressing 'Dolf.

"We are running awfully short, sir, you know," said 'Dolf.

"Never mind. He has none at all; so get him some at once."

'Dolf turned to obey, and in a few minutes some bread and meat and a bottle of wine were handed to the man in the canoe.

The fellow took it without any thanks, and in five minutes more had left the bay.

"Now to decide upon what is to be done," said Ned.

Then catching Harry by the arm, he added, excitedly—

"You saw the canoes of Tiger Claw?"

"Yes, I examined them carefully through my glass," replied Harry.

"Boaster—did you discover him? Was he one of them?"

"Not that I saw," replied Harry; "but poor Minnie I could make out distinctly."

"But he might have fallen in with the savages," said Ned. "The Spaniard did not see him alone on the river."

"He might," said Harry; "and if he did it would be bad for him if the Spaniard spoke truly."

"Perhaps," said Ned; "but I pray he may no longer be able to persecute poor Minnie. And yet, in the hands of Tiger Claw, what may she not be made to suffer? Oh, that I had remained near her!"

"Don't blame yourself, dear boy. Had you done so you might have shared the fate of Phopps, and made a miserable fellow of me for life."

Ned's hand slipped into that of his friend and rested there.

"Old man," he said, "if I have been cursed by having a bitter foe I am indeed blessed by possessing such a friend, and when I forget your friendship, may all honest men turn in disgust from Ned Nimble."

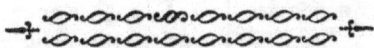

CHAPTER XXXVIII.

IN WHICH SALLY GOES UP AND JUMBO GOES DOWN.

ANXIOUS as Ned was to follow Minnie and endeavour to wrest her from the power of Tiger Claw, he was overruled by Sally Scrubbins, Jack, and Charley.

Sally had explained that the savages would have many customs to perform before Tiger Claw would dare force the poor girl to become his bride, and that if the Indians found they were not pursued they would be lulled into a feeling of security, and set a less strict guard over the white maiden.

So Ned's impatience became somewhat curbed, and he consented to remain where they were for a few days to recruit his own and Bircher's strength and allow the others to hunt on the island for food, with which to replenish their now somewhat scanty supply.

Bircher was stiff, weak, and ill from the effects of the blow which Bill had struck him, and though he did not confess how the bully had been enabled to escape, he did not give a false version of the affair.

He allowed Ned and the others to take it for granted that Ned's idea was the correct one; namely, that Bill had got his hands free and fallen upon the tutor unawares, and struck him down before he could raise an alarm.

Ned and Harry did all they could to ease his pain, and the kindness they showed and the sympathy they expressed for him often made Bircher think with regret of his conduct towards them when they were pupils at Pickleton Priory.

It was on the morning of the second day after the escape of Boaster that Jack, Charley, 'Dolf, Jumbo, and Sally went on shore in search of game, leaving Ned, Harry, and the Indians fishing from the boat in the bay, and Bircher tossing restlessly on his bed in the cabin.

"Now dis chile means to had a lot ob sport to-day," said Jumbo, as he tucked the one tail of his coat under his arm and rubbed his cheek with the barrel of his rifle.

"Guess we won't get much," said Charley, "while you're ashore."

"And why not?" asked the negro.

"Why not? Because you're so infernal ugly that you'll frighten everything away out of range of our guns," replied Charley.

"Guess dat's a lie," said Jumbo. "When de farmer wants to frighten de birds from his corn he makes up a scarecrow jus' like you. Guess dat farmer knows what he's about."

"That's 'cos he only wants to drive them away, not frighten the poor things to death," said Charley.

"Get out," said Jumbo. "Guess dis chile'll cotch more dan you will."

"You'll both cotch more than you'll like if you don't leave off growling and set to work," said Jack.

"Bress me now, what's bit you?" said Jumbo.

"Guess Sally's been gnawing him," remarked Charley.

"She'll be after clawing you if you ain't civil," said Sally.

"Shouldn't wonder but what you'd like to," said Jumbo; "women always likes to claw what dey flops dere 'fections on."

"You'd be a pretty beauty for a woman to have any affection for, wouldn't you?" said Sally.

"Guess dat's trufe," replied Jumbo. "Dis yer chile's good looks and mageristic bearing—dems de words, ain't 'em?"

"Oh, go and hang yourself," said Sally.

"Just lend us your neck den and I'll hang myself round it."

"No you won't," said Jack.

"Lor' now is you getting gealows?" said Jumbo. "Well, dat's only natral, for of course—oh, yar! what de debil's dat?" and Jumbo took a leap forward as if he had been shot.

Up from the grass in which Jumbo had stood rose the head of a small crocodile.

Sally gave a bound as the animal opened its jaws, and came down with all her weight on Jumbo's toes.

"Gor-a-mighty," cried the negro, "brest if I didn't tink it had got hold ob my leg."

"Oh, shoot it—kill it!' cried Sally.

'Dolf and Charley raised their rifles quickly.

But Jack, grasping his gun by the barrel, swung it round his head and brought down the heavy butt fair across the eyes of the horrible reptile.

The blow was a terrific one, but the crocodile made a snap at the gun and seized the barrel in its jaws.

Jack still clung to the weapon, and strove to tear it away.

But the crocodile's hold was too firm, and even Jack's enormous strength could not make it release its grasp.

'Dolf stepped forward, thrust the barrel of his gun between its jaws and fired.

Up flew the jaw of the reptile, showing its hideous teeth, and then down it sank dead in the grass.

"Well done, 'Dolf," said Charley, patting him on the shoulder; "couldn't have done better myself. You deserve a putty medal, you do."

"Paws off," said 'Dolf, shaking Charley's hand from his shoulder.

"As well throw pearls to swine," said Charley, "as bestow praise on a flunkey."

"I'll bestow something on you you won't like, if you don't mind what you are saying," said 'Dolf, as he commenced to re-load his gun.

"I accept no favours from my inferiors," said Charley.

"Your inferiors," said 'Dolf. "Well I like that."

"Glad you do; it's only right you should when a gentlemen condescends to praise a menial."

"You'll get my fist in your eye if you don't shut up," interrupted 'Dolf, angrily.

"My dear boy, do not imagine for one moment that I desire that my complexion should resemble in colour that of Jumbo's," said Charley, retreating a step.

"Then perhaps you'll keep civil," said 'Dolf, "or you'll get something you won't like."

They had walked on, leaving Jack and Sally some yards behind them, when suddenly three large birds rose in the air.

"There's a shot," said Charley.

In a moment up went their guns, and down came the birds floundering to their feet.

"Bravo!" said Jack, "that was a good shot."

"Guess dis chile killed 'em," said Jumbo.

"Why you fool, how could you kill them when you shot round the corner?" cried Charley; "you know you squint and can't see straight."

"Dat's trufe," said Jumbo; but den dese here birds squint too, and so they flied just in the opposite way dey wanted to—yah! yah!"

"Shut your mouth," said Charley, thrusting the barrel of his gun between Jumbo's teeth.

Jumbo did shut his mouth sharp, to the danger of breaking his teeth against the iron.

"What do you want to swallow my gun for?" cried Charley. "You are a hungry beggar, you are."

"Golly! what for you do dat?" inquired the negro, "tink my teefe want sharpening with dat ere. Don't you try dat game on again, 'cos if you do there'll be a row, suah."

"Thought there was now; you're halloaing loud enough," said Charley.

"Look here, you two fellows are always sparring," said Jack, "Hadn't you better fight it out and make an end of it?"

"I guess if dat low fellow gives dis yar cullered gen'l'man much more of his sarse, dis chile'll put him into dat hole full of water."

And Jumbo pointed to a water hole close beside him, on the surface of which floated green slime.

"What, you?" said Charley.

"Yes, sar, me," retorted Jumbo.

"Why I'd swallow you, coat and all," said Charley.

"Guess den you'd hab more sense in your stomach den eber you had in your head," retorted the negro.

At this there was a loud laugh.

"I calkerlate dat's one to dis gen'l'man," said Jumbo; "guess I had you there, you white trash."

"Here, hold on there about white trash," said 'Dolf. "I should fancy a white man was better than a black any day."

"Den I pities yer igerance," said Jumbo, with a lofty toss of the head.

"I shall have to thrash you before long that's certain," said 'Dolf, as he fired at a bird circling up from one of the trees and missed it.

Jack however brought it down.

'Dolf sank down on one knee to reload his gun, and Jack, laying his rifle down on the ground, ran and picked up the dead bird."

"It's a fine plump one," he said, as he placed it beside the others; "but we must try and find some larger game than this."

"Halloa! what's that there?" cried Charley, pointing up into the branches of a neighbouring tree.

Jack stooped to pick up his gun as the others tried to discover what was in the tree.

"I'll fetch it," said Charley.

Up went his rifle and he fired into the branches.

Down came something crashing through the branches to the ground.

"It's a cat," cried Charley.

"Cat!" echoed Jumbo.

"Cats!" shrieked Sally, all her horror of the wild cat showing in her face and voice.

And she turned to fly.

But Jack, still bending over his rifle stood in her path.

"Cats, cat's!" she shrieked; and taking a spring she would have leaped over Jack, but the conjuror rose to his feet and brought her up suddenly.

To save herself from being hurled to the earth, Sally seized 'Dolf by the hair, and gave it a tremendous tug, yelling the while—

"Cats, cats! oh Lor, it's wild cats!"

The disturbed and angry animals bounded to the earth with their teeth showing, and came towards her with gleaming eyes.

Swift as lightning Charley swung round his rifle and aimed a blow at the cats.

But the flight of the animals were swifter than Charley's stroke, and the butt of the gun missing the back of one of the cats, caught Jumbo across the waist, and doubling him up, hurled him backwards as if shot from a cannon.

"Gor' a-mighty! what's dat killed me, am it an earfquake?" he cried, as he toppled over the edge of the waterhole, and sank into the slimy pool, waving arms and legs wildly in the air till the green slush shut them from the sight of the startled and terrified Charley.

CHAPTER XXXIX.

IN WHICH BOASTER DISGUISES HIS BODY AND REVEALS HIS MIND.

BOASTER sat up and pressed his hands to his throbbing temples.

Could there be any doubt that it was Minnie whom he had seen in the canoe with Tiger Claw by her side?

No, he could not have been deceived.

But how came she there?

Alas! he could but too truly guess.

Tiger Claw had turned upon Phopps and stolen the girl.

And Phopps, what of him? The villain he had aided and whom he himself had determined to wrong or betray?

He feared the worst had befallen him.

If so he was alone, friendless, without means in a foreign land.

He sprang to his feet.

"I'll know the worst, I'll learn the truth," he cried; "come what may."

He staggered to where the canoe was, determined to push it into the stream and make his way to the Indian village.

"It cannot be far off here," he muttered. "I shall find the bay in which we landed if I keep close in the shore. Ah! what is this?"

He drew up a piece of canvas in the stern of the canoe and started back with a cry of joy.

There was a couple of rifles and a flask of powder.

He made a further search, and under another piece of canvas he came upon a tin box.

Opening it he found it contained biscuits.

This was indeed a fortunate find.

He was hungry, and began to eat.

He found a broken Indian spear lying along the bottom of the canoe, and a small can containing bullets under one of the seats.

"Food and arms," he said; "but I wish I had a knife; well I can make this spear-head do for one. Would I could bury it in the heart of Ned Nimble."

The words came through his clenched teeth like the hiss of a serpent.

And after much exertion he succeeded in breaking the blade from the handle.

The blade he thrust into his waist belt, and having satisfied his hunger, he pushed the canoe into the water and entered it.

Seizing a paddle he worked the light vessel down the river, keeping close to the shore, in order that he might land quickly should he discover Ned had come in pursuit of him.

Refreshed by the short sleep he had had, and the meal he had made off the biscuits, he paddled on till he reached the bay, in which with Tiger Claw and Phopps he had landed when they sought the village of Swift Arrow.

The bay was deserted now.

When last he had seen it many canoes floated on its bosom, now only his own was to be seen.

"From here," he muttered, as he secured the light craft to a tree on the shore, "I can easily find my way to the Indian camp, but will Swift Arrow receive me as a friend or a foe?"

He knew not of Swift Arrow's fate.

He decided it would be best for him to reconnoitre the village first, ere he made his presence known.

So taking the powder flask and one of the rifles, and placing some of the bullets in his pocket, he stepped ashore.

He remembered the direction in which he had gone with Tiger Claw, and following it, soon came to a spot from which a view of the Indian huts could be obtained.

Instead however of working his way out into the open, he bore away to the left into the forest, determined to come out upon the opposite side of the village as Ned and his friends had done when on their search for Minnie Sash.

He had just caught sight of the smoke of the Indian fires through the trees, when on looking down he sprang back with a startled cry.

At the foot of a large tree lay the body of a warrior, his hands and bosom covered with blood, and quite dead.

Boaster shuddered, and turned to hurry from the spot, but catching sight of the Indian's knife, he stooped down and secured it.

"I may want this," he said, as he placed it in his belt, and taking the spearhead therefrom flung it into some bushes.

"Was that some of Tiger Claw's work?" he muttered. "I must be cautious how I approach. I would go no further did I know for certain the fate of Phopps. I'd care not what it be, only that he is necessary to me in this vile place."

Cautiously he stole from the forest out on to the back of the village. .

But hastily he darted back into the shadow of the trees again as he perceived several squaws coming towards him.

They were talking and gesticulating excitedly.

As they drew near to where he crouched he heard what they said, and his cheeks grew pale and his limbs trembled.

They were discussing the fate of Swift Arrow and the white man Phopps.

Boaster now learned how Minnie had fallen into the hands of Tiger Claw, and how that chief had slain the wretched Phinicky when he swore that Minnie should become his bride.

But Boaster learned more than that; learned from the conversation of the squaws that the Indians had vowed to slay every white man who fell into their hands in revenge for the death of Swift Arrow.

The suspense of Boaster became fearful.

If they should discover him his fate was sealed to a certainty.

He would be consigned to the flames for which they were now visiting the forest to gather wood for the consuming of the body of the murdered Phopps.

For they believed that by burning the body of the white man the souls of Swift Arrow and his braves would be rendered joyous in the happy hunting grounds to which they had gone.

Boaster waited trembling till the squaws had passed on, and then he retraced his steps towards the bay.

But on his way thither he stopped beside the body of the dead warrior.

He stripped it of its headdress, its skirt, and moccasins, and hurried on again.

"I may find these things useful," he muttered; "they may conceal me alike from white foes and red."

On reaching the bay he sat down on the bank and examined the clothing of the dead savage.

"I thought so," he muttered, as from a pouch or pocket attached to the skirt he drew out several articles. "These pigments will disguise me, and I might pass even Ned and Harry without their having the least suspicion of who I am."

He washed the blood from the skirt and the moccasins, and then, stripping himself, he sorted the pigments he had found in the Indian's pouch.

Some of these he mixed with water, and smeared the paint over his legs, face, and body till he was of the colour of an Indian.

Then he painted his cheeks and forehead with red ochre in strips and crescents, after which he attired himself in the Indian's dress and surveyed his reflection in the water.

A smile of satisfaction passed over his features.

Then entering the canoe he hid his own attire under the canvas and exclaimed, as he pushed the vessel out from the shore—

"Now I can defy them all. Ned Nimble, beware! Vengeance will yet be mine!"

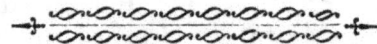

CHAPTER XL.

IN WHICH TIGER CLAW TELLS HIS LOVE AND MINNIE SHOWS HER SPIRIT.

THE moon sailed high in the blue heavens, and silvered the waters as they rushed madly on their way.

The roar of a distant cataract, mingled with the rustling of the leaves and the soughing of the branches as the wind tore through the mighty forest, and the bark of the wolf ever and anon broke upon the ears of the Indians grouped around a fire that threw its red glare out upon the moonlit waters.

At a short distance from the fire sat a white girl, her elbows on her knees, and her face buried in her hands.

She was sobbing audibly.

Beside her on the ground reclined the huge form of an Indian warrior.

"Why does the pale-face weep?" he asked, rising on his elbow and looking up at the bent head of the maiden; "why does she not dry her tears and let her eyes smile on Tiger Claw? Does the white maiden weep for the pale-face coward who stole her from the wigwam of her fathers?"

"No, no," cried the girl, taking her hands from her face, "'tis for my liberty I weep, not for him."

Tiger Claw gazed fondly into the face of Minnie Sash, but she turned her gaze away with a shudder.

"The white maiden shall not weep long for that," said the savage. "When she becomes the squaw of Tiger Claw she shall roam the forest and prairie at will, or guide her canoe over the great waters. She shall go where she will, and be as free as the waters or the winds."

"I can never be your squaw," said Minnie. "The pale-face weds not with the red man. Oh, you are a great chief, a brave warrior, and you will not war with a weak woman! Suffer me to depart. Let me go whither I will!"

"When our wise men have joined our hands, and you have vowed to weave for Tiger Claw the moccasin, and to feed the fire in his lodge, then shall the pale-face go whither she will, but not before. I have spoken."

And the savage chief rose angrily to his feet.

"And these are the words and intentions of the warrior chief, Tiger Claw?"

"They are."

"And you are resolved to force me to become your bride?" asked Minnie.

"Tiger Claw has spoken," he replied, haughtily.

"But only in jest," said Minnie, "for it is the coward alone who would wed a woman against her will, and you are a brave man."

"He must be a braver who would deny it," said the chief.

"Then I repeat you only jest when you say you will force me to become your squaw, for that would be the act of a coward."

"A coward!" cried the chief. "Tiger Claw is no coward. He has met his foes in the forest and on the waters, and his tomahawk has drunk their blood. He has faced the panther and buried his knife in his heart, and he has grappled with the bison and brought it to the earth."

"Deeds worthy of a brave," said Minnie, "but he is only a coward who wars with babes and women."

"Tiger Claw wars not with the pale-face maiden; he loves her and will share with her his wigwam."

"But the pale-face maiden loves him not," said Minnie. "She loves a noble youth of her own tribe, and would a brave chief tear her from him to whom she long since gave her heart?"

"Would the tiger rend the rattlesnake or the panther tear the life from the bosom of the lamb? Yes. Is Tiger Claw less brave and fierce than they? No. If the pale-face would take from him the maiden he loves he must bear her from his dead arms. If he seek her, the tomahawk of the brave shall cleave his skull or his knife lie deep in his heart."

Minnie shuddered.

"Heavens!" she cried, "you are a monster, and I hate you!"

Tiger Claw seized her arm.

"Pale-face," he said, "turn not the love of the chief to anger. His blood is hot. Beware!"

Minnie shrank coweringly beneath his fierce gaze.

"Oh, Heaven!" she cried, "save me from this man; save me, or let me die."

"Does the white maiden ask for death?" he said.

"I do," she returned, "rather than become the wife of such a man. Tiger Claw, be merciful, I cannot love you.

My heart is another's. Oh, spare me. I should die of very horror at the thought of becoming your squaw."

"Tiger Claw has spoken," said the chief, releasing her arm. "Again I say I have spoken."

"Then hear me speak," said Minnie, goaded to desperation. "I will never become your wife. You may kill me, but I will never be yours—never, oy the blue heavens above me, I swear it!"

"Pale-face, you lie!" cried the chief, stretching out his hand.

But ere he could grasp her, Minnie seized the warrior's spear and levelled it at his bosom.

"Touch me not," she cried, "or by Heaven I will bury this spear in your black heart and then in mine own!"

CHAPTER XLI.

IN WHICH IT IS A CASE OF PULL DEVIL, PULL BAKER.

For a moment all but Sally Scrubbins forgot the vicinity of the two wild cats in the sudden disappearance of Jumbo into the green, slimy waters of the forest pool.

As his black head, hands, and feet disappeared from view, Charley dropped his gun and sprang to the rescue of his friend.

Jack stood for a moment in surprise and hesitation.

'Dolf, still in a stooping position, could only gaze upon the spot where Jumbo had disappeared in astonishment.

But Sally heeded not Jumbo's mishap.

She had something else to think of.

She saw only one of the wild cats crouching for a spring, and all the blood in her veins seemed to turn to water.

"Cats! cats!" she gasped.

This animal had greater terrors for her than could even a grizzly bear or a boa-constrictor.

She stood fascinated, as it were, by the bristling tail and glaring eyes of the savage animal.

Up bobbed the woolly head of the negro out of the green slime.

"Gorra, catch hold of dis chile's hair!

Help! Suah, it's dead I am. Oh, yah, murder!"

Frantically Jumbo beat his hands in the air, and splashed them in the water, filling the eyes and mouth of Charley with the green slime as the white youth made a grasp at the negro's coat collar.

"Hole on! Quick, pull me out!" yelled Jumbo. "Dis chile a gone coon, suah, if you let's go."

"Hold your row, I've got you all right," cried Charley.

"Suah, but he'll nab me too," cried the negro. "Mussy, make haste and collar de biggest share of dis yar nigger."

"Hold yar jaw and be quiet, or I'll drop you back again," replied Charley, as he dragged Jumbo on to the edge of the pool. "Oh, Jerusalem!"

"Murder!" yelled Jumbo. "I'm dead, suah. Sabe me! sabe me!"

The head and shoulders of a crocodile shot up out of the green, slimy pool, and the horrid fangs made a snap at the thighs of the negro.

Charley gave Jumbo a desperate pull and a jerk forward as the reptile's jaws closed, only on the single coat-tail of the terrified black.

"Collar all de lot ob me, Charley,

collar all de lot," shrieked Jumbo; "don't let de beggar hab a share ob dis chile. Oh, yah! yah!"

Charley pulled frantically at Jumbo's collar, and the crocodile hugged fiercely at the coat-tail.

A desperate struggle ensued.

Charley strove might and main to drag his friend from the power of the reptile, while the crocodile tried to draw Jumbo back into the pool.

"Oh, if dat dere coat-tail would only go after its broder," gasped Jumbo.

"By Jingo, the collar's tearing off!" cried Charley. "Help, Jack, help, or Jumbo's a goner!"

Jack, recovering from his surprise, turned to help Charley.

But a sudden stop was put to his good intention.

At that moment the crouching wild cat took its threatened spring at Sally.

As the animal bounded from the earth Sally gave a loud scream, and turning, received the fierce brute on her skirts.

Terrified out of all reason, Sally uttered another loud scream, and bounded clean over 'Dolf's back, the snarling, spitting animal clinging to her with all its native ferocity.

As with extended legs she took her flying leap over 'Dolf, her boot caught Jack a blow in the chest that doubled him up, and knocked all the breath out of his body.

Hence, instead of hurrying to Charley's aid, he stood with his hands pressed to his waist, gasping heavily.

Away fled Sally, shrieking, she knew not whither.

Away with her, clinging on, tearing at her back, went also the wild cat.

"Help, s'cat, help!" shrieked Sally.

"Help, murder, help!" yelled Jumbo.

"Help here, good luck to you!" cried Charley.

"Gor-a-mighty!" yelled the negro, "dis chile's a—yah!"

Jumbo made a frantic grasp at Sally as she bounded past the pool.

The negro missed the girl, but seized the cat by the tail.

In his terror to escape the crocodile Jumbo caught at anything.

He held on like grim death.

And so did the cat.

Sally was brought up sharp.

She shrieked and tried to fly.

The cat spit and swore, and buried its claws deeper and deeper in her back.

Jumbo yelled and pulled at the animal's tail to drag himself away from his deadly assailant.

Charley tugged at Jumbo's collar till he drew it half over the negro's head, swearing all the while like a trooper.

And the crocodile, determined not to give up its hope of a meal, still clung to Jumbo's coat-tail, rising higher and higher out of the slimy water every moment.

Yells, shrieks, growls, oaths, and snorts rent the air.

The green, slimy water was splashed up over the sides of the pool, and into the faces of those on its bank.

The soddened earth was trampled into mud by the feet of the frantic strugglers, and the birds as they rose, frightened from the branches, added to the din and confusion by the loud flapping of their wings, and their discordant cries.

Suddenly a loud report rose over all as 'Dolf fired at the head of the crocodile.

The bullet, true to its aim, went crashing through the reptile's eye into its brain.

" Hurrah!" was the cry of both 'Dolf and Jack as they dashed forward, the servant holding his smoking rifle, Jack grasping his hunting-knife.

But ere they had taken a couple of steps the crocodile threw up its jaw and sunk like a stone beneath the slimy surface.

Down went Sally on her face.

Down across her came floundering the released Jumbo and his friend Charley.

Jumbo's whole weight fell on the cat, who, still clinging to the animal's tail, nearly twisted it out of its socket.

This the cat did not evidently like.

It released its hold of Sally's back, and twisting round as the negro rolled aside, fastened its claws in his dusky throat.

Jumbo gave vent to a series of yells, and rolled over and over on the earth.

"Murder! Take dis yar debbil off," he cried, in his pain tugging with redoubled vigour at the animal's tail. "Oh, yah, I'm killed, suah; get out, yer debbil, yah!"

Up to his knees he fought his way.

One hand grasped the cat's neck, the other still clung to its tail.

But he could not pull the beast off.

Its talons were fastened in his coat collar and his flesh, which it was rending with its sharp nails.

'Dolf was hurriedly loading his gun.

Charley was helping Sally to her feet.

Jack, with upraised knife, feared to strike, lest he should bury the blade in Jumbo's chest instead of the back of the cat.

"Golly, but I'll hab you off, you clawing debbil," yelled the black, writhing under the deep scratches the beast inflicted.

Up he sprang to his feet.

"Dar, take dat!" he cried.

He flung himself forward on his chest and stomach, and dropped with all his dead weight on the cat.

He had hoped to cause it to let go its hold, and crush the life from the animal's body.

But the animal was far too tenacious of life.

With its bones broken by the weight of the negro it still fought on.

Never had Jumbo had such a tussle before.

The blood streamed from his neck and chest.

And finally in despair he yelled out—

"Kill de debbil if dis chile's got to go under as well."

'Dolf had loaded his gun, and now pointed it at the cat.

Then he lowered it, saying—

"I can't, I shall kill you as well."

"It's got to be done," said Jack; "as well killed by a man as a cat. Look out, Jumbo!"

And the negro closed his eyes as Jack's knife came cutting through the air.

The cat gave an awful squeal, held on for a moment, and then released its hold.

"Dar now, guess dis chile knows how to kill a cat," said the negro, as he flung the animal into the pool; "knowed I could lick dat are clawing cuss in no time."

CHAPTER XLII.

IN WHICH THERE IS A LITTLE BIT OF A SCRAMBLE.

THIS cool remark of the negro's made Jack and 'Dolf stare.

"Well," said Jack, I'm blessed if I don't like that!"

"It's cool rather," said 'Dolf.

"Dat's trufe," said Jumbo. "Guess I'll trouble Miss Scrubbins for her han'kercher to bind roun' my froat whar dat cat tried to tickle dis chile."

Sally was sitting writhing on the earth.

"Is there anything else you'd like?" said Jack; "for if ever a fellow had cool cheek I think it's you. Her handkerchief indeed."

"Well, why cool?" asked Jumbo. "Didn't I take dat cat off of her and get all de scratches? But dere dat's jus' de way; help a poor debbil an' dey turns on you."

"You didn't get helped, did you?"

"What, me get helped!"

"Yes, you. Didn't I save you from being swallowed by the crocodile?"

"Lor' now, did you?" said Jumbo.

"Of course I did. If it hadn't been for me pulling you away you'd have been a gone coon afore this, I take it."

"Has you got de cheek to take de credit ob dat are?" asked the negro.

"Rather."

"Den it's like yer imperance, dat's all, an' I pities you," said Jumbo.

"What do you mean?" said Charley.

"Oh, ob course it was me you was so bery anxious about, wasn't it?"

"Who then?"

"It was dis here coat, dat's what you wanted to sabe. If yer could hab pulled it off, you'd 'a let dat are crocodile hab had what's in it. Get out, I knows you."

"I'll let the next one swallow you, see if I don't," said Charley. "you are an ungrateful pig."

"Dat's trufe," said Jumbo.

"I wish I'd let him gobble you up, blest if I don't."

"Dat's trufe again," returned Jumbo. "I knows dat 'cos you're such a greedy cuss dat den you'd ha' all dat we now shares atween us."

"It's a pity he hadn't made a meal of the pair of you," said 'Dolf.

"Lor' now, does you think so, flunkey?" said Charley.

"I don't know what use or ornament you are, either of you," returned 'Dolf.

"Dat shows yer igerance," said Jumbo. "Dere's a won'erful lot ob use and ornament about dis chile, though I guess I don't know dat dere's much about Charley."

"Well he's good enough to furnish a meal for a crocodile as well as you," said 'Dolf.

"Dat's where ye're wrong," said Jumbo, "'cos you see if dat are crocodile was ill and wanted a 'metic—dat's what you call it, ain't it?—why den he'd only have to swallow Charley, 'cos he's so 'fernal nasty, dat de reptile 'ud be sure to be sick. Guess dat's trufe, even if he didn't poison him."

"All right," said Charley; "want me to help you dress your wounds, don't you?"

"Gor' a-mighty, tink I wants to catch 'phobia? Guess dis chile ain't such a fool. But you can jus' take dat are shirt off, 'cos I don't want dis blue clofe to rub again dese here scratches."

"Don't you wish you may get it!" cried Charley, putting his fingers to his nose.

"Suah, dere dat shows your low breeding."

"Do you see any green in my eye?" said Charley.

"Guess dar's an awful lot on your face," said Jumbo.

"Ah, yes," replied Charley, wiping the slime from his cheeks, "I didn't mean that."

"Guess you don't know what you do mean," said Jumbo. "Gor-a-mighty, don't dese are scratches smart."

"Serve you right. What did you want to pull the poor cat's tail for?"

"Tink I was going to let de brute pull down Sally's back hair?" said Jumbo. "Guess I'se too much 'mirer ob de fair sex for dat. Golly, now, but dat jus' reminds me, Massa Jack, dat you'se got a bottle ob summat nice in yer pocket."

"Oh! I forgot," said Jack, pulling out a small wicker flask of brandy. "It will be very handy just now."

"Guess dat's trufe," said Jumbo.

"It's good stuff for scratches of wild cats."

"Excellent," said Jack.

"Den we'll use it for dat."

"That's what I mean to do," said Jack.

"Thank you, Massa Jack."

And the negro held out his hand for the bottle.

"What do you want?" said Jack, drawing back.

"Some ob dat are scratch medicine. Dat's what it's for, ain't it?"

"I said it was. Here, Sally, take a pull at this, old girl. It will put some life in you."

And he held the bottle to Sally's lips.

"Gor-a-mighty, don't you go for to drink it all," cried Jumbo.

"Shut up," said Charley.

"Hold hard dar," cried Jumbo. "Dat are stuff's too strong to drink much of."

"Is it?" said Sarah.

"'Spects it am—leastways all at once," said Jumbo. "Jus' let dis chile take a small pull, and den he'll gib it you back."

"Don't you, Sally," said Charley. "It's precious little you'll get once he lays hold of it."

"Dere now," said Jumbo, "don't I always share eberyting?"

"Oy, yes," said Charley. "You'll drink the brandy and give her the bottle. I know you; so you hold on to it," Sally."

"I mean to," said Sally.

"There's only a little drop," said Jack, "so you stick to that. You want it to compose your nerves."

"Guess dis are chile's nerbs wants a lot ob composing," said Jumbo, eyeing the bottle anxiously.

"Well, you'll have to wait till we get back to the boat to compose them," said Jack.

"Am dat so?"

"It is."

"Den I'm brest if you ain't a lot ob——"

"What?" cried Jack, turning on him quickly.

"What?" said Jumbo, retreating to Sally's side.

"Yes, what—what?"

"Wild cats—cats—wild cats!" yelled Jumbo.

"FLINGING UP HER HANDS, MINNIE TOOK THE DESPERATE LEAP."

PRICE ONE HALFPENNY
[Published Every Monday.]

At this Sally sprang to her feet and turned to fly.

Jumbo took advantage of her terror and drew the bottle from her hand.

"Where?—where?" cried Jack, looking round, as also did Charley and 'Dolf.

Jumbo jerked the bottle to his lips, and the spirit went gurgling down his throat.

So swiftly did he pour it down that in a couple of moments he had to pause for breath, and began coughing violently.

Jack sprang upon him and tore the bottle from his hand.

"Cats! where? I don't see them," he cried. "Come back, Sally."

"Eh?" said Jumbo.

Sally came back to Jack's side.

"Cats—where are they?" cried Jack.

"I don't know; guess there's plenty about, though."

"But where did you see 'em," asked Sally, peering around.

"See um? didn't see um," replied Jumbo.

"Then what did you say you did for?" cried 'Dolf.

"Didn't say I did," replied Jumbo.

"You infernal fibber, you did."

"Hear dat now," said Jumbo; "didn't say I seed wild cats."

"What did you see, then?" cried Jack.

"Dat are bottle," replied Jumbo.

"What's that got to do with cats?" asked 'Dolf.

"Yah, yah!" laughed Jumbo.

"Look here, what do you mean?" cried Jack, angrily. "What game are you up to?"

"Bress your soul, I ain't up to no game now. Yah! guess dis chile was though. I said dat you was all a set ob wild cats, and you all jumped and gib dis chile a chance to collar some of dat are med'cine—yah, yah!"

"What a sell," said Charley.

"Guess I hab yer dere."

"You won't have us again, though," said Charley; "we'll drink the brandy between us."

"Don' think you will," said Jack.

"Suah you won't," said Jumbo; "dis chile took good care ob dat."

Jack held the bottle up to his ear and shook it.

"Why, you greedy hound, you've drank it all," he cried.

"No, I didn't; Sally had her share."

"And now where's mine?" said Charley.

"And mine?" said Jack.

"Guess you'll hab to wait till you gets back to de boat," replied Jumbo.

"Well, that is a sell," said Charley.

"Guess that's trufe," said Jumbo.

"You ought to be poleaxed," cried Charley.

"Guess dat's trufe as well."

"I'm disgusted," said Charley.

"So am I," said Jumbo. "Guess you are 'cos you didn't get none, and it was bery good stuff."

"I'm half a mind to propose that we chuck you into the pool and leave you there," said Charley.

"Don't you tell lies," said Jumbo; "you'se awful bad you are, but you'se too 'cute to frow away what's so serbiceable to you. You knows dat if it wasn't for your being paternised by dis 'spectable cullered gen'leman nobody would look at such white trash."

"Oh, I like that," said Charley.

"In course you does; but you better be mighty civil, or I 'draws my paternage and leaves yer to sink down, down, down into the bery deepest deps ob—ob —ob—what the debbil am it called?"

"Bosh!" cried 'Dolf.

"Dat's it," cried Jumbo; "de bery deepest deps ob bosh, dar!"

And Jumbo drew his saturated coat over his scarified bosom, elevated his nose in the air, and turned loftily away.

Charley and 'Dolf laughed at the negro's antics.

"Guess it would lick you to cock your head up as high as that, wouldn't it, flunkey?" said Charley.

"But it wouldn't my foot," said 'Dolf.

And up he swung his leg and gave Charley so heavy a kick at the bottom of his back that that youth went flying forward after Jumbo, as if shot from a catapult.

The force with which his head and shoulders came against the centre of the negro's back, lifted Jumbo in turn off his feet.

Down he went and Charley went sprawling over him.

"Gor a'mighty;" cried Jumbo.

"What the devil!" yelled Charley.

The negro imagining it was an intentional assault, grasped Charley by the hair.

Charley, scarce knowing what he did, seized Jumbo by the wool.

Away they tugged at each others' hair, rolling over and over on the ground.

'Dolf shrieked aloud with laughter.

Jack followed suit, and Sally forgot her wounds and her fears in the comical combat, and joined her laughter with the others.

Charley and Jumbo soon began to realise the foolishness of their conduct, and letting go by mutual consent, rose sheepishly to their feet.

"Well, now, you fellows, if you've had your lark out," said Jack, "we'll attend to business. I think we've had enough play, so suppose we set to work."

CHAPTER XLIII.

IN WHICH MINNIE TAKES A BATH, AND TIGER CLAW TAKES STEEL.

AMONG the numerous hordes of savages that roam at will the prairies and forests of the new world, it would have been a difficult task to find a braver chief than Tiger Claw.

He had spoken truly when he said that he had fought his foes on land and river, that he had faced the panther, and brought to earth the bison.

Fear he had never known.

But now something akin to it he felt as he stood before the enraged Minnie, with his own spear meanacing his bosom.

Never had he quailed before man as he quailed before this slim tender girl.

Never could he have believed that woman could possess such courage.

But then he had never seen an Englishwoman driven to desperation.

His experience of the fair sex had been only among the wigwams of his people, where he had seen them cowering beneath the lash of their husbands, and meekly submitting to perform the most degrading offices.

No wonder then that for a time surprise held him dumb.

And that, when after a few moments he raised his hand to strike, it sunk again powerless to his side.

Surprise and rage gradually gave place to a feeling of admiration in his bosom.

But pity he had none.

The very courage and defiance of this girl only made him the more eager to possess her for his own.

Slowly he folded his arms across his broad bosom, and gave utterance to a sound that might have expressed contempt, but which was in reality one of admiration.

"By the great spirit the pale-face maiden is brave," he said.

"I am desperate!" cried Minnie.

"You are lovely," he replied.

"I am mad," cried Minnie. "Chief, you bid me beware. Oh, you know not what a white woman will dare when driven to desperation, or you would beware yourself. Nay, move not or you die!"

He recoiled the step he had taken, and stood gazing at her as the light of the fire played upon her pale face, and the spear head she still kept levelled at his bosom.

Tiger Claw gazed upon Minnie with admiration.

"Chief," she said, "I have implored your mercy, I implore it once again. Is the conquest of one weak woman so great that you will risk your life to torture her? I tell you I must go free, if it be only to the freedom of the grave. Suffer me to depart!"

"The pale face asks what the chief will not grant," he replied. "Let her demand all else, and she shall not ask in vain."

"I ask nothing but to be permitted to go hence unmolested," said Minnie.

"And whither would the pale-face go?" he asked.

"Anywhere so that it were from here, from you," she replied.

"The forests are full of beasts and reptiles," he replied. "Would the white maiden prefer death in the embrace of the bear or the folds of the snake to lie in the arms of Tiger Claw?"

"Yes, a thousand times yes," she replied.

"Then is the pale-faced maiden mad," he replied. "Let her lay aside the spear and be content with her fate, for she must become the squaw of Tiger Claw, and weave for him the moccasin."

"I say never," she cried. "Rather will I find release in the waters that flow at our feet. I can meet death, but never never accept life on such an alternative."

"The pale-face will not die; she shall live to kindle the fire in the lodge of Tiger Claw. She shall live to welcome him from the chase and the fight, and he will lay the scalps of his foes at her feet, and ask only in return her love."

Minnie shudderrd.

"Again, I say, let the pale-face lay the chief's spear on the earth, and let Tiger Claw see her smile again."

"Give me my liberty," she cried, "and I will smile upon you, bless you."

"Tiger Claw will not suffer you to leave him; he has spoken."

"Then thus do I take what you deny, cruel savage!" she cried, moving backwards towards the bank of the river. "This night I will go hence, even if it be to my death!"

"Hold!" cried the chief.

"Keep back, I am resolved!" cried Minnie.

"The pale-face is mad," he cried, making a grasp at the spear.

But quick as lightning Minnie sprang back, and again levelled the weapon at his chest.

"Advance, and your blood be on your own head," she cried.

"I offered the pale-face love and she asks for hate," he cried. "I would make her my squaw, and she spurns me. She shall be my slave; I have spoken."

He drew his tomahawk and whirled it round his head.

"Kill me," she cried, "it were mercy."

"Kill thee? no!" he replied, "but escape me, never. Down with that spear! Thou wilt not, pale-face fool? It is Tiger Claw who speaks."

And he severed the spear in twain with a blow of his hatchet.

Minnie gave a cry of despair.

Tiger Claw uttered a shout of triumph and sprang upon her.

But she eluded his grasp and flew shrieking to the bank of the river.

The chief bounded after her.

The cries of Minnie and the shouts of the chief caused the savages lying around the fire to spring to their feet.

But they did not move away from the fire, though they stood ready to do so at the first bidding of their leader.

As Minnie reached the bank the hand of Tiger Claw touched her shoulder.

By a superhuman effort she eluled his grasp, and turning, darted into the shadow of some bushes.

The tomahawk crashed through the bushes after her.

"Oh, Heaven!" gasped Minnie, "by death only can I escape him."

"The pale-face shall never escape," cried the warrior, as his hand touched her dress.

But she sped away, leaving a portion of her garment in his grasp, and turning again made for the river.

She reached the bank.

"Heaven forgive me," she cried, "it is my only refuge."

And flinging up her hands Minnie took the leap.

The chief darted out his hand to grasp her descending form.

But as he did so there was a thin streak of light behind him, and as a sharp instrument buried itself in his shoulder, his arm fell to his side, and he yelled out a cry of pain and alarm.

Then he sprang round to discover from whence the stroke came.

But a heavy blow planted between his eyes blinded his vision, and ere he could recover his sight, he heard a loud splash in the water at his feet.

"Save her, save the pale-face!" he yelled, and sank to the earth.

His cry brought several of his followers to his side.

Anxious eyes were bent upon the moonlit waters.

But nothing was to be seen save the moonrays reflected on the dancing wavelets.

The chief spoke a few hurried words.

The savages started away on all sides, while some of them threw themselves into the river.

The chief staggered to his feet. Blood was running from his shoulder, but he shook off the faintness that was stealing over him.

He bent down and peered into the stream.

His gaze searched in vain for Minnie.

One by one his followers returned to his side.

Their search for the assailant of Tiger Claw had been in vain.

The savages came back from their bath in the river.

The pale-face maiden could not be found.

She must have sunk.

The chief set his teeth together and suffered himself to be led back to the fire.

But where was Minnie, and who was it who had given the chief his wound?

Had Tiger Claw or one of his braves stood on the bank half-an-hour afterwards, the moon's rays would have revealed to him a canoe in which sat a young man with his face painted like an Indian's and wearing on his head a tuft of feathers, and a girdle of feathers round his waist, and in the bottom of the canoe lay the insensible form of poor Minnie Sash, and he might have heard the muttered words—

"Mine again, mine! Ned Nimble Bill Boaster will yet have his revenge!"

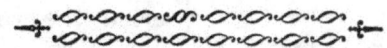

CHAPTER XLIV.

IN WHICH A START IS MADE AND DANGER LOOMS IN THE DISTANCE.

IN hunting, fishing, and preparing for a start for the camping-grounds of Tiger Claw, several days passed.

A large store of provisions had been obtained from the river and the island, and rest and careful attention to their wounds had restored both Ned and Bircher to comparative health and strength.

But the loss of the canoe was severely felt, for the boat was overcrowded, and Ned saw there was no help for it but to get rid of his Indian rowers, and trust to themselves to work the vessel up the river.

So calling the Indians around him he expressed his thanks for the service they had rendered him, and his regret at being compelled to part with them.

He gave the rowers double what he had agreed to do, and told them he must put them on shore and leave them to get back as best they could.

To this they made no objection, the receipt of a double reward making them greatly elated, and bringing down showers of thanks on the generous pale-face.

So everything being settled, shortly after sunrise the boat was pulled out of the bay into the wide river and rowed for the mainland, where the Indians were put ashore, their hands filled with presents from Ned.

Then Jack, Charley, and the others headed the vessel up the stream, and they were fairly started on their journey for the camping-grounds of Tiger Claw.

Though of course Ned was the head of the expedition, yet Sally, from her general knowledge of the river and the places on its banks, took command.

Under her directions the others worked.

Each took turn at the oars except Bircher, who, when not otherwise engaged, steered.

"Spose we'll hab to call her cap'n now," said Jumbo, turning to Charley.

"Course we shall," rejoined Charley; "we're under petticoat government now, you know, old son."

"Dis chile can't see dat."

"Can't see what?" said Charley.

"How we is under petticoat gubberment; 'cos there arn't a bressed petticoat aboard dis yar ship."

"What do you mean?"

"Ingin squaws don't wear petticoats; you don't call dat 'ere ting that Sally's got on a petticoat, do you?"

"What else is it, you fool?"

"Why a gownd what's cut short off at de knee."

"Well, that makes a petticoat of it, don't it?"

"Does it; den if dis yar coat-tail gets pulled off, dis yer nigger will be 'tired in a westcoat, eh?"

"Of course, it'll be a coat as comes to the waist, and that's a waistcoat, ain't it, eh?"

"Guess yer getting sharp, ain't you?" said Jumbo.

"Always was," replied Charley;

"wouldn't you like to have some of my sharpness, eh?"

"Don't know as I'd feel any better if I did," said Jumbo.

"Yes, you would; it would put a lot of life into you."

"Guess den dis chile'ul take a happorth if you got any to spare," said the negro.

"Ain't got none to sell, but as you're a friend of mine I'll give you some."

And Charley took a long pin from his shirt collar and held it so that, as Jumbo fell back in his rowing, the point ran deep into his back.

"Gor-a-mighty!" yelled the nigger, as starting up and letting go his oar he received a blow from it that lifted him over the thwart into Charley's lap.

The handle of Charley's oar caught him on the back of the head and knocked him off his friend's knee.

"What de debbil's dat?" cried the negro, as he sat up and rubbed his head.

"Look out!" cried Charley, "there goes your oar overboard."

Jumbo made a clutch at the oar as it slipped out of the rowlock.

As he did so he received a blow at the bottom of the back from the hands of Charley, and before he knew where he was he had shot head first over the side of the boat into the river.

All on board broke into laughter as the negro disappeared, but Ned ceased rowing and bent over to seize the negro directly he should come to the surface.

All on board were surprised to see the blade of the floating oar suddenly rise up in the water.

Jumbo had kept his hold on the handle, and his weight had caused the blade to rise and thereby force him still further downwards.

In a moment Ned realised the negro's danger.

If Jumbo did not let go the handle of the oar he would be drowned.

Would he do so, or would he lose his presence of mind and still cling to the end of it?

Higher and higher rose the blade above the surface.

Ned flung off his coat.

"Why don't the fool let go?" he cried.

"Because he is a fool, that's why," said Charley.

Ned hesitated no longer.

He sprang over the side of the vessel and disappeared.

Harry flung off his coat and stood ready to plunge in should Ned need his aid.

But in a moment down went the blade and up shot the head of the African.

Close behind it appeared the face of Ned.

"Hook that oar aboard or we shall lose it," cried Ned.

"Hook dis yar chile aboard," gasped Jumbo, "or golly you'll lose him, and he's worth more dan dat har oar."

"Do you want any help, Ned?" asked Harry.

"No, thanks, dear boy," called Ned.

Jack drew the oar to the side of the boat with the boat-hook, and 'Dolf and Harry grasped Ned and Jumbo and helped them over the side.

"All right, old man?" asked Harry.

"As a trivet," replied Ned.

"Why didn't you let go the end of the oar? you might have drowned yourself," said Harry, turning to Jumbo.

"Let go," cried Jumbo. "Golly, but I hole tight, an' if Massa Ned hadn't took me away I should ha' climbed up dat 'ere pole. Guess he likes to wet his clothes dat he cum after me."

"I calculate it's you as wants to spoil that coat," said Charley. "You are always a-doing something to injure it, you are."

"Go below, old man, and get some dry togs," said Harry.

"That's what I mean to do," replied Ned.

"An' what'll dis chile do for dry close?" asked Jumbo.

"Go without 'em," said Charley, "and serve you right for falling overboard."

"I guess dat you knocked me over."

"Get out. What do you mean?" said Charley. "If you would sit down on top of my fists when I was pulling why of course you'd be bound to be lifted off, wouldn't you?"

"Guess dat's trufe," said Jumbo, scratching his head; "but if some cuss of a muskito hadn't a-jumped on dis chile's back dis chile wouldn't hab gone ober."

"Oh, did a mosquito sting you?"

"Golly, didn't it," said Jumbo. "Jus' here."

"How did it feel?" said Charley, with a grin. "Did it sting much?"

"Almost as much as that," said Sally, bringing her hand down with all her force across the ear of Charley. "I saw your capers, you artful varmint, I did. You might have been the cause of the death of Master Ned and this stupid nigger."

"Here, I say," cried Charley, rubbing his ear, "what's that for? Just you cut it."

"You know what it's for," said Sally, "and I tell you I won't have none of your larks while I'm captain of this ship."

"Bravo, Sally!" said 'Dolf. "Show your authority."

"Mr. 'Dolf, you mind your own business, and leave me to attend to mine, if you please. I don't wan't none of your remarks."

"Sorry I spoke," said 'Dolf.

"Mr. Nimble has put me in charge of this boat," said Sally, "and I'm going to command her in a proper manner, ain't I, Jack?"

"Of course. Who said you wasn't? I didn't."

"And I didn't say you did. I saw Charley's little game if Jumbo didn't, and I won't have any such tricks played, so look out all of you."

"Well, I like your cheek," said Charley.

"And I like yours," said Sally, giving him another slap of the face.

"Here, I say, you Sal Scrubbins, cut that game, or I shall make you," cried Charley, starting up.

"What, mutiny?" cried Sally. "Here, Jack, pitch him overboard. I'll soon show him that the captain of a vessel is its king. Overboard with him."

"Golly, I'll help you," said Jumbo. "Guess dis chile's a-going to hab his revenge. Yah, yah!"

And Jumbo stepped towards Charley.

But as the negro put out his hand to grasp him, Jack caught hold of the tail of his coat and pitched him on to his back.

"A truce to this nonsense," he said. "There's a fleet of canoes coming up. We may have something else to do soon. Call Ned Nimble on deck."

CHAPTER XLV.

IN WHICH CHARLEY MAKES A WAGER AND WINS IT.

THE appearance of half-a-dozen canoes put a sudden stop to the proceedings on board the boat, and even Jumbo looked serious as he turned his eyes in the direction whence they came, and saw that they were crowded with Indians.

Sally watched them intently for some moments, and then, when Ned and Harry again appeared on deck, she said—

"Mr. Nimble, if those fellows yonder mean business with us we shall have to fight hard to prevent the loss of the boat, if not our liberty and our lives."

"Do you think they have seen us?" asked Ned.

"Of course they have, and what's more they are making for us too."

"They may be friendly to us," said Harry.

"They may," said Sally, "but I'd rather say they were not."

"Then we will prepare to meet them as enemies," said Ned. "Jumbo, a pair

of my trousers will not fit you, but as you have not been in the habit lately of wearing raiment of the most approved cut, I suppose you can make them do."

"Sartinly, sar," said Jumbo. "I ain't particular as to the length of them."

"'Dolf, give Jumbo a pair of my trousers and one of my shirts. Go with him and get them. Where's Sally?"

"Gone below," said Jack. "Shall I call her?"

"No, never mind. Mr. Bircher, I think we shall have to fight from the appearance of things."

"I hope not, Nimble," said the tutor. "Not that I fear an encounter, but I am not so well as I was yesterday, and should not be able to do justice to the name of an Englishman, you know."

Ned smiled.

"Oh, never mind, Mr. Bircher, you'll do to keep an arrow off somebody else if you ain't any good at fighting," said Ned.

"Don't, Nimble, don't. It's not a good thing to jest upon such a subject," cried the tutor.

"He's beginning to funk, Ned," whispered Harry.

"Beginning!" said Ned; "he began with his first fight, but he'll join in for all that when he's pushed to it. Even cowards fight, you know, when driven into a corner."

"That's true."

"Then let's get ready to give these fellows pepper if they molest us," said Ned. "I'll get the arms out ready."

Jumbo now returned on deck.

He was attired in one of Ned's shirts and pair of trousers, and evidently greatly admired himself.

"My!" cried Charley, "ain't we toffish."

"Did you 'dress dat 'mark to me, sar?" cried Jumbo.

"Lor', don't you think something of yourself now in other people's togs," said Charley.

"I tinks it's a great piece of imperance for ragged white trash to speak to 'spectable gen'leman like me. Jus' you member dis, I'se a——"

"Fool!" interrupted Charley.

"Dat's trufe," said Jumbo. "Doesn't you envy me now?"

"Envy you? No, I pity you."

"Pity! golly, I like dat. What for you pity a gen'leman like me?"

"Because you're obliged to wear other people's clothes."

"Dar yer wrong. Dis yer shirt and dese yer trousers is de property ob dis yer chile," said Jumbo.

"How do you make that out? Did Nimble give them to you?" asked Charley.

"Ob course he didn't. But den he couldn't be so mean as to take 'em back again, you know."

"Oh, yes, I forgot," cried Charley. "He'd be frightened to."

"Frightened?"

"Yes, after you'd worn 'em. Wouldn't care about catching the itch, of course not."

"Sar!" cried Jumbo, "do you mean to 'siniate dat dis chile's got de scratch?"

"You know you have," said Charley

"I say it's a lie, sar—a big, dundering big lie," cried Jumbo, indignantly.

"And I say it's truth," retorted Charley, "and I'll bet you my next share of grog that you have, and prove it too, there!"

"You will?"

"I will."

"Den dis chile bets you."

"Fair?"

"Fair, suah."

"You hear that, Jack?" said Charley.

"I hear," said Jack.

"Den yer a wetnuss to dat bet," said Jumbo.

"If you like," said Jack.

"All right," said Charley. "The grog will be served out direc'ly, and you'll see I've got to drink your share as well as my own."

"Is yer," said Jumbo. "Guess it'll take you a jolly long while to prove as I've got de scratch."

"Very well, wait till the grog comes, then Jack shall be umpire and decide whether I've won or not."

"Guess dis chile's sartin of a big drink dis time," said Jumbo. "Golly, wish I was as sure as Massa Ned will let me keep dese yer trousers. Dey fits me slick."

Harry meanwhile had been keeping watch over the approaching canoes, ever and anon turning a quick gaze upon the face of Mr. Bircher, which was momentarily growing paler and paler.

He could see that the Indians were armed, and evidently not on a very peaceful expedition.

"We shall soon be within range of their arrows, Mr. Bircher," said Harry. "But that would make little difference if we were only certain they meditated an attack upon us."

"How so, Honour?" asked the tutor, in a questioning voice.

"Because our rifles carry further than their bows," said Harry; "and we could pop them off before they could do us any mischief."

"It would be better then to take it for granted that they are not disposed to be friendly," said Bircher.

"It would scarcely be the right thing to fire upon them until we were certain of their intentions, Mr. Bircher," said Harry.

"Well—er—no, not exactly, but still

it's better sometimes to take things for granted and act accordingly," said Bircher.

"I don't think it would redound to our credit in this instance," said Harry, "for after all, despite their warlike appearance, these savages may have no intention of molesting us."

"Who do they intend to molest then?" asked Bircher.

"How can I tell?"

"It's somebody, or they would not be armed, and it's only natural to conclude that it's us."

"Still, it is uncertain, and we should give them the benefit of the doubt," replied Harry, firmly.

"And let them give us the benefit of a shower of arrows before we attempt to stop them," said Bircher.

Harry did not reply, for at that moment Ned came on deck, carrying with him several rifles.

"'Dolf," he cried, "fetch up the brandy and give each a glass; those canoes are getting precious near, and it won't be long before we shall have to open the ball."

'Dolf dived below.

"Jack, let each man have a revolver. Go and bring them up. You'll find them in the rack. Every one is loaded ready. We may have to use them if our rifles do not keep those red devils at a respectful distance."

"Here's the brandy," said 'Dolf.

"Give each his share," replied Ned.

'Dolf offered a glass first to Ned, then to Harry and Bircher.

The tutor took it with a trembling hand, and spilt a portion over his shirt front.

Jack returned with the revolvers, and giving one to each, together with a hunting-knife, drank his brandy.

"Now, you fellows," said 'Dolf, addressing Charley and the negro.

They advanced together, and Charley held out his hand for the glass.

"Jus' you wait," said Jumbo, pushing his hand back; "guess dis chile'll hab yours as well as him own. Don't you go for to back out ob dat bet, becos you won't. You've got to prove dat I got de scratch afore you smells dat glass."

"Yes, that's right," said Jack, "no backing out. How will you prove it Charley?"

"He can't," said Jumbo.

"I can," said Charley.

"Do it," said the nigger.

"So I will now. Jack, you've got t decide. Has Jumbo got the scratch o not?"

And he caught hold of Jumbo's shirt and tearing open the bosom, pointed t his lacerated chest.

"There's the scratch. I've won m wager," he cried.

"Give Charley two glasses and th nigger none, he has fairly lost his bet, said Jack.

Jumbo's jaw dropped, and Charle with a loud laugh seized the glass.

CHAPTER XLVI.

IN WHICH NED AND HIS FRIENDS MAKE THE ACQUAINTANCE OF TIGER CLAW.

THE astonishment so comically expressed in Jumbo's face caused Jack and 'Dolf to roar with laughter, in which Charley joined as soon as he had drunk his own share as well as the negro's.

"I calculate, old man, I won that bet square and neat; didn't I?" said Charley.

"Well," said Jumbo, "if dere'd been any justice in dis yere blessed world dat 'ere brandy 'ud choked you. I guess I done with you now, done with you for eber."

And Jumbo cast a longing look at the

bottle in 'Dolf's hand and turned awa with a heavy sigh.

Jack informed Ned of the whol affair.

"Poor beggar, tell 'Dolf to give hir a glass," he said.

And he joined Harry.

"I can't make those fellows out," sai Harry, pointing to the canoes; "the are fairly within range of our rifles, an if we were certain they meant mischie we ought to give them a volley."

"They seem very quiet," said Ned.

"Yes; and that's what makes m

bt their intention. We are not up their tactics, unfortunately."

"Sally is, though."

"Where is she?"

"In the cabin," said Ned, "where I pe she will remain, out of danger."

"That's just what she won't do, Mas-Ned," said Jack, coming to his side. That girl never kept out of a row if could poke her nose into one. She s always in hot water in England."

"She is better where she is if it comes a fight," said Ned.

"So say I. But she will have her own y."

"Then I pity you, Jack," said Harry, ghing.

"Halloa!" said Ned, "what are those lows up to?"

The Indians were fitting arrows to ir bows and the canoes were spread-g out.

"Take to your arms, lads," said Ned, nd lay low, the ball is about to open. o not fire till I give the order, and en let each shot tell."

Bircher flung himself quickly down on e deck.

The others grasped each a rifle, and ouched low under the bulwarks.

Jumbo excepted, who having received s ration of brandy, was too busily en-aged in jeering at Charley to heed ed's order.

"Dar, you white cuss," he cried. Guess dis chile ain't got de worst of it ter all. Got my share, didn't I—yah! lways mean to hab my share, I does—h! Oh!"

A shower of arrows came whirling rough the air, and the negro bounded couple of feet from the deck as one of em cut away a portion of his ear in s flight.

"Golly, I'm killed, suah," he cried, as s hand went up to his ear and his nees came down on the deck. "What e debbel——"

"Fire!" cried the voice of Ned.

Up sprang each from the deck and a olley of bullets was sent among the In-ians.

"Down, and load quickly," cried Ned.

A yell broke from the savages as the aden messengers of death came plung-g amongst them, and two of their umber pitched out of the canoes into e water.

But the others fitted arrows to their bows, and another shower was sent at the boat, accompanied by a fearful yell from fifty Indian throats.

As Ned had said, Bircher would find his courage as soon as the fight began.

His paleness fled.

His face flushed, and his teeth set hard together.

Quickly he loaded his rifle, and crouch-ing behind the low bulwark waited the order to fire.

The second flight of arrows sped harmlessly on their way.

Again came the order to fire.

Again the report of seven rifles rang through the air, and as many bullets carried wounds and death into the mass of savages.

Again yells of pain and fury arose from the Indians, mingling with the splashing of heavy bodies as they fell into the water.

"Keep low," cried Ned, "the beggars are coming on. Do not waste a shot. Wait till I give the order to fire again."

Just peeping over the top of the bul-warks Ned watched the movements of the savages.

Bang!

A puff of smoke rose from one of the canoes and a bullet struck the side of the boat within a dozen inches of Ned's head.

"Whew!" whistled Ned, as he drew back rapidly. "Some of the beggars have got firearms."

"All the worse for us," said Harry. "Be careful, Ned; the next shot may come nearer than the last."

"All right, dear boy. See that tall fellow in the stern of the longest canoe? That's he who fired."

"He is loading his rifle again. I'll give him a shot before he can finish it."

Harry glided the barrel of his rifle over the side, took aim, and fired.

"Missed him," said Harry, "confound it!"

"Never mind, old man, you've winged the other by his side."

"Try your luck, Ned, while I load up."

Ned brought his rifle to bear upon the savage, but as he fired the canoe swerved round and another occupant of the vessel received the shot in his side.

Meanwhile the savages were not idle.

Again a flight of arrows came whizzing through the air.

But this time, evidently by the order of the Indian with the rifle, they were shot higher, so as to fall on the deck of the boat.

"Fire!" cried Ned again, as the arrows struck the sides and deck, doing no more damage than pinning the coat of Bircher to the planks.

Up sprang the white men and Jumbo, and poured in a volley.

"Down," cried Ned, "and load!"

Down they sank in a moment, without stopping to see the effect of their fire.

But it was pretty clearly told by the yells of their enemies.

"I'm glad Sally keeps out of this," said Ned to Harry.

"So am I," replied his friend.

"Wonder who that fellow is?" retorted Ned; "he's evidently the chief of that howling mob. Look at him now he stands up; he's every inch a man, isn't he?"

"He is indeed a noble-looking chap," said Harry; "what a carriage! Have you got him in range, Ned?"

"I think so," replied Ned; "now."

Ned fired. The Indian shook his head and clapped his hand to his cheek.

The Indian raised his rifle quickly and fired.

Ned felt the bullet whistle past his ear.

"Bravo," said Ned, "a splendid shot."

"Almost too warm, old man," said Harry, drawing Ned lower down to the deck.

As he did so another loud yell broke from the savages.

Ned looked up quickly.

The whole fleet of savages was bearing swiftly down upon the boat.

"Ready, boys," cried Ned; "they mean to board us; give that tall Indian a volley; he bears a charmed life whoever he is."

"That is Tiger Claw. To fall into his hands is certain death."

Ned turned at these words and saw Sally standing behind him.

In his surprise at learning that the brave chief at whom he had fired in vain was no other than the abductor of Minnie Sash, Ned stood glaring at Sally, quite forgetful of the mark he presented to the rifle of Tiger Claw or the arrows of his braves.

Nor was he reminded of this till Harry drew both himself and Sally down to the deck.

"Tiger Claw! The wretch who slew Phopps and tore Minnie from his arms" he cried at last.

"Yes, Tiger Claw," returned Sally, "the red warmint who wanted to make me Mrs. Tiger Claw, and from whom I had escaped when you found me surrounded by wild cats on the island, that's him, and I only hope my Jack will get hold of him that's all."

"Tiger Claw!" repeated Ned.

"Yes, him as wanted to make me his squaw after he'd killed my husband; not as I cared for the departed, oh dear no, but though he's a handsome Indian is Tiger Claw, he's a wild one, and 'ware hawks to us if we fall into his hands."

CHAPTER XLVII.

IN WHICH JACK AND SALLY SCRUBBINS ASTONISH THE NATIVES.

NED cast a quick glance at the savage chief, and as his gaze rested on that determined face he felt that indeed it would be a fearful fate to fall into the hands of Tiger Claw.

"Go below, Sally," said Harry, "he will recognise you if you stay on deck, and if we have to knock under to this savage you may escape him again as you did before."

"Go and hide?—not if I knows it,"

said Sally; "I'm going for his scalp this time. Want me to be Mrs. Tiger Claw does he? I'll claw him if I can."

And Sally flourished an umbrella which she held in her hand.

"Not with that, surely?" said Harry as he hurriedly loaded his rifle.

"With this and nothing else, my boy," replied Sally.

"Don't you go spoiling my umbrella," cried Bircher; "there's many a slip bewist the cup and the lip, and if we should be suffered to escape I may require the services of that old friend, so pray put it back again from where you took it."

"It is anything but a formidable weapon," said Ned; "but pray be advised, Sally, go below and leave us to do the fighting."

"Not if I knows it," said Sally. "I ain't a girl of that sort, oh, dear, no, and as for this not being a good weapon wait and see if it ain't. I'll astonish you with what I'll do with it, see if I don't."

"If you won't go below, pray keep out of danger all you can," said Ned; "give them another volley, lads, and then we must trust to knives and revolvers if they effect a footing on this deck."

The savages were now almost close to the boat.

Under the direction of Tiger Claw the canoes had borne down on the boat, and when within a short distance they separated so as to surround it, those who were not rowing sending shower after shower of arrows from their bows.

The whites gave them another volley, Charley receiving the bullet from Tiger Claw's rifle in return, which passed through his rimless hat, close enough to his head to cause him to fall to the deck.

"Golly, am you dead?" cried Jumbo, dropping down beside him.

"Yes, quite," returned Charley. "Can't you see I am?"

"Guess it's trufe, I can," said the negro, "so as you're dead, get up, and don't play possum."

And Jumbo gave him a kick in the ribs to accelerate his movements.

Charley was on his feet in an instant. There was no time to reload.

The canoes, nearly half emptied by the rifles of Ned and his companions, were now close alongside, and the yelling savages, throwing aside their bows and arrows had drawn knives and tomahawks, and were climbing up the sides, bow and stern of the boat.

"Down with them!" shouted Ned, clubbing his rifle.

"Beat them back into the water!" cried Harry.

"Gib 'em gumbiles on de top ob dere heads!" yelled Jumbo.

With clubbed rifles the crew of the boat battered away at the heads and hands of the savages as they made frantic efforts to reach the deck.

Bircher forgot his wounds and his nervousness, and where he could reach a head he hit it, and hit it hard.

The yells of the Indians were truly deafening.

The splashing of the water as body after body fell back beneath the heavy blows of the defenders, was continuous.

But still the savages swarmed up the sides.

The tall form of Tiger Claw sprang over the low bulwark, and his clubbed rifle warded off the blows that Harry and Ned aimed at him.

Before his towering form Ned and Harry were compelled to fall back, and up behind him and on to the deck swarmed his yelling followers.

Now the tide of battle changed.

The savages could no longer be kept at bay.

"Shoulder to shoulder, boys," shouted Ned. "If we must die, we'll die fighting—shoulder to shoulder."

Fighting at every step, and retreating slowly on all sides, the companions of Ned drew back till they formed a compact knot in the centre of the vessel.

"Would to Heaven you had gone below!" cried Ned to Sally, as he saw the eyes of the chief fixed upon her, and detected that Tiger Claw had recognised her.

"Let me alone," said Sally.

"Down with your rifles, and trust to your revolvers and your knives," cried Ned.

In a moment the rifles were flung aside and their revolvers were in their hands.

"Give them pepper," cried Ned.

Ned and his friends opened fire, and the Indians fell back before the terrific volley that was fired upon them.

But now several of those who had been forced back into the water climbed upon the deck and the fight was renewed.

But the revolvers kept them off.

Much to the surprise of Ned, as the Indians raised their tomakawks for a throw, the chief bade them hold, but Sally guessed the reason.

"He wants to make sure of getting hold of me," she cried; "and if they throw their hatchets one might hit me."

"Thank Heaven for that," cried Ned, "or we had been done for ere this."

"Confound the gingham, it won't open after all," cried Sally, who had been making frantic efforts to open the umbrella. "And, oh, didn't I expect to give 'em pepper."

At length all the chambers of their revolvers were emptied, and the whites had only their knives to meet the onslaught of the Indians, whose numbers were yet formidable, despite the fearful slaughter that had been going on.

Still unscathed through all that deadly volley stood Tiger Claw.

Now realising the helplessness of the whites he gave a quick order, and with upraised tomahawk and a demoniacal yell he sprang forward at the head of his braves.

His descending arm, as it aimed a blow with his hatchet at Ned's head, was caught in the hold of Jack and twisted till the tomahawk fell from his grasp, and then the conjuror seized the chief with the other hand, and flinging him off

his feet held him above his head as if he were an infant.

This feat of strength so surprised the Indians that they stood for a moment thunderstruck, and in that moment Sally succeeded in forcing open her umbrella, and shrieked aloud—

"Now, you red beggars, I'll give you a taste of my patent mitrailleuse."

And the surprise of Ned and his friends was quite equal to the consternation of the Indians as volley after volley of bullets was poured into them from the bottom of the umbrella at every movement of Sally's hand.

With yells of terror the Indians sprang over the side of the boat into their canoes, Sally pointing the umbrella towards them, and firing at them as they scrambled over.

"How do you like it; ain't it jolly?" cried Sally.

Jack hurled Tiger Claw violently to the deck, and bent over the powerful Indian chief, as huge volumes of smoke curled up over their heads.

CHAPTER XLVIII.

IN WHICH SALLY HAS SOMETHING TO SAY, AND SO HAS TIGER CLAW.

THE terror with which Sally's novel weapon inspired the savages and the sight of the overthrow of their redoubtable chief, Tiger Claw, rendered them almost powerless, and when Ned and his friends flung themseves upon them, they leapt the bulwarks and tumbled headlong into the water or their canoes.

Seizing the paddles they sent their light boats away from the side of Ned's craft, for nothing could withstand the volleys poured into them from that umbrella.

In less than a minute there was not a savage within range except the dead and wounded that lay upon the deck, the furious but now powerless Tiger Claw, and an Indian warrior whom Jumbo was lugging one way by his hair and Charley pulling the other way by his heels.

"Hurrah!" cried Ned, wiping the perspiration from his face with the back of his hand, "victory is ours. But Heavens! the boat is on fire!"

He dashed forward with Harry to find that it was only a straw mattress into which a wadding from one of their guns had fallen and set it on fire.

To bundle it off the deck into the water was the work of a moment.

"Thank Heaven, it was not the boat in flames," said Ned. "It was a fierce fight, dear boy, but we've won the victory."

"Thanks to Sally," said Harry, "but for her magic umbrella we might now be crying on the other side of our mouths."

"My umbrella, if you please, Honour," said Bircher.

But Harry paid no heed to this remark, for he darted away with Ned to where Jack stood, his foot pressed on the throat of Tiger Claw, and threatening the savage with his own hatchet.

"What shall I do with this fellow?" asked Jack; "brain him with his own tomahawk?—it is to him we owe this scrimmage."

"For our safety's sake it were perhaps best," said Ned, "and yet I do not like to counsel the slaying of a defeated and powerless man."

"You would not let him escape so that he might attack us again?" said Jack.

"I have heard that even the red man respects a promise," said Ned.

"Bosh," said Sally, "he might if he promised to kill you or even eat you, not else; and as to this varmint, ugh, you beast!"

And Sally, who had closed the umbrella, gave the Indian chief a dig in the ribs with its ferule.

"Does the pale-face think to make Tiger Claw show fear?" asked the prostrate chief.

"Oh, so you know I'm a pale-face, do you?" said Sally; "remember me, don't you? Of course you do, and I remember you too, you villain, for didn't you kill my poor departed husband?"

And Sally again gave Tiger Claw a dig with the end of the umbrella.

"Ugh!" grunted the chief, "the scalp of Red Feather hangs in the smoke of my lodge; it is good."

"Oh, you cannibal," cried Sally, "not that I want his scalp, oh, dear no, I was only too glad to get rid of him; you might have made a tooth-brush of it for all I care, but I owe you one, you red-skinned, ugly brute, I do."

"Shut up," said Jack; "what does he care for all your palaver?"

"Oh, of course; perhaps you'll say he didn't care for me neither?" said Sally; "then why did he want to make me his squaw?"

"I don't know," said Jack; "because he was a fool."

"Jack," said Sally, "don't you go to aggravate me; you know what I am when put on my mettle."

"Who's a aggravating you?" said Jack; "only I don't like to hear you talk about dear departeds and coves that wanted to make you their squaw, it riles me, it does."

"And don't you think it riled me?—me, Sally Scrubbins, a true-born Englishwoman—to be insulted and considered only fit for an Indian's squaw? Oh, my blood biles, that it does."

"Then get away and leave us to settle what's to be done with this fellow," said Jack.

"Done?" cried Sally, "why what should be done to the nasty wretch as wanted me to be his wife?"

"Cook his goose," said Jack, "to be sure."

"Then why don't you do it, and not stand there and let the red warmint smile up at you like that? Oh, I'd like to scratch his face, I would."

And Sally shook her fist at the prostrate chief.

Tiger Claw smiled tauntingly.

"Leave the chief to us, Sally," said Ned, gently pushing her back.

"Oh, of course," said Sally; "I ain't wanted here, oh dear no."

"Now, Miss Scrubbins," said Bircher, deprecatingly.

"Shut up," said Sally, thrusting the tutor aside, and striding indignantly to the bows of the vessel.

Charley and Jumbo having tugged away at their captive till they had nearly pulled his head off his neck and his legs off his body, swung the savage backwards and forwards and then flung him over the side into the river.

Having done this and seeing that the savages in the canoes were speeding away with all their might, they strode up to where Ned and the others stood round the prostrate chief.

"Again, Master Ned, I ask you what's to be done with this fellow?" said Jack, who felt terribly incensed against Tiger Claw for presuming to fancy Sally for a squaw."

"And again I reply that I do not like to slay a captive," said Ned; "had he fallen in fair fight I should have been glad, but now to take his life is to lower ourselves to his level."

"That is true, Ned," said Harry, "and yet what can we do with him? We can't keep him prisoner, and if we let him go we may have cause soon to repent doing so."

"He'd be down on us again in no time," said Jack, "he came after that girl of mine, I take it, and he'd be after her again, see if he wouldn't."

"Then he don't know as much ob her as we do, eh Charley?" said Jumbo.

"Guess not," replied Charley rubbing his cheek.

"You cannot look upon him with greater aversion than I do," said Ned; "for it is he who has stolen away Minnie Sash."

"Then kill him; he deserves death," said Jack.

"His death will not restore Minnie to me," said Ned. "No, hold your hand, Jack. I must know where he has taken her and what may have been her fate."

As the chief heard Minnie's name his eye flashed, and he set his teeth together.

He guessed then that Ned was the white youth to whom Minnie had given her love.

His savage nature felt joyed at being able to wring the heart of his conqueror.

"Tiger Claw," said Ned, "where is the pale-face maiden you carried off from the village of Swift Arrow? Remember you are at my mercy, and your life will depend upon the truth of your replies."

"Does the white boy love the pale-face maiden?" asked the chief, trying to raise his head, but being prevented by Jack's foot.

"He does. She is more to me than a dear sister, and I have come over the great waters to seek her. Tell me where you have taken her?"

The Indian only smiled.

"Speak!" cried Ned. "Where is she?"

"Can the horse feed while the rider holds its head?" asked the chief. "Can the chief talk when his neck is pressed by the foot of the pale-face?"

"Take off your foot, Jack," said Ned. "If he attempts to escape we can shoot him."

Jack sullenly obeyed.

The Indian sat up.

He would have risen higher, but Ned pressed his revolver to his head, saying—

"The chief can talk and sit. Answer me. Where is Minnie Sash, the pale-face maiden you tore from the white man Phopps, in the village of Swift Arrow?"

"How should Tiger Claw know?" asked the chief.

"Because she is his captive," replied Ned.

"The white man speaks false," replied Tiger Claw. "The Indian knows not where to find the pale-face girl."

"You carried her away from the village," cried Ned. "Don't lie to me, for we saw her in your canoe, sitting by your side."

"The white man's tongue is straight. The white girl did go with Tiger Claw."

"Then why lie to me?" asked Ned, fiercely.

"Tiger Claw scorns to lie," retorted the savage. "He speaks truly when he says he knows not where she is."

"What mean you?" said Ned. "You confess the poor girl was your captive, and then you say you know not where she is. You play with your own life, chief. Refuse to tell me where you left her and you die. Speak truly and, much as you have made me suffer, I will spare your life."

"The pale-face has given his promise to the red chief," said Tiger Claw. "The Indian spoke truly when he said he knew not where she is, and he speaks truly when he tells the white man that the girl he loves sought death in the waters of the deep Orinoco."

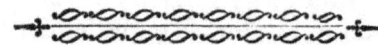

CHAPTER XLIX.

IN WHICH CHARLEY PULLS IN FUN AND JUMBO HITS IN EARNEST.

"DEAD!"

The word burst from Ned's lips, as clasping his hands to his forehead he fell back white and horrified.

"Dead!" echoed Harry. "Minnie dead!"

The heartrending tones, the white horrified look on Ned's face so startled Jack that he paid no heed to the crouching chief, who, seeing the gaze of the powerful man turned from him, bounded like an arrow to his feet.

With a cry of surprise Jack turned upon him.

But even as he did so the savage snatched his tomahawk from Jack's grasp, and eluding his clutch, sprang backwards and leaped upon the low bulwark.

"Shoot him down! He will escape!" cried Jack, as he bounded towards the savage.

"Pale-face!" yelled Tiger Claw, "go join the white maiden who scorned the love of Tiger Claw."

"'GO IT, YOU CRIPPLES, AND I'LL PLAY YOU A HORNPIPE,' CRIED CHARLEY."

As he spoke he hurled his hatchet at Ned, who stood paralysed as it were, at what he had heard.

That moment had been Ned's last but for Jack.

The conjuror made a clutch at the legs of the chief as the weapon left his hand.

The savage in eluding the grasp flung up his arm, and thus sent the tomahawk flying high over the head which he had meant to cleave in twain.

As the weapon left his hand he threw himself backwards into the water.

"Escaped!" cried Jack.

They all dashed to the side as Tiger Claw disappeared beneath the surface of the water.

"Confound him! why did you not let me kill him?" cried Jack.

"Because that's my job," said Sally. "I owe him one and I'll let him have a lot if— oh, there he is."

The head of the Indian rose some yards from the boat.

Sally raised the umbrella, pointed it at the head of Tiger Claw, and opened it.

"There," cried Sally, as a dozen puffs of smoke burst forth and formed into a cloud at the end of the umbrella, "you wanted Sally Scrubbins; now you've got enough of her."

The shoulders of Tiger Claw shot up out of the water as a loud yell broke from his lips.

Then his hands were flung violently above his head and down he sank into the waters to rise no more in life.

Sally's aim had been true.

Tiger Claw, the destroyer of her Indian husband, had perished by the hand of his victim's unwilling bride.

"He's gone," said Jack.

"No mistake about that," said Charley. "By Jingo! Sally's the girl to do it."

"She jus' am, an' not no mistake," said Jumbo. "Guess we'll hab to learn how um make dat parashute shoot like dat. Golly, but it fire slick."

"Cheer up, dear boy," said Harry, laying his hand on Ned's shoulder.

"Oh, Harry, only to think poor Minnie——"

Ned broke off suddenly, turned his face away, and strode to the cabin.

"It is hard, upon my soul it is," said Harry. "Here, you fellows, heave these savages overboard while I go and comfort Ned."

"I'll see to them," said Jack.

"All right, Jack. Ned is cut up at what he's heard."

And he followed Ned to the cabin.

"Bear a hand here," cried Jack. "Now, Jumbo, sling that carcase overboard."

"Golly, guess dat's jus' de job I'm fond on," said Jumbo. "Now den, you lazy white trash, jus' you collar his legs."

"Who are you calling white trash?" said Charley.

"Don't you stop to make not no remarks at dis chile, but 'tend to your work."

"Oh, you be blowed."

"Now den, jus' you mind what you're arter. I don't want dese here trousers spiled," cried Jumbo. "You's only gealous as you ain't got 'em, or you'd be more 'ticular how you shoves dis here dead Injun agin 'em."

"I'll shove him down your throat if you don't hold your jaw," cried Charley.

"Golly, I'd jus' like to see you do dat."

"I will, too, if you don't close your tater trap. Now then, over he goes."

Over went the dead savage, another followed, and another, till the deck was cleared.

The blood stains were mopped up, and then 'Dolf, at the suggestion of Charley, procured some brandy, which was handed round.

Meantime a look-out had been kept by Bircher to watch the movements of the canoes, and give note if they showed any signs of returning.

The Indians, however, did not attempt any further molestation of the boat.

Sally's patent mitrailleuse had evidently too much terror for them.

Bircher looked ruefully at his umbrella, the naked ribs of which he could see through the cut and burnt covering at the bottom.

"It's quite spoilt," he said, shaking his head, "quite spoilt."

"Look here, you old grumbler," said Sally, "you'd have been spoilt if I hadn't hit upon the idea of making it into a mitrailleuse."

"Well, yes, perhaps I might; but that gingham cost me seven and sixpence," said Bircher.

"What?" said Charley, looking up from examining the new instrument of warfare, "seven and sixpence? Walker."

"What do you mean by Walker?" asked Bircher, indignantly.

"Oh, ain't we innocent?" said Charley.

"I don't understand your low slang," said the tutor.

"Of course not.   So very refined, ain't you?"

"Pray keep your conversation to yourself if you cannot talk to me in a proper manner," said Bircher.

"Oh, I'm a proper sort of chap I am. I don't borrow an umbrella and then say I gave seven and a kick for it."

"Do you insinuate that I would stoop to theft and falsehood?" cried Bircher, angrily.

"Oh dear no, not at all."

"Then what do you mean by saying that I stole that umbrella?"

"I—I say so?" cried Charley, in pretended surprise and indignation.

"Yes, yes."

"Oh, Mr. Bircher, Mr. Bircher," cried Charley. "You, a gentleman of respectability, to say that I said you stole it, when I only said you had borrowed the gingham. Oh, how could you be so cruel? You stab me in a tender part, and if I'd tears to shed I'd cry a bucketful."

"Guess dere'd be a awful mess if you did," said Jumbo.

"Oh, if I did," said Charley, "but then I can't—my indignation has dried up the springs from whence the tears are drawn, and my sobs are dry as a red herring when he finds himself laid on a gridiron."

And with an expression of comic grief Charley flopped his head down on to Jumbo's shoulder.

"Here, hole up! Golly, don't you go a veeping on de collar ob dis here shirt, or yer'll take all de starch out ob it."

"Oh, my lacerated heart!" cried Charley.

"Gor-a'mighty, wake up!" cried the nigger, "ye're a rubbing yer head agin dis lacerated ear; hole up, d'ye hear?"

"Ear, I hear," said Charley, jobbing his skull against the cut ear of the negro.

"Gor-a'mighty, dis ear won't neber hear no more, suah. Get away, or golly, I gib you something you won't like."

"Oh, let me weep," moaned Charley.

"Guess dis chile 'uil make you roar if you don't get off. Won't you go? Den take dat."

And he gave Charley a punch in the ribs.

"Take this, certainly," said Charley, making a grab at Jumbo's ear. "I've got it."

"What de debbil—hole hard—oh!"

"Well, ain't I holding hard?" said Charley. "I can't hold much harder."

"Hole hard, I say. Hole hard, you white cur," yelled Jumbo, dancing about with pain.

"So I am, can't hold any harder," said Charley, "unless I pull it off."

"Tarnel tunder," yelled Jumbo, "dis chile no stand dis."

"Sit down, then," said Charley.

"Brest if you don't lay down," cried the black. "You pull my ear, den I hit your nose. Dere, how you like dat?"

And Jumbo gave Charley's nose a punch that set it bleeding and caused him to relax his hold.

"What did you do that for?" he cried, fiercely.

"Jus' to open de springs where de blood comes from, and let you weep. Yah, yah, you pull my ear, I punch your nose, dat's fair—yah, yah!"

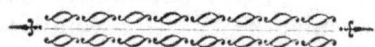

CHAPTER L.

IN WHICH NED TAKES HEART AMD MAKES A RESOLVE.

"Look here, old man," said Harry, "I don't believe that Minnie is dead. I've been thinking it over, and I've come to the conclusion that she is still alive and a captive."

Ned shook his head.

"Why should the Indian have said so then?" he asked.

"I don't know why, of course, but I won't believe she is dead. That savage expected to escape, and thought perhaps to prevent you searching further for the poor girl. Depend upon it, I'm right, Ned; Minnie is yet in the land of the living."

"Oh, if indeed she be, what must she be suffering?" said Ned.

"Perhaps not so much as we fear," replied Harry. "I wouldn't give up the hope of finding her if I were you. I'd carry out the programme to the end, and have more proof than the Indian chief's word before I gave up all as lost."

Ned pressed his friend's hand.

"Harry," he said, "you put new life and hope in me. I will have further proof that Minnie is no more before I give up all hope of ever seeing her again."

"Bravely spoken," said Harry, "and come weal, come woe, I'm with you to the end."

Again their hands joined in a fervent pressure.

"We shall soon reach the camping grounds of Tiger Claw's tribe," said Ned, after a pause, "and there we may find confirmation or denial of the chief's assertion."

"And possibly meet with less trouble than if that ferocious chief were alive and kicking," said Harry.

"Thank Heaven, he did not effect his escape. If Minnie indeed lives, she will have one persecutor the less," he said.

"That's true, thanks to Sally and her wonderful instrument."

"We must examine that, dear boy. Whoever would have thought of an umbrella being put to such a use?"

"Why nobody of course but Sally Scrubbins," replied Harry. "By the way, Ned, we'll hear what her opinion about Minnie is. She knows what these red fiends are better than we do."

"It would be as well to have her opinion," said Ned. "I'll go and talk to her."

As he was about to leave the cabin, Sally came down, carrying with her the umbrella.

"Sally," said Ned, "we owe our lives to you."

"Don't talk nonsense, Mr. Ned."

"But it's not nonsense," said Harry. "If it had not been for the way in which you showered bullets at the savages, we must have been overcome by numbers."

"Get out," said Sally, "you'd have beat 'em."

"I doubt it," said Ned. "But whatever made you think of fashioning such an instrument as that?"

"I don't know," said Sally. "I suppose it was seeing that box of small revolvers you had here. I thought what a lark it would be to fire them all off at once, and then I tried to think how it could be done, and could see no other way than by fastening one to each of the ribs of Bircher's umbrella, and attaching strings from the handle of the ging- to the triggers of the revolvers."

"And a capital idea too," said Harry,

"Yes, it answered first rate. All that had to be done was to cut away the cloth round the bottom of the umbrella, and then as it was opened it pulled the strings, the strings pulled the triggers, and then 'ware hawks didn't the Indians get it rather."

And Sally who had been showing how the thing worked, while she explained its construction, laughed till the tears ran down her cheeks.

"I mean to take out a patent for this if ever I get back to England," said Sally.

"Not a bad idea," said Ned.

"You ought to make your fortune out of it," remarked Harry, "or at least get enough to furnish a nice home and set Jack up in business."

"Go along with you," said Sally.

"I shouldn't wonder but you will," said Ned, "but only think what the government might give you for the patent of an umbrella mitrailleuse. They might arm the British army with it—who knows?"

"Go on, Master Ned. Poke your fun at me if you like," said Sally.

"But I'm not poking fun, Sally."

"We owe our victory to you," said Harry, "and I shall kiss you for it."

"Lor', now," said Sally, slipping aside as Harry flung out his arms to grasp her.

"You dear creature, why what the devil ——"

Harry looked up to find Jumbo in his arms.

Jumbo was equally as much surprised as Harry, which surprise was greatly increased on hearing Ned and Sally fairly scream with laughter.

"What for you catch hold ob me like dis, Massa Harry?" cried the negro.

"What do you mean by coming here, you ugly black rascal," returned Harry. "How dare you thrust your ugly black body into my arms?"

"I frust my brack body into your arms?" said Jumbo. "Jus' you hear dat! Golly! tink it was him frust him white arms roun' dis chile's brack body."

"Get out," said Harry, turning away.

"Sartinly, sar; but brest if um didn't fink you was going to kiss this yer nigger."

"So he was, Jumbo," said Sally.

"Neber; you don't say so?" said the black. "Dis chile objecs to dat. If him wants to kiss anybody I guess he'd better kiss you."

"How dare you?" said Sally. "As if Master Harry would think of such a thing now."

"If dis chile ain't quite a fool him guess dat's what he war arter. Golly! dis nigger's sorry him poke his head in de way, so he take him hook so him no see where Sally flops her 'fections."

And the negro dashed out of the cabin.

"Oh, blow it," said Harry, "that was too bad."

Sally laughed.

"Never mind," she said; "what was you saying, Master Ned?"

"We were speaking about your patent mitrailleuse."

"Oh, it's scarcely worth talking about," said Sally, "though it's a bit of a curiosity, I think."

"There's a deal of novelty in that invention, after all," said Ned.

"Ask the Indians who saw it if there ain't," said Harry, with a smile.

"I will when I get another chance," said Sally. "But I say, now, won't it be a first-rate gun to keep off wild cats. I do believe they could not frighten me if I had this umbrella fully charged."

"Capital," said Harry, "I hope you'll get plenty of chances of using it on them."

"If I do, 'ware hawks to the cats," said Sally. "I hate 'em worse than savages, I do."

"Now, Sally, what is your opinion? You heard what Tiger Claw said about Minnie?"

"I did, and he's learnt what I thought of him."

"Yes, but with respect to Minnie Sash. Do you believe he spoke truly when he said she had perished?"

"Do I believe him?"

"Yes."

"Not a blessed word he uttered."

"You think she lives then?"

"I do."

"Why? Give me your reason for thinking so," said Ned.

"Well, I've got two or three reasons, you see," said Sally.

"What are they?"

"The first is, that I've heard you say as Minnie was a very pretty girl."

"But pretty women die as well as plain ones."

"That's quite true," said Sally, "but then men are generally more careful of them than they are of the ugly ones, you know; and that rascal Tiger Claw had an eye for beauty I can tell you."

"We have proof of that in his desire to get hold of you," said Harry.

"None of your chaff, Master Harry," said Sally. "I may be passable, but I know I ain't got any beauty to boast of."

"I shouldn't like to say so if Jack was behind me," said Ned.

"Oh, Jack's a fool—he's no judge," said Sally. "But if Tiger Claw took a fancy to Minnie, and we know he did, he'd take precious good care of her, you may depend on that."

"But may she not, on finding herself in the power of such a wretch, have sought her own death?" said Ned.

"Women, you know, are like cats in some things, they're awful tenacious of life. A young girl ain't so fond of dying as to kill herself to get away from a fellow she don't like, or I'd have done it, shouldn't I?"

"But all are not alike," said Harry.

"Pretty much when you come to killing yourself," said Sally. "She wouldn't do that I don't believe, leastways if she was in her right senses."

"Ay, but if her captivity, if the cruelty of Tiger Claw had driven her mad?" said Ned, with trembling lips.

"Well, of course it's hard to say what other people might do," said Sally, "but I only know when I get mad I go for the one as made me so. I don't hurt myself, oh dear no, but I just wire in to them and let them have it."

"Poor Minnie, she is so sensitive, so nervous," said Ned.

"Ah, so was I once," said Sally, "but when my fellow servant made eyes at Jack and said she meant to take him away from me, I tell you that took all the nervousness out of me, and I went for her hair quicker than Tiger Claw ever went for a scalp. Don't you think women are quite such chickens as they look."

Harry laughed, and even Ned smiled.

"I shouldn't believe she'd kill herself unless I see her do it," said Sally, after a pause. "Hope don't always die out of a woman's bosom, even in the darkest moments of despair. Life's sweet, you know, and like wild cats women will fight for it. I wouldn't believe she was dead till I saw her corpse, and that's flat."

"Nor will I," said Ned, "and in spite of all, I'll find her living or I'll find her dead."

CHAPTER LI.

IN WHICH THERE IS A CONSULTATION AND A DECISION.

NED was firmly resolved to have confirmation of Minnie's death or never turn back till he had rescued her from the hands of those who held her captive.

Filled with this determination he kept on his course towards the hunting-grounds and camping-place of the followers of the red chief Tiger Claw.

What effect the fate of that brave savage would eventually have on the band, he knew not.

But Sally Scrubbins, when Ned suggested that perhaps he might be able to make friends with them, intimated that his chances of doing so were very remote.

"Then my fears for poor Minnie are enhanced," he said. "They may revenge their defeat and the fate of Tiger Claw on the dear girl."

"They may the more firmly resolve to prevent her escape," said Sally, "but they will not offer her any violence."

"You think not?"

"Of course I do," said Sally. "Why there ain't a brave among them who wouldn't make her his squaw, and if one of them should hurt her he'll have the rest down on him like a flash of lightning. Don't I know 'em?—rather!"

"I would our party were stronger," said Ned. "We cannot hope to meet with the same success in a fight ashore as we gained on the river."

"It's stratagem that will do it if it's done at all," said Sally, "unless you could get one of the tribes to help you."

"Could that be done, think you?" asked Ned, eagerly.

"I don't see why it shouldn't," replied Sally. "There's scarcely one in these parts that have not been conquered by Tiger Claw, at one time or another."

"And hence would fear the prowess of his braves," said Ned.

"Yes, and only long for a chance to revenge themselves," replied Sally. "Now if you could manage to make friends with one of these bands and get them to assist you in an attack, Minnie might be rescued."

"You think so?"

"I do."

"Why? Give me your reasons, Sally."

"Well, you see, Master Ned, the reds, although they don't admit it, have a good deal of fear of the whites, and a lot of respect for their pluckiness, and though they mightn't care to have a tussle with their old foes singly, they wouldn't hesitate if they had got half-a-dozen pale-faces to assist them."

"Do you know of a band who would listen to overtures if I made them?"

"I think I do. A tribe under a young chief called Flying Deer. His father was slain by Tiger Claw in their last battle."

"And where is he to be found?" asked Ned.

"A day's journey beyond the camping-ground of Tiger Claw, on the opposite side of the river."

"And you think his hatred of those who defeated his people may induce him to aid me?"

"Yes, if his band will let him."

"Oh!" cried Ned, and a shade of disappointment passed over his face, "then his people may refuse, though he himself be willing?"

"That's it. You see a council would be called, their medicine men would be consulted, and if they said the signs were against it the band would not consent."

"Then really it is the medicine men who give the decision."

"Yes. The Indians have great faith in their powers, and he who can pretend to be greatest in signs and portents, and succeed most in working upon the fears and credulities of the poor, ignorant fools, gains the greatest power over them."

"Then I am afraid our hopes in that direction are gone," said Ned.

"Don't be too sure of that, old man," said Harry. "I believe if it hadn't been for Jumbo hitting Swift Arrow we should have had the whole of that chief's followers at our back and Minnie in our possession now."

"It was an unfortunate circumstance," said Ned.

"It just was, for it seems that Jack was just getting those reds to believe he was a most wonderful medicine, and in a short time they would have been ready to fall down and worship him."

"Could Jack's tricks prevail, I wonder, with Flying Deer and his people?" asked Ned.

"A lot more than fair words and promises of revenge would do," said Sally. "They are such awful superstitious beggars that a well-arranged bit of hanky-panky would go further than anything I know of to bring 'em over to your side."

"Then we'll try it," said Ned. "I'll speak to Jack about it."

"And if he tries it keep with him yourself, Ned, and see that he don't get spoiled as he was before."

"I tell you what, Master Ned," said Sally, suddenly, "if you could only pretend to be a great medicine yourself, now that would be best."

"But I can't, you see, Sally, if it requires any conjuring to make me so. I can't do any of the hanky-panky tricks, you know."

"Can't you, though," said Harry. "Ask Bircher."

"Ask Bircher," said Ned. "Why ask him?"

"Because he knows you can."

"Bircher does?"

"Yes; didn't you fit a big brass ball in his eye and pitch him into a bucket of water in no time?"

Ned laughed.

"I didn't mean for you to come the hanky-panky," said Sally; "but if you pretended you assumed the power to summon demons to do your bidding and then pretended Jack was a demon and ordered him to do certain tricks, it would go down the swallow of the Indians like oil."

"If you think so, Sally, I'll work up something, I and Jack together. How long will it take us to reach the camping-ground of Flying Deer?"

"I reckon we are nearly a day's journey from the falls," said Sally. "Three miles this side of them we sha'l have to land and make our way on foot, unless we get a boat below the falls, and that ain't likely."

"And then it is fifty miles," said Harry.

"Yes. Had we canoes they might be carried overland for about five miles and then take to the water again, but the boat could not, and must be left behind."

"That is unfortunate," said Ned.

"Very," said Harry. "Are there no means of procuring canoes on the other side of the falls?"

"Not unless you could find some hidden in the banks belonging to Indians on the shore, or could entice some savages ashore and take their canoes from them," said Sally.

"That would be a most unjust thing to do," said Ned.

"Rather," put in Harry.

"Well, it ain't quite the right thing," said Sally, "certainly; but needs must, you know, when——"

"No, no," said Ned, interrupting her, "nothing can excuse doing that which is wrong."

"Sorry I spoke," said Sally.

"Couldn't we build a raft?" asked Harry.

"Of course we could," said Ned. "I never thought of that."

"Nor I," said Sally.

"Then that gets over the difficulty," said Ned.

"But how about the boat?" asked

OR, THE SECRET OF THE PHANTOM CAVE.   137

Harry.   "It might be stolen while we were gone."

"Not much fear of that," said Sally. "Some place can be found to hide it in."

"But the Indians might discover it," said Ned.

"They might.   But the banks of this river ain't quite so much inhabited as Cheapside or the Seven Dials."

"Not by a lot," said Harry.

"It's a chance if even a red man would come near it in six months," said Sally, "so you need have no fear about leaving it."

"Besides, we could leave some one on board it," said Harry.

"Who?" asked Ned.   "Bircher is the least use to us, and yet he'd be the worst to leave behind."

"What do you say to Charley?" asked Harry.

"He wouldn't, he might be handy to us, you know."

"Or Jumbo, then.   He couldn't spoil the whole affair as he did before."

"I don't believe he'd stay," said Sally. "Those two rascals would pine to death I believe if they were separated for a day."

"Then what do you say to 'Dolf?" asked Harry.

"The faithful fellow would refuse," returned Ned.   "He considers I am in his charge, and would not let me go into danger without following me."

"Then who could be induced to remain behind?" said Harry.

"I don't know, unless you would, dear boy," said Ned.

"You could more easily induce a shark not to swallow you when he had got you in his mouth," said Harry.   "I stay and know that you might be running into danger?   I'd cut my head off first."

"Of course you would," said Ned, "I knew that.   So we shall have to leave the boat to look after itself after all."

"It won't run away," said Sally, "and nobody would run away with it.   You'll find it where it's left when you come back again, never fear."

"When we come back," said Ned. "Perhaps we may never come back—who knows?"

"Here, I say, Ned, don't talk like that," said Harry.   "If you've any fear——"

"Fear!" cried Ned; "no, no, Harry, I fear nothing, but we are not the rulers of our own destinies, and who of us can say what to-morrow may bring forth?"

Then springing to his feet, he added—

"But come what may I'll save poor Minnie or I'll perish in the attempt."

CHAPTER LII.

IN WHICH ONE IMPOSTOR FOOLS ANOTHER.

IT was a week later when an Indian village on the left bank of the Orinoco presented a scene of the greatest excitement.

The men were assembled in front of their lodges, while their squaws and papooses crouched in the lodge openings, looking half eager, half frightened towards the river, on the bank of which the village was built.

Several warriors leaning on their spears stood round an old Indian who was gesticulating wildly, and as he paused ever and anon in his antics, gave utterance to loud growls of approval.

Suddenly every tongue was hushed, and the squaws craned their necks through the openings of their lodges, as through a belt of trees some fifty yards from the village arrived half-a-dozen red warriors.

Following them came what at first appeared to be an Indian squaw, but which, on closer examination, proved to be a white woman with tattooed cheeks, and attired in Indian costume.

Behind her walked a man whose attire was the wonder of the red-men, and the admiration of their squaws, and who attracted more notice than the woman.

This was 'Dolf in full livery, and in a moment he won the title of the man butterfly.

Behind him walked three persons attired in black coats, the eldest of which wearing spectacles, was instantly named by the squaws Double Eyes.

As the party reached the space before

the lodges, the Indians joined their fellows, except one, a tall young chief, whose handsome features and muscular limbs proved him the firmest built and most handsome savage of all assembled.

He held up his hand as if for silence, and the squaws who had begun to congregate round the door of the centre lodge ceased their chattering.

"Flying Deer," said the chief, "thought the tongue of the white squaw was crooked, and he went with her to the river that he might see for himself the great white medicine of whom she spoke; and that my brothers may see themselves how true were the words of his messenger, I have brought him to our lodge."

He waved his hand and Ned stepped to his side.

A murmur ran through the assembled Indians, and the old savage who had been gesticulating so wildly, stepped forward and peered into Ned's face.

"Ugh," he growled in a tone of disgust. "A boy whose arm has not the strength to throw the hatchet. Ugh! Is this the white medicine."

And he laughed derisively at Ned.

"He does not believe in your power, great chief," said Sally, bending before Ned in pretended adoration. "He persuaded this noble chief, Flying Deer, to drive your humble messenger from his presence this morning when I came here in obedience to your command to solicit the friendship of the brave Indian warrior for the great white medicine."

"If words failed to satisfy then let deeds convince him," said Ned. "Were he not himself an impostor he would not argue that I was one."

"Does the pale-face accuse the Great Bear of being an impostor?" cried the medicine man.

"He does," said Ned; "and it is the knowledge that you have long been pretending to powers you possess not that has induced the great white magician to visit these parts, and prove to those who believe in you that you only pretend to that to which you have no claim."

"Let the pale-face beware, lest the Great Bear summons the demons of the woods and waters to destroy him."

"Call them if you can," said Ned.

"Woe to the pale-faces did the Great Bear lift up his voice. The white boy would fall at the feet of the medicine to rise no more."

"Again I say call forth the spirits whom you say you have the power to summon. Let them come singly or in legions, and the white magician will defy them. Call them forth, I say."

"Is the pale-face boy tired of life ere it is scarce begun?" cried the medicine.

"Not a bit of it," replied Ned; "but I'm quite willing to lose it if you can put your boasted power into practice."

"The pale-face is mad. The great medicine has but to hold forth his hand and mutter a few words to slay him and his people. But the medicine is kind to the white man, and he will spare him."

Ned laughed aloud.

Turning to Flying Deer he said—

"Chief, as my messenger told you, I came hither to show you and your people that you have been deceived by the pretended power of this man. As the king of all the magicians of the white men and the medicines of the Indians I have been deeply offended that he should pretend to a power he does not possess."

"Ugh!" cried the chief.

"Were he what he pretends to be he would not talk thus, for he would know that I am the great chief of all the medicines in the world."

The chief recoiled as Ned said this, and the women who heard the words seized their papooses and hurried frightened into their lodges.

"He is," cried Sally, "the great magician king, and we are his slaves."

"We are; all—all!" cried Harry, bowing almost to the ground; 'Dolf Bircher, and Sally following Harry's example.

"Ay, all are my slaves, vile pretender," cried Ned addressing the Great Bear, and waving his hands above his head. "Who dare say I am not what I am? None, none!"

"None, none!" cried his fellow conspirators, bowing again to the ground.

The Indians gazed upon him terrified.

Even the Great Bear stood speechless and confounded.

"Unbeliever," cried Ned, taking hold of the arm of the Great Bear, "can you summons the beasts of woods and prairies to prove your power?"

"I can."

"But they will come not at the bidding of a false prophet."

"They will not come at thine," cried the Great Bear.

"'Tis false!" cried Ned. "Vile wretch, this to show thy dupes thy falsity and my power."

He waved Sally and the others back and then placing his fingers to his mouth, blew a loud shrill whistle.

"Let a bear obey the summons of the great white magician, his lord and master."

"He comes, he comes!" cried Harry.

"He comes, he comes!" echoed Bircher, 'Dolf, and Sally.

"Go hide thyself, false medicine," cried Ned, "lest in anger my servants slay you."

Out from between the trees opposite the huts crawled a huge black bear."

Having got free of the timber it raised itself on its hind legs and bowed its head several times towards Ned.

The Indian chief uttered an exclamation of surprise.

The medicine turned and fled in terror.

Several of the warriors would have done the same, but Ned called out—

"Fear not; he shall not harm you. Stay and see the power of the white magician;"

The Indians returned and stood close together as if in fear the white man would forget his promise.

Ned made a motion to the bear, and it stood erect again, licking its paws.

Then Ned addressing the young chief, said—

"The false prophet has fled; his tongue was crooked. But let him go; no longer can he deceive you. Let my red brother see the true power of the great white magician."

Again Ned placed his fingers to his lips, and this time he blew three distinct whistles.

"From the slime of the banks washed by the waters of the Orinoco, come forth thou terror of rivers," cried Ned.

"Come, come!" echoed the conspirators.

"He comes, he comes!" cried Harry. pointing to the river.

With exclamations of surprise the Indians saw crawling up the bank a large crocodile.

As the fearful object came towards them, opening its awful mouth at every step, the savages raised their spears, and some of the women who had returned again to the doors of their lodges fled back shrieking.

"Again I say fear not," cried Ned. "Lay down your arms. I will not let him harm you."

The Indians began to murmur and look at their chief as if for instruction.

"What, do you murmur?" cried Ned, angrily. "Do you doubt my power to prevent harm coming to you? I, whose word the beasts of earth and water obey?"

The chief motioned with his hand, and every spear fell to the earth, and then down bowed every head to the dust in adoration of the supposed power of the great white magician.

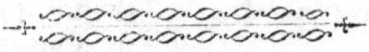

CHAPTER LIII.

IN WHICH THERE IS A DISPLAY OF FIREWORKS FOR THE BENEFIT OF GREAT BEAR.

NED was well pleased at the fear which his pretended power inspired, a fear which was shared equally by the chief and his subjects.

To further his purpose Ned knew he must rather intensify then weaken their terrors and admiration.

The crocodile having placed itself alongside, the bear stood erect on its hind legs.

"Who dare doubt the great magician's ability to bring even the beasts and rep-

tiles to do his bidding?" he said, looking round at the savages.

"None," replied the chief.

"He who can summon them from their lairs, can make them perform at his will," said Ned. "Shall the great magician bid them amuse the Indians?"

"Yes," said the chief; "but make them not angry with the red-man, oh pale-face medicine."

"They will not dare do only what I

bid them. Slave, come hither!" cried Ned, addressing Sally.

At his feet lay several small pebbles, these he picked up and gave to Sally, then pointed to the crocodile.

Sally advanced to the crocodile, and threw the pebbles one by one into the huge mouth.

"Change them to balls of gold," said Ned, "and throw them forth."

In a moment ball after ball rolled out of the huge mouth to be caught in the claws of the supposed crocodile, and thrown into the air.

Then, to the wonder of the Indians, the balls were caught and flung by the supposed monster over and around its head.

Ned whispered to Sally, who, taking a long knife from her belt, threw it at the bear.

The animal caught it in its paw, and placing its point on the tip of its snout balanced it there.

In speechless wonder the Indians sat and gazed at the play of the two animals, when all of a sudden there was a noise in the branches, and out into the open bounded a wild pig.

It made straight towards were Bircher, 'Dolf and Sally stood, its teeth gleaming and its tail erect.

"Kill it, stop it!" cried Harry.

And somebody did stop it.

That somebody was Bircher.

The pig darted between the tutor's legs, and made a snap at 'Dolf's heels.

Away flew his spectacles and down went Bircher with a yell, sprawling backwards over the pig.

Snap came the pig's jaws on 'Dolf's heel.

'Dolf screamed out and made a clutch at Sally, who made a bolt to get out of the animal's way.

But she was pulled up sharp, for 'Dolf had made a grab at her shoulder, and catching hold of her head-dress of featthers, stopped her flight for a moment.

Only for a moment. Away came her feathers, and down over her shoulders streamed her back hair.

And down went 'Dolf too, backwards, down on to the pig's back with all his weight.

The cries of the whites and the savages, and the squeals of the wild pig, were something awful for a moment.

Over rolled 'Dolf off the pig, which now seemed about as frightened as any one had been, and only too eager to escape.

It bounded towards Ned, but stopped dead short at sight of the bear and crocodile.

Fortunately it did so, or the savages might have smelt a rat.

That moment's hesitation dissipated any doubt as to the genuineness of the animals.

"Kill it!" cried Ned.

The crocodile aimed one of the gilt balls and struck the pig between the eyes.

And the bear, catching the long knife in his paw, as it fell from his snout, flung the weapon with such precision, that it buried itself to the haft in the animal's chest, and giving an unearthly squeal, it rolled over dead on the ground.

Pointing to the pig, Ned cried—

"See, the white magician has provided a feast for the Indians. He forgets not those who admit his power."

'Dolf who had edged up to the side of Ned whispered—

"I thought I was a goner."

"Guess you nearly made goners ob us," came in a whisper from the bear's head.

"You nearly spoilt the show," sounded low down in the crocodile's mouth.

"Shut up," cried Ned, "or you'll crab the whole affair. They don't sniff a mouse yet, and I don't want them to. Go on with your hanky-panky, Jack; make them forget it."

"All right," replied Jack. "I've got the tow fixed in my gills. Just shove a fusee down my throat, and I'll manage to strike it on my teeth."

Ned placed his arm in the crocodile's mouth, and while he held it there he addressed the Indians—

"Has the Great Bear power to do this?" he said; "if he has, let him come forth and place his arm in this reptile's jaws, and draw it forth, as I do, uninjured."

"Where does the great medicine hide his head?" said the young chief, looking round. "Brothers, if the Great Bear has not deceived us, he will come forth and do the bidding of the great white magician."

"He dare not," said Sally; because

he has ever spoken with a tongue that is crooked."

"Why comes he not forth to show his boasted power?" said Ned, leaning on the shoulders of the bear, and placing his hand on the snout of the hairy animal. "Is Great Bear a coward as well as a liar, or does he fear the white medicine he pretended to despise?"

"Let him come forth, or my braves shall cut out his tongue, and his body shall feed the flames," said Fying Deer. "Drive out the medicine, I say. Let no squaw shelter him in the lodge of one of the braves of the Flying Deer."

At this there was a commotion at the entrance of one of the lodges, and a couple of women were seen dragging out into the open the terrified Great Bear.

A yell of derision broke from the Indians.

"Come forth, coward," cried Flying Deer.

"Coward am I none. The Flying Deer speaks not truly when he says the Great Bear is a coward," said the medicine, as he was forced into the centre of the throng.

"All ready, Jack?" whispered Ned.

"Yes," came from the crocodile, in a whisper.

"All right, Jumbo?"

"Guess this here bear are," was the reply, in a low tone.

"Then when I get that red beggar close up here, mind you both spit it out hot and strong."

A chuckle came from the mouths of the bear and the crocodile.

"Be careful," said Ned, "and mind you don't betray yourselves."

"Leave dis chile alone," said Jumbo.

"No fear about that," whispered Jack.

"Can you see what the red idiots are up to?"

"Yes," was the low reply of both the supposed animals.

"All right, then. Are you alight?"

"Yes."

"The Great Bear has seen the white magician's power. Let him now show his own if he have any, which I deny," said Ned, speaking in a loud tone. "If he refuse, then has he only played upon the fears of his people and should be driven from their lodges in shame."

"And he shall," cried the young chief. "I have spoken."

The medicine of the tribe knew what was meant by the words and looks of Flying Deer.

He knew that if he refused to place his arm in the mouth of the crocodile, and his hand in that of the bear, he would be set down as an impostor, and not only driven from the lodges of his tribe, but slain by those into whose hearts he had so often struck awe and terror.

He might escape from the beasts or demons, whichever they were, but from his own dupes never.

Slowly he walked towards Ned, and at last stood in front of the bear and crocodile.

"Spirits who work the will of the white magician," cried Ned, "the Great Bear ridicules your master's power and your ability to avenge the insults the red imposter has heaped upon us. See, with all his boasted courage he hesitates, fearful of the vengeance he defies."

One moment Great Bear hesitated, then he sprang forward with a loud yell, with both arms extended to thrust into the mouths of the beasts, now opened to their utmost width.

Then a shriek of mingled fear and agony broke from his lips, a shriek that was uttered by every Indian present, as a volume of smoke and sparks were belched out upon him from the mouths of both the bear and the crocodile into the face of the red medicine.

CHAPTER LIV.

IN WHICH A LITTLE MUSIC GOES A LONG WAY.

To see fire and smoke issue from the mouths of the bear and the crocodile was not only more than Great Bear could stand but the rest of his tribe also.

The squaws shrieked in terror.

The savages bounded away towards the forest, and even the brave young chief, Flying Deer, was not slow in following them.

A panic had seized upon the whole band, brave as they were.

Men whom the most severe torture, the most appalling death would have failed to terrify, fled from the sight they had witnessed.

No longer could they doubt the power of the white magician—the youth who could call beasts from the forests, reptiles from the waters, and compel them to spit fire and smoke at his bidding.

And so they fled, the screams of the terrified squaws, as they crouched under the skins in their lodges, following their husbands and fathers in their mad flight.

"Well," said Ned, "I rather think that astonished them."

"Golly! it jus' did dat are; but dere's a lot ob cuss' sparks a burning ob dis chile's shoul'ers. Jus' pull dat big lump of tow out ob dis bear's gills, Mars'r Ned. It hab got a-fire at de wrong end and dere won't be not no wool on dis nigger's head, suah."

"Can't you pull it out yourself?" said Ned.

"It won't come. It's got stucked somewhere. Yah! Oh, dere's all my wool a burning. Oh, yah, oh!"

"Hold your row," cried Ned. "There, it's all right now, ain't it?"

"Guess it am; but don't dis wool ob mine smell down yer in dis bear's carcuss."

"Hush! don't talk. As soon as those fellows get over their fright they'll be back again."

"I jus' fink we gib 'em fits. How's you getting on dar, you ole crocodile?"

"Shan't be sorry when I get out of this," said Jack; "the confounded tail gets in my way. I say, Ned, just roll those balls down my throat while you've got a chance. I don't want to lose them."

"All right," said Ned.

And picking up the gilt balls he rolled them down the mouth of the crocodile, where Jack caught them and shoved them in his pockets.

"It's awful warm in this suit, Master Ned," he said, "and I shall be glad when I can get out of it."

"I won't keep you in it longer than I can help, Jack," replied Ned; "but we must keep it up till I can bounce Flying Deer to aid us to rescue Minnie."

"Of course," said Jack. "Do you think they'll want any more frightening?"

"No, I don't, but I ain't sure. As soon as I can induce them to come back we'll try if we can't amuse them and put them in a good humour. But I must go after them and persuade them to come back."

And Ned turned to go.

"Ned Nimble?"

"Who spoke?" asked Ned.

"I—Charley. I'm here, just inside the wood. I want you."

Ned strode towards the sound.

"What is it, Charley? Keep out of sight. I'll call you if I want you."

"It was nearly a case of run for me," said Charley, "when that brute of a pig made a dart out of here."

"Well, keep out of sight. I'll give you the signal if you're wanted."

"There's a litter of young pigs here. You might call on me to bring one of them out, you know, if you wanted to astonish the natives again."

"All right, I'll remember. Now be careful."

And Ned started off.

As he passed Sally, 'Dolf, and Bircher he said—

"Keep together. You come with me, Harry. We must get those niggers back again, or we shall have had our trouble for nothing."

"That's true," said Sally.

"If I can prevail on them to come back I'll get up a dance with Jack and Jumbo, and 'Dolf and you, Sally, shall be their partners. Then they'll see, or fancy they see, that I can make the brutes playful as well as vicious."

"That's your sort," said Sally. "I'm on for a jig."

Ned and Harry hurried away past the huts, bidding the women within them have no fear, since the beasts dare not harm them unless he bade them do so, and requested them to call their husbands back.

But they would not leave their lodges, so Ned and Harry hurried on, and soon saw some of the savages on the edge of a belt of timber.

"Come back," cried Ned. "I swear by the great Manitou that no harm shall befall you."

This oath, so sacred to an Indian, decided them, and the savages, looking and feeling ashamed of themselves, followed Ned back to the opening in front of their huts.

When all were assembled save Great Bear, who was nowhere to be seen, Ned, standing in front of Flying Deer, said—

"Chief, you have seen the power of the great white medicine, and how he can compel his wishes to be done?—how he can reward those who obey and punish those who refuse to heed his words?"

"The white medicine is a great chief; all other chiefs are his slaves," said Flying Deer.

"Then let Flying Deer and his braves listen," said Ned. "The great chief Tiger Claw, who slew the father of Flying Deer, offended the white medicine, and now he lies dead at the bottom of the river."

"Tiger Claw dead?" cried Flying Deer; "and I had sworn his scalp should hang in my lodge. The spirit of my father will mourn in the happy hunting-grounds that his son killed not his foe."

"Not if you do that which I shall command you," said Ned.

"Let the great medicine speak his will."

"In the lodges of the braves of the dead Tiger Claw is a white maiden whom the chief made captive. Flying Deer must place himself at the head of his braves and take her from them, and give her into the hands of the white medicine, who will aid him to revenge on the tribe of Tiger Claw his father's death and their own defeat. I have spoken."

"Flying Deer hears, and he and his braves will obey."

"It is well," said Ned; "but fail not to set forth to-morrow for the camping-grounds of your foes, or the white medicine will bring upon Flying Deer and his people a terrible punishment."

"Flying Deer will obey. I have spoken."

"That is well. Now will I show you yet more of my power; but fear not. Those who at my will can spread terror and death will also at my bidding make happy. Flying Deer has pleased the great medicine by his promise to rescue the white maiden, and he will bid his slaves please the bold chief and his braves and their squaws."

So saying he strode away, and walking to where the bear and crocodile were lying, said in a low voice—

"Jack and Jumbo, get up a dance to put these red fools into a good humour. Don't forget to chuck your legs about. 'Dolf and Sally will join in."

"All right," said Jack, rising; "but this here tail of mine won't let me dance much, I think."

"And dis yer chile ain't good at de dubble-shuffles when dere's no music. Wish we'd got dat 'ere frying-pan and dem sarcepan-lids here. Dere's a lot ob melody in a frying-pan."

"When a steak's frizzling in it," said Jack; "but we'll have to jig without music. Call up our partners and let's get to work."

Ned called Sally and 'Dolf and bade them do their best.

"What are we to do for music?" said Sally.

"I've got it, Master Ned. Shall I bring out my instrument?" called Charley.

"Yes," replied Ned. "What is it?"

"You'll see in a minute."

"Now, then, go it," said Ned, and he walked over to the side of the chief.

Jack and Sally, and Jumbo and 'Dolf, took up positions opposite each other, and at a signal from Ned began to dance in the most active manner, throwing their legs and arms about as if they were mad, and when they had got well into it out sprang Charley from the belt of timber with a small pig held firmly under his arm.

"Go it," cried Charley; "here's a splendid organ, and first-rate music to dance to. Bircher, rattle out a few notes on your hat — tambournine, I mean."

Bircher whipped off his hat and began beating away at the crown of it.

"Now go it, you cripples," said Charley. "Step out, Bircher, and move your legs. Shame a steam-engine. Go it, and I'll play you the sailor's hornpipe, highland fling, and an Irish jig, all in one."

And pressing his elbow into the pig's ribs and twisting the tail of the young porker, there issued such a series of squeals, grunts, and squeaks that the Indians rent the air with peal after peal of laughter.

CHAPTER LV.

IN WHICH MINNIE FINDS HERSELF IN STRANGE QUARTERS WITH AN UNPLEASANT COMPANION.

WHEN Minnie Sash opened her eyes it was to find herself in darkness, and to hear a rushing, thundering noise in her ears.

Her head throbbed with a maddening pain, and her limbs were cramped and cold.

She tried to realise where she was, and how she came there, but for a time everything seemed a blank to her, save the pains in her temples and her limbs, and the thundering noise that rang in her ears.

"Where—where am I?" she moaned.

Softly though the words were uttered, they came back to her ears in loud echoes, and with a distinctness that caused her to start to a sitting posture, and clasp her hands to her head.

"What can it mean?" she gasped. "Do I dream?—am I mad?"

"Mad, mad, mad!" came the words from a dozen different points.

The poor girl trembled, and over her cold body crept a moisture, brought forth from every pore by fear and terror.

With her head clasped in her hands she strove to pierce the darkness, and then like a flash came back to her recollection her flight from Tiger Claw and her headlong plunge into the waters of the Orinoco.

Now she remembered all, but where was she?

"Is this death?" burst from her lips at last.

"Death, death, death!" was repeated on all sides.

In the horror these words inspired she sprang to her feet, and stretched forth her arms in the darkness.

"Oh, merciful Heaven?" she cried, and fell forward in a swoon.

When again consciousness returned, she opened her eyes to find an Indian bending over her, her head supported on his arm, his face almost close to hers.

At his feet a fire was burning, the flames of which lit up a strange, wild scene.

It was more like the fairy scene of some gorgeous pantomine than aught else.

Pillars of crystal were on all sides, and festoons of the same hung from the roof, and each reflected back the light of the fire, and seemed to dance in its rays.

A moment the poor girl gazed wonderingly upon them, and then her eyes rested on the face bent over her, and she gave utterance to a loud shriek of terror.

But she closed her eyes and shuddered as shriek after shriek, in tones of thunder, rang through the place.

"Fear not," cried a voice in her ear, "you are safe."

Echo repeated the last word.

Trembling she again looked up.

"Who are you? Where am I?" she gasped.

"Where Tiger Claw will not dare follow you," was the reply.

"Who are you?"

"One who saved you from death in the waters of the Orinoco, and brought you here," was the reply.

"What place is this? Why have you saved, why brought me here?" cried Minnie.

"I only know that it is a cave I discovered by accident when my canoe shot over the falls, and I thought that both of us had perished," replied the Indian.

"But who are you? Your voice is not like an Indian's. It is like one who —who——"

"Ay, who?" he asked.

"A villain—Boaster!" she cried.

"Boaster!" thundered the echoes.

"You are right," he replied; "it was no Indian who saved you from death, but a white man—one who loves you."

As the echoes repeated the words Minnie tore herself from his grasp and sprang to her feet.

"Oh, Heaven, better death a thousand times?" she cried.

He rose and stood before her.

"'ADVANCE ONE STEP, AND I HURL HER BODY INTO THE FOAMING WATERS,' CRIED BOASTER."

The firelight played upon his painted features.

"Is that your gratitude," he cried, "for saving you from death, or worse than death, at the hands of Tiger Claw?"

And he put forth his hand to grasp her.

But she sprang back with a shriek that echoed and re-echoed through the place.

"Touch me not, touch me not," she cried. "Oh, Heaven, why was I not suffered to perish ere the hands of such a wretch could rob death of its willing victim?"

And then, overcome with weakness, she sank to her knees on the icy cold floor of the cave.

"Minnie," said Boaster, "I had hoped for better treatment than this for what I have done."

"Done," she moaned, "oh, what have you done but that I should loathe and curse you?"

"Saved you from Tiger Claw!" he replied; "saved you from rushing unbidden to your Maker's presence, risked my life for yours, and watched and tended you here while you raved in delirium, and is this my reward?"

He took her hand, but she wrested it from him and crouched shuddering to the earth.

"Minnie," cried Boaster, "do not hide your face from me; I have been cruel but I was driven to it by one who hated me and one whom I hate; but I love you, Minnie, love you as I never even loved my mother. I have risked my life for yours, will risk it daily, hourly, but for one kind word, one smile from you!"

"You have saved me," she said, "and you ask my thanks; rather take my curses! But for you I had been happy in England; but for you I had never meditated self-murder; but for you I— oh, Heaven help me, why did I not die, why did I not die?"

"Because it is Heaven's will that you should live to forgive and bless me," said Boaster.

"Bless!" she cried; "bless the wretch to whom I owe all my sufferings, all the indignities through which I have passed; bless the villain who has brought me here to this wild spot that he may torture me with his odious professions of love? Away, the blood of your vile confederate is on your hands and soul! Away, away!"

She waved him back, and looked wildly around her.

The place terrified her.

She knew that she was alone with a desperate, unprincipled wretch.

She felt that she was as weak as an infant, and at his mercy.

Too well she knew his character, and her heart sank in despair.

Could she escape?

But whither?

Wildly her eyes roved through the arches of stalactite into the gloomy depths beyond.

Whither did they lead? And what meant that thundering noise of falling waters?

All these thoughts flashed through her aching brain in a moment.

The next she turned and fled.

But scarce had she taken a couple of steps when her strength deserted her, and uttering a cry of despair she sank in a heap upon the floor of the cave.

Boaster sprang to her side.

He bent over her and raised her in his arms.

She was powerless to resist.

"Oh, let me die, let me die!" she moaned, as her head sank upon his breast and her eyes closed.

He drew her to the fire and placed her beside it, and taking her hand in his chafed it between his own.

"Cold," he said, "cold as her heart towards me; I could pity her but for him. She says it is I who have brought all her sufferings upon her. She lies! 'Tis he, Ned Nimble. But for him she had never been carried from England, but for him she might now be happy. Curse him, I must even torture what I love to be revenged on him I hate!"

"Wretch!"

It was in a faint voice that Minnie uttered the word, but the echoes of the place sounded it in his ears in tones of thunder.

"Wretch!" he repeated; "but who made me the wretch I am? The boy who loves you, Minnie Sash, loves you to madness, and whose love you return. He insulted me, taunted me, struck me, and I swore to be revenged; to make him suffer in tenfold agony what I suffered! and I will do it, though in doing so I heap crime on crime upon my guilty head and plunge my very soul to perdition!"

CHAPTER LVI.

IN WHICH MINNIE FINDS HERSELF ALONE WITH THE DEAD.

THE fainting Minnie heard the words which Boaster uttered, and while the echoes rang through the stalactite cavern, insensibility once more stole over her.

Still holding her in his arms, Bill Boaster gazed long and anxiously into the white, upturned face.

At first he thought she was dead, so cold and rigid was her form.

But bending his head till his cheek rested on her lips, he felt by the soft breath that fanned his face that her heart still beat.

He drew a sigh of relief.

Villain as he was, he had learned to love her, and could Minnie have been prevailed upon to return that love, he would have even forsworn his revenge on Ned.

For one word of love from her lips, one smile of affection from her eyes, would have made him her slave, so deeply, so intensely did he love her.

It was to be revenged on Ned that he had aided Phopps to bear her from her home.

At that time he would not have hesitated to kill her, but now he would die almost for a smile from her.

Her beauty had charmed him.

Her love was what he panted for now more than revenge on Ned.

But that love he felt could never be his, and so the passions that she might have torn from his heart only rankled the deeper.

Oh, that he could rend her lover limb from limb before her eyes, how gladly he would do it; but fiend as he was, he would not lay the weight of a single finger in injury upon the girl he held in his arms.

"I will not harm her," he muttered; "no, no, but I will slay him she loves, and then, when she knows he is no more, her heart may soften towards me."

And he kissed the pale, cold lips of the insensible girl.

He would not harm her—as if words were not sometimes more cruel than blows, threats more hurtful than dagger thrusts.

He drew her nearer to the fire, and placing her beside it rose to his feet.

"I must seek fresh fuel and food," he muttered. "She will return to consciousness soon, and will need refreshment. When she is strong enough I must take her from this wild place, but whither—ah, whither?"

He cast another look upon the prostrate girl, and satisfied that she gave no immediate signs of consciousness, he turned and passed under the arches, and was soon lost in the darkness of the cavern.

The fire burnt lower, and one by one the glittering pillars of stalactite became wrapped in gloom, till at length only those nearest to the dying embers reflected an occassional glare that leaped from amid the white and red ashes on the floor of the cave.

Gradually Minnie showed signs of recovery.

Her limbs trembled.

A sigh broke through her parted lips.

Her eyelids quivered and opened, and the vacant look slowly faded from her eyes.

Then a violent shiver shook her whole frame, and she sat up and gazed around her.

"Was it all a dream?" she muttered.

The echoes repeated her words.

"Oh, no," she said; "it was alas! too true. But where is he? Am I alone?"

"Alone," came in loud echoes back to her ear.

"Thank God! May I never see him more!" she continued. "But oh, this fearful place, which seems as though it were haunted with phantoms. Can I not leave it? Can I not escape from him?"

"Escape from him?" repeated the echoes.

"Oh Heaven, give me strength and I will try!" she cried, rising with difficulty to her feet, and peering into the darkness on all sides. "If there was an entrance there must be an exit. Oh merciful Heaven, grant I may reach it ere he returns to stay me!"

The echoes rolled back to her ears, but she paid no heed to them, and stepped forward.

She passed under an arch whose festoons of crystal faintly reflected the dying firelight, staggered forward with outstretched hands past several columns till she found herself in a darkness as dense as a tomb.

Then she paused and leaned up against one of the pillars that felt to her touch like ice.

The cold was intense.

She looked back but the fire had died out, and all was darkness before and behind her.

With throbbing brow and tottering limbs, Minnie once more pushed on, keeping her hands extended before her in order to guard against any obstruction in her path.

Ever and anon she ran against one of the icy pillars, but still keeping her hands in advance, she shielded her face and body from injury.

" Her course was naturally slow and whether she was keeping in the same direction, or in rounding the pillars was retracing her steps, she could not tell.

In vain her eyes sought for some ray of light.

Not a gleam lit up the Stygian darkness of that awful cave.

Hope which had sprung to her heart, now gave place to despair, and she sank down on the cold floor, feeling that it was useless for her to go further.

"Oh, that I had died ! " she moaned; "for this is worse than death."

"Death ! "

The word seemed to be shouted back in her ears in tones of thunder, and Minnie clasped her hand to her head in horror.

She feared that madness would seize upon her, so fearful, so awe-inspiring were her surroundings.

Clasping her hands together, she cried in her agony—

"Oh, this is awful ! I seem to be surrounded by mocking phantoms. I shall go mad ! oh, I shall go mad ! "

Mad! mad! mad! came back in thunders from all sides.

With a shriek of horror Minnie sprang to her feet, and fled from the terrible sounds.

Ere she had taken a dozen steps, she was brought up sharp by striking against some object in her path, and throwing out her arms grasped at what ?

Horror of horrors ! a human hand.

Not warm and soft, but hard as stone and cold as death.

In her terror she stumbled forward, and her other hand rested on a human face, cold as the hand she had grasped— the face of a corpse.

With a shriek she strove to tear herself away, but could not.

Her whole frame seemed to have become paralysed.

In her terror she shrieked aloud.

And her shrieks echoed and re-echoed, as if from the throats of ten thousand demons.

Rendered desperate by the intensity of her horror, she again strove to flee from the spot, but turning, found her limbs entangled in something, and struggling to free them, fell.

In making a clutch to save herself she seized upon she knew not what, and pulled it down upon her.

But in a moment she realised what she had done, for an icy-cold hand rested upon her arm, and a dead marble-cold face lay across her own.

Frantically she threw up her arms to push it from her, and in so doing realised that she grasped a corpse.

All strength left her.

She was powerless as the dead to move hand or foot.

The weight of the fearful body seemed pressing her down further and further into the earth.

She tried to shriek.

She could utter no sound.

Her breathing grew painful.

A red mist seemed to rise in the darkness and float before her eyes.

Her blood seemed to turn to water in her veins.

The very pulsation of her heart grew fainter and fainter at each beat.

Then all was darkness and oblivion.

How long she remained thus she knew not.

When she opened her eyes a faint light pervaded the place, but which momentarily grew fainter and fainter as she recovered consciousness.

But oh, to what horrors did she awake?

To the knowledge that she was held

to the floor of the cave by the weight of a dead body.

In the faint light she could dimly make out that it was the corpse of an Indian that lay across her bosom with a weight which was indeed fearful.

As her eyes wandered round horrors seemed to increase, for turn her gaze which way she would human forms stood or lay before her, as if carved in stone.

But the light—whence came it?

As this thought flashed through her mind she put forth all her feeble strength and rolled the body off her.

It sank with a noise as of a huge stone falling on stone.

Minnie staggered to her feet, and with wild eyes glared in the direction where the light was brightest.

A shudder ran through her frame and she would have shrieked but that her tongue clove to the roof of her mouth.

For on either side of the cave were ranged dead bodies of Indians placed in every conceivable position, bodies petrified to stone and impervious to decay.

While she gazed in awe upon the scene the light faded out and she was left in darkness and alone with the dead.

CHAPTER LVII.

IN WHICH NED AND HIS FRIENDS PART FROM THEIR DUPES.

If the Indians had been terrified at seeing fire and smoke belched out of the mouth of the supposed bear and crocodile, they certainly had a set-off against their fears in the mirth-provoking antics they now performed.

Round and round, backwards and forwards went the dancers to the accompaniment of Charley's improvised instrument.

Surely never did crocodile or bear fling their legs about before as they did now.

Nor ever was heard such a variation of notes in pig music as Charley managed to extract from the young porker.

Bircher too could not keep his legs still.

As he beat his knuckles on the top of his hat he set his legs in motion, and warming to his work danced as excitedly as 'Dolf or Sally.

Ned did not think it wise to carry the game too far, so raising his hand he called in a loud voice—

"Enough!"

The dancers paused.

Charley ceased to twist the pig's tail, and Bircher to beat his hat.

Even the pig itself hushed its squeals and lay quiet and exhausted in Charley's arms.

"Spirits, you have done well," said Ned. "Reptile, back to your river's slime. Bear, to your native woods."

Jack bowed his head and dropped on all fours."

Jumbo followed his example.

Then the crocodile crawled away towards the river bank, and the bear into the timber and were both soon lost to view.

Ned beckoned Charley to approach.

"Chief," he said, "here is another pig to furnish a feast for your people. Eat and dance to-night, but at sunrise to-morrow be on the war-path to avenge your father's death and rescue the white maiden."

"The chief has spoken and his tongue is straight," said Flying Deer.

"Camp near to the great falls and there the white magician and his spirits will meet you and your people and lead you to victory."

"Flying Deer will obey the words of the great white chief."

"Fail me and I will send lightning to blight your corn and foes to lift your scalps. I have spoken."

"The Flying Deer will not fail the white medicine. He speaks not with a crooked tongue."

"It is well," said Ned. "At the falls we meet again in three suns. Farewell!"

Ned motioned Harry and the others to precede him and stalked from the spot.

The Indians remained where they had stood and watched the party of whites till the forest hid them from their view.

When the trees had completely shut them out from the gaze of the savages, Ned paused, placed his hands on his hips, and laughed.

"Oh, what a sell!" he said, after a moment. "Could you have believed it, old man?"

"Blest if I could," replied Harry. "You fairly bounced them into a belief that you were what you pretended to be."

"Cheek did it," said Charley. "Guess I'll have to sing small after that."

"You don't know 'em like I do," said Sally. "They're the easiest to fool, though they're precious hard to lick."

"That was a capital idea of yours and Jack's," said Ned.

"Of course it was," said Sally. "But where's that crocodile of mine got to?"

"And my bear?" said Charley.

"They'll join us at the spot where we landed. I arranged that with Jack and Jumbo. Let's get on. Those savages must not get a chance to have their peepers opened."

"Quite right," said Sally. "But you needn't fear. They won't think of following and prying into the doings or sayings of such a wonderful medicine as you've bounced them you are."

"I don't believe they smelt the slightest sniff of mouses," said Harry.

"I was fearful they would, though, when that pig came bounding on to the scene. Did he get a good grab at you, 'Dolf?"

"No, I managed to get my leg clear before his teeth snapped on it," said 'Dolf.

"I'm glad of that," said Ned. "Bircher got a nasty fall, though."

"Not much, Nimble," said the tutor; "the only damage done is to my trousers, but a needle and thread will soon put them to rights."

"Then none suffered; that's good," said Harry.

"Oh, yes, one did," said 'Dolf.

"Who was that—Sally?"

"No, the pig to be sure. I weigh ten stone, you know."

"Ha, ha," said Ned, "and the pig felt that weight very much when you came down on him, I reckon."

"Poor piggy," said Charley; "he didn't feel it long."

"No," said Ned, "for Jack and Jumbo made short work of him."

"And those reds will make a meal," said Harry.

"So much for poor piggy," said Charley. "But you haven't complimented me upon the talent I showed in working that organ. How did you like the music, Master Ned?"

"About as well as the pig did," said Ned. "It hurt the porker and I'll swear it hurt me."

"That's because you haven't got an ear for sweet strains," said Charley. "Never were sounds so celestial poured from the pipe of a pig before. I fancied I was being wafted on the wings of——"

"Shut up," said Harry.

"Well," said Charley, "if you can't appreciate the beauties of——"

"I can appreciate pig roasted, that's all," interrupted Harry. "I shall never look on pork again without fancying I can hear that horrid squeal."

"Horrid squeal," said Charley. "Oh, Master Harry, it was as good as a dose of medicine to me. Why, haven't you ever heard that—

If you'd soothe your aching breast,
And lull your troubled soul to rest,
Then catch a porker young and strong,
With tail that's curly, not too long;
One you can hold well in your fist,
And round about your fingers twist,
Then wind, as if 'twere twine on reel,
And list the music of his squeal.
  Oh, it is delightful,
  Yes, it is delightful.
'Twill make you feel to hear him squeal,
  There's nothing so delightful."

"Well," said Sally, "I always thought it on you, that I did."

"Thought what?" said Charley.

"As you'd been brought up a street nigger. But I suppose you ran away with the halfpence and pawned your banjo, and that's how you came into these outlandish parts."

"I guess you're wrong there, old girl," said Charley.

"Old girl, indeed," said Sally. "I'll have you to know I'm not——"

"Not quite seventy," interrupted Charley. "I know that, you are fifty-two, I think you said, next birthday."

"Look here, Mr. Imperence, you won't live till next birthday if you come any of your chaff with me."

"Order, order," said Ned. "Let dogs delight et cetera, but we mustn't quarrel."

"Course not, Ain't we the happy family ?" said Charley.

"Guess dat's trufe," said a voice, and Jumbo came out of a clump of bushes.

He was instantly followed by Jack.

Each of them carried their disguise in their arms.

"That's right," said Ned. "Now we are all together again, let's get back to the raft."

CHAPTER LVIII.

IN WHICH JUMBO MAKES A LITTLE STIR.

HAVING reached the raft in safety, the party embarked on it, and after a journey of a few miles, landed some little distance back from the beach, after having secured the raft so that it could not float away.

They had left their boat some distance from the falls, as Sally had suggested, and after rounding the cataract, had felled timber and made the raft.

On this they had proceeded the rest of the way to the camping-grounds of Flying Deer.

On their journey they had slain a bear and a crocodile, and the skins of these animals had been dried and made to serve the purpose to which we have seen them put with such success.

Having partaken of food, Ned and his party sought rest, for at sunrise they intended to again take to the raft and set out on their return journey.

At the same time Flying Deer had promised that he would place himself at the head of his braves, and lead them towards the hunting grounds of the followers of the late Tiger Claw.

There was no fear of the savage chief and the whites coming in contact till they reached the falls, as Flying Deer would proceed by land after crossing the river in his canoes, while Ned and his party would go on as far as they could by water, keeping well into the shore.

At daybreak a hurried meal was taken and Ned and his friends went again upon the raft, and set sail.

As they proceeded on their journey, Ned turned to Harry.

"If all goes well we shall soon know for certain the fate of poor Minnie," he said.

"Yes," replied Harry, a few days now will prove whether she is still a captive, or—"

He paused.

"Dead !" said Ned.

"No, I believe Sally was right in saying she is still alive."

"Why then did you hesitate ?"

"I don't know, Ned," replied his friend, " unless it was the fear I felt that though still living she might not be in the hands of those we are on our way to seek."

"In whose then if not in theirs ?" asked Ned, quickly.

Harry shook his head.

"I can't tell ; it was only a fancy, that was all."

"Not Boaster's ? " said Ned.

"I never thought of him," replied Harry ; "besides, he would not dare to seek her there."

"I wonder where he is now ? " said Ned, after a pause.

"I wonder ?" was Harry's reply.

"Perhaps he is with the savages with whom we first met him," said Ned.

"Perhaps he has shared the fate of his vile confederate," returned Harry.

"Who knows but you are right ? " said Ned.

"If so, he would well deserve it," remarked Harry. "He would get no sympathy from me whatever his fate might be."

"He has been a cruel and bitter foe to me and mine," said Ned.

"That he has, dear boy, and so he will remain if he is still alive," said Harry.

"I could forgive him for any injury he might inflict on me, but on Minnie, never," said Ned. "If he lives, I wonder shall we ever meet again ?"

And Harry not returning any answer, Ned fell into a reverie.

The raft, under the impulse of oar and sail, drifted on.

The sun was hot, and Jack had made a sort of cabin for Bircher and Sally by stretching canvas over some pieces of timber, under which they could sit, sheltered from the hot rays that poured down upon the river.

Bircher was sitting with his elbows on his knees, and his chin resting on his hands, gazing on vacancy.

The tutor's thoughts were far away.

He was thinking of his wife Mary.

Sally was sitting with her head leaning against one of the pieces of the timber that supported the canvas, with her eyes closed.

The heat had evidently caused her to slumber.

Both could be seen by those in front of the raft.

Jumbo had been watching them for some time.

Suddenly he looked over at Charley and said—

"Dis chile guess dere's a lot ob courting a-going on in dat are cabin."

And he gave a wink and nodded his head towards Jack.

"More than I'd like my sweetheart to be up to," said Charley; "and that Bircher a married man too."

"Dat's where it don't look 'spectable," said Jumbo.

"And she's going to get swished some day to Jack."

"Guess she'll lose her chance ob collaring dat crocodile if she don't be careful."

"Just look at 'em now," said Charley. "Oh, ain't they billing and cooing. Blowed if I'd stand it; would you, Jumbo?"

"Guess I wouldn't if I was 'trofed to her. Oh, no, not dis yer nigger."

"There, look at him! Did you see him wink?" said Charley.

"Wid bofe eyes. Oh, de wicked old sinner!"

"And got a wife of his own too. It's shameful."

"Guess dat's trufe, and dat are ole crocodile neber to see it."

"Oh, he twigs right enough," said Charley. "I'm up to his game."

"Lor', is you? What is it?"

"Can't you see."

"Not a bressed bit."

"He'll let 'em go on with their courting, and then he'll get up a breach of promise case ag'in Sally. I can read his little game."

"What's de good ob dat, eh? Dey can't deworce a gal what ain't married"

"Who said anything about a divorce?"

"You did."

"No, I didn't. I was talking of a breach of promise."

"Well, ain't dat all de same?"

"No, you fool."

"Here, I say, don't you go for to call me names or dere'll be a breach ob deworce atween us."

"Now, then, you two, you're at your rows again," said Jack, suddenly turning on hearing Jumbo's raised tones.

"In course we is. Tink I'm going to be hinsulted by dat common white trash?"

"Who's a-insulting on you, you lowbred nigger?" said Charley.

"You is."

"What's it all about?" asked Jack.

"About Bircher and Sally," said Charley.

"What about them?" asked Jack.

"Jumbo says Sally's awful sweet on Bircher."

"Dat's a lie," cried the black. "I said dey was a-biting each other, acos dey hated each other like pison, and den you said Jack was a-going to get a deworce from Bircher. Dere, dat's de trufe."

"Well, you are a——"

"Guess I am dat," interrupted the nigger.

"Look here," said Jack, "just you two fellows let Sally alone."

"Who's a-touching on her?" said Jumbo.

"I didn't say you was," remarked Jack; "but perhaps you'll not make so free with her name."

"Dar, you see, Charley, jus' what I tole you."

"What did you tell me?"

"Dat you'd make Jack awful gealous if you said anyting about dat are gal ob his."

"Why, you black cuss, it was you who——"

"Dere now, don't you go for to open your mouf to put your foot down him frote, cos if you was on'y to tell half what you been saying to dis chile about her, dat Jack 'ud be so awful mad dat he'd chuck you off de raft into de river."

"What's he been saying?" cried Jack, angrily, seizing Jumbo by the collar. "Tell me, you black whelp, or I'll shake the life out of you."

"Guess he didn't say not nuffin," replied Jumbo. " Yah, yah ! "

"Go to the devil," cried Jack, giving Jumbo a drive, and turning angrily away.

"Dis chile felt orful dull ; guess him much better now," said Jumbo. " Dese here little 'fairs does break do 'notony of dese here hot days."

CHAPTER LIX.

IN WHICH SALLY SCRUBBINS MAKES A DISCOVERY.

NOTHING interfered with their progress, and the falls being reached the raft was abandoned, and a few miles brought Ned and his party to where their boat was hidden.

They found everything on board as they had left it, and were only too glad to be once more on its deck.

Guns and revolvers were loaded, and Sally paid great attention to her mitrailleuse.

Every preparation was made to meet and combat a brave and determined foe.

The roar of the falls sounded loud and near, and when the sun went down, from the deck of the boat the whites could see the glare of the fires of the Indians on the shore.

"Heaven grant Flying Deer may not fail me," said Ned, "for on him and his braves I centre all my hopes of rescuing my beloved Minnie."

"He will not fail us," said Sally. " Revenge is too sweet to the red man to let any obstacle stand in the path of obtaining it."

"But," said Ned, suddenly, "how shall we know of his presence ? Fool that I was. I never arranged a signal with him to proclaim when he had reached the scene."

"And a good job too," said Sally.

"How—why ? "

"If you had you'd have knocked on the head at once the magician dodge. As long as he fancied you were what you pretended to be he'd think you must know when he arrives."

"Ah, true. true. What's best to be done, Sally ? "

"Send a scout ashore to watch for his coming."

"Yes, of course. Who shall I send ? " said Ned. " I'll go myself."

"No," said Sally, " I'll go. I am a better woodman than you are."

"You are a woman, and I cannot suffer you to place yourself in danger unless others are near to aid you."

"Let me alone," said Sally. "I'm good enough for any danger with my mitrailleuse, so say no more about it. Master Ned Nimble, I'm the scout, so there ! "

"But Sally ——"

"Never mind any buts, Master Ned. I'll just take my twelve-barrelled umbrella—and that's worth fifty buts—and I'll go ashore at once, for I'm a bad judge of Indian travelling if Flying Deer and his braves ain't pretty near here now."

Ned still protested, but all to no purpose.

Sally would listen neither to him nor Harry, and when Jack proposed that he should go instead, Sally flourished the umbrella in his face and cried—

"Look here, Jack, you know what sort of a gal I am, so you shut up, or it'll be the worse for you. I said I'd go, and I'm going, and not fifty wild cats will turn me when my mind's made up, so there ! "

And so Sally went ashore.

She was better acquainted with that part than any of the others could have been, for she had wandered through its forests and along the bank of the river right up to the falls, and knew where the cave was situated where the Indians buried their dead and where the medicines of the tribe retired to learn from the spirits whether good or evil would attend the expeditions of the band.

This cave was held in great awe and reverence by the savages, and all but the medicines gave it as wide a berth as possible, for whoever ventured into it vowed that they had heard voices of thunder and horrid noises, and seen the fearful shapes of the guardians of the dead.

Indeed it was only when chased by

some wild denizen of the forest that any of the tribe had dared venture within the awful precincts, and the stories they told of what they had seen and heard on their return, had given the cave a reputation so fearful that nothing short of almost certain death would tempt a savage warrior to intrude upon it.

Its entrance was in the densest part of a dark belt of trees that stretched down almost to the river's edge, but how far it extended none knew, unless it was the medicines, and if they knew they never told their fellows.

Even Tiger Claw, bold warrior that he was, had never gone further than its entrance, and his stout heart had been appalled on hearing his own words come back to him in tones of thunder.

No wonder then that Sally, who was almost as superstitious as an Indian, and who had heard the fearful stories of the phantom cave, had no desire to go too near it.

She made her way slowly through the forest, keeping ears and eyes open for any sound or sight that might reach them.

She knew that Flying Deer would endeavour to steal as near the encampment of his foe as he could during the darkness and then camp till Ned should join him.

Grasping her mitrailleuse firmly, and listening for the slightest sound that would indicate the vicinity of man or beast, she made her way through the trees and undergrowth, which her eyes, now accustomed to the gloom, permitted her to do with comparative ease.

She had travelled thus for about half-an-hour when a crackling sound broke on her ears.

She paused and drew up close to the huge trunk of a forest giant, and almost held her breath lest it should betray her presence.

She listened intently.

"If an Indian he is no foe to the tribe who camps yonder," she thought, " or not even the breaking of a twig would betray his presence."

Once more came the crackling sound, and this time almost close to her.

Her hand sought the knife in the belt at her waist.

Her heart beat quickly.

Another moment, with palpitating heart and strained eye, she waited, and then up before her loomed the figure of a man.

She could see that he was an Indian by the feathers on his head.

But his movements were not those of a savage.

In wonder she gazed upon him, as with something in his arms he moved between the trees.

Suddenly his foot struck a protruding root or a stone, and he stumbled, and as he staggered to regain his balance, he muttered—

"Confound it! I have missed my way and Minnie will be frozen to death if I do not find the cave soon."

Sally's hand fell from the hilt of her knife, and it was with difficulty she repressed the scream that rose to her lips at the mention of the name and the tones of the man's voice who had uttered it.

She set her lips hard together as she followed with her eyes the form of the man through the gloom of the forest, and then, when she could see him no longer, her lips parted, and she tottered from the tree.

"'Tis he, I'd swear it," she muttered. "That pretended Indian is the wretch who struck down Bircher on the boat. Yes, it is Boaster, and the poor girl is in his power and he has hidden her in that awful phantom cave!"

CHAPTER LX.

IN WHICH NED PAYS A VISIT TO THE PHANTOM CAVE AND IS BROUGHT UP SUDDENLY.

SALLY decided to return instantly to the boat and acquaint Ned with her discovery.

Announcing her presence upon the bank by an agreed signal, she got on board and asked for Ned.

"What is it, Sally? Has Flying Deer arrived?"

"I have seen nothing of him or his braves," replied Sally, "but I've seen and learned what is of more importance to you than all the red men in America."

"What?" asked Ned, eagerly.

"I've seen that villain Boaster."

"Boaster!" asked Ned and Harry in a breath.

"Yes, and from his own lips learned that the girl you seek is no longer with the Indians."

"Then she is indeed——"

"Stop!" interrupted Sally, "she ain't dead; she's alive, as I said she was, and Boaster told me where she is to be found."

"Boaster told you?" said Ned.

"There, keep yourself cool now and I'll tell you all about it."

Ned promised, and Sally then told him how she had come across Boaster disguised as an Indian in the forest, and the words she had heard him mutter.

"Then he himself, the villain, has Minnie captive," said Ned.

"Yes, evidently, and he has concealed her in the terrible phantom cave, the entrance to which he was in search of when he passed me in the forest."

"Then we must not delay a single moment, lest he bear her away from it," cried Ned. "Sally, you know where this cave is situated; you must conduct us to it."

"But surely, Master Ned, you would not dare enter that fearful place?" cried Sally.

"I'd plunge into the depths of Hades to rescue Minnie from that villain," cried Ned.

"But the phantoms, the awful phantoms that inhabit it?" said Sally.

"Bah!" cried Ned. "Show me where to find this cave, and though a legion of fiends barred my way I'll enter and tear Minnie from that scoundrel's power."

"I'll show you the cave, Master Ned, but I would not enter it for worlds."

"Only point out to me where it lies, and I will ask no more."

"Indians are camped near it," said Sally, "and should they see you?"

"No matter, Sally, were they a thousand times as numerous as they are, they should not stop me."

"But if you wait the coming of Flying Deer——"

"I will wait for nothing," said Ned, "I must away at once."

"I'm with you, old man," said Harry.

"And so are all of us," said Bircher.

"Now look here," said Sally. "If you won't wait for Flying Deer and his braves, the fewer of you who go the less chance of being seen by the Indians."

"That's true," said Ned. "I will go alone, at least, alone with Sally as a guide; more may give Boaster a suspicion of the vicinity of foes, and he may be off with the girl. I and Sally alone will go to the cavern."

"I won't go nearer than a dozen yards to it," said Sally. "Ugh! the very thought of it makes me shiver."

"It is dark, then?" said Ned.

"I've heard it's black as pitch."

"Then I'll take a torch," said Ned.

"How can you carry a torch and fight Boaster too, if you happen to meet him?" asked Harry.

"I did not think of that."

"You'd better let me come, Ned. I could be torch-bearer, you know, and besides, I should be at hand to fight for you if needs be."

Sally bent her head and whispered to Ned.

"If you've made up your mind to go into that cave, you'll have to be pretty careful, both of Indians and that villain, who has tried to make himself look like one. Boaster knows Harry's voice as well as your own, you'd better get Jack or Charley to go with you."

"Then I'll take Charley. I don't expect to encounter any one but Boaster, and him I can fight by myself. Charley need only give me light to know and see what is to be done."

"Well, if phantoms——"

"Nonsense," said Ned. "I'll go and arm myself while Charley gets a torch, and join you directly."

"Well, I don't know what to think of it," said Sally; "I hope no harm will come to Ned, but I'm awfully afraid I am."

Ned had bid Charley follow him below, and in a few minutes they returned to the deck, Ned armed with revolvers, and a knife and Charley with a knife and revolver, and carrying a torch in his hand.

Ned motioned Sally to precede him, and stepped ashore.

Very silently and cautiously the three

ade their way towards where the camp
res of the Indians were burning, keep-
g just within the edge of the forest,
ll at last Sally paused, and turning
asped the hand of Ned.

I dare not go any further," she whis-
ered. "You see that black trunk right
fore us?"

Ned said that he did see a blighted
ee.

"That tree never puts forth a leaf,"
ail Sally. It stands on the right of the
itrance to the cave. The entrance is
idden by thick bushes which you must
ush through to reach it. Heaven guard
ou, Master Ned. I dare not go further.
ll wait here your return."

"Never mind, Sally, we'll go on alone.
'ome, Charley."

"Don't light the torch till you are be-
ond the bushes, or the Indians will see
he flare."

Without a word in reply Ned pro-
eeded towards the blighted tree that
tood towering high above its fellows, its
lack bare branches spreading far out on
ll sides.

They reached the bushes, and parting
hem forced their way right up to the
ree.

Then their eyes, accustomed to the
loom, made out the black yawning
pening by its side.

Boldly Ned stepped within it, followed
fter a moment's hesitation by Charley.

"Light the torch," said Ned, in a whis-
er.

"Light the torch!"

The words seemed to be thundered in
heir ears by a thousand demon voices.

For a moment Ned was startled, then
he burst into a laugh.

Peal after peal of laughter rolled back
o their ears.

"Good Heavens!" cried Charley,
'what can it be?"

"Echoes, you fool!" said Ned.

Thus reassured Charley struck a light
and set fire to the torch.

They strode forward, and Ned saw that
they were in a large stalactite cavern, the
air of which was bitterly cold, and the
sound of rushing waters fell on their
ears.

Pillars of crystal reached from floor to
roof.

Suddenly Ned paused and cocked his
revolver.

The next moment he lowered it, for
the Indian he had discovered crouching
at the foot of one of the pillars he saw
was a corpse.

Another and another met his gaze, and
then he realised that he was in the burial
place of the dead, and that the corpses
were turned to stone by the action of the
air in the cavern.

"And is it to this place that the
villain has brought Minnie?" he
said.

"Minnie, Minnie!" echoed on all
sides.

As Ned paused to listen to the echoes
a scream broke on his ears, and springing
round a huge pillar he saw before him a
dense curtain of water descending from
the roof.

Scarce did his eyes rest upon it than
the scream was repeated in a thousand
echoes, and then mingled with them the
cry—

"Ned, Ned! Oh save me, save
me!"

And up from the earth bounded a
female form with outstretched arms.

"Minnie, Minnie!" cried Ned springing forward.

But ere he had taken two steps the
tall figure of an Indian sprang between
them, who clutching the girl round the
waist, held her back, and levelling a revolver, cried—

"Back, Ned Nimble—back! Advance
one step and I scatter your brains and
hurl her body into these foaming waters!"

Ned recoiled in horror as he recognised
in those painted features, his remorseless
enemy Bill Boaster.

CHAPTER LXI.

IN WHICH NED SEEKS MINNIE BUT SEEKS HER IN VAIN.

MINNIE struggled to tear herself from the clasp of Bill Boaster, but in vain.

The bully's arm tightened round her waist till she felt as though she were in a vice.

With a devilish look of triumph on his painted face, Bill kept his pistol levelled at the head of Ned.

Ned dared not fire.

He feared to pull the trigger lest he should shoot Minnie instead of her persecutor.

Bill divined his thoughts.

He could see the working of Ned's features in the glow of the light cast by the torch in the hand of Charley.

"Take yourself off, Ned Nimble," said Boaster. "You can do no harm to me, while you may cause the death of her. Better give up your pursuit of both myself and Minnie, you only waste your time and indulge in hopes that never can be realised."

"Coward and villain!" cried Ned.

"Go on," said Boaster, with a laugh. "I am used to your railings, Ned Nimble, and they have no more effect upon me than does the wild echoes of this cavern."

"Release that girl, I say," cried Ned.

"Not at the bidding of a legion, much less at thine," cried Boaster.

"Release her, I say, or I'll fire," cried Ned.

"If you do, your bullet will rest in her breast, not mine," said Boaster.

"You double-breasted mongrel," cried Charley; "you second-hand slab of a curse, don't shelter yourself behind a woman's petticoats; let go the girl and fight like a man."

"Oh, is that your advice, you dirty rascal? Ned Nimble's pride must have fallen greatly when he chooses the dregs of an American jail for his friends and advisers."

"I'll shove this torch down your throat, you painted image," cried Charley.

"Peace," said Ned. "Once more, Boaster, I bid you release that girl."

"And once more I say I will not," replied Boaster, "and now take yourself off, or I'll drop you with a bullet from this revolver."

"Oh, Ned, save me, save me," cried Minnie.

"Move not," cried Boaster. "You know me, Ned Nimble, so move not, I say; the first step you take in advance, and I'll fling her body into the torrent."

"You dare not, coward that you are, you dare not," cried Ned.

"I dare, and I will," said Boaster.

"Mercy, mercy," moaned Minnie.

"Mercy!" cried Boaster, "for you, yes; for Ned, no. Never shall he tear you from me; to possess you is half my revenge, and sooner than lose it I would leap with you into that boiling flood and in my dying agonies strangle you lest he should rescue your living body."

"Oh, Heaven!" gasped Minnie.

"Coward, let your revenge be centred on me," cried Ned; "release her and then take your vengeance on me. Release her, we are armed alike, and let Heaven decide between us."

"You are artful, Ned Nimble," said Boaster, "in not mentioning the aid you will get from your most respectable companion."

"By Heaven he shall not raise a finger against you; the quarrel is ours, and alone we will decide it," cried Ned.

"Ned Nimble," hissed Boaster, "I swore when we were at school together that I would not strike at your face but at your heart; I now strike at you through her, and I triumph in the knowledge of the pain I inflict upon your soul now."

"Oh you base inhuman monster!" cried Ned.

"Rail on; words are harmless," said Bill. "Minnie, the girl you love, is in my power, in my grasp; from neither shall she ever escape, and never, Ned Nimble, shall you ever again clasp her in your arms but as a corpse."

"Heaven help me," gasped Minnie "would, would I were dead!"

"Oh, say not so, Minnie," cried Ned; "I will yet save you from this human fiend."

"Never!" cried Boaster; "never, by Heaven."

"You lie, villain," cried Ned, raising his revolver, "this shot shall—"

"Slay her!" cried Boaster, as he swung the form of Minnie round before him

Ned let fall his hand.

"Why don't you fire, Ned Nimble?" cried Boaster, tauntingly.

"Monster, devil," yelled Ned.

"Ha, ha, ha!" laughed Boaster; "has Ned Nimble turned liar as well as fool, that he makes a threat and then refuses to keep it?"

"Villain, but that I might kill her I—"

"Just so," said Boaster, tauntingly; "you fear to kill her; now begone, for only as a corpse I swear will I ever surrender her to you."

"Kill me, Ned, oh kill me!" cried Minnie, "but oh, do not leave me alone in the power of this wretch. It were mercy rather to die by your hand."

"Oh Heaven help me!" cried Ned, again raising his revolver and once more lowering it; "I cannot fire, I dare not."

"You dare not," repeated Boaster; "then get you hence and leave us to ourselves; I told you the hour of my triumph would come, and it is arrived at last."

"Wretch!"

"As you will," said Bill, "perhaps I am a wretch, but remember, Nimble, it was you who made me what I am."

"A coward will always find an excuse for his cowardice, and a villain for his villainy," said Ned, "but once more I say release that girl."

"You only ask in vain," replied Bill; "she is dearer to you than all the world, hence the possession of her makes my revenge on you the greater; I tore her from you to minister to my revenge, to keep her from you enhances it, and I will keep her, Ned Nimble, while life lasts, and count every moment of exis-

tence a stab at the heart of the man I hate."

"Ned," cried Minnie, "fear not for me. Rather death a thousand times than life with him; fear not to take the life I could myself freely resign. Fire, Ned; fire, and God bless you!"

"Minnie," cried Ned, in choking accents, I cannot, cannot."

"But I can and will," cried Charley.

And jerking up his weapon fired.

Ned flung himself upon him.

"For Heaven's sake hold!" he cried, grasping Charley's hand.

A cry broke from Boaster, a shriek from Minnie.

Let go, you fool, I've winged him," cried Charley.

Ned obeyed.

Boaster had fallen to his knee.

Minnie wrested herself from his hold and sprang towards Ned.

"Saved, saved!" she shrieked.

"Lost," yelled Boaster, bounding to his feet and seizing her in his arms again.

Ned and Charley again raised their weapons.

But Boaster held the girl clasped to his breast, and walking backwards drew her with him.

"Fools," he cried, "you have not yet and never shall tear her from me!"

And raising his hand he fired under Minnie's arm.

The bullet struck one of the columns.

Ned and Charley both held their weapons levelled towards him.

But he kept his body so covered by that of Minnie that they dared not fire.

Boaster continued to discharge shot after shot, but the struggles of Minnie prevented his aim from being true.

At every shot he retreated backwards nearer to the waterfall, and stood close to it as he discharged his last shot.

"Now," cried Ned, "his weapon is empty and Minnie is ours."

"Never!" cried Boaster; "she is mine in life and death for ever.

And raising Minnie in his arms he sprang backwards with her into the roaring waters.

CHAPTER LXII.

IN WHICH JACK AND JUMBO GO IN SEARCH OF NED AND FIND SALLY.

" Guess as how dis yar chile don't understand all dis here bobbery, does you, Massa 'Dolf? " asked the negro.

" Who's bit you ? " asked 'Dolf.

" I didn't say as how I was bit, what for you tink I did ? "

" Well, what are you hammering at then ? " said Ned.

" Guess dis chile ain't a hammering at not nuffin."

" Then what do you mean ? "

" What for Massa Ned take dat are Charley and leave dis most 'spectful nigger here for ? " said Jumbo.

" Oh, because you're a fool, I suppose," said 'Dolf.

" Guess dat's trufe," replied Jumbo, " but dis yer nigger feels hisself 'sulted to tink dat Massa Ned prefer dat ragged dirty white trash to dis 'spectably tired gen'leman."

" Well, you have got something to be proud of since Ned rigged you out in some of his left off togs."

" Don't you turn up dat ugly snout ob yours 'cos you didn't get your perquisites. Guess dat's what you are riled at."

" Yes, a lot of good they'd do me here," said 'Dolf.

" Dey does dis chile more good ; Lor'-a-mussy now, if I was only in New York wouldn't dem bressed gals be a running after me in dese here trousers."

" Don't know," said 'Dolf ; " don't think any girl would be fool enough to run after you."

" Why not, eh ? "

" Because you're too much like the devil," said 'Dolf.

" Guess dat's trufe," said Jumbo ; " but dis chile feel very much put out dat Massa Ned should take dat are Charley what ain't wuth not nuffin, can't make it out not nohow."

" He took him because he's so precious ugly he'd frighten the demons in that cave Sally talks about," said 'Dolf.

" Never thought ob dat," said Jumbo.

" It was no good his taking you, one devil ain't frightened of another, you know."

" Ob course, dat's de reason he left you behind," said Jumbo ; " but dere's one bressed good ting about it."

" What's that ? " asked 'Dolf.

" I'll hab Charley's share as well as my own when de time comes round to share out de grub."

" Don't think you will," said 'Dolf, " for I don't mean to share out any grub till Ned comes back."

" Suppose him no come back ? " asked Jumbo.

" Then no grub."

" Golly, guess den I'll hab to eat dose here trousers ; halloa ! who's dat knocking at de door ? "

A hand came heavily down between Jumbo's shoulders.

The negro turned to see Jack.

" What for you hit dis bear, you ole crocodile ? " said Jumbo.

" To wake you up," said Jack.

" Guess dis chile weren't asleep," said Jumbo. " Don't you take such liberties wid de back ob dis yere shirt, you nearly pull de collar off it."

" I'll pull your head off if you don't hold your noise," said Jack ; " I want to talk to you."

" Well, den, don't you talk wid your fist ; what you got to say ? "

" I want you to come ashore with me."

" What you going to do ? "

" I don't feel comfortable about Ned, and I'm going to look after him and Charley."

" Ob course you don't care about Sally, oh, no."

" I care for them all," said Jack ; " I've been talking to Harry and Bircher, and they've agreed that you and I should go ashore and do a prowl round."

" Guess I'm ready."

" But I ain't, no more are you yet ; we are going in our new suits."

" Eh ? " said Jumbo.

" I'm going in my crocodile skin and want you to go in your bear skin."

" What for ? "

"'WHAT DE GROUND JUMP UP AT DIS OLE BEAR FOR?' CRIED JUMBO."

"So as to make the Indians if they should see us fancy we are animals to be sure and give us a wide berth. So get your skin on and put a revolver in your belt in case we should need it."

"Guess I'll do dat same," said Jumbo, darting below.

Jack followed him.

In a short time they returned to the deck attired in the skins, and with a revolver and knife hidden beneath them.

Harry, who had been talking with Bircher, came to their side.

"You think you could find this cave, Jack, from what Sally told you?"

"Yes, I fancy so," replied Jack; "she said it was close to that high tree which we saw to-day stripped of every vestige of leaf."

"Be careful," said Harry; "I can't help feeling extremely anxious about Ned, or I would not urge you to go after his refusal to let anyone else accompany him. Of course you have no superstitious fears with respect to the place?"

"Not a bit of it" said Jack. "I never saw anything worse than myself."

"If anything should have happened to Ned you may be able to learn it or render him assistance."

"I'll do it if he needs it," said Jack, "never fear."

"Guess dis chile won't be far behind," said Jumbo.

Harry wrung Jack's hand and they parted.

Jack and Jumbo to go ashore and make their way to the cave, and Harry to take charge of the boat and wait impatiently the return or news of his friend.

It was darker on shore than on the river, and though Jack felt certain he could make his was through the forest to the tall, blighted tree, he soon found out his mistake.

After half-an-hour's travelling through the woods, and occasionally dropping down on all fours when they fancied they heard a sound other than the wind sweeping through the forest, both Jack and Jumbo were fain to admit they did not know in what direction they were going.

They looked round in search of the camp-fires of the Indians, but they were no longer to be seen.

They wandered on till they came to a space more clear than others they had passed through, and searched for the blighted tree.

It was not to be seen.

"Confound it!" said Jack, "I'm up a tree."

"Guess dat's a lie," said Jumbo. "Dat 'ere tail ob yours, you ole crocodile, wouldn't let you get up one."

"I'm all afield, I mean," said Jack.

"What's dat, you'se afield? Guess you is as much a field as you is a crocodile. Don't you try to make dis ole nigger beliebe dat."

"You're a fool," said Jack.

"Guess dat's trufe for once you spoke," said Jumbo.

"What the devil's best to be done?"

"Golly, dat's jus' what I was tinking."

"I can't see that tree."

"No more can dis chile."

"I don't know where to look for it, either," said Jack.

"Guess I do."

"Where?"

"Up a tree," replied Jumbo.

"That's right; climb one of them and look round."

"Hope I won't tear this yer suit," said Jumbo, as he essayed to climb a tree.

But all in vain with that skin on his limbs.

"That can't be the wind roaring like that," said Jack, suddenly.

"Guess not," said Jumbo; "dat's water."

"Why we are getting closer to the falls," said Jack.

"Well, and ain't dat de way we got to go? Jus' you gib us a bung up dis yer tree."

"Yes, of course; I've got in a fog," said Jack.

Jumbo made another attempt to climb the tree, and Jack gave him a hoist.

"Confound this tail! What the dickens has got hold of it now?" cried Jack, as he was pulled backwards.

"Oh, de debbil!" cried Jumbo, and losing his balance, came to the ground, and turned clean head over heels. "What de ground jump up at dis ole bear for?"

"Oh," cried Jack, "an Indian!" making a clutch at his knife.

"Drop it," said a voice, "or I'll put a dozen bullets into you with my patent **mitrailleuse.**"

"Sally!" cried Jack and Jumbo in one breath.

"Reckon that's me, you pair of fools. If I'd been an Indian you'd been corpses, and no mistake."

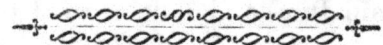

CHAPTER LXIII.

IN WHICH THERE IS MUCH FEAR AND A LITTLE MYSTERY.

"Oh, Sally, I'm so glad we've found you," said Jack.

"Rather say you are glad I've found you," returned Sally. "I thought you were wild animals at first, and if I hadn't been afraid of bringing the Indians down on me you'd have got a dozen or two of bullets a-piece in your bodies."

"I'm glad you didn't fire," said Jack.

"Guess dis chile 'ull say ditto to dat are."

"I should have done so, I expect, if you hadn't spoken. Then I knew who you were."

"Guess we're awful glad we did speak den. If I'd only gib a growl—oh, Lor'!"

"I should have let fly if you had," said Sally, "and chanced it. Now what are you both doing here and in those skins?"

"Looking for Ned. Where is he?" asked Jack.

"Being gobbled up by the goblins, I expect," said Sally.

"Don't be a fool," said Jack.

"She can't help it," remarked Jumbo.

"None of your imperence," said Sally.

"Dis chile's sorry he spoke."

"Then don't speak again."

"But where is Ned?" asked Jack again.

"And Charley?" put in Jumbo.

"They went on to the cave, and I have been waiting here for them, but I'm afraid we shall never see them again," said Sally, sadly.

"Why, do you think the Indians——"

"Indians? No. They wouldn't dare go near it; but the demons——"

"Now, Sally, do be a sensible woman. You know there are no such things."

"I don't know nothing about it. All I know is that that cave is haunted, and I fear that Master Ned and Charley will never come out of it again alive."

"Then they shall dead," said Jack, "for I'll fetch them out."

"Oh, don't, don't!"

"Nonsense, Sally, where is this cave? I could not find it, nor yet the blighted tree."

"It's over there; but don't go near it, Jack, don't."

"Sally, would you have me desert the friend who brought me here—brought us together again."

"But the cave, Jack—if you go into it I may never see you more."

"Don't be so silly. The sounds with which it is filled come from other than demon throats. Now how can you be so stupid when you know that Boaster must have been in it himself?"

"That's true," said Sally; "but then he's a bad 'un, you know, Jack, and may have sold his soul to the evil one, and so have been allowed to roam in and out it at will."

"Pshaw!" said Jack. "Come, Sally, where is this cave?"

"Oh, Jack!"

"Never mind 'Oh, Jack,' but tell me, or I shall think you are quite indifferent to what Ned's fate may be."

"You know better than that," said Sally. "There's the tree, and the cave is just beside it."

"The tree; where?"

"Look up."

Jack did so.

"Why, we're close to it, and we've been looking everywhere for it."

"Except in the right place," said Sally. "But don't go, Jack, stop with me."

"Rather come with us," said Jack.

"I dare not."

"Then we go alone, for if anything has befallen Ned I should never forgive myself for not being near to protect him."

"No more would dis chile," said Jumbo.

"Come, Sally, be a woman," said Jack: "what need you fear with me by your side?"

And Jack flung his arm round her.

Sally hesitated, then suffered herself to be persuaded, and tremblingly pointed out the way to the cavern.

Jack parted the bushes as Ned had done, and drew her towards the opening.

"I cannot enter it, Jack, I cannot," she whispered.

"Nonsense," he replied.

"But it is pitch dark."

As if to belie her words, a light suddenly appeared within the opening of the cavern.

Jack had drawn her into the black mouth of the cave, and Sally, alarmed by the sudden appearance of the light, uttered a slight scream.

A thousand voices seemed to echo it in tones of thunder.

With a shriek of horror Sally bolted from Jack's hold and fled away into the forest.

Jack turned to pursue her, but stopped dead short as a voice exclaimed—

"Look out, Ned, there's a bear in the opening."

"Stop, stop!" cried Jack; "don't fire for Heaven's sake, it is Jack and Jumbo."

Ned and Charley had raised their weapons to fire, but at the sound of Jack's voice lowered them.

"All right, Ned," cried Jack; "we came to look after you in disguise. Sally's frightened and took her hook. I'll be back directly."

And Jack sped after Sally, whom he found clinging to a tree a little way off, and trembling violently.

"Silly goose," he said, "it's only Ned and Charley," and he drew her back to the opening of the cave.

"She was frightened at the echoes, for that's all they are, I expect," said Jack.

"That is all," said Ned.

Charley held his torch so that the light fell full on Ned's face.

It was deadly pale.

"It frightened me to death nearly," said Sally; "and oh, ain't Master Ned awfully frightened too."

"No," said Ned, "but I'm broken-hearted."

Sally forgot her fear in sympathy for Ned.

"What—what is it, Ned?" she said. "Have you found her?"

"Yes," said Ned, "I found poor Minnie, found to lose her."

"Lose her?"

"Alas! yes, for ever."

And Ned bowed his head on his hands.

"Good Heavens, what do you mean?" asked Jack.

"Alas, my friend, poor Minnie is no more!"

"Dead?" cried Jack and Sally in a breath.

"Yes, for how could she live in that boiling flood? But come," he added, "let me show you her grave."

He took the torch from Charley's hand and led the way into the cave.

"Fear not," he said, "at the sights you will see here. The place is used by the Indians for the receptacle for their dead, and those you will see about the place can harm neither you nor I, for they are only the petrified bodies from which the soul has fled."

He led them on through the pillars and under the festooned roof.

Sally shuddered and clung to Jack, and even Jumbo kept close to Charley's side.

The place had more terrors for them than admiration, though the stalactites, glistening in the torch light. formed a scene of surpassing splendour.

But that splendour was destroyed by the presence of the dead that lay around them.

The roar of the falling waters at the end of the cavern, the weird shadows and loud echoes, appalled the heart of the superstitious Sally, and she trembled so violently that Jack feared she would be unable to proceed much further.

At length there came a turn in the cave, and the sheet of falling, foaming water was before them.

"Behold poor Minnie's tomb," said Ned, holding up the torch; "behold where innocence and guilt lie buried together. Oh, Minnie, Minnie, my happiness is buried for ever in your watery grave!"

While Ned pointed to where the water disappeared in the floor of the cavern, and the misty spray danced like milliards of diamonds in the torch light, the curtain of water parted in the centre, and the form of a man bounded on to the floor before them.

"Boaster," cried Ned, as the torch fell from his hand in his startled surprise, and the cave and its occupants were plunged into darkness.

CHAPTER LXIV.

IN WHICH NED MAKES A SEARCH AND A TERRIBLE DISCOVERY.

SALLY clung tightly to Jack's arm, and cried in trembling accents—

"Oh, we shall all be carried off by the demons, I know we shall. Oh, that was one of them who looked like Boaster, for didn't Ned say the villain was drowned ?"

"Don't be a fool," cried Jack. "Let go. Get a light, some one."

"Oh, yes; do get a light," cried Sally.

"Ain't I trying to ?" said Charley. "Where have I put the matches ?"

"Ugh, oh, murder !" shrieked Sally, clinging round Jack's neck.

"Don't be frightened, Sally, it was only I who touched you."

"For Heaven's sake, quick with a light," said Ned.

The next moment Charley had struck a match, and as it lit up, Ned looked towards the spot where Boaster had stood.

Nothing met his gaze but the curtain of water.

He looked round.

Boaster was nowhere to be seen.

Once more the cave was flooded in the light of the torch, but no Boaster could oe discovered.

"Strange ! Where could he have gone ?" cried Ned.

"It was not him, it was only his ghost," said Sally. Oh, Ned, come away irom here ; do come away."

"Away, away !" rolled in echoes round the cavern.

"I cannot make it out," cried Ned. "It's like a dream."

"It's the work of demons, Master Ned," said Sally. "It was a phantom we saw, and if we do not leave this place at once we shall fall victims to the vengeance of the spirits, whose home we have disturbed. Oh, Master Ned, do let us go."

"I begin to fancy Sally's right about that fellow being a demon," said Jack,

"for no living man could come and go as that fellow did."

"There is some mystery in this place," said Ned, "and by Heavens I will fathom it."

"Don't be a fool, Master Ned ; leastways, don't try to destroy yourself and us too, but come away at once," cried Sally.

"Away at once," repeated the echoes.

"Don't you hear ? " cried Sally. "Oh, do be wise and go away."

"Go away," repeated the echoes.

"Sally, it is nothing but the echoes of this wild cavern. If you and Jack fear them, go. I will remain and try to discover how Boaster hid himself in that moment's darkness. It was he, and alive, and if he still live, why should not poor Minnie ? "

"Don't think it, Ned, don't think it," she cried ; "you only tempt fate and call for punishment on your own head by remaining here. Come, come."

"Go," said Ned, "but here I stay till I know more of this place, and have satisfied myself whether that was Boaster in the flesh or the spirit I saw just now."

"I don't go and leave you here," said Jack.

"Guess I'll say ditto to that little speech," said Charley ; "though it's a rum affair, and I don't tumble to it a bit. Let Sally go and wait for us in the forest."

"No, no," said Sally, "if you will stop, so must I. I daren't go and wait outside by myself now."

"No harm will befall you here," said Ned ; "leastways, if it does, it will certainly be from human hands."

"I ain't afraid of human, not with my patent mitrailleuse," said Sally, "but I've mortal fear of ghostesses."

"Then if you fancy again that you see

one fire at it," said Ned, "and you will soon dispel the illusion. So pluck up a little spirit, Sally, and help me to find out where that villain can be hiding, and how he managed to escape what seemed to be certain death."

Sally gave a shiver and clung close to Jack.

"I'd give you a dose of brandy, Sally, to put courage into you if I'd got any," said Charley.

"I'm sure I'd like a drop," said Sally, "that I would."

"Can't be accommodated," said Charley; "but Jack can give you a quid of tobacco instead."

"Beast!" said Sally.

"Hold the torch here, Charley," said Ned; "there must be something strange in this water."

"How so?" said Charley, as he held the torch so that Ned could examine the falling water.

Ned looked long and searchingly at the descending sheet, and then peered down to where it disappeared at his feet in a foaming mist.

"Well?" said Jack.

Ned shook his head.

"It is a natural cataract," he said.

"And a precious long and heavy one too," said Jack.

"Can it be possible that we all fancied we saw Boaster spring through it?" said Ned; "for it does not seem possible it could have been true."

"Oh, Ned, depend upon it that what we saw was one of the demons of this awful cave," said Sally.

"But that I was brought up in a Christian country, and have been to school," said Ned, "I might believe it was so, but knowing as I do that there are no such things as demons and phantoms, either we were all labouring under some hallucination or it was Boaster himself in the flesh who confronted us."

"Then where is he, and how did he come through that mass of water?" said Sally.

"That is what I want to find out," said Ned.

"And what you'll never do," said Sally; "leastways, not till you are dead and turned into a ghost as he has been."

"I can't see how anyone could pass through such a flood of falling water as that," said Jack.

"Nor I," said Ned.

"Nor I," replied Charley. "It's a licker to me, and no mistake. We saw him go down, and how he got up again from that place—there, I give it up, blowed if I don't."

"Guess as dis yar bear says ditto to dat are obserwation," put in Jumbo. "Golly, but it are a licker, an' no mistake."

Charley held the torch down close to the floor of the cave, to show the apparent depths into which the cataract descended.

"I give it up," said Jack.

"I guess that's what we'll have to do," said Charley.

"I gibs it up and I gibs it down," said Jumbo. "Guess 'tain't no use dis chile to speckerlate about it."

"You may give it up," said Ned; "but I don't yet awhile. I'll first explore every portion of this cave, and then if I fail to discover Boaster hidden somewhere about it, I'll——"

"What?" asked Jack and Sally in a breath.

"Never mind now. Let's go all over this place first. Keep your weapons ready, for we may get a shot or a stab at any moment," said Ned.

And taking the torch from Charley's hand, Ned held the flaming brand high above his head, and moved back from the cataract.

"Follow me," he said, "and keep your eyes and ears open. Don't be surprised if Boaster should spring out upon you from behind one of these pillars."

"If he does," said Charley, "I'll have another pop at him, and with better effect next time, I hope."

Sally held her mitrailleuse ready, and looked nervously about her.

Even Jack, bold and powerful fellow that he was, felt his hands tremble, and his knees quiver, as he followed close to Ned, who flashed the torch first on one side and then on the other.

The further they proceeded from the cataract, the wider grew the cavern.

The pillars of stalactites became more numerous and massive, and on all sides flashed in the torchlight, till the cavern seemed filled with diamonds.

It was a magnificent sight.

But in the present state of mind of

Ned and his companions, it had no charm for them.

The further they proceeded the more numerous became the dead bodies of the Indians.

Here they reclined against the pillars; there they lay stretched upon the floor without the slightest appearance of decay.

More like statues carved in stone were they, than forms that had once had life and motion.

Not a word now was spoken.

Even Ned himself felt awe-stricken at the scenes around him.

They made a circuit of the cave.

They peered round every pillar.

They penetrated every recess.

They examined every figure, standing, sitting, or lying.

But not a glimpse did they get of Boaster.

They came upon the dead embers of a fire, and kicked aside the ashes to see if beneath them there was any trap that might lead to a hiding place.

Finally after examining every part of the cave, they stood once more before its entrance.

Then did Ned speak, and his tones rang out in strains of agony as he held the torch forward—

"The entrance is blocked up! Boaster has escaped, and consigned us all to a living tomb!"

CHAPTER LXV.

IN WHICH ALL ARE SHUT IN—AND NED SHUTS HIMSELF OUT.

WITH feelings of mingled horror and despair, Jack, Sally, Charley, and Jumbo realised the truth of Ned's assertion.

With perspiring brows and fainting hearts, they saw the opening to the phantom cave had been closed up by a huge piece of rock, which they dared not hope their united strength could move away.

How it had been placed there they knew not.

That one man's hand could have placed it in the opening, was of course beyond belief.

But that it had been so placed by Boaster's instigation, Ned doubted not.

And if so, he must have friends and accomplices, but who were they?

Ned's thoughts flew to the Indians, whose camp-fires he had seen on the way to the caves.

But Sally did not believe that the rock had been placed there by human hands.

Neither did Jumbo, whose limbs trembled beneath his bear skin, till he could scarcely stand.

"Gor'-a-mighty," he gasped, "dis yer bear's a dead nigger, for sartin, and de debbil has gorne and done dis for suah."

"I said we'd suffer for daring to intrude into this demon's den," moaned Sally. "That was a fiend after all and not Boaster, and he's lured us to destruction. Oh Jack, Jack!"

And Sally sobbed on the shoulder of the crocodile.

"Don't cry, Sally," said Jack, pressing his cheek to hers, for he had thrust his head through a slit in the neck of the skin. "If we've got to perish, we shall do it like the babes in the wood, together."

"And dis poor ole bear ain't got no baby to die wid," said Jumbo, shaking his head, which was also thrust through the hole in the neck of the bear skin.

"Shut up!" said Charley; ain't you got a whole family in me; ain't I been a mother and a father to you, and a sister and a brother, as well as an uncle and a aunt, you ungrateful cuss, you?"

"Golly! But what's de good of all dat now?" said Jumbo.

"Ain't I here to share all your griefs and miseries?" said Charley.

"Guess you'll hab the biggest share den," said Jumbo. "You always collared de biggest lot, and you're so greedy, you'll hab it now."

"Do not give way to despair," said Ned; "we are entrapped and things look bad for us I admit, but while there's life there's hope."

"Guess dere's a lot ob life now, but berry little hope," said Jumbo, "and soon dere'll be a lot ob def, and what's de good ob hope den? Dis chile don't tink ob hope nohow."

"And to think that after all it's come to this," said Sally; to meet after so many years only to die in each others arms!"

And Sally sobbed more fiercely on Jack's bosom.

"Why don't you come and comfort dis yer nigger?" said Jumbo; "you talk about sharing de grief ob a poor ole bear, and you don't sling your arms over him at all."

And Jumbo put his paws round Charley's neck.

"Just you lay dis here nigger's head on your buzzim, you cole-hearted white ——,"

"Get out," cried Charley, giving Jumbo a jerk off him; "do yo you think I want any of your fooling now?"

"For Heaven's sake cease this nonsense!" said Ned; "instead of trying to make things worse, help me to discover how to get out of this accursed place."

"You'll never do it, Master Ned, never; it's the vengeance of the offended demons who haunt this terrible cave."

"Sally," said Ned, angrily, "I am ashamed of you. Were you an Indian squaw such superstition might be pardonable, but in an Englishwoman, oh, for shame!"

"Dat's just it," said Jumbo. "In a poor ole nigger bear it am all right, but in a crocodile and a woman it's a shame, and dis chile's ashamed ob you bofe."

Sally, shamed by Ned's words and manner, checked her sobs, and then Jack said—

"What can be done? We cannot hope to move that rock."

"We have not tried yet," said Ned; "and we don't know what we can do till we try."

"Then we'll try," said Jack, gently pushing Sally aside, and proceeding to take off his disguise.

"Guess dis chile'll hab a hand in dat," said Jumbo.

And he too began to get off the bear's skin.

"That's right," said Ned. "It is time enough to give way to despair when all chance of escape is passed."

Ned stuck the torch in an opening in the wall near to the entrance, and Jack and Jumbo, having divested themselves of their skins, our hero said—

"Now, Sally, do compose yourself and listen to me."

"I'm listening," said Sally.

"We are going to make an effort to remove the rock from the entrance; if we succeed we may find ourselves confronted by a still greater danger, which we must prepare to meet."

"What danger do you expect?" asked Jack.

"Boaster, and perhaps a troop of savages at his back," replied Ned; "so stand ready, Sally, to pour into them the contents of your mitrailleuse."

"If they are men I can do it, but——"

"Now, Sally, you vex me," said Ned; "do as I bid you, if we move that rock and there should be anyone beyond it to attempt to bar our passage, fire upon them, be they men or devils."

"I will," said Sally.

"It will be our only hope of escape," said Ned; "and if you hesitate it will be you who will be to blame for any harm that may befall us."

"I'll do it, Ned," said Sally, desperately. "It can't make it worse for us, so I'll do it."

"There now, boys; put your revolvers where you can snatch them up, and let's see if we cannot make for ourselves a way out of here."

His words seemed to put new heart into them.

"Now, then," said Ned, "all together."

The four men brought all their power to bear upon the rock, but in vain.

It would not move an inch.

"Again," cried Ned.

Again they tried.

But with the same result.

Never did Jack put forth his enormous strength with greater will than he did now, but it availed nothing.

The huge stone stood as firmly as a mountain.

"It's no go," said Ned. "It won't move."

And he wiped the perspiration from his face and sighed.

Sally sank down on the floor of the cave.

"I knew it," she said; "I was sure of it."

"I fought it, brest if I didn't," said Jumbo.

"Guess we're 'tarnaily blocked up,"

said Charley, "and gone coons and no mistake."

Jack said nothing, but stook shaking his head and looking at the mass of stone.

"Friends," said Ned, "I imagined at first that this was the work of my enemy, and that he had been assisted in preventing our escape from this place by the Indians whose fires we saw, but now that I can realise the enormous weight of rock that lies there, I have come to a different conclusion."

"What is that, Ned?" asked Jack.

"That the rock has fallen from above and blocked up the opening, and that Boaster had no hand in its being there. Indeed, I doubt that he left the cave by that way at all."

"But if what we saw was he, how else could he leave it?" asked Jack. "We have searched the place from end to end, and there is no other way out of it."

"As far as we know," said Ned. "But a suspicion has dawned upon me—a suspicion that I will change into certainty. If there be another way of get-ting out of this place I will find it, or in the attempt I will perish."

So saying Ned took the torch in his hand.

"Follow me, friends," he said, "follow me back to where we saw tha wretch whose villainy brought us here

Jack raised Sally to her feet and sh clung trembling to his arm.

"Come on, you old rascal," cried Charley, seizing Jumbo by the nose and pulling him forward. "Blest if you ain't turned black in the face with fright."

"Let go ob dat yer nose," yelled Jum-bo. "Golly, let go, I say."

Ned led the way back to the cataract, and then he turned to Charley.

"Take this torch," he said, "and I will know whether we are doomed to perish or permitted to escape. No words. I am resolved. I will lead you from this prison or be the first to fall!"

And springing to the edge of the chasm he bounded upwards and leaping forward disappeared from the horrified gaze of his companions in the swiftly descending waters.

CHAPTER LXVI.

IN WHICH BOASTER IS SURPRISED AND TERRIFIED.

MINNIE gave herself up for lost when Boaster, grasping her tightly in his arms, sprang with her into the waterfall.

The shriek she uttered was stifled by the roar of water that fell upon and around her, and she closed her eyes in insensibility.

But the last hour of poor Minnie had not yet come.

Instead of sinking with Boaster down into unknown depths, the bully landed upon firm ground, a curtain of water closing him from the view of those who stood on the other side of it paralysed with horror.

Nor had Boaster himself expected to perish in that leap in the cataract.

The cavern in which he now stood was the one into which he had first entered when his canoe, shooting the falls, had been driven into the cave hidden from the river by the descending sheet that leapt over the rocks above.

In that cave both he and Minnie had perished for want of food—for his canoe had been shivered to atoms against the water entrance to the cave—but that while half concealed in the darkness he had seen a man, carrying a covered light in his hand, spring through what he believed to be only a portion of the falls under which he had passed.

Boaster had crouched low over the body of the insensible Minnie, and the man had passed him by either without seeing him, or if he had observed him, had doubtless believed him to be the body of a dead Indian.

Suddenly the light disappeared, and Boaster scarcely knowing whether his senses had not really deceived him, waited long and anxiously the man's return.

Time passed and still the place in which Boaster found himself was in darkness, and the only sound that broke the stillness was that of rushing water.

At last he had risen, and knowing

that the pouch of the Indian skirt he wore contained the means of obtaining light he struck one, and setting fire to a piece of tinder which fortunately had remained dry, he blew into a red glow, and by the faint light searched the floor of the cave around him.

For a long time in vain he searched for something to kindle into a flame.

At length however he lighted upon a piece of rope, or rather thick string that had been washed into the cave, and lain out of reach of the falling waters till perfectly dry, and this he kindled and blew into a flame.

Now he could search further, and he came upon a broad piece of the side of his wrecked canoe.

Saturated as it was he could not hope to set it on fire, but he could use it for another purpose than for obtaining a light.

He stepped close up to the falling waters through which he had seen the man enter the cave, and thrusting it forward with one hand, while he held his fast consuming string in the other, parted the waters with the broad plank.

The weight of the descending stream almost tore it from his grasp, but he held it so as to throw the water off on either side of the plank, and with a cry of mingled satisfaction and surprise, he discovered what he had half suspected, that it was but a thin curtain of water falling through the roof, and that beyond it lay another and a vaster cavern.

By the time he had made this discovery the weight of the water tore the piece of timber from his hand, and he detected the light creeping out of the gloom, and quickly extinguishing his own, he crouched down again over the body of Minnie.

There was something so strange and suspicious in the movements of the bearer of the covered light, that he feared to make his presence known and ask his aid.

This fear increased when he made out by the light, that the man carried in his hand a long knife, and that its blade was covered in blood.

Closer and closer to the ground crouched Boaster.

But his gaze never wandered from that evil-looking face, and those red wet hands and blade.

On towards the curtain of water came the man, and when he reachd it he paused, held his band and knife in it, and suffered the water to wash frm them the stains of blood.

As he stood thus, Boaster hard him mutter—

"The secret is safe enough fom him now; dead men can neither rob nor betray. He's done for, and now we can start on our cruise without fear of being sold by a traitor. Good-bye, Back Pedro, we'll come and look at your corpse when we return in a month or so—ha, ha!"

And as Boaster crouched horried, the man and the light passed throgh the crystal curtain, leaving the cave n darkness.

Base as he was, Boaster had at shuddering with horror for some time, then he again struck a light, and igniting the remainder of his piece of string, looked around him.

On one side was the thin curtain of water, through which the man had passed; on the other the huge cataract, beneath which his boat had been driven after descending the falls.

And away to the right and left of him darkness and continuous space.

He looked down at Minnie.

She still lay like one dead.

Not once since he had sprung into the river after her, when she took that fearful leap to escape from Tiger Claw, had she opened her eyes.

Would she die, or could he save her? —save her for himself and be revenged on Ned.

This thought gave him courage.

She needed warmth to revive her.

Beyond that curtain of water might he not find material for building a fire?

The string burnt to his fingers.

Another moment he would be in darkness; he dare hesitate no longer, and he sprang through the crystal curtain.

But he was again in darkness.

Once more he obtained a light, and holding his glowing tinder to the floor, he saw several dried osiers or twigs lying about.

These he swept into a heap, and after awhile kindled into a flame.

Then, as the wood crackled, a thousand echoes filled the place, for a time terrifying him, but after awhile he realised what the strange sounds meant, and als the forms of the Indians by whom he had found himself surrounded.

Here and there he found strewn about dried branches that had evidently formed at some time hurdles for the carrying of the bodies into the cave, and by the light which these gave he explored the place as hurriedly as he could, to see if there was anyone to molest him.

Finding none but the dead, and discovering the entrance that led to the forest beyond, he returned to where he had left Minnie, and taking her in his arms he sprang with her back into the cavern, where his fire still burned.

Before this he had lain her, placed more osiers on the flames, and sat down to watch and wait.

Gradually life came back to the poor girl, but reason had fled her brain, and she raved in the delirium of brain-fever.

For long days he watched and tended her, removing her to that part of the cave where we first saw her after her escape from Tiger Claw, paying occasional visits to the forest at night for fuel, or stealing by day upon the Indian village for food.

Several times he had passed through that curtain of water, and tried to discover whither the man had gone on his murderous errand, but in vain.

But he had learned the secret of the double cave, and that knowledge enabled him to elude Ned and Charley when Minnie was all but in their grasp.

To Minnie he had never revealed the mysteries of that crystal curtain, and no wonder that the poor girl believed her doom sealed when she found herself borne into the falls as the youth she loved dashed forward to tear her from the arms of her persecutor.

In the agony of that moment her overwrought feelings had given way, and insensibility, if not death, had steeped her senses in utter oblivion.

For a time Boaster waited, a malicious smile on his face, a feeling of demoniacal triumph in his heart, and he would have laughed aloud at the thought of Ned's confusion and defeat, but for the fear that his voice might reach his ears through the crystal curtain and betray its secret.

An hour at least he crouched beside Minnie in the darkness of that inner cavern, and then he rose to his feet.

"The fool has gone to weep over he supposed death by now," he muttered, "and I shall be troubled by him no more. Oh, Ned Nimble, how I glory in the misery you must suffer! I could wish you dead but that I know your agony is ten thousand times worse than death."

As he finished muttering he sprang through the curtain of water into the other cavern.

The smile on his face gave place to a look of terror, the joy in his heart to a feeling of dismay, as he saw just before him the hideous forms of a bear and crocodile, as he believed, about to devour Ned and Charley.

As the place was plunged into darkness, he turned and sprang back into the inner cave.

CHAPTER LXVII.

IN WHICH THERE IS FEARFUL SUSPENSE AND AN AWFUL TRAGEDY.

IN his terror lest the supposed animals should pursue him, Boaster caught up the body of Minnie, and despite the darkness of the cavern, fled along it, expecting every moment to hear the roar of the bear behind him.

The motion awoke Minnie to partial consciousness, and she uttered a scream.

Ere its sound had fully died away, a light flashed before Boaster's eyes, and faint though it was, he recoiled several paces.

In his surprise he let Minnie slip from his arms to the ground.

Before him, at some short distance, appeared an opening, and through this opening streamed the light out into the darkness of the cavern.

Wildly Boaster gazed towards it, and his heart seemed to cease to beat.

In the rays of that light he saw several moving forms, and one of them peering out in the direction of the spot where he stood paralysed almost with terror and surprise.

In a moment Bill Boaster realised that he gazed upon the place whence the man he had seen on his first coming to the cavern had disappeared from his view.

Then as the remembrance of that blood-stained knife, and the words its owner had uttered flashed through his mind, he placed his hand over Minnie's lips.

"Not a word—not a breath, or we are lost!" he whispered.

Boaster drew her farther away from where the stream of light fell along the floor of the cavern.

What were that group of men, and what were they doing there?

Would they discover him?

If so, how could he escape them?

If seen he dared not seek safety on the other side of the crystal curtain.

To retreat was death, to advance was perhaps worse.

Cold drops of perspiration stood on Boaster's brow.

All the triumphant feelings of joy and revenge that so short a time before coursed through his heart were fled, and fear, horror, and despair took possession of his soul.

He kept his hand pressed on Minnie's lips.

Though moments only passed, yet ages seemed to roll by, as Boaster gazed to-wards that lighted opening in the cavern partially blocked up by the body of a man as he peered out into the darkness before him.

Then a gruff voice fell on Boaster's ears.

"It must have been fancy, mates. Nobody could have got into the cave with that rock lowered over its mouth, and if any redskin has come to life, I calculate he ain't up to the secret of the water curtain. Get out, it's nothing. So go on with the trial, and don't keep the cap-tain waiting for his ticket to old Nick."

There was a roar of laughter in reply to this, and then the man drew back from the opening and the light disappeared.

Boaster drew a breath of relief.

He drew his hand from Minnie's mouth.

"Speak not, breathe not!" he whis-pered; "we are surrounded by danger and death!"

"Ned, Ned!" moaned Minnie.

"Fool! silence!" hissed Boaster. "Would you destroy us both?"

"Wretch!" said Minnie. "Oh, Heaven! am I still in your power?"

"Girl!" hissed Boaster in her ear. "I love you to madness, but by Heaven I will kill you if you speak!"

"Kill me—in mercy kill me!" she gasped.

"No, no," he said, quickly. "I would save you, for I love you. Oh, Minnie, be merciful to me! 'Tis for your sake —yours! I pray you utter no sound."

"Let me go to Ned—let me go!"

"Oh, Heaven, she will bring ruin and death upon us both," muttered Boaster.

"Ned! Oh, Ned, where are you?"

"I must be cruel to save her and my-self," muttered Boaster. "Minnie, blame me not—blame only yourself for this."

He thrust one hand over her mouth and with the other tore away a portion of her dress.

Then he thrust the linen between her teeth, and fastening it behind her head, gagged her mouth.

Having gagged Minnie's mouth, Boaster tore another slip from her dress and tied her hands behind her.

"Minnie," he whispered, "you make me cruel where I would be kind; I who love you so madly."

He pressed his lips to her cheek and rose from his knees.

"She cannot run from here nor cry for help," he thought. "I must know what fresh danger surrounds us."

Tremblingly he stole towards where he had seen the light.

As he drew nearer, the sound of voices reached his ears.

Excited now by curiosity he crept on till he stood close to the opening, and putting forth his hand he incautiously touched something that yielded to the pressure of his fingers.

It was a kind of curtain that shut out those beyond from the cave in which Boaster stood.

A thin stream of light gleamed out as the curtain moved beneath the pressure of his fingers, and through the crack Boaster saw about a dozen men assem-bled, seated on casks and chests, and on the ground in the centre of them lay a man bound hand and foot.

All save the bound man were armed with knives and revolvers, and a more desperate-looking set of ruffians it was impossible to imagine.

Fascinated, Boaster forgot his fears and his danger, and placing his eye to the crack he made by pushing the curtain slightly aside, he glared in upon them.

He nearly betrayed himself by the start he gave as one of the men stood up suddenly, and he recognised the ruffian he had seen with the dripping knife and red hand.

"Well, mates, I take it we're all agreed the captain shares the same fate as Pedro. We know now that he sent that Spanish cuss to rob and perhaps betray us, and that between them they meant to collar all for themselves."

"He did," said one. "We've got plenty of proof he meant to play us false, and I for one say let him die the same death as Pedro and share the same grave with his fellow-traitor. Are you all agreed, mates?"

"All, all," cried the assembled ruffians, drawing their knives.

"Then let him first look on his comrade. Lift him up, mates."

The men lifted the bound man up, and standing him on his feet held him there while the ruffian who had last spoken flung up the lid of a huge chest and revealed the body of a dead man lying therein.

"He intended to rob and then betray us, and you were to share all our plunder with him," said the ruffian, addressing the bound man; "but we found him out in time, and my knife stopped his tongue and his breath together."

The man shuddered.

"Ah, you may well tremble, Captain Rolfe," said the fellow, "for now you know that there's no mercy for you. As long as you were true to us we were true to you; but you intended to play us false, and your punishment must be——"

"Death!" cried every voice in the assembly. "Death to the traitor!"

A dozen knives flashed in the torchlight, and then descending were plunged into the shoulders, breast, and back of the doomed man.

CHAPTER LXVIII.

IN WHICH BOASTER BECOMES A GREATER VILLAIN THAN EVER.

As a shriek of fearful agony burst from the lips of the murdered man, the curtain before the opening moved aside, and paralysed with horror at the sight he had witnessed, Boaster fell forward into the midst of the assembled murderers.

A moment and panic-stricken the ruffians stood, their blood-stained knives held before them.

Then a howl of fury broke from their lips and they sprang forward.

"A spy, a spy!" they shouted. "Stab him! kill him! He has learned the secret of the cave—he will betray us! Death to the spy!"

Another moment and the knives would have found a sheath in Boaster's bosom, but a loud and piercing scream pealed through the cave, and right into their midst plunged a female form shrieking wildly—

"Ned, Ned, save me! save me!"

It was Minnie.

She had burst the bonds that secured her arms and torn the gag from her mouth, and fled, shrieking for Ned to save her, not knowing—not caring whither she went.

The upraised knives of the assassins remained suspended in the air as they gazed wonder-stricken upon the young and lovely vision that had sprung into their midst.

Ere the ruffians had recovered from their surprise at the second unexpected appearance in their midst, Bill Boaster had sprang to his feet.

"Men," he cried, in a loud, firm voice, "I am no spy, no enemy to you. I would be your friend—your comrade. I am a hunted, desperate man, with every man's hand against me and my fingers at every man's throat. You have slain a captain who would betray you—rob you of your share of your plunder, and you have done wisely."

Minnie, dazed at finding herself in such company, had stopped, terror-stricken and speechless.

Boaster, without waiting for a remark, went on quickly—

"That I am no spy, no enemy to you —nay, to prove that I am your friend— know that this secret hiding-place for your plunder has been long known to me. I could have shot down or given up to justice yonder man when he slew Pedro the Spaniard for intending to rob his comrades. That man was in my power, and I could have killed him as he washed his red hand and blood-stained knife in the falling waters some time since.

"No wonder you look so strangely at me, friends, and marvel at my words and my presence here in this disguise," continued Boaster, quickly, not giving the surprised men time to speak. "Had I wished to rob or betray you, how easily could I have done so? But no, I desired to join a band of such bold and desperate men, and it is to ask you to let me become one of your bold band that I am here now, here at the moment when such ghastly proof as that lies before us that a traitor's doom is a traitor's death."

"Who are you?" cried one.

"How came you in this cave?" asked another.

"Who is this girl?" questioned a third.

"I will answer all you ask," said Boaster.

"Go on," said the man whom he had seen at the crystal curtain long before.

"I am an Englishman," said Boaster, "who left my country to be revenged on one I hate. You who know what it is to have a foe, must know how sweet is revenge."

"We do."

"Well, then, in the pursuit of that vengeance I tore this girl from her home and the arms of her lover, and in bearing her from him and those who would wrest her from me I was thrown by accident into this cave. Here by accident I learned your secret. It would have made me rich for life, but I would not take advantage of my knowledge, for you, like me, were men whose hands are ever at the throat of his fellow-man. Shall I ask your friendship in vain?"

There was no reply.

"Men, I have broken the laws of honour. I am an outcast from society, stained with crime, but I have proved true to those, who like myself, have placed themselves beyond the care or sympathy of honest men. In one sentence, I, who would crush an honest man, have scorned to rob rascals like myself, or I should have wronged you. I have shown you friendship where others have become your enemies. There is the hand of a friend; will you take it?"

He held out his hand.

"We will," cried the man he had before seen; "you have shown good will to us, and Tom Stockton for one tips you his flipper."

And he shook Boaster's hand.

"And you, and you?" said Boaster, offering his hand.

"Yes, yes," was the reply.

And one after the other, the ruffians shook him by the hand.

Poor Minnie, she gazed upon the scene before her like one in a dream, and her gaze resting on the bleeding body of the murdered man, a mist of blood seemed to float before her eyes.

Like a crushed lily she lay there in the centre of that gang of ruffians, powerless to speak, powerless even to weep.

"You've learned some of the secrets of this cave," said Stockton, at last, "but I guess not all."

"What's that?" asked Boaster.

"The Devil's Bay, where our ship rides at anchor."

"I admit it," said Boaster.

"But you'll soon learn it," said Stockton. "Now mates, listen to me, our captain's paid the penalty, and as there's sure to be more blood-letting if we vote one of the crew to the post, what say you to making our new comrade captain of the 'Black Viper?' You can see he is no seaman, but that he can soon learn to be. We must have a commander, and I vote for him. Give us your name, lad."

"Bill Boaster."

"Bill Boaster for captain of the 'Black Viper!'" cried the men, without one dissenting voice.

"I will be your captain," said Bill.

"Give him the oath," said Stockton. "We're short-handed, and can't afford to kill each other, boys. Let him swear to be true to us, and we to him, and then we can start without a fight or feeling of jealousy.

"Give it him yourself, Tom," cried one.

"Then swear to be true, and remember that to betray or wrong us is death," said Tom. "Swear on the wet blade of every man's knife, and remember that to fail to keep your oath is death."

"I swear!" said Boaster, and he bent his lips to the still wet knives; "I swear!"

CHAPTER LXIX.

IN WHICH THERE IS MADNESS AND DESPAIR.

A CRY of horror echoed through the cave as Ned disappeared in the swiftly descending waters.

"As I suspected," he muttered; "that sheet of water falls through the roof, and divides the cave, and Minnie has not perished, but where is she?—whither has he taken her?"

He glared round him in the darkness.

"Ah," he cried, "there is a light yonder. Boaster, villain, Ned Nimble is on your trail, and will tear that poor girl from your arms or perish in the struggle."

As he uttered these words he loosened his knife in its sheath and bounded towards the distant light.

But suddenly he paused as he saw within its glow the forms of several men.

Then he bounded forward again as a loud piercing scream in a female voice echoed through the cave.

Clutching his knife fiercely he sprang forward, but the light was suddenly shut out and a roar of gruff voices reached his ears.

"Kill him! Stab him? Death to the spy!" were the words he heard uttered in tones of fury.

He staggered forward in wonder till he stood just without the curtain before the robbers cave, and then as the words of Boaster rang out loud and clear he paused and listened.

Wonder-stricken and horrified he stood without the curtain while Boaster spoke and then like that villain he softly pushed the curtain aside until he could see into the interior of the robbers' rendezvous.

His heart sank within him as his gaze fell upon Minnie crouching on the floor and Boaster in the centre of a group of murderous-looking ruffians whose sanguinary blades were presented for him to kiss as he took the oath to be true to them.

Desperate, as he was, Ned saw how useless, how mad would be any attempt made to bear Minnie from their midst.

"Oh Heavens!" he gasped, "I am more powerless to aid her than ever. Oh, why do I not rush in among them and kill that villain? What holds me back? Oh Minnie, Minnie, it is you, for your sake I dare not."

And then his gaze rested on the horrified face of the poor girl whose vacant maniacal stare rested on the bleeding form at her side.

The body of the murdered traitor captain whose place Bill Boaster had sworn to fill.

With a start Ned raised his white agonized face as the harsh voice of Tom Stockton broke on his ears.

"Now, that's settled mates," said the ruffian. "This young fellow has taken the oath and we've elected a captain without our fighting each other. It won't do to stop here palavering for a month or we shall lose this tide and that means a good chance of losing that little haul we expect."

"Wall I guess you're about right thar, Tom," said one with a nasal twang that proclaimed him a Yankee. "We'll have to be slick and skedaddle sharp if the 'Black Viper's' got to overhaul that yar Britisher afore she sights land. Tarnel thunder, but the 'Viper' 'll have to glide along like greased lightning if she comes up with her now."

"We've got to chance it," said Tom. "However we're bound now for 'Frisco and California. Whether we overhaul the 'True Blue' or not it will be as well to take half our hidden wealth aboard as was agreed on."

"Hear, hear," said the others.

"And also half the arms and ammunition, for we're short of both on board. So while you Sam Snarl, introduce our new captain and his sweetheart to the 'Black Viper' we'll get rid of these dead uns and overhaul the arsenal and treasure chest."

"Guess I'll do that thar," said Sam. "Now, captain, shall I carry her aboard for yar, or will you sling her across your shoulder? 'Tarnel thunder, just ain't she a beauty!"

And Sam stooped as if to lift Minnie from the floor.

But Boaster pushed him aside and placed his arm round Minnie's form and lifted her to her feet.

The next Number will contain the conclusion of "Ned Nimble Amongst the Indians," and the opening chapters of "Ned Nimble Amongst the Mormons." Order Early of your Bookseller.

A shudder ran through her frame and she raved—

"Oh Heaven, Ned!—blood!—murder! Ha, ha, ha!"

At the mention of his name Ned clutched at the curtain to draw it aside and spring to her aid despite the certain death he would meet.

But as that maniacal peal of laughter broke from her lips and told but too surely that reason had fled its throne, his whole frame became paralysed with horror and with a gasping sob he sank to the ground in a heap.

Ned could only glare through the crack into the cavern, only follow with his gaze that bitter and revengeful foe as he followed Sam through an opening on the other side of the chamber, and hear the triumphant and fiendish laugh of Bill Boaster as he bore the girl from the sight of her stricken lover.

Like one in a dream Ned saw the ruffians break in the heads of some of the casks, and take therefrom swords, knives, pike-heads, rifles, and revolvers.

From others he observed them extract bags and bars, the very sight of which made their villainous eyes sparkle, while some of the men rolled small kegs along the floor of the cave to the opening opposite that where Ned sat crouched behind the curtain.

The men came and went, bearing away with them various articles, till at length Tom Stockton flung down the lid of a heavy chest with a bang, and turning to his comrades said—

"There, mates, we've taken enough on board to last us if we shouldn't make a good haul on our cruise. I reckon we've took half of everything, arms and bullion. We'll leave the other till we come again."

"Or somebody else comes," said one.

"That ain't likely."

"So we thought afore, and yet Pedro and the captain—

"Well I take it, mates, that what they got for trying it on will stop any one else, seeing as how they're sure to go under if they do. It's safer here than aboard by long shots. If we sink in a squall or get overhauled by a crusier, then the lot's gone to a dead certainty."

"That's true," said the man who had spoken before. "We've got half left here if the worst comes to the worst."

"Well, I think the worst will be for the fellow who thinks to collar it all. He'll get more steel than gold for his pains, I take it. Howsoever, mates, lest any fool should fancy he could come the artful over us, we'll leave a notice to say as how he's bound to suffer for it if he does."

And opening the chest again, Tom searched among its contents, and finally drew forth a sheet of paper.

Then stooping he dipped his finger in the pool of blood on the floor of the cave and ran it over the paper, which he had placed on the lid of the chest.

"There," he said at last; "there's the warning, and that's my seal."

And he drove his knife through the paper and pinned it to the lid of the chest with the sanguinary blade. "Now come on, lads, let's aboard."

With a laugh the men followed him, and the only occupant of the robber chamber were the dead Pedro and murdered captain.

For some time Ned sat glaring into the cave.

At length he staggered to his feet, and throwing aside the curtain entered.

He looked at the paper on the box, on which was written—

"Death to him who robs this cave! Beware! Touch not or you die! As sure as a knife holds this paper, so surely shall it be sheathed in the heart of him who would rob the Black Vipers! Beware!"

CHAPTER LXX.

IN WHICH THERE IS A PARTING AND A MEETING, AND A TERRIBLE VOW IS REGISTERED IN THE PHANTOM CAVE.

"Oh Heaven!" cried Ned, "would I could awake and find it all a dream. But alas! it is too true. I have run the fox to earth, and when I thought I had torn my sweet dove from his claws, my foe and his victim find shelter in the lair of the tiger, and I am further off than ever from the realisation of my hopes. Oh, cruel bitter disappointment."

"Yeo—yo-ho!"

Ned sprang round at the sound.

Then darting through the opposite entrance he found himself in a narrow passage, at the end of which several yards away he could see the light of day.

He bounded along the passage, and in a few moments stood on the margin of a large rocky basin or bay, across which was gliding as graceful a schooner as ever he set eyes on.

Every object on her deck was visible but on one object alone Ned's eyes centred.

It was the form of a man attired as an Indian, holding in his arms the drooping figure of a young girl.

It was Bill Boaster and the drooping girl in his arms was Minnie Sash.

Ned drew his revolver and levelled it.

"Though I kill her in his arms," he cried, "that villain shall die!"

Ned pulled the trigger.

There was no report.

The revolver was empty, and with a bitter groan of despair Ned flung the weapon into the bay, and covered his face with his hands.

When he again looked up the bay was deserted, the ship had disappeared, and Minnie Sash was lost to his view.

With throbbing brain and aching heart Ned retraced his steps through the passage to the cave, and taking a lantern which had been left burning on the chest, he made his way back to the curtain of water.

Having reached the fall he bounded through it, wondering how his presence would be received by Jack and his friends, but to his surprise he saw them not.

While wondering where they could be, the sound of shouts and firing met his ears.

He hurried along towards the entrance of the cave.

Bang, bang!

What could it mean?

Ned hurried on, and suddenly a shout went up.

"It moves, it moves! Hurrah!"

And then as Ned reached the spot he saw the stone roll away from before the entrance, and in the archway stood grouped not only Jack, Sally, Charley, and Jumbo, but Harry, 'Dolf, and Bir-

cher, each wringing the others' hands and capering for joy.

"Ned, where's Ned?" cried the voices of Harry and 'Dolf.

"Here; he is here," cried Ned, springing forward.

A shout of joy rang out from the men, a scream of terror from Sally, who tore through the opening, and with her umbrella was the next moment lost to view in the wood beyond.

While Jumbo started off in search of Sally, hurried explanations took place, and great indeed was the surprise and indignation of Harry and the others when they learned what had befallen Ned and poor Minnie.

By the time Ned had told his story Sally returned in company with Jumbo and when she found that Ned was indeed in the flesh, she flung her arms around his neck and kissed him fervently.

In answer to Ned's inquiries, Harry said that they had become so anxious on board lest harm had befallen him, that they resolved to leave the boat and search for the cave.

On their way they heard firing, and discovered that the Indians had arrived and had attacked the band of Tiger Claw without waiting for the appearance of the white medicine.

The savages had been taken by surprise and finding after a desperate struggle that they were beaten, some of them made for the cave, and thus gave Harry and his companions a clue to his whereabouts.

They had, however, been unable to remove the stone before Flying Deer's braves discovered them, and they had taken to flight, followed by their enemies.

It was the firing of the Indians that Ned had heard while in the cavern.

While endeavouring to remove the stone in order to search the cave, Harry and his companions had by their voices made their presence outside known to those within, and their united strength being brought to bear upon the rock, had yielded just as Ned had made his appearance.

"What will you do now, dear boy?" asked Harry at last.

"Follow him, if need be to the end of the earth," replied Ned; "I swore to tear that poor girl from his arms, and will do so, or give up my life in the attempt."

'But you know not whither they have led," said Harry.

"Not for certain, but I think towards San Francisco. Never will I give up the pursuit while life shall last. Firmer than ever is my resolve to track that wretch to his doom, and avenge in his coward blood the sufferings of myself and that poor, ill-fated girl."

"And I am with you, Ned, to the last," said Harry, grasping his hand.

"And all of us," said Bircher.

"Thanks, Bircher, thanks," said Ned.

"And I guess this coon's in that little swim," said Charley.

"And dis yar ole bear," said Jumbo; "I can't tink ob leabing dis yar white muss, 'cos you see de shadder ob my 'spec-ability——"

"You're a fool," said Charley.

"Guess dat's trufe," said Jumbo.

"I needn't say I'm going," said Sally, "leastways, if you'll let me, Master Ned."

"Of course you'll share Jack's fortunes," said Ned; "but I implore you, kind friends, not to sacrifice your own comforts for me."

"We shan't do that," said Jack, "because you see me and Sally is going to get married as soon as we can find a minister, and I am sure I shall be as good a man married as I hope you have found me single."

"Be it as you wish, friends," said Ned; "let me tell you that we shall want for nothing, not even the wherewithal to procure a good ship, arms, and provisions, for I have found the means to obtain all, and at the same time make the rascals who will aid Boaster in his villainy pay for his destruction. We will away from here as soon as we have placed the treasure I have discovered on board, to hunt the rascal to his death."

"And we'll never rest till we have done so," said Harry.

"Then come with me, and I will show you all the secrets of the phantom cave, and the haunt of the villains of whom Boaster has become chief; follow, and fear not."

Ned led the way to the water curtain, explained its mysteries, and sprang through it.

Harry and the rest followed him, not even excepting Sally.

In a few moments they stood in the robbers' haunt, beside the victims of their cruel vengeance.

"Here is their hidden treasure," said Ned, "of which, despite their threat, I shall take charge, and which you shall all share with me. Here are the arms and ammunition, and this is the defiance and the oath of Ned Nimble; write it down on the paper, Harry, while I repeat it; write it in the blood of their murdered victims."

Harry drew the knife from the paper, and dipping the handle in the gore at his feet, wrote as Ned spoke.

"I, Ned Nimble the Avenger, devote the treasures found in this cave to hunting to death Bill Boaster and the assassins under his command, and by the aid of Heaven I will fulfil my vow of vengeance!"

"There," said Ned, "is my seal to the compact."

And he plunged his knife through the paper and pinned it to the chest.

"And mine," cried Harry, as he drove his knife beside Ned's.

"Now to get these treasures to our boat and set sail," said Ned. "But first let us join hands here upon the spot where poor Minnie was driven to madness by the persecution of a villain and the horrible sights she was forced to see, and swear, come weal, come woe, to save her living or avenge her dead!"

Grasping each others' hands the friends fell upon their knees, and swore the bitter and binding oath of vengeance.

They rose to their feet, all save Ned, who still remained on his knees, his hands and eyes still raised.

"Bill Boaster," he cried, "you triumph now, but the hour shall come when your smiles shall turn to tears. Never did sleuth-hound track murderer to his doom with surer fate than I will hunt you to your death. Tremble, villain, for Ned Nimble is on your track, and never will he rest till he has fulfilled his bitter oath of vengeance!"

Then he rose, and proceeded to lay bare the robbers' treasures.

When all the treasure had been stowed on board, the vessel was cast loose and headed down the river.

Then Ned grasped Harry's hand, and in a husky voice said—

"The race has begun that must end in death. It is either Boaster's life now or that of NED NIMBLE!"

COMPLETE PLAYS

FOR HOME AMUSEMENT.

ROADSIDE INN.
JACK CADE, THE REBEL OF LONDON.
ALONE IN THE PIRATES' LAIR.
TOM DARING; OR, FAR FROM HOME.
THE GIANT OF THE BLACK MOUNTAINS; OR, JACK AND HIS
    ELEVEN BROTHERS.
KING ARTHUR; OR, THE KNIGHTS OF THE ROUND TABLE.
THE SKELETON HORSEMAN; OR, THE SHADOW OF DEATH.

Each of the above Plays contains Sixteen Sheets of Characters and Scenes, price 4d. plain; 8d. coloured; postage 1d. extra; or can be had mounted and cut ready for use, price 2s. 6d.; postage 3d. extra.

THE FORTY THIEVES.
BLUE BEARD.
THE MILLER AND HIS MEN.
MAZEPPA; OR, THE WILD HORSE OF TARTARY.
HARKAWAY AMONG THE BRIGANDS.
ROBINSON CRUSOE.

Complete Plays. Each containing about Twenty-four Sheets of Characters and Scenes, price 6d. plain; 1s. coloured; or, mounted and cut ready for use 3s. 6d.; post free, 3s. 9d.

BOOKS OF THE PLAYS, 1d. each.

STAGE FRONTS, 1d. plain, 3d. coloured; mounted 6d. WOOD STAGES, 1s. 3d.
THE NEW FOLDING WOOD STAGE, 1s. 6d. LAMPS, 3d.; post free, 4d.
SLIDES, 4d. per dozen; post free, 6d., per dozen.
EXTRA SHEET SIDE WINGS, &c., 2d. plain; 4d. coloured.

Any of the above may be obtained through any Bookseller, or a parcel can be made up and sent per carrier if desired. If the Wood Stages are required by parcel post, an additional 5d. must be included.

Models for Building.

Old English Farmhouse. Coloured, One Penny.

The Interior of a Village School. Coloured, One Penny.

Kenilworth Castle and Maypole Dance. Coloured, Twopence.

Gothic Castle and Tournament. Twopence.

Village Smithy. One Penny.

Last Castle of the Knights of St. John. One Penny.

Old London Bridge, with Boats, &c. Plain, One Penny; Coloured, Threepence.

Thames Embankment and Cleopatra's Needle. Plain, One Penny; Coloured Threepence.